SHE
SHIFTERS

SHE SHIFTERS
LESBIAN
PARANORMAL EROTICA

EDITED BY
DELILAH DEVLIN

FOREWORD BY
KATE DOUGLAS

CLEiS
PRESS

Published in the United States by Cleis Press, Inc., 2246 Sixth Street, Berkeley, California 94710.

Printed in the United States.
Cover design: Scott Idleman/Blink
Cover photograph: Eryk Fitkau/Getty Images
Text design: Frank Wiedemann
First Edition.
10 9 8 7 6 5 4 3 2 1

Trade paper ISBN: 978-1-57344-796-6
E-book ISBN: 978-1-57344-808-6

Contents

vii   *Foreword* • KATE DOUGLAS
xiii *Introduction*

1   *The Night Crow* • PAISLEY SMITH
16 *Verde* • ANNA MEADOWS
30 *Nine Days and Seven Tears* • J.L. MERROW
38 *Sweetwater Pass* • ANGELA CAPERTON
51 *Scorched Retribution* • CHRISTINE D'ABO
65 *Thwarting the Spirits* • MICHAEL M. JONES
80 *She's Furry Yiffy* • ADELE DUBOIS
96 *Totem* • KARIS WALSH
106 *Sneak* • GISELLE RENARDE
121 *Purrfect in Venezia* • MYLA JACKSON
137 *The Dragon Descending* • SACCHI GREEN
148 *All the Colors of the Sun* • VICTORIA OLDHAM
162 *The Handler* • TAHIRA IQBAL
178 *Bound with Bronze* • CHRIS KOUJU
194 *Catnip* • DELILAH DEVLIN
212 *Belling the Kat* • J.L. MERROW

219 *About the Authors*
223 *About the Editor*

FOREWORD

Kate Douglas

I've always loved fiction. There's something about those larger-than-life characters that truly appeals to me. When I was little I read animal stories. I took the things I read—from the dogs', cats', horses', and other critters' points of view—and grew up loving animals. Those stories made it perfectly obvious to me that our four-legged friends think and have their own language in real life, just as they did in the stories I loved. But I never really thought of the stories I read as lessons learned. They were fantasy, and the stories made me feel good.

As I grew older, my focus turned to science fiction—amazing worlds with unique settings and characters that totally enthralled me. I know that even today my fascination with the space program and the possibilities inherent in paranormal fiction go back to those books I loved, the ones that stretched my imagination and made me wonder if the impossible might really exist. Stories by Robert A. Heinlein, Arthur C. Clarke, and Anne McCaffrey, among so many others, removed the boundaries and limits that society, by virtue of its existence, creates. But lessons? I was entertained, but not actually learning, right? Not forming my opinions based on fantasy, not learning more about who I was, what I wanted, what my future might hold.

When I first began writing fiction, I had no idea my stories revolved around common themes—not until I started receiving fan mail from readers who wrote to tell me what they had learned from my books, who said that my sensual tales of shapeshifters overcoming whatever life threw at them had left them feeling empowered. Many readers related personal stories of heart-break and loss and then wrote of their own victories—victories they said came from the lessons of love and acceptance they found in my books.

They're learning something? Feeling empowered by my stories? But how? I write erotic paranormal romances. There's no message there, none intended, right?

I had no idea how wrong I was, nor did I realize that my own life experience, my own core beliefs—many of those beliefs forged in my earlier reading—were so much a part of my stories. I didn't set out to write stories with a message, nor did I intend to write anything that could possibly be construed as life lessons, but that's what stories do. I know that now, because my readers made me see the impact that the fictional stories we read can have on our lives.

I write of the redeeming power of love and the need for us to love ourselves before we can freely love another. I write of men and women who have suffered, but have gone on to find the strength to believe in themselves, to believe they are truly worthy of love—and to choose partners who are worthy of their love. But most of all, I write about acceptance. That love in and of itself is what matters. Paramount in my stories is the concept that we are all worthy of love, that gender, race, religion, and all the other things society tries to throw in our way as barriers to love are foolish—though I have to admit, they do create wonderful themes around which to build our tales.

Since I write romances, it's often sexual attraction that brings my protagonists together, but what keeps them together is stronger. It's honor and integrity, it's putting the one you love first and wanting their happiness above all else. It's accepting that person exactly as they are—not asking them to change to fit an ideal rather than their own reality. I write my stories around these themes because they're important to me—I had no idea how important they were to my readers.

Readers' letters also made me look much more closely at the stories I choose to read as well as the ones I write. I made a most surprising discovery: those same messages of love and acceptance, of honor and integrity, abound in the books on my "keeper shelves." That led to another question—are my core beliefs something that sprang from within, or were they, at least partially, the result of the books I've read over the years? Did I choose those tales of love and acceptance because I agreed with them, or did I read them and learn?

I believe fantasy—beyond what it teaches us about life—can often provide the direction we need to get our lives on track, to figure out those things about ourselves that we either like or hope to change. It helps us accept who we are and why we are the way we are, and if we are foundering and can't quite figure out what's important, they can often point us in the right direction.

Love and acceptance are popular themes in our culture, in our lives, and in our fantasies. Why fantasy? Because we don't always automatically find love or experience acceptance in our real-world existence, and yet we continue searching. It's a visceral drive within us, to know that we love, that we are loved—that we are capable of loving even when the object of our desire isn't quite what we expected.

Sometimes the stories we find in fantasy offer solutions for our own reality, a blueprint for accepting not only ourselves but those around us, and most especially, those we love.

Within the pages of books, through the imaginations of others, we can find answers to questions, examples and lessons for living that translate from the fantasy of the impossible or entirely improbable, to the reality of our own existence, our own personal experience. Life doesn't come with a guarantee of *happily ever after*, or even *happily for now*. What it does come with is the option of choice—the chance to choose our own path.

But how do we know what to choose, what direction we should take? That's where fantasy gives us analogous guidelines for real life. Like the parables of old, stories of love and acceptance, of overcoming long odds, of finding love in the least obvious of places with the most unlikely of partners, can be translated into real life lessons.

She's fallen in love with a shapeshifter, but his or her shape is worlds apart from our heroine's. Will she have to change to suit her lover's needs, or be strong enough to stand firm and say, "Love me as I am"? She's found love but it's not the partner her family would choose, not the proper consort in this fantasy world—does she give in to outside demands, or follow her own path, find the inner strength she needs to choose love?

Our protagonist's fictional choices translate into life lessons in reality for the reader. Stories filled with emotion and passion, with adventure and danger and convoluted relationships are still rife with empowering messages. Messages that resonate with readers, that offer subtle guidelines and life lessons they can translate into real life experience. The choices that give our protagonists their happily ever after can help us build a foundation for our own decisions, our choices and the way we deal with our most intimate relationships in the real world. They can be a guideline, a template, a warning—even the story that ends badly can be a lesson, if only in caution, in making smart choices.

We are the sum total of all our experiences. We learn from our families, our friends, from school and work and life in general, but never forget the lessons we take from the reading we do for pleasure. Fantasy can be a powerful instrument in real life choices, teaching, even as it entertains. I remember, in a conversation one time, trying to explain my core beliefs of the human sexual condition, and I realized later it's a philosophy I've come to almost entirely through my reading. It's simple, really, when you think about it, but love is love, no matter the gender, the race, or any label you choose. The rest is friction.

So, I invite you to sit back, maybe pour a glass of wine, get comfortable, and open the pages ahead. You'll find tales of love, of acceptance, of challenges met and fears overcome. And maybe you'll take away a lesson or two. It might be fantasy, but believe me, it matters.

INTRODUCTION: THE SHAPES OF DESIRE

The concept of shapeshifters—beings both human and animal—ignites our imaginations with visions of primal passions and insatiable hungers. Most commonly seen as dark, masculine demons, I felt shapeshifters were in need of a metaphysical overhaul—a new feminine/Sapphic blending of physical power and inescapable desires.

So, I sent out a call for submissions and asked writers to re-imagine common myths. Traditional lycanthropes and feline familiars were welcome—if told with a fresh twist. However, I wanted new, inventive tales celebrating feminine power, lust, and erotic love.

Above all, as always, I wanted a surprise.

Writers took my suggestions to heart. Rather than an in-box filled with werewolf stories that my friend Kate Douglas already does so well, I read stories filled with cats, snakes, mice, cobras, seals... So much variety of species, and from such a rich mixture of mythologies, that choosing among them was painfully hard.

In the end, I chose the stories that touched my emotions. Those that painted a lushly erotic picture and made me smile or cry. I'm a pretty jaded reader. If a story can affect me, I figure others will appreciate it, too.

Usually, the idea of shapeshifting creatures is meant to elicit shivers of horror. But imagine the possibilities if the animal lurking under the skin of a woman is searching for love. Even a demon with fangs and fur can long for a tender caress. Imagine again, a human who discovers her most erotic fantasies embodied in a wild, untamable lover.

Inside *She Shifters*, you'll discover how it feels to be embraced inside the warm, feathered wings of a phoenix, explore faded memories of a past life to find your one true love, race through a rain forest morphing from tiger to kingfisher, and watch your lover surrender her seal's pelt to walk hand in hand with you along a cold and lonely shore.

Love comes running, slithering, flying—in all shapes of desire.

Delilah Devlin

THE NIGHT CROW

Paisley Smith

"Even the ravens of the Tower sat silent and immovable on the battlements and gazed eerily at the strange scene. A Queen about to die!"
—George John Younghusband

Y ou are now free to move about the cabin."

I retrieved my MP3 player from my purse, plugged in the earbuds and leaned my seat back, trying to get comfortable for the long flight ahead. Overnight from Atlanta to London. I'd lost my fucking mind.

I exhaled the breath I'd been holding since takeoff. Now that the monstrous jet had climbed and leveled to cruising height, some of my tension melted away. Already, the sleep aid I'd taken just before boarding started to take effect.

Part of me didn't want to sleep. Ever. Not after the dreams I'd been having. Although I'd always been interested in psychic phenomena and past lives, these dreams had rattled me to the core.

They'd compelled me to buy a plane ticket and travel to London, where perhaps I could sort out what was happening to me.

My eyelids grew increasingly heavy, and my breathing deepened. All over the jet, passengers switched off their lights and settled in for the flight. I blinked, fighting the urge to doze. My gaze drifted to the couple beside me, obviously honeymooning and glowing with new love. Surely it would be safe to relax here, in the midst of all these people.

I snuggled against the tiny pillow the attendant had given me earlier. Yes. I could sleep here—even knowing my dark lover would come from that long-ago time to haunt my dreams again.

"Touch me," my lover pleaded, her voice but a broken whisper as she took my hand to guide it under her nightrail to the soft thatch of curls between her thighs.

I did not need coaxing. Love surged as I sought her delicate folds in the darkness. Her breathing hitched and her thighs parted for my touch. Already slick with her juices, my fingers slid easily over the swollen pearl, and then into the wet velvet of her sheath. Her hands drew me closer under the covers and I realized I could not get close enough to her. The need to fuse with her body, nay, her soul, rose hard within me.

Light from the fire flickered, casting her face in a glimmer of shadows, but I did not miss her impassioned expression. Sweet lavender emanated from her luxurious, inky locks. With her lips parted and her wealth of black lashes resting against her cheeks, I found her incredibly beautiful. Bewitchingly so.

I ached to kiss her, and I craned my neck until my lips

brushed hers. Her eyes flew open, and we stared at each other for several steep seconds until she lifted her chin, fusing her mouth with mine.

Wild desire raged inside me. Still kissing her, I compelled her onto her back and I moved over her, parting her knees with mine, opening her treasures to my touch. My tongue slipped between her lips, and she accepted it, grasping my head in her hands, spearing her fingers into my hair to hold me captive.

She did not have to hold me. My heart was already her willing prisoner. As much as I wanted to please her, I wanted to protect her, to secret her away from this place and hide her from the world. From court. From him.

I thrust my fingers in and out of her, intent on feeling her come undone at my touch. My shoulder dropped and I explored deeper, finding and stroking the swollen pad secreted in her channel. Mewling cries spilled into my mouth. Her fingers clutched harder. Her body trembled beneath mine. Hot wetness gushed around my probing digit, and then her body went rigid. I muffled her cries with my kisses to keep from alerting the others, but she would not be silenced.

She tore her mouth from mine and a long, low moan escaped before I clamped my free hand over her lips, stifling the sound. "Quiet, my lady," I whispered, even as I peppered her cheek and neck with kisses.

Tremors shook her slender body in rippling waves. I eased my hand from her cunny and brought it up to cup one of her breasts, delighting in the diamond-hard nipple pressing into my palm.

How had this happened? How had I fallen in love with a woman?

An unattainable woman.

Her eyes opened, and she gazed up at me. "Would that I

found such pleasure in my husband's bed as I find with you,"
she whispered, her voice hoarse.

Fear seized me. "Silence. You speak of treason."

"Speak it. Commit it. My darling, Fortune, I cannot deny
my heart."

I held her black gaze, my own heart overflowing with
conflicting emotions—love and terror. Innately, I knew danger
loomed. Whispers traveled far at court. Already he looked to
replace her.

"Kiss me," she murmured, drawing me to her. "Kiss me,
sweet Fortune."

I exhaled. "My love," I muttered before my lips closed on
hers once more, knowing what I must do.

Kill him.

My eyes snapped open. My heart hammered. No longer was I
in a shadowy bedchamber. The honeymooning couple snoozed
beside me. A flight attendant eased down the narrow aisle.
The monotonous roar of the big engines vibrated through me,
ripping me from my dream lover's arms and seating me firmly
in the present. I blew out a breath, trying to will my pulse to
return to normal.

Again, I had dreamed of a raven-haired, black-eyed beauty.
In the dream, I knew her well. I *loved* her. I blinked, trying to
recall the location, knowing only it was in a castle bedroom.
A fire burned low in the hearth. I closed my eyes, grasping at
elusive details. Thick, richly embroidered velvet curtains draped
from a canopy overhead. The bed linens were fashioned of the
finest linen, and the pillowslips were emblazoned in gold thread
with an initial I couldn't quite remember.

I only guessed the location was England from my lover's
accent. Her strange manner of speaking hailed from centuries

past. It was almost as if she were calling to me from another time and place.

But why?

And who was the man I would kill for this woman? The memory and strength of my conviction sent a shudder racing down my spine.

I shifted in my seat, once more chiding myself for coming on this fool's errand. What did I hope to find in London?

I'd maxed out my credit card to purchase plane fare and a hotel—all because of a series of recurring dreams. Anyone who knew me would think I'd lost my mind.

Hell, *I* thought I'd lost my mind.

But a dark thought lurked. What if I found my dream lover in England? What then? How could I explain the drive that compelled me to travel across an ocean to find her?

I snorted. This was silly. There was no real woman. I knew better. At the very least, I hoped to make some sense of these crazy dreams that plagued me.

I hoped to make them stop so I could return to my normal, lonely existence working in the Tennessee State Museum, restoring old clothes and flags. Trying to keep from focusing on the dream, I mentally went back over the last items I'd restored. A trunk had been donated by one of the oldest families in Nashville. Some of the items inside had traveled over with the first settlers from England. At first glance, I'd guessed some of the fabrics to be nearly five centuries old.

My expertise lay in fabrics and clothing dating from the mid-nineteenth century. I knew little about anything as ancient as some of the items in the trunk, but I hadn't been able to resist the cardinal sin of touching one of the ermine-trimmed pieces with my bare fingers.

Cold realization washed through me. That was the night my

dreams began. Had touching that fur triggered something in me? I'd never been one to have supernatural experiences, but I had to admit, the idea of past lives fascinated me.

I ruminated again over the dream details I could remember. I had referred to my lover as *my lady*. If my theory about a past life was correct, had I been nobility of some sort? She definitely had been. I bit my bottom lip wondering about the fate of her husband. I'd intended to kill him. I could even recall the determination I'd felt in the dream.

I blinked sleepily. The pill I'd taken still had me under its spell. As much as the dreams aroused me, they also disturbed me deeply. But I had little other choice than to try to find a comfortable position and close my eyes.

I stood in a desolate clearing. Only a small fire cast an eerie glow on an array of items I had readied. A shriveled bird's foot. A mass of curly reddish gold hair. His? Other powdered substances that emitted foul odors when I threw pinches of them into a cauldron of boiling liquid. Over and over I chanted a phrase I could not understand. "Chun an bandia, Molaim a anam. Saor in aisce mo banríon a bheith liom."

I tossed in the severed bird's foot and a vile smoke arose from the pot, reaching into the night sky until it became a part of it. Triumph surged through me. It was done.

Now she would be mine.

And he would die.

"Please replace all trays and return your seat to the upright position."

I jolted awake, once more shaken by the utter vividness of my dreams. My hand trembled as I raised my seat back. I couldn't believe the turn my dreams had taken. They'd become sinister, shadowed with a shroud of intrigue and darkness. Who was the man my dream-self wanted dead? And more importantly, who was the bewitching lover haunting not only my dreams but my fantasies as well?

"Fortune," my lover whispered breathlessly as she pushed the door shut behind us.

I could not wait to be in her arms, to hold her. To touch her. Dressed in forest green velvet with her raven hair smoothed back under a bejeweled French hood, she looked like a queen.

Precious stones gleamed as she lifted her hands to my face. "They are all away at the joust," she said, her dark eyes searching mine.

I shook from the sensation of her cool hands on my cheeks, her fingers lifting my chin so that she could kiss me. Our lips met, softly at first, and then she stepped closer and a little moan spilled into my mouth before her mouth plied mine and her tongue slipped inside. I clung to her, raking my nails in the nap of the velvet, brushing my thumb over the tiny pearls embroidered on the collar of her gown.

She dragged her lips away, and then went to secure the door. My heart beat as quickly as a rabbit's as she turned to me. Dampness gathered at the juncture between my thighs. I could hardly swallow as she started toward me.

"I want you naked," she said, her voice but a whisper.

Immediately, I tugged at the ties securing the top of my gown. She turned me and roughly unlaced my bodice, raking it down along with my thin linen chemise. From behind, she cupped my naked breasts in her hands and squeezed them. My eyes closed, and I leaned against her, luxuriating in the perfect pinch and tug working my nipples into erect, sensitive points.

My channel constricted wildly, and with a little shake of my hips, the gown whispered down my legs and pooled at my feet. She inhaled sharply, and I turned my head to kiss her mouth. Her hands anchored me. One continued to knead my nipple and the other ventured lower. Warm fingers threaded into my thatch and searched until they found my aching clitoris.

I whimpered, and as she pressed and circled me, a shudder rippled through my body. I wanted her naked as well. To feel her skin against my skin would be heaven. I turned in her arms. I'd dressed and undressed her hundreds of times—but never for this purpose. Never in broad daylight. I could barely swallow as she turned and lifted the curtain of her hair off the laces of her gown. Gooseflesh broke out along the slender nape of her neck, and I pressed a kiss there, shocked at the sudden jolt that passed through me at the contact.

As soon as I freed her from her heavy gown, she stepped out of it and pushed me onto the bed. All at once, her hands and mouth were everywhere. My lips. My neck. My breasts. The curve of my belly. Between my legs.

I bit my bottom lip to stifle a cry as she shouldered between my thighs and her mouth closed on the hidden flesh there. My legs flew open wide, exposing my folds to her erotic attention. I held her head, raking my fingers into her silky hair. My heart soared. I could not believe that this powerful, beautiful woman wanted me—would risk her life to have me.

Terror surged, but I forced it away in the wake of her insistent mouth. Her tongue swept through my slit, darting into my opening to explore and taste before tantalizing my clitoris once more. Her lips plucked at my needy flesh, causing the muscles in my legs to grow taut. Pleasure detonated in rhythmic blasts through my body, each one more devastating than the last, driving me higher and higher.

When her finger worked its way inside me, I arched toward

her, grinding my cunny into her mouth. Shaking, I clutched my own breasts. Her finger stroked my rigid nubbin, stoking an already uncontrollable wildfire raging inside me. The soft wetness of her mouth was the most exquisite sensation I'd ever known. She murmured something—a term of endearment—and the vibration from the sound sent me reeling over a precipice.

I spiraled, feeling as if I had no handhold to cling to. Ecstasy shattered me. Each spasm sent bliss winding around my spine and shooting through my limbs. I couldn't breathe without moaning. "My lady," I managed, but the words came out in a strangled whisper.

Her head lifted, and intoxicated, I gazed into her black eyes, my passage still milking the finger embedded deep inside me. Her mouth glistened with my dew. "Taste me," she uttered, moving up to rake her nude body against mine.

Hard nipples scraped my belly and breasts. Her mouth captured mine, and I kissed her, tasting my own essence. This is treason... Again, I stifled my inner voice and moved with her, rolling her onto her back. I didn't know how much time we had, but I burned to kiss every inch of her body, every dip and hollow, every lush swell. Her skin was fragrant and sweet and decidedly her in those places hidden by her clothes. I breathed it in as if I could breathe her spirit into me.

"Fortune." My name spilled from her lips when I slid my hand between her legs.

Her dew-soaked folds opened for me, and I caressed her there, delighting in her heat against my palm and the feel of the thudding pulse of her clit against the ball of my hand.

Her heels scrabbled for a hold on the bed so she could rock into my touch. "I cannot forbear my desire a moment longer, sweet Fortune," she pleaded, pushing my shoulders. Her head lifted off the pillows. "Taste me thus, my love."

I kissed each puckered nipple and then moved between her legs, admiring her femininity before burying my face there. She cried out. Her knees raised. One hand fisted in the covers. I inhaled her and let my tongue slide languidly through the narrow slit, laving her folds and the hard ridge cresting her sex. I could not get enough of her.

With a growl, I pushed her thighs open, spreading her wide. Kneeling, I bent over her and sucked at her flesh, plucking it with my lips, plunging my tongue into her passage, and then tormenting the sensitive strip connecting one orifice to another.

When my finger joined my tongue, she let out a whimper. Her shoulders rose from the bed, arching back the long column of her graceful neck. Her beauty staggered me, and I closed my eyes to concentrate on her pleasure. Sucking her swollen pearl, I thrust my finger into her again and again, letting my free fingers fall to tease her rosette.

Her backside rolled up, toward me, and I coated a second finger with her juices before I wriggled it into her bottom. She thrashed her head from side to side and encouraged me. "Yes! Fill me. Oh merciful heavens…"

Her cunny gripped me like wet velvet, soft and yielding. Her other hole, in stark contrast, was slick and so tight I feared my persistent thrusts would hurt her. She caught her knees and pulled them up to her chest, opening herself to me. The sweet sound of wet suction and my lady's moans filled my ears.

I lifted my face from her center, only so I could finger her harder. Faster. The muscles in her face tensed, and then a ragged breath expelled from deep in her chest while her two openings squeezed my fingers in rhythmic succession. She'd found bliss.

Sudden pounding sounded on the door, and I jumped back from her. Our wide gazes locked.

"There has been an accident, Your Majesty!" a man's voice

cried from the other side. "The king has been injured and is feared dead."

I awakened, sitting upright in the bed. A woman on the television chatted about the latest indiscretions of some pop star—and someone was knocking on my door.

I eased out of bed and pulled on a robe before padding across the carpeted floor to peer through the peep hole. Someone from the hotel stood in the hallway so I opened the door.

"As you requested upon your arrival, I made reservations for you to tour the Tower this afternoon," the young man told me as he presented me with a ticket laid across a silver platter.

I raked my mussed hair out of my face. "Yes. Yes. Thank you." I took the ticket, tipped the bellhop, and then closed the door. Yawning, I strolled into the bathroom and began getting ready to go.

I don't know why I'd been so drawn to the Tower of London—other than I felt an odd sort of familiarity about the place. Silly. It was a place I'd never been before.

But that last dream had confirmed that the Tower might be the best place to start if I wanted to figure out what—or who—was causing these dreams.

Half an hour later, I'd presented my ticket and stood on Tower Green, gaping at the ancient stone structures and Tudor architecture surrounding me. Crenellated towers rose all around me, blotting out modern London. Had it not been for the throng of contemporarily dressed tourists, I would have felt as if I'd been hurtled back in time.

Now and again, my focus clung to the wavered glass of a window or a stone archway, and my insides jellied as eerie memories lurked just out of my grasp. Had I somehow been here before? In another time, in this place?

My feet numbly carried me across the grounds toward a glaringly modern monument in the center of the courtyard. The faraway sound of a rhythmic drum echoed in my head, obliterating the sounds of chattering tourists and outside street traffic. My vision blurred and for an instant I saw the ermine collar of a cloak in front of me. I blinked to dispel the intruding images.

As I neared the monument, my stomach knotted. My knees shook. This place held some significance for my dream-self. But what?

The loud caw of a raven sliced through the damp air, drawing my attention to the bell tower of Chapel Royal of St. Peter ad Vincula. I looked skyward to see the imposing bird stretch its black wings and sail down to the monument where it perched on the chrome railing.

Caw! Its jet gaze locked with mine, and for an instant, I almost thought the creature recognized me. I stopped in my tracks and stared, wary of it. Ravens were far larger than the crows to which I was accustomed. I could easily see how they'd become the subject of evil omens in gothic literature.

The bird lifted one blue-banded foot and let out another gurgling croak. As if drawn magnetically, I stepped toward the animal. It leaned forward, spreading its sooty wings as if to embrace me.

"Shoo!" one of the liveried tour guides said, running at the bird and waving his arms. "Off with you!"

The raven gave voice to several short, shrill calls, flapped its great wings and soared back to the roof of the chapel. I stared, stunned, feeling as if I'd come close to this mysterious thing I'd sought.

"Those birds bite," the guide said. "Best not get too close."

* * *

My attempts had failed miserably. I had wanted to protect her. Instead, my spells and incantations had placed blame on her. She'd been the one accused and convicted of witchcraft, of adultery. I'd stood by, knowing those accusations were meant for me, and had only held my tongue at the command of my queen. Heartsick, I stood on the scaffold behind her, my gaze fixed on the sumptuous ermine of her collar, on her slender neck, which was about to be severed by the burly, hooded executioner she herself had requested from France. My insides trembled, and I fought back the tears.

I'd begged her to let me come forward, to admit my wrongdoings, but she would not hear of it. Instead, she'd whispered to me one request.

Free her.

I shook as Mistress Lee stepped forward to collect my lady's cape. She gave me a reassuring glance as she removed her headdress, and then calmly tucked her raven tresses under her white cap.

Shaking madly, I looked away, trying to pretend I wasn't standing here, that this wasn't happening. That my beloved Anne was not about to die.

My gaze locked on the Tower ravens who sat, perched high above, watching the spectacle below with dispassionate interest. With her gleaming black hair and quick, dark eyes, Anne reminded me of those birds. Majestic. Shining and shrouded in mystery.

I loved her. I had loved her even before she had invited me into her bed to comfort her, to lie with her as a husband lay with a wife. I inhaled a faltering breath, knowing what I must do—knowing how I could keep her.

I chose one of the ravens, and as my lady knelt to pray— to die—I commended her soul to the breast of that bird.

* * *

My eyes snapped open, and I drew in a sharp breath as Tudor England once more became my stark, modern hotel room. Everything was suddenly clear. I'd been one of Anne Boleyn's ladies-in-waiting. I'd been her lover. And a witch.

I gulped, still trembling, still feeling as if I stood on the scaffold alongside her. And then cold realization shook me to the core. The raven I'd seen at the Tower was her. My Anne. My lady.

A stifled sob choked in my throat, and I brought my fingers to my lips. Something moved out of the corner of my eye, and I startled. I looked quickly toward the flimsy curtains covering the balcony door.

A raven perched on the iron railing. Without hesitation, I flung back the covers and darted to the door, wrenching it open.

The bird stared, and once again, lifted her banded foot.

Not breathing, I cautiously approached and peered at the band which bore the name *Anne*. I'd never before touched a wild bird, but I reached out and stroked the satiny head. She turned toward my palm, her eyes closing as she received my caress.

Tears welled and rolled down my cheeks as centuries-old heartache flooded me. I took the band in my fingers and ripped it in two, casting it aside. My lips moved, and I began to speak words I didn't know. "*I scaoileadh tú, a ghrá*. I release you, my love."

With a raspy caw, the raven opened her wings, and as she leaped down onto the balcony, she transformed, her wings becoming the belled sleeves of a luxurious black velvet gown, the feathers on her head lengthening into waist-long locks of gleaming hair, the beak shortening into a narrow nose, and the eyes, as dark and black and knowing as before.

I should have been amazed by what was taking place before

me, but instead, joy filled my heart as she took one step toward me and enveloped me in her arms.

"My Fortune," she said, her voice rough from centuries of disuse. "I knew you would find me."

And then our lips met in a kiss tender with love remembered. She was safe. She was whole, and she was finally mine.

VERDE

Anna Meadows

The whole town blamed the *quetzal* for the drought. There had been no rain for months, and every time a cloud crossed the open sky, they waited until it dissipated into wisps. Afterward, someone always claimed to have seen the green bird the night before, and the rest would nod and agree that yes, that was why, and they must all carry their pistols in case one of them should see it again.

Round-bodied and jeweled with short, bright feathers—save three long ones for the brushstroke of its tail—the *quetzal*, native to the cloud forests, had no business in a *mesa* town. A bird of such color did not belong in the desert. Ristra had gone half the summer without electrical storms, which always brought downpours on the thirsty land. It was a few weeks into that dry season that the *quetzal* first appeared.

A dozen strong men had seen her. Each had fallen sick with *susto* days later, the blue sky still flat and smooth as a wedding sheet.

They had first thought the bird was a male—the female *quetzals* did not have tails as long as a cat's—but then they saw the blue feathers mixed in with the green, and the gray-brown of the undersides of her wings, and they feared her all the more. A female had no right to such tail feathers, thin and curved as the arc of the moon two nights after *la luna nueva*. She must have stolen them from her mate after she killed him, said the sick men's wives, and now she had come for their husbands.

Others said that sometimes at night they saw a copper-skinned woman darting naked between the trees, her hair fanning out behind her like a single dark wing. They called her a *nagual*, and the whispered word spread throughout town, paling those who first heard it like the mention of *la llorona*, the weeping woman whose shrieks could be heard when the desert winds blew hard enough to turn the air gold with dust. There had not been talk of the *nagualli* near Ristra for generations, not since the old Mixtec woman had cast out those wicked beings who turned to wolves or birds at night. But *la vieja* had been dead ten years, and now a *nagual*, this one half-woman, half-*quetzal*, had come to dry out the land.

The *quetzal* was quick, appearing only as a shimmer of color as it fluttered between the trees, feeding from the few red peaches or Satsuma plums that hadn't withered in the heat. From the wild avocado trees she chose fruits too small and hard to be picked, swallowed them whole, and spat out the pits, each clean as if they'd been scrubbed. When they grew into saplings days later, and the peaches and plums burst into full harvest, the people of Ristra thought her even more evil, and would not eat the new crop. If they saw her, they shot at her, but she always vanished. They threw stones from the dry riverbed, and her soft cry was their only reward before they lost sight of her green wings. No one as yet had been able to reduce that winged demon to the weight of her flesh and the emerald and pink coral of her feathers, but whoever managed it first would be a hero.

They thought it would be Sam Colton. The woman made her living off a scant half acre of fruit trees, so they figured she'd be willing to kill the thing with her bare hands.

However, half the town still called her Samantha, so she wouldn't answer their pleas past the demands of common courtesy. It was bad enough that bills and junk catalogs still showed up in the mailbox bearing her full name. Besides, as far as Sam could tell, the bird wasn't hurting anybody. She only pecked at peaches small enough to get her beak around, and against the sky she looked like green topaz in a clear stream. The only *nagualli* Sam believed in were the occasional horses or cats that vanished for days before appearing back in their stable or at the foot of their owner's bed just after midnight.

The man who almost killed the *quetzal*, in fact, didn't own a pistol. Jasper Harris lived out near the reservoir, which had seen a ten-foot drop since the start of the year. But Jasper was blind enough to take it for a lake, and though Ristra was hundreds of miles from the nearest swamp, he'd been raised in a bayou so thick with alligators that he couldn't walk to school without seeing the slow blink of their eyes just above water. He'd been bit so many times he'd learned to grab the palatal valve at the back of the animal's tongue. He'd push on the flap of soft tissue, and once enough water rushed down the back of the alligator's throat, it'd snort and let go. Their teeth left him with a mess of scars, but once he figured out how much women liked running their fingers over them he stopped minding.

The waters around where he'd grown up bloomed with algae growth every year, so when he thought of alligators, he remembered them bright as sod grass. All the *quetzal* had to do was peck at a Santa Rosa plum that had fallen to the ground, and

Jasper was sure as anything that she was a young alligator come to finish the job.

Her beak was deep into the tart fruit, and that extra fraction of a second it took her to catch the shadow of Jasper Harris's cane was enough time for him to swing it down.

He saw the red flash of her chest when she flailed, but assumed it must have been the blood of her last meal, and with an "Oh, no you don't," he hit her again until she lay still. He left with a satisfied huff, walked to his back door, and had a heart attack from the effort. By the time the neighbors found him, the *quetzal* was gone, and Jasper Harris had died with the contented smile of having gone before the beast of his youth had the chance to kill him.

Sam Colton lived close enough to that same reservoir to see the shimmer of the water beyond her rows of Blushing Star peach trees, but these days the waterline had fallen so low she had to take a walk out to the bank to catch a glimpse of the blue. When she saw the ambulance, she figured the heat must have gotten the best of Jasper Harris. Without the electrical storms, Ristra blazed during the day, though overnight it got cold enough that Sam slept dressed in a flannel shirt.

Sam said a prayer, first for Jasper Harris's body, and then for his soul when she saw the women cross themselves, first one, then three more, like it was catching. The last of sundown flashed in the water, and Sam walked the path along the dry creek bed back toward her fruit trees. The sky was deep as iolite by the time Sam heard the animal's cry.

It sounded, at first, like the whimper of a young dog. But as Sam followed the sound into the dark, she heard a weak music in it, the treble syllable that belonged to no creature but the winged. She searched for the pale neck of a black-billed swan or the red body of a cinnamon teal. However, the shimmer of motion she found was green, the bird's feathers catching the light of the first stars like a million shards of jade.

The *quetzal* trembled, its call fading. Her eyes shined up at Sam, round and dark as polished onyx. She flailed one wing, but the other lay curled and limp beneath her. Her chest was fuchsia as a prickly pear flower, so Sam couldn't tell if she was wounded. *Quetzals* were weak fliers, Sam had heard, but they could get off the ground for short bursts.

Sam could almost hear her father telling her to leave the bird where it was, but the man had never followed his own advice. He'd let Sam's oldest sister keep a runt of a rabbit she'd found in the rows of Elberta peach trees. He'd turned a blind eye when his wife took in a pig too small for its mother to feed and gave it milk with an eyedropper. So Sam spread her father's jacket over the ground and lifted the bird onto it.

The *quetzal*'s body was solid and heavy as a cat's. The bird screamed at being touched, but quieted when Sam laid her down on the duck cloth. "Hey," she whispered. "It's all right. I'm not gonna hurt you."

Damned if she could promise more than that. Short of setting the paw of a favorite cat growing up, Sam was no doctor, and there wasn't a vet in the county she could trust not to kill the bird at first sight. Stories about that *quetzal* had spread fifty miles in every direction. By now every town had its own. Sam had taken five crates of peaches to a market just west of Ristra, and the grocer wouldn't pay her until she promised to be wary of those green wings. Later the same week, she'd driven three towns to the north to pick up a stock of canning jars, and the woman swore that the dreadful creature had slit a man's throat with her longest tail feather, clean as if it'd been a blade.

The churches were no help either. The priests would cut out the *quetzal*'s heart and burn it with the egg of a blue hen, because they were sure it would bring rain. Even the women who knew to call her Sam instead of Samantha wouldn't listen. A couple of weeks earlier, when Sam had mentioned that all the *quetzal* had done was make a wrong turn flying somewhere, they called her a "silly boy" and asked if she wanted to come in for *jamaica* and *tortas de aceite*. If they had the chance, they'd take the bird to the back of their land so Sam wouldn't hear it screaming when the knife went in.

Sam crouched and stroked two fingers over the soft blue down on the back of the bird's head. "You and me got some bad luck, huh?" she said, and gripped the jacket by the collar. She dragged it as gently as she could manage, kicking rocks and dead roots out of the way so they wouldn't jostle the injured bird. She carried her inside and set her down on her grandmother's quilt, folded over four times. The *quetzal* had lost either the strength or the inclination to scream again.

Even injured, with her weight slumped to one side and her wings crumpled against her body, the *quetzal* was the most beautiful thing Sam had ever seen. It made her wonder how everyone had got to hating her so much. If there was anything Sam knew about people, it was that they always liked something pretty. Her mother had known it too; it was why the woman cried whenever Sam's father took her to get her hair cut short or bought her a new pair of blue jeans. She'd go on about how no one was ever gonna marry the girl if she grew up looking like that, and why couldn't he let her just be pretty like her sisters? "You got five daughters, Edda," he'd say. "If one of them wants to be a son, you can damn well share." Her father won too; Sam had barely outgrown her first pair of overalls by the time she knew how to tell a Roza peach from an Autumn Red by the scent of the blossoms.

The *quetzal* was green as malachite, the feathers closest to her skin flashing a peacock's blue when she shuddered. Among her emerald feathers, her chest looked like a handful of beautyberries nestled in bright leaves. A patch on her crown was the same dark pink. The inner down of her tail feathers matched the pale blush of moonglow fuchsias.

All her colors made Sam think of the poem Jorge Vasquez, the drunk, had scratched onto the tavern wall near the phone booth, a line at a time in the weeks before he'd died. Sometimes Sam would buy him a *cerveza* so he'd let her watch him dig the knife into the paneled wood. She would ask what it meant, and Jorge would slur, half in Spanish, half in English, that she only needed to watch and see. After he was gone, Sam spent hours leaning on the side of the phone booth, her Spanish broken enough that she could only make out a few words at a time.

Verde que te quiero verde. Bajo la luna gitana.

Green, I want you green, under the gypsy moon.

Con la sombra en la cintura, ella sueña en su baranda, verde carne, pelo verde, con ojos de fría plata.

With the shade on her waist, she dreams on her balcony, green flesh, green hair, with eyes made of cold silver.

Un carámbano de luna, la sostiene sobre el agua.

The icicle moon holds her up above the water.

She'd jotted down a few lines and taken it to the branch library two towns over, and the woman at the desk had told her the poet's name. "Lorca," she'd said with a wistful glance up to the ceiling, like she was remembering an old friend.

Sam gave the bird water, and then cut open a peach and offered her the two pink halves. The *quetzal* nipped at the sunburst of red in the center, and then slept. The slow rise and fall of her wings told Sam she was still alive.

Sam ate the peach half the bird had not touched, fell onto her bed without taking off her jeans, and dreamed of green wings spreading out as big as clouds across the cornflower sky.

When she woke, the *quetzal* was gone, and in her place a woman lay curled on her side, her cheek burrowed into the folds of Sam's quilt. Sam blinked until the muscles around her tear ducts ached. The woman did not vanish.

At first glance, her naked body looked soft, like it was holding to the last traces of baby fat, but her breasts and hips were too full for her to be that young. Instead, it was the same roundness, compact but full, that Sam had felt when she'd carried the *quetzal*. The woman's hair, black as the reservoir at night, shielded her breasts and caught the light, glinting flashes of green and peacock blue.

The woman gasped awake. Her eyes snapped open, and the color of the irises threw Sam, stripping away the last of her reluctance to believe that the woman in front of her had, the night before, been the winged creature. At first Sam thought of the woman's eyes as a reddish sort of brown, then maybe a kind of red-violet, but the longer she stared, the more they blazed back red. Not the crimson of a loon's eye, but the deep rose of cold raspberries, the same color the feathers on the *quetzal*'s chest had been. The woman's mouth and the tips of her breasts were the same berry pink.

The woman's body tensed. Her hand slowly curled into a fist and uncurled, and she dragged herself, a centimeter at a time, off the quilt and onto the wood of the floor. A band of bruising crossed her back, already dark as blackberry wine.

It took the chill of a draft from under the door for the woman to remember her own name. *Graciela*. Her mother had never called her the full name, not even when she'd done something wrong. Those times, she was "Grace." All others, she was "Ciela." Now she remembered the man's cane coming down on her, the fragile skin beneath her feathers taking the impact as she heard the echo of her mother's voice, "Grace, Grace, Grace," until the sky had gone dark.

But now, again, she was Ciela, her skin raw and new, the tangles of her hair her only clothing. She could have covered herself with the blanket beneath her, but she couldn't take hold of the fabric. Each time her fingers closed, the calico slipped from her grasp.

The boy who had taken her from the side of the dry riverbed crouched near her, forearms on the thighs of his jeans. But enough of the buttons on his shirt had loosened in his sleep that she could see the shadow one breast cast on his sternum. A woman, much older than the boy she'd first thought she was. She wore a cotton duck jacket that smelled like the peach she had given Ciela the night before. Ciela had seen her with her fruit trees, and had seen her carrying a shotgun to scare off the crows. She had never aimed it at Ciela. It was how Ciela remembered her, because the others always did.

Sam wrapped a bag of frozen blueberries in a kitchen cloth and set it against the bruise on the woman's back. "Do you speak English?" she asked.

The woman winced at the cold, but tilted her head, barely a nod.

"Yeah?" Sam asked. "What's your name?"

The woman's head lolled to one side. Her hair fell away from her temple, revealing a new wound, red and wet as the inside of a cherry. "Ciela," she said, so softly that Sam had to read her lips to make out the sounds.

Sam smoothed a few strands of dark hair away from the cut. The *quetzal* had had no ruby feathers on her head, only blood staining the green. "I'm Sam," she said.

Ciela tried to pull her limbs closer into her body, but her muscles gave out, and her body went slack.

"I'm gonna help you," said Sam. "I can help a person easier than I can help a bird." She gathered her off the floor and put her into her bed, half-expecting the woman to burst into feathers when she touched her. Sam covered her with her grandmother's quilt and got to work on the wound, cleaning it first with water, then with a little of the rubbing alcohol she splashed on all her own cuts. She'd never needed anything gentler.

This time the woman did not flinch or startle. A single tear streaked across her cheekbone like a drop of polished quartz. Sam was about to tell her she was sorry when Ciela said, "Thank you."

Sam blotted the last of the blood. She would have taken the drop of quartz with it, but it was too beautiful to brush away.

Ciela's eyes closed, sealing away the pink topaz of her irises.

"Where'd you come from?" Sam asked.

It came back to Ciela slowly, like film developing and then, just as quickly, yellowing with age and sun. It always did when her human skin returned. Her mother had had her heart broken by a local man when Ciela was barely seven, and shortly before eating enough moonflower to kill her overnight, she took her daughter to a *bruja*.

Ciela played with the kitten on the *bruja*'s floor while the two women discussed what the girl should be. The *bruja* shuffled through a stack of cards, so old the corners were worn soft, each painted with a different creature. She thought Ciela would make a fine pony, but Ciela's mother shook her head; just as many colts were *calaveras*. Ciela's mother thought she should be a cat, so she would never need anyone, but the *bruja* lifted a thin finger to the kitten in Ciela's lap. Cats did not start out as cats, but as kittens, blind and weak. Ciela's mother would not have that for her daughter.

The *bruja* continued to shuffle the cards, until a round bird, bright and green, appeared at the top of the deck. The women lifted their eyes from the table to each other's faces, and it was as though a dark wick, stubborn and wet, had suddenly caught the flame. *Quetzals* were lonely and wary of all others, and if they ever mated, it was for life. They were beautiful, but with a song too ordinary to lure men into the hills.

Ciela had thought they were playing a game. Theirs were the last voices she remembered before the morning she awoke, dew-wet and trembling, in an avocado tree, her body small and trapped in a coat of dark feathers she kept trying to shake away. But it stayed.

She remembered, also, the witch asking her mother if she would ever like the *remedio* to be broken. Her mother answered, "Yes, if she is loved," and the way she said it sounded like *un cuento de hadas*, a fairy tale that would never be.

Ciela had stayed a *quetzal*, only a *quetzal*, for so long that when she first emerged again in her human body, she barely recognized it. She could not know how many nights passed between each time she appeared again in her own skin, but each time, her breasts and hips were a little more distinct from her waist, and the soft hair between her legs was soaked with her own longing.

She hated her mother for bringing her to the *bruja*, and in her worst moments, hoped she had suffered through the night before the moonflower and thorn apple killed her. There were no other *quetzals* in the desert, and even if there had been, they, like the other birds, would have known she was a *nagual*, and not one of them.

In Sam's arms the night before, wearing her feathered body,

Ciela had felt a careful affinity for the woman, like a kitten might feel in the hands of a boy who was gentle but whom she did not know. Now, despite the pulse of blood in her temple, Ciela wanted the woman called Sam who sat near her on the edge of the bed. She didn't care if a stripe of bruising stung on her back; she wanted to unfasten the rest of the buttons on Sam's plaid shirt and see the breasts that cast shadows on her sternum. She wanted to take off her jeans and find the hips she should have known could not have belonged to a man; they were sturdy and muscular, but too full. She wondered if the hair between Sam's legs would match the dull gold that was just long enough to fall into her eyes.

Ciela lifted her hands to the thighs of Sam's jeans, slowly, so she might not notice. She had caught her reflection in the reservoir once, and she knew she was no longer the soft brown and cream she'd been as a little girl, with hair dark as *cacao*, and her palms and feet a little paler than the terra cotta of her limbs.

Now she was a strange red-eyed thing, with the colors of the *quetzal* wings staining her hair even when she shed her feathers.

Sam's fingers stilled when she felt Ciela's hands on her. Ciela pulled her forward and kissed her, and there was nothing Sam could do but fall, bracing her hands on the bed to keep her weight off her. Sam struggled to say something, but Ciela wrapped her legs around Sam's body, gripping her with her thighs. Ciela took hold of Sam's lips with the berry-red of her own, and all Sam could think of was green, and the gypsy moon, and the icicle sky. The green and blue in Ciela's hair darkened almost to black, but Sam could find it still as she ran her fingers through it. Her eyes deepened to brown, leaving a ring of pink sapphire just at the edge of the iris, as she stripped off Sam's jeans and parted her shirt to find her breasts.

Sam kissed the rose-gold of Ciela's breasts, one at a time, and took in the scent of cinnamon and wet petals that was strong on her skin. *Verde. Verde. Verde.* Even with skin instead of down, and soft thighs instead of tail feathers, Ciela's body held all the bright beauty of the *quetzal*'s green and red.

It came quietly at first, the soft tapping of a few fingers on Sam's roof, the rustling of leaves under the weight of new water. But then Sam and Ciela heard the rain beating the ground into life, soaking dried roots and flooding the underground rivers.

Ciela felt herself blooming open, her thighs parting a little more without her meaning them to. That slight rise in her hips weakened Sam's shyness, and she came, her wetness spreading over the space between her legs and then rushing out onto the damp velvet between Ciela's.

That embarrassed Sam at first, letting it out like a man would; it hadn't happened since she was young, first learning to touch herself in the dark of her bedroom when she was sure her sisters were asleep. But Ciela tilted her head back, her hair spreading out over Sam's pillow, and her lips parted, her next breath laced with pleasure.

The rain was filling the dry riverbed. The ground grew drunk on it, like it was the *mezcal* of the bluest agave. The water, warmed by the heat of the ground, rushed out over Sam's half acre of farmland, reviving the peach trees so the boughs reached toward the slate-blue sky. The branches shuddered with such excitement that they almost burst into flower out of season.

Days later, when the reservoir had filled and the creek bed had risen almost to its banks, Sam gave Ciela one of her father's shirts, long enough that with a belt she could wear it as a dress, but short enough so the women from the church might cluck their tongues anyway.

She took Ciela's hand and led her into the town, shaded with fresh leaves. The wells were full, the priests told Sam. The women's sick husbands had woken with an appetite for twice their usual breakfast, and no one had seen the *quetzal* since the night before the rain began. They told the strange girl holding Sam Colton's hand that she was lucky, that if she had come to visit a week earlier, she would have found Ristra as dry as the moon, but that now it was wet, and living, and green, all of it green.

NINE DAYS AND
SEVEN TEARS

J.L. Merrow

Y ou don't get seals on the Isle of Wight, *Briony Brain-Dead.* It was probably a rock. A big, fat rock." Col punctuated his words with wide-armed gestures, and when he'd finally shut his stupid mouth, he blew out his cheeks.

I pretended to yawn. Maybe I wasn't a stick insect with a pair of melons for boobs like all the girls in the porno mags he kept hidden in an old Airfix kit box under his bed, but so bloody what?

Maybe I'd skip pudding tonight, though. Well, depending on what it was. Mum did some great puddings.

"I know what I saw, all right? Anyway, they had a bloody whale in the Thames. Why can't we get a seal blown off course 'round here or something?" I didn't even realize I was standing there with my hands on my hips until he started mimicking me. I shoved my fists in my pockets and stomped along the sea wall away from him.

God, I hated this place. Nothing here but sand and sea and

people who remembered every daft thing you did when you were a kid.

All right, I didn't hate the place. Maybe I even loved it, with the fresh island breezes and the smell of the sea everywhere you went. But I didn't love the lack of opportunities and the narrow-mindedness.

There's a reason the word "insular" comes from the word "island."

I was stuck here, fresh out of Uni with a degree no one wanted and no bloody job. Not likely to find one round here either, but I'd have to be mad to leave home without some money coming in, wouldn't I?

Col didn't care. He had it all planned out. He was going to finish at the tech college and get a job stacking shelves some-where, and live at home so he could spend his pay drinking with his mates every Friday night with just enough left over to take his girlfriend out somewhere cheap on Saturday.

I hated her as well. Sharp-faced little cow in skinny jeans, always offering to lend me her clothes like she couldn't see there were three sizes between us—and that was on one of my good days.

If she'd been here, she'd have been laughing at me, too. But I knew what I'd seen. I'd seen a seal. Beautiful, it was, with eyes you could dive right into. It'd looked straight at me, head cocked like it was studying me, and then it ducked back under the waves. I'd looked for ages, trying to see it again, until Col came up and asked me why I was staring out to sea like a zombie had come up and eaten my brain. Not that it would have been more than a snack—according to my bloody brother.

I didn't hate Col. Not really. I just didn't like him very much, that's all.

* * *

I came out again after tea. I'd had two helpings of jam roly-poly, just to prove Col hadn't gotten to me, so I needed the walk. And I wanted to see if she was there again.

I'd decided the seal must have been a she. Too graceful to be male, she was. Maybe I'd only seen a sleek head and the curve of her back as she dived, but I knew she was grace itself. I wanted to see her again. I wanted to watch the sunset gild her fur while I stood on the beach like a love-starved sailor of old, seeing mermaids in the gloaming.

I'd forgotten it would be high tide by then.

The wind was whipping up the waves to crash against the sea wall, sending up clouds of spray that spattered my face and left me tasting salt on my lips. There was no beach left at all, and the gulls were circling high above me, crying at its loss. I shivered, hoping my seal had found somewhere safe to rest for the night.

I turned to walk back home—and almost bumped right into her. Not my seal, of course. A girl. Well, a woman, really; just about my age, to look at her. She'd pulled down the top half of her wetsuit to show her black swimsuit underneath, swelling with the curve of her full breasts.

"Hello," she said, smiling at me. "I'm not quite sure where I am."

"Sandown," I said. "Well, Yaverland, really, this far down, but you won't have heard of the village." And I blushed, because there she was, a beautiful woman come out of nowhere, and there I was, getting pernickety about parish boundaries.

She cocked her head to one side, her dark, wet hair drifting in the wind like seaweed in the swell. "Yaverland? I like the name."

Her accent was strange—reminding me of all those Scandinavian crime shows on the telly, though my swimmer would fill out a Faroe sweater much better than what's-her-face in that Danish show.

"Where have you come from?" I blurted out.

"Oh, my boat's out there," she said, waving an arm vaguely out to sea. I looked, but I couldn't see a single light. "Like I said, I think I got lost."

"You swam in from a boat?" My heart felt cold as I looked at the waves thundering against the breakwaters, crushing driftwood to pieces. "You can't go back in this sea!"

"It's all right," she said, her hand soft on my arm. "I'm a very strong swimmer."

"Look, why don't you come back to my mum and dad's? They're out—it's ballroom dancing night. You can have a cup of coffee and—" *And I can try and stop you swimming to your death.*

She looked at me for a long, long moment. "You're sure? That's very kind of you. I'm Freyja."

"Briony," I said. "And, um, my brother Col's going to be home, but just ignore him, okay?"

"Ah! I know—I have lots of brothers." She slipped her hand into the crook of my arm and we set off back home, my skin tingling every time our hips brushed.

Col didn't even look up from his PlayStation when we walked in the door. I didn't want to talk to Freyja with guns blaring in the background, so I took her in the kitchen, ducking under Dad's freshly ironed shirts hanging by the door. We sat at the little wooden table with the wonky chairs, breathing in the scents of fabric softener and the lasagna left over from tea.

"How long are you going to be here?" I asked, as I handed her a mug of coffee made with hot milk to keep out the chill.

She smiled crookedly. "I can't stay. I need to get back to

Hvammstangi—I really shouldn't be here at all. I don't know what drew me down here." As she spoke, she laid her hand, warm from the mug and from the heart of her, on my arm.

I placed my own hand over it and twined my fingers into hers, my stomach feeling like it was full of little fishes darting joyfully in all directions.

"But I'm glad I came," she whispered.

"Me too," I said, and I leaned over the table and dared to kiss her. She tasted of salt and fresh air and freedom, and I pulled her to me, not wanting to let her go.

Her breasts were warm and soft against mine, her skin like velvet. She clambered onto my lap, still half in her wetsuit like a butterfly coming out of its chrysalis, and we clung together, wordless, until she rested her forehead on mine. "I have to go. I'm sorry, Briony."

I tried to stop her. "No, you can't go." I pulled at her wetsuit, but she looked so sad I dropped my hand. "I wish you'd stay," I whispered, defeated.

"Remember me," she said softly. "Remember me, and perhaps we'll meet again."

"When?"

"Nine days' time, if you still remember me. Nine days' time. I can stay that long."

"Then why not stay with me?" I begged.

"I can't," she said. "But I can come to you once more."

I walked her back to the seafront. The wind was quieter now, and the sea was soft and welcoming.

Freyja put her hand to the zip of her wetsuit. "Don't watch me go," she said.

So I turned and walked away, but the splash I listened for never came. For a moment I thought she'd changed her mind, but then I heard her voice on the wind as if a gull had carried it to me.

"Nine days," she called. "Remember that, Briony. Nine days and seven tears."

There's a lot you can learn in nine days. You can learn all about the different types of seals and where they live. You can learn that Freyja's an Icelandic name, and Hvammstangi is a small town in their north. You can learn that Iceland's a much more tolerant place than some islands you could think of.

You can realize that if you have to spend many more months here you'll go mad, and that while hope can inspire you, it can hurt you, too.

It was a calm, clear night when I went back down to the sea, Mum's apple crumble and ice cream a cold comfort in my stomach. Nine days, she'd said, and here I was. Maybe I'd already gone mad. After all, who'd seen her apart from me? Col hadn't even noticed her passing through.

It wasn't hard keeping her second condition as I sat on the sea wall with my legs dangling over the edge, hugging myself while I let my tears drop into the water. Harder to keep to seven, they flowed so fast, but I hoped she'd forgive me.

I thought I saw my seal, but she was gone before I could blink—and then Freyja was beside me, her wetsuit half undone once more.

"You didn't forget," she whispered, and she was crying too.

I pulled her close to me, the soft warmth of her flesh revitalizing me. "You're like a hot spring," I told her. "Warmed by the spirits of the earth."

Freyja cocked her head on one side and smiled. "And you're a rock for basking on, heated by the sun."

"Come and bask with me," I said, and we stood and walked back to my parents' house.

I didn't disturb them, watching telly with Col. I took Freyja straight up to my room. I peeled off her wetsuit, and her swimsuit too, and left them on my bedroom floor. My breathing hitched as I kissed her full breasts and the curve of her stomach, her body all softness and warmth. I traced her contours with my tongue, which tingled from the sea-salt on her body, and I kissed her lower still, where the milky white of her skin gave way to darkness and musk.

I found where the heat of her was centered, and as she opened for me like a sea anemone, she arched her back and hummed with pleasure. The scent and the flavor of her almost overwhelming me. I tongued that hard, crimson bud again and again, until Freyja shuddered and came, crying out softly in an ancient language I longed to understand.

"You make me so hot," she whispered, but her white fingers felt cool on my heated skin, like the lap of the sea on a hot summer's day. They rippled over me, bringing life and yearning to every part they caressed, and then they dove inside me, darting in and out with a touch that both burned and soothed.

I gasped as her mouth closed over my nipple, feeling the heat of it deep within me. Her tongue teased me without mercy, but I ached for my loss as it left me—only for my Freyja to murmur soothing sounds as her dark head dipped lower, her silky hair flowing like water over my body. I had to stifle my cries in case Col might hear as she found me again, this time right at my center. She sucked on my clitoris as her fingers moved within me, bringing me higher and higher on a wave of sensation, and I cried aloud as I crested that wave and broke, tumbling down to float on smooth water, little ripples moving me still.

Afterward, I held her in my arms, and we basked together in a tangle of cool sheets and warm bodies. "I'm going to see you again," I told her.

"I can't stay," she said sadly, her hair caressing my skin like warm, dry sand as she shook her head.

"I know," I said. "But I'm going to see you again."

If I were a man, I might have stolen her wetsuit as she slept and never let her swim away from me.

But I'm not a man, and despite my name, I'm not one to cling onto what's not mine by right. So I kissed my love in the dawn's pink glow, and I walked her down to the beach before anyone was up. I turned my back once more as she swam away while the gulls mourned for the both of us.

But then again, what do gulls know? I booked a flight to Reykjavik with my credit card and started looking for a job there over the Internet.

"Why do you have to go to Iceland? There's nothing there," Col grumbled as I packed my bags.

"Well, it's like you said. You don't get seals on the Isle of Wight." I shut my case with a snap, and Col sneered at me and twirled a finger round by the side of his head, muttering "Briony Basket-Case."

And I smiled and started counting the days until I'd see my selkie again.

SWEETWATER PASS

Angela Caperton

My papa always called me a bent branch—strong enough, fully leaved, but not quite right. I was always the one who scratched at the windows. It was me who tipped the pastor's hat from his head if I could get away with it undetected. Bent branch—the limb on the tree that needed constant trimming.

My marriage to Albert had been a disaster. Papa hoped that marrying me into the McCray family would give our family some legitimacy in Somerville, but Albert wasn't as simpleminded as Papa had thought. Albert noticed almost at once that I wanted Sarah, our maid, more than I wanted him.

Albert fired Sarah. He beat me.

Maybe he was just that simpleminded. It was always the small things that hooked him. He didn't see beyond my desire for Sarah, didn't see how his boot in my belly dissolved my restraint, didn't see the wolf and marten in the open door.

My family left that night, headed north and west, my bruises just a shadow on my skin, the blood in my throat still acidic and bitter.

Three months later, Mama, Papa and Lonnie, my pup brother, were leaving Iowa, the wagons' creaking and groaning as natural as the rustle of the tall grass, the smell of livestock and poorly bathed men and women almost a comfort.

"We gonna see wild Injuns, Mari?"

"Mr. Blocker says we may. Says we'll be lucky if they don't scalp us all." I poked Lonnie in the ribs. I loved my brother, eight years my junior and the first of us born in the United States of America. I always wondered what he would be when he grew up.

"They won't catch Papa. He's too fast!"

"No...but you know them Injuns value pup scalps more than anything. You'd best behave so Papa and Mama don't just sell you to them."

Lonnie's eyes grew big as plates, but then he scowled and socked me in the arm. "Well, better a pup than a widow!"

Lonnie couldn't have known how well he aimed, nor would he know the strange dullness of the piercing. Widow, yes. Mournful, well, less than would be acceptable to the neighbors, I was sure.

I took off my bonnet and used it to fan myself. The sun baked us, and the air lay so still that the dust settled exactly where it rose. Lonnie picked at the laces of his shoes, head down, his tawny hair too long, curtaining his face from me.

I ruffled his mane. "I'll bet you that when we reach California, I'll find a gold nugget before you do."

Lonnie looked up, his eyes bright as stars. "No, you won't! I'll find one the size of a melon! You wait and see."

"Bet ya."

Lonnie scrunched up his face. "A week's worth of wood cuttin'."

"And when I win, it will cost you a week's worth of clothes washin'."

He spat in his hand. I spat in mine.

Bound. Bet.

Family.

There were nine other families in our train, almost thirty wagons, plus goats, cattle, and stubborn sheep that the dogs constantly nipped at to keep moving. At the head rode Mr. Blocker. Sometimes, I saddled the mare Papa bought for breeding stock instead of riding in the wagon with Lonnie. The buckskin didn't cotton to me, and I really didn't blame her, but I'd learned not long after my first change that most prey animals wouldn't like me much. The mare and I came to a grudging understanding late one May night—I wouldn't rip her throat out and she'd let me ride her on occasion.

Bound. Bet.

Family.

I sat on the mare, the saddle warm between my thighs, and rode up to Mr. Blocker at the head of the long line of wagons.

"Miss Mariann," he greeted me, his smile more of a leer.

"Mr. Blocker. Mr. Anderson said that we might be stopping at a creek later today?"

"Yes, miss. It's about three hours ahead at the low part of Sweetwater Pass. We'll stop there for the night. Hopefully, the Injuns won't make trouble."

"Trouble?" I'd learned over the weeks we'd been in Mr. Blocker's care that "Injuns" were a constant threat that grew bigger with each cup of whiskey. My eyes started to roll back into my head until I realized I didn't smell spirits on his breath. He was serious.

"Yes, ma'am. This here's a bad part of the trail. Sioux all around us, but down in the valley, there's another tribe's territory."

I looked back at the wagons, the ambling livestock, the men on horses.

"Is there real danger?" A knot began to form in my belly. I knew the sensation, I knew the sting of fear, but it had been so long since I'd felt it so purely.

Mr. Blocker leaned toward me, his breath acidic with chicory and the rot of meals long past. "I ain't gonna lie to you, Miss Mariann. Every minute we're at that creek, we're sittin' ducks."

"Who are they? Apaches?" I had always heard they were the worst.

"No, ma'am." He laughed a little. "Not this far north. No, I reckon these are Sioux as much as they're anything, but there's lots of kinds of Sioux. Some of the Injun scouts I've known call these folk witches."

I tried to suppress a snort. I knew that word sometimes just meant "different." We'd heard it often enough back home.

Mr. Blocker must have heard me. "Go ahead and laugh, missy, but three months back, two wagons came through here with a bad guide, and I know personally the man who found 'em. Them folks wasn't just scalped." He paused a moment, dabbed his forehead with a stained rag, and measured me with his blue eyes. His spoken reply barely rose above the clop of hooves. "They was skinned."

I pulled up on the buckskin mare and let Mr. Blocker continue forward, the wagons creaking past me. My family was near the end of the train, and I didn't move until Lonnie's young whoop dragged me from a cold well.

"My turn, Mari! Let me ride now. I'm tired of drivin'."

"No." I rarely denied Lonnie anything he really wanted, but I needed the heat between my legs, the animal contact through the leather. Mama and Papa were in the wagon behind Lonnie, eager to embrace the west as our new home, to snap the leash on their nature and be part of this rolling, rattling village of nine families. I couldn't bring myself to tell them what Mr. Blocker had said. This poor wagon train seemed like our last hope. Where else could we go?

We camped that night along the creek, fires glittering in the trickling water as families and hands gathered to eat meals. Laundry hung on leather cords to dry; dogs yipped to keep cattle and sheep tight on the banks.

Papa dozed as he leaned on our good saddle, stretched out by the fire. Lonnie had already yawned three times. Only Mama watched me as she dried dishes after dinner and put them in the pack. The night would be warm, surprisingly so considering we were still at a good altitude and we had not felt a warm night yet.

So Mama watched me—sharp-eyed, keen but quiet—ever the marten. "Don't find trouble in the shadows, daughter," she said, her Welsh lilt intoxicating.

"None seen in shadows, Mama." She knew me.

Twelve years old, back in Tennessee, sleepy and cold, I'd seen the cat by chance. Our sheep ranged in the woods, scattered by a storm that felled trees and smashed the paddock fence. Like Mama and Papa, I was out in the woods after the wind and crashing lightning had stopped. I was the one who found our ram, his throat clutched in the jaws of a beautiful animal, tawny coat, black-touched ears, its eyes like amber, its wisdom deep as molten earth.

Panther.

Aunt of my skin and my heritage.

I only half remember the changing, that first moment when cloth and skin fell away and a pelt became my shield against the air. Mostly, I recall the breath over my tongue as I ran—

and other tastes. Mama and Papa were with me after that first time.

Mama held me close as I wept and shook when my vision came to full color again, and the panther's fur had melted back into my skin. When Deacon White killed the panther a week later, everyone said it was the biggest cat anyone in the township had seen in at least a generation.

I mourned the panther's death, not really understanding the kinship between us, but knowing that something important had happened. As I grew older, I knew that she had blessed me.

In the oddness of that spring season—the new hair in my private place, the swelling of my chest—turning into a panther was only part of what my mama called the change. I had a whole new life—a whole new way of looking at the world. It took me over a year to stop crying every time the moon pulled the panther out of me and another year to learn how to resist the moon's summons, though sometimes even now the moon wins. In the fall, Mama and Papa took me hunting for the first time. The hot blood from the mole I caught christened my throat and sealed my fate. Every sound, every scent of the woods became mine. I saw deep into shadows in shades of gray, savored each bunch of muscles, every crunch of leaves beneath my wide paws. By winter's end, when I changed, I became the cat, insatiable for freedom, fearless and fast.

Two weeks later, I kissed Bonnie Swanson, a tender press of our lips in the alleyway behind her pa's bakery. I tasted her, rough sugar that burst on my tongue. I measured her pulse with mine, and savored her breath against my cheek. Her heart sang my favorite song, the beat as joyful as any Saturday night band music.

That summer, Bonnie was married to Jessup Markham two weeks after she'd turned fifteen. We shared one last kiss the morning of her wedding, Bonnie dressed in a light yellow, crisp cotton dress, carrying a simple bouquet of phlox, trilliums, and yellow poppies. I tasted our tears in the simple stroke of our tongues. She left her home to go to the church and didn't see her brother staring at me, revulsion and lust like lightning and thunder on his face.

Time flowed, places melted into memory, one thing after another, one place after another until the wagons and the pass.

Mr. Blocker's voice rose from the nearest gathering of folk, a fire circle of stories, louder than the wind in the brush, and the gurgling creek. Among the people, one of the Crow guides told stories. The two Crows were brothers and were the only Indians I had ever talked to. They both seemed nice and smart and they talked English better than Papa did. They were funny too. I couldn't hear the words, but the men laughed and I knew it wasn't a story for women's ears.

If I were the panther, my ears would be sharp enough to hear, but then I wouldn't care. This was a wide valley, the white-tipped mountains distant before and behind us, full of rich forest. I knew I would find wild lands in California, but they might not be this wild. I might never have this chance again. Papa knew. Mama knew. Lonnie whined.

Don't find trouble in the shadows.

I moved as quiet as my reflection in a mirror, light on the pads of my bare feet as I crept away from the camp. When I reached the brush not far from the creek, I shed my nightdress. Cool air kissed my skin and pulled my nipples to hard plugs. Overhead the moon approved, shining its blessing upon me. The air caressed me like warm hands on my skin. I slid a finger between my legs, still human, and touched the wet slickness that the night coaxed in me. The ground thinned beneath my feet, the night became alive under my veil of flesh. I burned with the sudden craving that always preceded the change, my own stroke unsatisfying. I conceded that in Albert's horrible attempts to mount me even he had found the sweet spot sometimes.

Still stroking, I slipped out of my skin, uncurling into the cat. I welcomed the dense fur, the blunt nose and keen eyes, my hands and feet now pads that tingled with the vibrations of life beneath the dirt. The first burst of overwhelming humanity almost made me retch—fry pans close to rancid with old fat, the acrid burn of greasy smoke, cattle, sheep, and horse dung, too much body odor, too many liquored breaths.

One of the dogs began to bark, and I ran silently, weaving through the tangle of brush and tree effortlessly, the path clear before me—to my eyes, my nose, and my ears. I smelled deer and my mouth watered. I sniffed for rival cats. I knew panthers were far more common in the west than back east, and I welcomed the fight.

I smelled something else. A cat, but different. The scent drifted from the direction of the creek, a beckoning that made my whiskers twitch. I slid under bushes, between branches, stepped over twigs and settled my paws on soft, night-dewed leaves until I reached the edge of the stream.

I saw her there, silver in the moonlight, rich beyond all the metal fields of the west. She crouched by the pool, soft ears tipped with arching tufts of hair that framed a perfect face, bright eyes, a sleek nose, her tongue curling under to pull water into her whiskered mouth—a petite lynx, compact huntress and beautiful beyond my dreams. Watching her, I felt heavy and clumsy, too big for my soul, too cumbersome to cross into the light and join her, our whiskers tipping into each others, bunched muscles rippling under our mother moon.

Her scent summoned me, a delicious mix of earth and sweet corn that pinched my stomach with hunger and wet my mouth with want. My nose twitched and my claws turned into the earth, kneading the ground as I wavered. I sank into a crouch, legs trembling, heart pounding as fierce as the mountains. I stretched my senses and tasted her essence on my lolling tongue. I should run, I thought, before she sees me.

But I was too late, and I had no desire at all to run.

She, beautiful she, was like me.

Trembling, I stepped beyond the brush, half-concealed by leaves and branch. My size and strength could crush my delicate huntress, but she looked at me with shining eyes and no fear. She stood tall, her little body solid and true. She sniffed the air, her whiskers like little moonlit whips as she scented and assessed.

I stepped toward her, closing a distance too broad, wanting just the hint of her heat before she melted into the night and into my dreams. She didn't run away, but instead stood straighter, not quite arched, no hunched subservience, no cowering away from my size. She sniffed the air again, opened her mouth, and pulled my scent into her body. Something so simple, so instinctual and my chest swelled with caught breath.

Foolish and filled with fanciful flutters of stomach and pulse, I took one more step and melted, rising in the light, naked and open to her, my pelt a memory as my nipples hardened in the cool night. My womanhood slicked with a passion beyond my skin, real as my bones.

Her nose twitched one more time. Her ears folded back, then rose to tufted triangles of curiosity. Her golden gaze locked on mine, and in her eyes I saw flashes of pride and strength, musical acceptance and reverent dance. Wisdom like smoke and stubborn flame tipped the corners of her mouth, and passion, earthbound and heavenly, shimmered over her body as she stood, tall, bronze, with midnight hair past her waist, her little breasts peeking from behind the curtain. All her fur fell away except the moon-silvered, ebon patch between her legs.

I wanted to touch her there, to nuzzle and lick.

She reached out, inviting me, her fingers slender and curled slightly, a generous cup I imagined on my breasts. "Come. The water is sweet." She spoke beautifully with an accent that sounded like the French women back in Iowa.

"You are with the wagons," she said, her tenor curious and critical.

"Yes. My family travels to California."

She tilted her head, almost smiling. "Gold?"

"My brother wants to find gold. My father wants to make furniture." I looked down a moment, then stared into her shining eyes. "We all want to find a place where we can...run."

She stood as still as an oak, her face open, light, her eyes full of wonder and acceptance.

"Come. The water is sweet."

I followed her without a thought. I had a thousand questions, but didn't want any answers. All I wanted was her.

And sweet water.

We made no sounds, our feet as light as the cats inside us. When we reached the creek, she turned, the moonlight tipping her nipples and eyelashes in pale silver. I sucked my tongue before I spoke, not wanting the spit to drain over my lips. Hungry, starving, she smelled of life and danger and something amazingly new. I wanted it all.

I wanted her.

"I *am* thirsty." I heard the words as they left my mouth and knew they sounded ridiculous, but in her dark eyes, I saw understanding. She thirsted too.

Enough of the panther still lay upon me that my senses probed the night around us, painting a picture of light and sound and scent. I saw us as though from a distance, two women bathed in the muted cream and ash of the night, painted by the shadows of trees, alone with the moon and the stream. And I saw her before me, almost close enough to touch. I stepped closer, both of us on the cool, sloping bank. A foot away from her, she burned hotter than any campfire.

I wanted her to touch me, but I also saw that she awaited me, so I reached out, across an expanse big as the sky, wide as the continent. I had never felt anything as fine as the smooth warmth of her arms, muscled and firm. Bolder, I stroked up her shoulder, down the curve of her breast. When I touched her nipple, I saw her eyes turn dangerous and wild.

She reached up, her fingers long, her nails blunt and worn with life, but I felt the claws within. I needed the claws. Would she pierce my skin and pull a howl from me?

Our foreheads pressed, the touch innocent but vital, and as our breaths mingled, I knew I had found everything I wanted, that we would finish the night in sweat and heat. She gripped my waist, kneading the soft flesh above my hips, her fingers primal, her strength arousing. She pulled me against her, fur to fur, our sexes tangling. I'd never been so wet between my legs.

She smelled of everything I wanted, grass and air, warm flesh and salty pleasure, and stronger, a hint of warm honey. Our noses traced lines up our cheeks, and when our lips met, the world opened to me, unexplored, mysterious and full of wonder. Her tongue flicked mine then pressed, a fullness more complete than any promise said before a preacher, the bond as sweet as summer plums. Her fingers ignited my need, turned my center to liquid that flowed to my sex, pearling the curls.

My hands were made to explore her curves, the sensation of her skin under my pads raced excitement through my bones to feed the growing ache in my core. Her warm, firm muscles and her scent drove me wild. When my fingers brushed her sex, the stiff fur parted easily to my probing. Wet, hot, her folds beckoned me. I gripped her waist and slid down, kissing her nipples, enjoying the curl of my tongue around the stiff tips. I sucked, my teeth gently pulling, and her gasp of pleasure bolted joy through me. Her fingers tangled in my hair, pulling me to her, to her heart, to her being.

I knelt, crushing the grass. I cupped her butt and kissed her belly, followed my fingers' trail to the nectar I needed more than air. As my tongue tipped past the curls, I tasted heaven, sweet and true, alive with a passion I knew only in dreams. Sweet, wondrous ambrosia, all mine. I tongued her deep, tracing the folds, my lips caging the bud, my mouth demanding surrender.

I wasn't gentle or demure, I starved for her. Her hands held me to her sex, and my mouth ravaged her. Relentless, I flicked and lapped and nibbled. I sucked her juices and savored the building quiver in her thighs, in her belly, and when her panting turned to whimpers, then to growls, I drank deeper, my tongue a plow, her sex my field. This was my new world, this was my treasure—this beautiful, sensual woman, this sister of the earth. I lapped, a cat at cream, until she screamed and shook, and sank to the ground beside me, holding me in shaking arms.

Beyond the creek the moon slid behind a cloud, but it didn't matter. I held her close, and she me.

After a long time, she whispered, "Your wagons will pass free."

"They are not my wagons," I said, aching with my need for the words to be true, but I knew in my blood they were.

She kissed my breasts, and then my lips, looked into my eyes with a gaze that pulled my soul from its roots. "The wheels cut the earth. This time, I am not sorry."

I saw the sea in her eyes, saw the trees my father would make into chairs and tables, the sturdy home we'd build in California. I saw my brother grown, a young girl on his lap, bouncing on his knee. I saw Mama grey, her eyes still keen as any marten, and my bald father's plane turning wood to useful art. I saw myself, by the sea, with the memory of sweet water, of her, incomplete.

"I'll come back." I almost cried the words.

"I know," she answered.

And the moon, escaped from the clouds, accepted my promise.

I knew, without a doubt, I would return to Sweetwater.

SCORCHED RETRIBUTION

Christine d'Abo

C aity ignored the flip of her stomach as she entered the The Dragon's Den bar and walked in a smooth path toward one of the booths. A quick look around the place as she navigated past chairs filled with patrons told her nothing much had changed since she'd left.

Ten years. Her breath hitched and her heart pounded—she was finally home, back to the one place she shouldn't have left. She'd traveled, worked in both small and large cities over the years before setting her sights on completing her university degree. Not that any of it mattered—the pull to come back was too much.

Caity slipped into the middle booth, her jeans snagging on the knotted wood of the seat as she shifted into place. Falling down in a nervous heap wouldn't set the right tone for her return. Though it was doubtful anyone in the crowd would even notice her arrival, let alone her subsequent breakdown.

"Caity?"

It was a challenge not to roll her eyes. Instead, Caity ignored the voice and concentrated on getting her mind centered. If she was going to be successful, she couldn't be distracted.

"Caity McKenzie? Oh my God, it is you!"

This must be karma. Caity smiled at the woman and tried to remember her name. Sonya, Sasha, Sara...

The brunette turned her chair, the scrape of wood on wood echoing in the bar. "It's Sabrina Cochran. We went to high school together."

"Hi, Sabrina. How are you doing?"

The last thing she wanted to do was engage in a bunch of idle chitchat with someone who never gave her the time of day before Caity had become one of the village's more interesting residents. But she'd have to handle the villagers for the next few hours to finally see an end to her heartache.

She'd do anything to win her lover back.

Somehow, she managed her end of the conversation while scanning the room for the one person who'd brought her here. The reason she'd taken a sabbatical from her PhD studies to come home. The creature haunting her dreams and ruining any chance she had at a normal life.

"Oh! You might want to know that Lynn passed away a few years ago."

Caity snapped her attention back to Sabrina. "What?" She hadn't anticipated that. Lynn had warned her about the necessity back in the early days, but Caity hadn't considered the implications. Did that mean Lynn had moved on?

The brunette must have sensed the shift in Caity, a smirk appearing on her lips as she leaned forward. "Yeah. The rumor is she killed herself. Some niece has taken over ownership of the bar. So there's no one left to pick on you and make you blush."

Caity's sexuality had never been much of a secret growing

up. And while it made her life a living hell, the novelty of being a lesbian in the village quickly wore off as she got older. No one had been surprised when she'd packed her things and headed south to Toronto. If anything, she knew they'd most likely wondered what had kept her in the small northern Ontario village for as long as she'd stayed.

But she sure as hell knew the entire population would have been shocked if they'd known the real reason for her running away. And why she'd come back.

Licking her lips, Caity relaxed the tension in her back. "What's the niece's name?"

"Quinn. She's nice enough. Mostly keeps to herself. At least she hasn't changed the bar from what Lynn did."

God forbid Lynn—Quinn—make any changes to her precious bar. "I'll have to say hello."

Further conversation was cut short when Sabrina's companion got up to pay and someone turned the jukebox on. It was easy to turn around and sink into the darkness and noise of people laughing, living their lives. Her whole return had been surprisingly easy, given how things had ended.

"You're new around here." A paper coaster landed on the table in front of her. "What can I get you?"

Caity looked up into a familiar pair of golden eyes, and her world stopped.

The face was different, younger than Caity remembered, but still older than her. It would be easy for people to accept Quinn as Lynn's niece, given the resemblance and obvious age difference. Humans were able to brush away anything unexplainable with the thinnest stroke of logic.

But she knew better.

Even if Quinn's face was completely different—if she'd changed her hair from the glorious coal black to blond, Caity still would have recognized her. The pull remained, the invisible strings wrapped unknowingly around her body, snaring her to this woman. To this magnificent, terrifying, stunning creature.

Quinn was giving her a way out—though Caity wasn't sure why. She could pretend she didn't know who it really was standing in front of her—with her black T-shirt stretched tightly over her breasts, low-riding jeans hugging her hips, fire in her eyes—and get on with her life. Caity had done it once before. Walked away.

She wasn't making the same mistake twice.

Caity straightened her back, folded her hands in her lap, and lowered her gaze submissively to the coaster before her.

"It's nice to meet you, *Quinn*."

The hitch in the other woman's breathing was the only indication that her emphasis hadn't been missed. "I'll get you the usual."

No question, no choice. Coming from any other person, Caity would have been furious at the presumption. But Quinn was the reason for her return, the void she'd tried to fill for the past ten years of living in the big city. Caity accepted the statement with a single nod of her head.

A few minutes later, a glass of red wine was placed on top of the coaster. A hand covered hers, squeezing enough to dig Quinn's long, red nails into her skin. "You're not moving from this booth. You can get up to pee if you need to. The bar closes in two hours."

"Yes, ma'am."

Caity settled her mind, drank her wine, and waited, excitement and hope warm in her chest.

Quinn sent three refills to Caity over the next two and a half hours as the bar patrons slowly filtered out into the warm summer night back to their homes and their beds. The alcoholic buzz did little to dull Caity's anticipation of upcoming events, nor was it enough to completely relax the tension from her body.

She listened to Quinn joke and tease the staff as they cleaned up the bar. It should have been odd that no one approached her, encouraging her to leave. Then again, she wasn't looking at them, her gaze fixed on the table, and couldn't have seen anything Quinn was doing to deter them.

It took her a few minutes to realize the last of the staff had gone, and she was finally alone with the woman she'd been unable to escape. Quinn—the woman she couldn't be without.

The soft thuds of footsteps caught her attention. Caity shifted her gaze enough to see Quinn standing by the back door.

"I know it's been a while for you." Quinn's voice sounded rough, deeper than it had when the others were present. "But I have rules. You've broken far more than I could possibly count."

There was no point in apologizing. Quinn wouldn't believe it, and for the most part, Caity wasn't sorry for leaving. She'd had to get out, away from the village and everything that it represented. She'd needed time to get her head around what her life was becoming. Then she'd needed time to accept her role.

Words were meaningless. Actions, however...

Her legs only shook a little as she got to her feet and walked meekly over to Quinn. Not once did she look up, scared to see the expression on the other woman's face. Caity paused only long enough to open the door to the back before making her way through the storeroom and out into the backyard.

The moon was out, illuminating the trees and casting long shadows across the yard. Caity was relieved to see things hadn't changed with the passage of time, and easily found the path that led to the clearing.

She didn't need to see Quinn to know the other woman was following at a distance. Caity pulled her shirt off, letting it drop on the path as she continued on. The air was cool, and her nipples hardened instantly on exposure. Her bra fell next and the breeze rolled across her skin, eliciting a shiver.

The path emptied into a clearing. The rock circle stood much as it had when she'd turned eighteen and had been here the first time. The wooden stake in the middle still held the long chains, silver cuffs dangling from the tips. Yanking on the button to her jeans, Caity kicked off her sneakers and carefully walked barefoot to the circle.

She had to be naked. She had to be submissive. Most importantly, she had to be willing.

The metal was cold on her skin as she clicked the shackles into place. If things went her way, they wouldn't stay there long, and Quinn would free her. Giving the restraints a testing tug, Caity finally let herself relax. She'd come back home to offer herself up on a plate to the woman she'd walked away from.

She would finally make the sacrifice she couldn't ten years ago.

Letting out a huff, Caity turned and pressed her back to the wood and focused her gaze on the path. There was no movement for several minutes, which wasn't surprising given who she was dealing with. Quinn would make her wait. Unlike the first time she'd found herself in this position, Caity wasn't afraid.

The villagers didn't actually believe there was a dragon who lived in the mountains dwarfing their homes. It was a legend, like Ogopogo or Loch Ness, to pull in the tourists in the summer. The dragon festivals were an excuse for hikers to congregate and youths to drink themselves stupid.

And every few years, some unlucky person would be brought to the stake in the woods, shackled tight, and offered up as a sacrifice. A prank by high school kids looking to haze the class nerd, the quiet girl, anyone different.

Just like they'd done to Caity.

Only that time the dragon came.

The rumble echoing in the quiet night air could have been mistaken for thunder, if not for the cloudless sky. Vibrations ran up Caity's leg, shaking her skin and ramping up her anticipation. Her pussy dampened at the thought of what would come. She needed to be strong, give Quinn what she demanded if she was to get what she wanted in the end. Another rumble was followed by a third, until the thuds lost their distinction from each other and crashed through the calm.

Caity's breath caught at the first sight of the dragon's head emerging from the forest and into the clearing. Even at this distance, she saw the glow from her eyes and the glimmer of her scales in the moonlight. The dragon didn't stop her approach until the tip of her snout reached the edge of the rock circle. A super-heated blast of air blew across Caity, chasing away the chill.

Why have you come back? Quinn's voice sounded in Caity's head.

"I told you I would." Knowing this wasn't the time for submission, that the dragon had to understand her reasons, Caity held the ancient creature's gaze. "I'd never intended to hurt you."

The dragon's eyes reflected the creature's age and loneliness. Her scales, once bright, had lost their sheen. Quinn was beautiful, though. Her muscles were full, projecting strength. Her black wings tucked neatly to her sides, fanning out a few inches in annoyance.

You broke our pact.

"I asked for a little time."

Ten years is not a little time.

"You're a dragon. I didn't think it would be that long for you."

We'd bonded. You left me without my heart.

"I know." She was sorry for that, though she couldn't vocalize it. "But I have come home. I'm here now for you. If you'll have me."

The roar shook the trees surrounding them. Caity cringed, turning her face away from the creature's rage. *You left me alone! I chose you above the others to be mine, and you walked away. Why should I take you back?*

"Sorry." What little strength she had remaining evaporated beneath the dragon's anger. Caity slid to the ground, sitting on her legs, and sobbed. "Sorry."

You will be punished.

Words that should have been a threat felt like a blessing. Punishment implied redemption, something she wanted more than anything. Caity looked up at the dragon and wished she could wipe the tears away. "Please."

On your feet.

It was difficult to force her muscles to cooperate. She tried to do as she was told, but her knees buckled and the best she could manage was to get to her knees and press her bare chest to the wood. Her back now exposed, Caity hugged the wood as she emptied her mind, praying Quinn gave her what she needed.

A high-pitched whine cut through the air, preceding the snap of the tip of Quinn's tail against Caity's skin. The smooth-scaled tip was thicker than a normal whip, but the dragon controlled every inch of its length. Instead of falling away, Quinn kept her tail in place where it landed.

You're soft.

Caity swallowed hard. "I haven't been with anyone else."

The dragon's silence spurred her on. "Even the thought of it was...it felt like betrayal."

The next crack of her tail landed across the fleshy part of Caity's ass, pulling a surprised cry from her. *Why did you leave me?*

Another snap, along the curve of her waist. "I was losing myself in you. It was like I no longer existed, and that scared the hell out of me."

Three more snaps. Caity barely had time to breathe in between, forcing her to gasp for air. The tears flowed unchecked down her cheeks to drip onto her chest. Her ass and back burned from where the dragon's scales had bit into the skin. The sting helped center her mind, focusing her on what was important— Quinn.

Why did you come back?

"I missed you." Her whisper carried on the still evening air. "I needed to come home."

The sound of Quinn's body shifting, the snap of bones and muffled moans forced her to look at the dragon. When Quinn passed through the rock circle, she brushed the tips of her fingers along the stone. Coal-black hair danced in the air as the breeze kicked up, haloing the dragon's human form.

Caity held still, scared to breathe for fear of ruining the spell they both seemed to be under. She lowered her gaze and waited. The touch of Quinn's fingers along the path of one of the whip marks sent a burst of want spidering through every inch of her body.

"And why should I take you back?" It was odd hearing Quinn speak and not the rumble of her dragon voice in her head. "Why shouldn't I cut all ties and go in search of another mate? Someone who actually wants this?"

With a lick of her lips, Caity closed her eyes and knew this was the moment she'd both longed for and dreaded. "I have no reason. You are within your right to throw me away."

Strong fingers wound in Caity's hair, and the yank, when it came, stretched her neck back at an awkward angle. Forced to meet Quinn's golden gaze, Caity knew she'd been a fool to run in the first place. How could she leave the woman who'd captured her heart as she'd opened her eyes to the wonders of the universe?

"You will do what I say." Quinn reached down with her free hand and cupped Caity's cheek. "If you please me..." She shook her head. "Turn around."

It was a struggle to do as the dragon commanded—Quinn hadn't released her hair, and the cold made her legs numb and unresponsive. She stumbled, but the chains held her body up, stretching her out and giving her momentum to spin herself. Not once did the dragon break eye contact. The intensity of her gaze brought a blush to Caity's face.

"I couldn't be with another." Quinn tugged on her hair. "You knew my race bonds with their chosen ones. You *knew* I was alone." *Always alone.*

"Let me prove myself to you." Caity shuffled as close as Quinn's grip and the chains allowed. "Please, Mistress."

Fire flared in Quinn's eyes. "You lost the right to call me that."

Caity whimpered. God, she knew it wasn't going to be easy, but she had no idea where to start. With nothing to lose, Caity pulled against Quinn's grip and pressed her nose into the curls of her pubic hair.

The unmistakable scent of the dragon's arousal slammed into her like a bat to the head. The pain of her hair being pulled wasn't a deterrent. She nuzzled her nose into the hidden folds of Quinn's cunt, seeking out her prize.

The dragon didn't stop her, but neither did she assist Caity in any way. If she wanted this, to work her way back into the dragon's life, she needed to earn it. Closing her eyes, Caity pressed her mouth where she knew Quinn's clit was hidden. With a lick of her pointed tongue, she lapped at the folds, swallowing down the unique taste of her mistress.

Everything narrowed down to that moment, that connection and Caity's need to win her way back into the dragon's heart. Tang burst across her taste buds as she licked and teased Quinn's clit. The dragon didn't move, didn't respond in any way for what felt like eternity. Concentrating, Quinn doubled her efforts and began to use her nose along with her tongue to drag a reaction out of the dragon.

The slight shaking of Quinn's thighs told Caity she was making progress. Moaning against her pussy, Caity yanked on the chains preventing her from touching the thing she most wanted to. She pulled back to look up at Quinn.

"Mistress, release me?"

"No."

"I want to touch you. Make you feel good."

"*No.*"

This time when Caity yanked on the chains, pain flashed through her shoulder muscles and into her chest. "Tell me, then. I need to know how to fix this."

The growl when it came shook the trees circling the clearing and vibrated through Caity's body. Quinn shoved her back, sending her into a heap against the stones and wood.

"You're mine." Quinn grabbed Caity's leg and lifted it up. "You thought you could walk away from me and find some other life?"

Quinn dropped to her knees and shuffled forward. Caity's chest tightened, her breathing starting to come in gasps as she watched her lover move into position—moving to claim her.

Thank God.

Lifting her leg to curl it around Quinn's back, Caity shifted her lips to lift her pussy enough to brush against the dragon's. Their simultaneous moans blended together, making the best music Caity had ever heard.

Quinn ground her cunt down, sliding their clits together, mixing their wetness and binding them as one.

"Don't you dare leave me again." Quinn's voice was barely a whisper. She moaned as she swiveled her hips once more. "Never, ever again."

"I won't. Promise."

Words stopped, and Caity focused on the pleasure. Every brush of her clit against Quinn's brought her another step closer to release. Ten years was too long to go without contact. Too long to be separated from the woman she'd loved. But she'd hold back until Quinn gave her permission, her blessing for this to become something more than physical release.

Quinn rode her body hard, grinding and humping her until sweat covered Caity's body. Her body tingled where the dragon touched her. Quinn's nails dug into the flesh of Caity's thigh as she squeezed it, using the limb as leverage to push their bodies together. Sweat mingled with tears on Caity's cheeks and slid into the corners of her mouth.

She hadn't realized her eyes had slid shut until she felt the sharp pinch of her nipple. Quinn smiled at her surprised gasp and gave her another hard tweak. The roll of her nipple between Quinn's fingers sent another jolt of pleasure to her cunt. The rough contact ramped up her desire, and Caity knew she wouldn't be able to hold out much longer. Instead of begging, she bit the side of her cheek and prayed her lover would understand.

Quinn released her nipple, leaned in and caught Caity's bottom lip in her mouth. The points of her teeth dug into the flesh even as Quinn increased the pressure of her pussy against Caity's clit. Turning her head, Caity opened up and gave everything she had left to the dragon. The kiss scorched her soul, re-branding the dragon on her heart.

The flare of approaching orgasm seized Caity's muscles. She closed her eyes and tried to distance herself from it, needing to hold off, wanting Quinn to come first. But when sudden warmth pressed against her mind, there was no holding back.

They'd only done this once before, and back then Caity hadn't understood what was happening. She did now. With a deep breath, she relaxed her body and allowed the dragon to enter her mind.

Every nerve exploded with pleasure. Caity felt Quinn's pleasure and...her relief at having her human back. The dual sets of sensations of pleasure—nipples scraping against each other, clits swollen and hard, cunts begging for release—rolled over Caity. Eyes wide, she silently begged Quinn for what she couldn't vocalize.

"Come for me," the dragon whispered against her lips as she ground down one final time.

The scream wrenched from Caity's chest as pleasure cascaded through her, over her, obliterating every thought from her head. She bucked her hips, squeezed her leg around her lover's back trying to pull her even closer. Wet covered her thigh, easing the way even more for Quinn. The dragon bit down on Caity's shoulder as she came. Her body flared with heat, the metal of the cuffs holding Caity to the wood was suddenly too hot against the sensitive flesh of her wrists. But she didn't say anything, simply waited for the dragon's pleasure to subside.

With a groan, Quinn dropped forward, bracing her weight

on her hands. Their minds were still joined, and for the first time in years, Caity felt a sense of peace.

Quinn turned her face and licked at the spot where she'd bitten her. Caity sighed, happy to have her lover's mark once more on her skin. They stayed that way a moment before the dragon moved to release her from the chain. Pain lanced through her shoulders and it took both of them to lower her arms to her sides.

"I forgot how much that hurts."

Quinn chuckled. "Then don't leave and we won't have to do this again."

"I won't."

Quinn sat down and pulled Caity onto her lap. There was something beautiful about being held by this creature, this woman who was older than anyone fully appreciated. Caity had been wrong in walking away. Quinn would never allow her to lose herself, to forget who she was as a person. Quinn needed her to remind her of the joys of life. Caity would never fail her again.

"Did you find what you were looking for?" Quinn's question was nearly lost, spoken against her hair as she placed kisses to her head.

"I did."

"Good. I want to hear about it. About where you went and what you saw."

Caity pressed her head to Quinn's shoulder and looked into her golden eyes. "Let me tell you."

THWARTING THE SPIRITS

Michael M. Jones

In the city of Puxhill, there is a park. Crowded by day, deserted by night, it's a patch of green set against the urban jungle. Tonight, with the full moon shining overhead, impossibly out of their natural habitats, a mongoose and a cobra fought with tiring implacability.

The cobra was a textbook example of its species, nearly eight feet long with a magnificent hood and cold eyes. It would not have looked out of place wrapped around the god Shiva's neck.

The mongoose was short and slender, brown of fur and long of claw, and likewise far from home.

They wrestled and leaped, paused and charged, slithered and struck. Evenly matched in speed and ferocity, neither seemed capable of gaining the advantage for long. A keen-eyed watcher who got past the impossibility of the scene might have picked up on several things. First, that both creatures were significantly larger than most of their kind, possessing preternatural presence and power. Second, that while they struggled with all their strength and cunning, neither actually seemed intent on winning. Though compelled to battle, they refused to carry it to its natural conclusion. The blood flew from a multitude of wounds, but none were by any means fatal.

At last, the night ended. The moon set and the sun peeked over the horizon. As dawn broke, the two creatures reeled apart as though repelled, putting a good distance between them. The sun's rays flowed through the trees, striking one and then the other.

Changes began. Bodies twisted, bones cracked and elongated, scales shed and fur fell out. Claws and fangs retracted, and their many wounds healed as though never inflicted. It was a swift, brutal process, over in a minute, and it left behind a pair of naked, exhausted women in place of the creatures.

The cobra was the first to recover, picking herself up off the ground to brush away the grass and dirt. Tall and lithe, radiating a queenly grace, she was all sinuous curves. Her skin was a smooth bronze, her eyes wide and dark, her lips full, currently pursed in something between frustration and amusement. Long dark hair tumbled luxuriously down her back, stray waves falling to not quite cover small breasts. Even naked, she exuded confidence. Those who knew her would have recognized her as Purnima Gurtu, a graphic designer for a local advertising agency. They'd finally know why she never joined them for drinks on the nights of a full moon.

The former mongoose was several inches shorter, with a stockier, though equally sleek, build. Her skin wasn't quite as dark, and the stubbornness to her features made her look defiant and a little aggravated. Glittering dark eyes and brown hair cut to the nape of her neck echoed her animal alter ego. She wasn't so confident in her nudity, immediately turning away with an arm over her breasts. This was Hala Laghari, a research librarian for nearby Tuesday University, and she really wasn't happy.

"This can't go on," Hala said, voice clipped with annoyance and embarrassment. She bent over to retrieve a small backpack from where it had been stashed in the nearby bushes.

Purnima paused to ogle the other woman's round backside as it was unwittingly offered. "I agree. It's not doing either of us any good. Sooner or later, it'll all end in tears." She moved to grab a small duffel bag from where she'd hidden it.

For several moments, the women distracted themselves by slipping on the clothes they'd put aside hours before. Purnima's movements were slow and languid as she slipped into matching silk purple bra and panties, before adding an ankle-length multi-colored skirt, a low-cut light blue shirt, and well-worn sandals.

Hala was much more awkward, moving with furtive speed. First, plain white cotton underwear, then a long-sleeved brown shirt, blue jeans, and sneakers. Finally, with a great deal of care, she wrapped her hair in a black hijab, tying the ends of the scarf securely. Once she was properly covered, she relaxed a little.

They finished straightening up as best they could, looking around to make sure they hadn't missed anything or been spotted. Early-morning city sounds echoed from the nearby outskirts of the park, as Puxhill properly came to life. Their gazes met, and an awkward moment of silence was broken only when Purnima spoke. "So. Breakfast, then? The usual place?"

Hala dipped her head. "I will meet you there shortly."

Purnima's eyebrow quirked. "Prayer first, of course." She was well-used to Hala's ways. The teasing came out of habit.

Hala puffed indignantly. "Though my family cast me out for loving as I do, and I transform into a monster every month, I will not abandon my faith. I merely...make adjustments under the circumstances, and pray Allah will forgive my irregularities."

"Easy, my dear, I'm not judging you," said Purnima, tone softly soothing. "I will order for you and see you soon." She bestowed a fond smile upon the other woman, almost reaching out, but rethinking it. Instead, she bowed her head, turned, and left.

Hala closed her eyes for a long moment, breathing deeply, before departing as well. The rising sun took no notice of them.

The Dashen Diner was a small place, a hole in the wall that had served the Caravan Street community for decades, with little thought given to décor or ambience. You got good food at cheap prices at all hours of the day, and that was that. When Hala finally walked in, Purnima had secured a booth near the window, where she could watch the street and the early-morning traffic. There was a scattering of other patrons, a mixture of those up too late and those up too early. In one corner, a pair of scruffy men argued with a waitress over whether their cat qualified for the children's menu, and asked for their coffee to be brought by the pot. At the counter, a notorious talk show host chatted animatedly with a sleepy pair of prostitutes over slices of blueberry pie, apparently regaling them with exaggerated tales of his own prowess. Elsewhere, several college students desperately quizzed one another about differential equations. It was just another morning.

Hala slid in across from Purnima, smiling with more warmth. There was coffee waiting for her; she took it between her hands gratefully, breathing in the steam rising from the top. "You are too kind."

Purnima sipped at her own cup. "After the night of the full moon, it's the little things that make me feel human." She sighed, putting the cup down. "This has to stop, Hala. How long have we been at this?"

Sobered before she could even enjoy her coffee, Hala stared into its swirling depths. "Just over a year," she murmured. "Three nights a month, for thirteen months and counting. Ever since we first met." She raised her suddenly challenging gaze to meet Purnima's. "Ever since the Bifrost Books mixer. Ever since, in a moment of foolishness and ill judgment, we fell into bed together."

The shared memory crackled like electricity between the two women. A night of burning passions set against a wrath-of-God thunderstorm. Intermittent lightning casting wild shadows against the walls of a hotel room. Limbs entangled, chests heaving, bodies sliding. Soft lips, slick skin, taut nipples. Vanilla and jasmine and the musk of arousal. Low, heated cries of passion, and a seemingly endless series of orgasms. Curling up together under rumpled blankets, impossible to tell where one woman ended and the other began. One perfect night of wild abandon.

Purnima's skin darkened with the memory, her eyes flickering; she didn't look away. "It was the best night of my life," she said. "We connected so well. The sex was mind-blowing. You fit against me like it was meant to be. It felt like the start of something."

Hala gave Purnima her best silent look. Neither of them could forget the next night, the first of the full moon. How unfamiliar forces had raged screaming out of the depths of their souls, their conscious minds fleeing under the onslaught. Their bodies had twisted and reshaped, instincts overriding intellect. In a cruel mockery of the previous night of lovemaking, they'd fought with unrelenting hatred. Only a miracle had prevented tragedy that first night, as the cobra and the mongoose clashed. "It was the start of something," she said, bitterly. "How long before one of us kills the other?"

They'd agreed to keep their distance for the nights when all was normal, for a variety of reasons. The relationship that could have been, reduced to this: three nights of feral combat, three mornings of recriminations and regret. "It's getting harder to hold back," admitted Purnima, glancing away shame-facedly. "I dream of sinking my fangs into your neck, wrapping my coils around you. I yearn for your death."

Hala looked down, finger tracing the rim of her coffee cup. "I wake up with the taste of blood in my mouth. This is never going to stop, Purnima. Never. I've researched until my eyes about bled, exhausting hundreds of sources, and nothing."

"We'll find a way," Purnima promised. Seizing Hala's hand, she kissed each fingertip in turn. Hala was too surprised to protest. It was a bold move, given the state of their relationship, and she didn't let it linger. Instead, she released the hand and stood, throwing down money for their coffee. "I have to go. But we will find a way."

Hala remained long after Purnima stalked out. Her fingertips tingling, she replayed the moment in her mind with surprising pleasure. *Please*, she begged silently, *let us find something. It would destroy me if I killed you.*

"Couldn't help but overhear you," drawled a voice. It was one of the scruffy guys, an olive-skinned, gold-flecked-eyed man of indeterminate age and a fondness for jeans and plaid. He'd come to lean against the side of the booth while she was lost in her thoughts. "Don't get upset, li'l lady. I've just got good ears, and I'm a bit nosy." He lowered his voice. "If you've got problems of a magical nature, I've got a name and address for you."

Hala studied him fiercely, trying to read any guile or malice in his openly earnest expression. No, she decided, he might have been an eavesdropper and a busybody, but there was something trustworthy about the man. He had a wildness to him, but his intentions seemed straightforward. She made her choice. "Go on. I'm interested."

* * *

An hour later, Purnima met Hala outside Desiderata. It was either a pawnshop or antique store, depending on who you asked, its dusty windows full of old junk and curiosities. Hala greeted her with a slight smile. She'd explained what little she knew over the phone. Wordlessly, they went in.

The proprietor was a few years older than either of them, short and slender with pale skin, dark eyes, her black feathered hair streaked with red. She had the same wildness Hala had spotted in the man at the diner, the same wildness she recognized in Purnima and herself. She sat at the counter, reading a newspaper; when they came in, she looked up, head cocked birdlike to the side, and stared unapologetically. "Help you with something?" she asked. "I'm assuming you're not here to pawn something. Call it a hunch."

"We were sent here by a guy named Raoul," Hala said tentatively. "He said you could handle...unusual things."

The woman groaned, rubbing at her temples. "The Coyote Brothers are back in town? Lovely. Was this something they caused?"

Hala shook her head, swiftly. "No, it's not like that. They merely pointed us in the right direction."

"That's something, at least." The woman hopped down from her stool, and flipped the sign on the door to "Closed." "My name is Isobel Sparks. Call me Izzy. Tell me what's wrong."

They explained everything. About the cobra and the mongoose. About their thrice-monthly fight to the near death. About their fears. Izzy offered them tea or coffee, but neither took her up on it. Occasionally, she asked for clarification, eyebrows twitching thoughtfully with each answer.

Afterwards, she sat, rubbing her chin. "It sounds to me like you two somehow got entangled in a free-floating, generational curse. I can just imagine. You come from different cultures and traditions, but you both have a healthy dose of the animal spirits in you. Folks like us, we tend to gravitate towards one another. So totally by accident, you meet. Your spirits collide, things kick into high gear, next thing you know, they're reenacting something from centuries ago with you caught in the middle." She whistled. "Raven's balls, that's an icky one."

Hala fidgeted. Purnima stood dead still. They watched and listened while Izzy spoke, half to herself, half to them. "There's only three ways to break something like this." She listed them on her fingers. "You can get as far away from each other as possible, stretch it until it snaps. It's anyone's guess as to how far is far enough. Downside is, you can never see each other again for fear of resurgence. Do nothing and it eventually runs its course, most likely killing one or both of you in the process." She paused.

"The third?" pressed Purnima.

"You overload it." Izzy's grin was almost reckless. She brought her hands together to signify two forces colliding. "You find a way to supercharge the curse, and it'll collapse under its own weight and significance. Kablooey."

"But how would we do that?" asked Hala.

"I can't help you there. It's not in my skill set, and I don't have the tools. This is way beyond my experience. But I know just the right person. You're in luck, it's the right time of month to talk to her." Izzy wrote down a name and number on the back of a business card, and gave it to Hala. "Tell her this clears us for the Lexington thing."

"What do we owe you for your help?"

"Normally, I'd charge you a favor each, but since you actually gave me advance warning that the Coyote Brothers are back in town, I'll make it one favor between the both of you. And I promise, it'll never be anything illegal, immoral, or against your religion."

"Deal!" exclaimed Hala and Purnima as one.

As they left, they heard Izzy muttering about getting the emergency kit ready. Just in case. Stupid Coyotes.

"There's a woman with issues," murmured Purnima, wryly.

Hala had to agree, a surprised laugh escaping her.

Phoebe Masters was a tall, pale woman, silver-haired and violet-eyed. She hosted a late-night program on a local classical radio station, and agreed to meet Hala and Purnima in the midafternoon, well before sunset. When they joined her at the Dashen Diner, it was impossible to miss her. Even dressed in jeans and a sweatshirt, she had a presence about her, a magnificent radiance that made them want to bow down, to acknowledge some ineffable quality. Just sitting in the booth, sipping at her tea, she was regal. *No*, corrected Hala's mind, *she was like a goddess.*

They settled in, side by side, across from Phoebe, studying her curiously. Apart from the indescribable aura and unconventional attractiveness, she seemed normal enough. How could she help them? Introductions were made, drinks were ordered; only after the waitress had come and gone again did Phoebe get down to business. "You have a problem. And Isadora Sparks thinks I can help."

Purnima straightened up, trying to project confidence, something in short supply at the moment. "She said it would clear your debt for the Lexington thing."

"Mmm, that. Well worth having that issue dismissed. Tell me your story." Phoebe's voice was cool and soothing, but carried an inescapable weight, like the incoming tide. Once again, Hala and Purnima took turns explaining their dilemma. Silent, impartial, majestic, Phoebe drank it in without interruptions. At some point, Hala took Purnima's hand, their fingers interlacing on the tabletop. Phoebe's gaze caught that as well.

When they'd finished, Phoebe smiled slowly; it was as though the moon had come out from behind the clouds. "I think I understand."

Hala's hand tightened against Purnima's, who squeezed back in response. They waited for Phoebe to continue.

"Though I am not what I once was, I still have some say over what happens under the full moon." Phoebe's tone was soft, wistful, and far-away. "I can...strengthen you. I can ward off the moon's influence for a time. A single night, never to be repeated. One night in which you might find what you seek." The purple in her eyes had faded into silver like her hair, round and full. "What you do with the time is up to you, but I would use it wisely. It won't come around again."

Hala and Purnima didn't even stop to think. "Do it," said Purnima, the pleading in her voice undermining the insistence.

"Please." Hala shuddered with the sudden knowledge of who and what Phoebe was. In a world where shapeshifters lived and loved, how much stranger could it be for the moon to walk as a human?

Phoebe placed one cool hand over theirs. "So be it," she murmured. "One night to do as you must. A gift to you, my dear children." Warm energy spread through the union of hands, sinking into bones and muscle and blood, sweeping through the women with surprising speed. Hala's nerves tingled, her core pulsing as the energy, almost erotic in its strength and allure, coiled deep within her, taking up residence in her very soul. From the way Purnima squeezed her hand, Hala knew she'd felt it also. It was...pure.

Phoebe broke the contact, leaning back to regard them with ancient, unfathomable eyes. "The moon will rise soon. Your time is limited. Were I you, I'd not waste a second."

"How can we thank you? How can we repay you?" asked Purnima quickly.

Phoebe shook her head. "This is a gift. Or, if you would, an apology. Even I don't know what originally happened, but it's not right that you were swept up in something that's far outlived its purpose. This will make things right." Her smile was a flicker. "I hope." She lifted her tea, bringing it to her lips in a clear dismissal.

Hala and Purnima exchanged looks. Then, still holding hands, they left the Dashen Diner with as much haste as their dignities would allow. Behind them, Phoebe Masters watched them go, as distant and cool as the moon itself.

A single night in which to run from each other—or come together. They hotly debated their options for several long minutes, painfully aware of time's passage as the sun slipped towards the horizon. Truthfully, the decision was never in doubt. Purnima sealed that when she suddenly seized Hala by the shoulders, delivering a sizzling, passionate kiss that left them both stunned and breathless, while city-jaded pedestrians swerved around them.

They chose the hotel they'd used the first time they'd been together. Not only was it a good way to avoid nosy roommates, it seemed appropriate to come full circle. It didn't take them long to catch a taxi, to get a room, to stumble through the door and kick it shut behind them. Only monumental willpower had kept their hands off one another this far, some brief concession to public image and decency, and the knowledge that once started, they'd never stop until satiated.

Yet once alone with each other, they hesitated. Hala felt the mongoose clawing within her, aching to break free, to hunt and fight and feed. It sensed its enemy's presence, an inexplicable compulsion driving it into a bloodlust. The moon tugged at it, trying to set it free, but Hala fought back, strengthening the barriers against its frenzied strength. She looked into Purnima's eyes, and there was the cobra, rearing up magnificently, hood flared, tongue flickering, venom dripping from its fangs. It was ready to lunge forward, to strike at its prey. It was likewise thwarted.

Fists clenched. Bodies tensed. Chests heaved with deep breaths. The full moon rose outside, silver light streaming through the picture window to bathe them both. They finally crashed together, with human passion instead of feral obsession. Mouths clashed in a hot, demanding kiss, lips parted and tongues danced. Fingers clawed at clothes, raking at backs as they embraced, bodies fitting as one.

The cobra and the mongoose paused in their efforts to escape, surprised by their initial failure, baffled by their hosts' actions.

Purnima finally broke the kiss, eyes wide and lips swollen. "Hala," she said. One, simple, profound word. It meant everything.

"Yes," Hala said. An offer and an acceptance. A question and an answer. A statement and a reply. She took Purnima back into her arms. Together, they peeled away layers of clothes. Fabric puddled around their feet, or it was tossed carelessly aside. Hala stepped away to solemnly remove her hijab, shaking her hair free in a frighteningly intimate way.

She turned back and met Purnima's dark, intense eyes, held by the gaze. It stripped her bare in soul as well as body, but for once she didn't mind. In this moment, in this space, nothing could separate them. One woman reached out, the other took her hand; they moved toward the bed, collapsing onto it in a fluid tangle of limbs. Purnima's mouth glided over Hala's neck and throat, teasing with teeth and tongue, breath hot against electrified skin. Hala's fingers traced over Purnima's breasts, coaxing dark nipples into erectness, drawing a moan of pleasure out as well.

As they stroked and touched one another, they jockeyed for position and dominance, their warring animal spirits refusing to back down.

It was Hala who did the unthinkable by yielding first, though it was in no way a surrender. It just meant her allowing Purnima to roll on top, to straddle her victoriously, to lean down and capture a nipple in her mouth, tugging at it with her teeth. The electric thrill that raced through her sent Hala into shudders of joy; she forgot all about trying to claim the upper hand. Instead, she arched upwards, offering herself eagerly to Purnima's questing fingers. She was hot, wet, aching with anticipation, and she granted her lover the freedom to do what she would.

When the tongue flicked against her clit, she squealed with delight, fingers digging into the bed under her, body tensing. It had been a long time since she'd felt anything so fiercely; all she could do was let the sensations race through her. Tongue and fingers teased and entered her, licking and sucking and stroking. Her breath came short and fast, one moan after another, the orgasm building rapidly until it exploded forth, stealing away her senses. Her head swam with ecstasy; she drifted for a moment until Purnima relented, pulling away to let her recover. Hala urged her upwards for a kiss, so she could taste herself on the other woman's lips. It was exquisite.

The cobra and the mongoose were...at a loss. The spirits shifted restlessly in the space they occupied, silent questions flying back and forth through the ether. This was beyond their sphere of knowledge.

Hala kissed Purnima once again. "My turn," she murmured

with a chuckle. One hand slipped between the other woman's legs, parting her to explore her warm depths. Purnima stretched and rolled under the delicate touch, like a snake adjusting its coils. Slowly at first, building in pressure and tempo, Hala rubbed her clit, while blazing a trail of kisses across Purnima's breasts and stomach. As the other woman writhed and whimpered, Hala slid down to lap at her pussy, drinking freely of her arousal and her need. She'd wanted this for so long; it felt like a miracle to actually be here, doing this, instead of trying to kill her.

Purnima wasn't shy as she drove her hips upwards, even as Hala buried her face between her thighs, tongue driving deep and fast, roaming up to the clit and back down again. When she added several fingers, burying them in a slow, deliberate thrust, it pushed Purnima right over the edge into an orgasm she muffled with a hastily grabbed pillow. Hala basked in the result, only letting up when Purnima begged for mercy, shuddering from the strength of her release.

The mongoose and the cobra were...changed. They no longer hated one another. The drive to fight, to dominate, to kill—it was greatly diminished, and fading fast.

Still not satiated, still not done, Hala and Purnima cuddled for several minutes, exchanging light kisses and soft caresses, lost in one another's embrace. Hands glided over curves, over sweat-slick skin, through loose hair. When they were ready again, they shifted into a position where they could take each other simultaneously, licking and fucking with enthusiasm and skill, each buried in the other's pussy. Working in unison, they reached another series of slow, powerful orgasms, ones that rippled through body and soul, leaving them almost too satiated to move afterwards.

The mongoose and the cobra gazed at each other from across a void, all traces of hostility, of hatred, of violence gone. There was understanding, acceptance, even fondness instead. Whatever had driven them was long gone.

Bathed in moonlight, exhausted, satisfied, Hala and Purnima curled together in bed, Hala tucked into Purnima's arm, head resting on her shoulder. "This is going to change a lot of things," she said.

"Like whether we can make things work now that we're no longer at each other's throats?"

"And whether we're ready for something longer-term. More public. More...everything. You barely know the day-to-day me."

"I'm certainly willing to try if you are," Purnima assured her. "After all this effort, it would be silly not to."

Hala chuckled, twisting to give her a kiss. "I guess this really is the start of something." Inwardly, she winced, realizing she'd missed evening prayer. *But*, she thought, *Allah will understand. This was...important. Essential, even. For both of us.* She was a wayward child, but a faithful one.

The moon had no comment.

In the city of Puxhill, there is a park. Sometimes, when the moon is full and no one's around, a cobra and a mongoose sneak out to play. They fight, or hunt small animals, or curl up together. They're far from home, and their relationship would seem to challenge nature's way, but they're as happy as can be. Only a few people know the truth, and none of them are talking.

SHE'S FURRY YIFFY

Adele Dubois

Anika lifted the cold glass of beer from her drinks tray and served the tourist at the twenty-dollar slot machine without spilling a drop. His hand brushed her thigh before sliding a tip into her shorts pocket. She would have made him sorry for groping her, but for the aroma that drifted past. Frozen in place, she raised her head and sniffed.

Beneath the odors of cigarette smoke, sweat, and snack bar food, she picked up a scent that compelled her to follow. Female. Not yet in heat, but soon. Though she'd inhaled that smell only once before—on the Appalachian Trail where she jogged each day behind her Mt. Pocono cottage—the tag would remain part of her DNA forever.

Tucking her empty tray under the arm of her white uniform blouse, she inhaled again and tilted her head to listen for movement below the earsplitting din of slot machines. She tracked the scent across the casino floor in her red high heels, and moved stealthily through the crowd, following footsteps she could not see, but sensed.

There. To her right, a long golden tail flicked above shapely legs. A slash of fabric barely covered a tight, round butt. The woman she sought entered the convention room.

A sign posted at the entrance read: *Welcome Fur Con XXX.* Anika pulled the digital order pad from the waistband at the small of her back and held it out as if reporting for duty. Though she hadn't been assigned the casino's Furry Lifestylers event this time around, she doubted anyone would question her presence. Chin raised, Anika strode through the entryway and into the lighted ballroom.

Plush toy vendors, photographers and artists called out like carnies to passersby, lending a street party atmosphere to a room pulsating with rock music. Conventioneers dressed in anthropomorphic fursuits resembling moose, wolves, dogs, wild boar, red foxes, cats, apes, bears, and more, mingled. Some donned head-to-toe zoot suits like mascot costumes. Others wore only fake ears or tails and face paint with street clothes. Since Fur Fans were predominately male, she supposed a YIFF—Young Incredibly Fuckable Furry—could have her pick here.

The assault of colors and the smells of body heat and fluids, blended with artificial fur and chemical dry-cleaning solutions, overwhelmed her delicate senses, and she nearly gagged in response. She covered her mouth and took shallow breaths while she closed her eyes until she adapted to her environment. By the time she lowered her hand, the distinctive scent she'd followed vanished. *Damn.*

"*Mundanes* aren't supposed to be in here," a masculine voice said behind her. His tone sounded more flirtatious than threatening. Furries had a reputation for friendliness, so he was probably harmless. She'd learned that, and the lingo, the first time she worked a Fur Con, months before her life-changing event.

Anika turned toward the man dressed in moose costume from the neck down and forced a polite smile. He wore long, thick antlers over his neatly cut brown hair, possibly to signal a YIFF looking for a big cock. Fur Con XXX was for mature conventioneers looking for fun and hook-ups, unlike the family-friendly Furry events held elsewhere.

Anika touched her tongue to her bottom lip. She could almost taste the animal he pretended to be, but not in the way he might wish.

"She obviously works here, idiot," the wolf-clad male next to him replied. "Can we get drinks?" He gave her a friendly *tailwave* with the long gray plume he pulled from behind his back. "That is, unless you're feeling *yiffy*. Blue-eyed blondes with great legs and big, uh…are my weakness."

Anika knew he wasn't referring to the YIFF acronym. *Yiff* in its many grammatical forms had its root in one word. Sex.

She eyed the faux wolf and noted the SPH—strategically placed hole—in his costume to accommodate fucking. *Not a chance*. She hadn't had sex with a guy since high school, and had been mostly celibate since Lori moved to Seattle eight months ago for a job promotion. The move was a transparent excuse to break up with her following Anika's attack in the woods.

What hurt most was that Lori didn't deny the abandonment. "I can't handle it," was all she would say. She'd refused to make eye contact before she walked out the door. Anika had been inconsolable for weeks afterward.

Since then, she'd been alone, but her need for companionship had become a painful ache that tormented her night after lonely night. Her rare one-night stands had been disasters of epic proportions. The women had run from her house and refused to return her calls. There simply weren't many choices for a lesbian with her particular new…penchants.

Anika returned her best fake smile to the Furs. After years of practice as a casino waitress, her sincerity could be convincing. "I'll have to pass on the yiff, since I'm on duty, but I'll be right back with those beers, guys." *Yeah, right.*

Booths lined one side of the room where conventioneers posed for color portraits or bought Furry-related souvenirs. Snack concessions lined the opposite wall, wafting scents of popcorn, hot dogs, and pizza. Conventioneers ate or drank with their faux animal heads tucked under their arms or between their feet, adding a touch of comedy to an already surreal scene.

At the center of the room, portable bars had been set up between gaming tables and slot machines. Costumed attendees filled every seat. Behind the public areas, semi-private alcoves and lounges dotted the perimeter for more intimate entertainment. Total privacy required a retreat to hotel rooms.

Anika headed in the direction of the semi-private areas. She planned to search each section, and then move to the center of the ballroom, until she found the woman whose scent she'd recognized as her own.

Furpiles of snuggling, dry-humping bodies reclining on the sofa and carpeted floor inside the first lounge proved interesting, but failed to deliver the odor of the woman she sought. Some participants *skritched*—groomed—one another. Others relaxed on love seats. A few were getting *yiffy* while the others watched.

Anika stood, transfixed. A full-figured female, wearing nothing but rabbit ears, a black leather bra, fishnet pantyhose topped by a thong, and black heels, formed a sandwich with two large, costumed males.

The lion behind her rubbed his body along her back and then pressed his groin into the hollow at the base of her spine. While he ground against her, the man dressed as a coyote rubbed the full length of his costumed form along the front of the woman's nearly naked body.

The trio found a rhythm and began undulating until all three panted and moaned. The woman raised her hips against the coyote. "*Murrr,*" she crooned low in her throat before she giggled. *Murrr* was the Furry sound offered to indicate pleasure. She groaned and writhed while the scents of arousal filled the air. Anika knew that *spooge* would soon follow.

As the woman drew closer to orgasm, the heaviness in Anika's abdomen and the tingle in her breasts grew stronger. She licked her lips and fought off the urge to bite down and taste blood.

She turned away from the ménage for her own protection. Sexual pique had changed for her after her encounter in the woods. Genital stimulation failed to be enough anymore. She needed her teeth and nails to bite and scratch and draw blood while she climaxed. Finding a partner who shared her predilection had been impossible.

Maybe that would change when she met the woman with her twin scent. She hoped for that, more than she'd ever wanted anything.

She took a last look at the Furries playing sex games and moved on. If that female wanted real animal action, she could have given it to her. But they were only acting out parts. If any one of those Furries came face-to-face with a genuine anthromorph, they'd shit their zoot suits.

The lion grunted and cried out. The scent of *spooge* grew stronger.

Anika hurried away, aroused and agitated. Her nostrils flared and a low growl formed in her throat. She cleared it and forced herself to focus on her objective. She scanned the room while she passed a small group of Fur Fans waiting to have their caricatures drawn by an artist. They chatted and petted one another while they waited their turns.

She inhaled deeply and picked up a scent thread. Puma. And pussy. Wet and hot. Anika licked her lips and increased her pace. The hairs at the back of her neck prickled, and her nipples tingled. Mental images of a feminine pink tongue flicking over the tips nearly caused her to stumble.

"Easy there, Vixen," a tall elk said as she regained her balance. Anika cursed under her breath for losing focus. She should know better. If she hadn't fallen while daydreaming during her jog a year ago, she wouldn't be in this predicament.

Scientists and wildlife experts refused to believe the rumors that mountain lions had returned to Pennsylvania's Appalachian Trail, but she knew better. The big cats had been declared extinct in the Pocono Mountains since the early twentieth century. Indistinct photographs taken by tourists and reports of sightings by locals to prove their return had been dismissed as hoaxes.

Since the authorities refused to believe pumas had wandered back east from the west, who would believe a demon hellcat had made its home among the Pride? If she hadn't scrabbled off a cliff's edge and catapulted into the river when it pounced, her corpse might have been the proof they needed. The unnatural being—part animal, part human—had left a mere scratch on her torso as a token reminder.

After that day, she'd been...different. Her senses had sharpened, and her sleep patterns had changed. She hadn't shapeshifted while awake, but did so most nights in her dreams.

While asleep, she watched her body transform from her womanly shape into a lithe, but powerful, golden beast. Her muscles stretched and her bones reconfigured until she cried out with pain. Then she'd watch while she hunted inside the forest with single-minded purpose—to kill the demon cat who had possessed her. Sometimes, she'd wake in her bed dirty, bloody, and exhausted, unable to deny the reality or futility of her situation. She was leaving her house to track the monster.

Her despondency returned at thoughts of living and hunting alone indefinitely. There was strength in numbers. She had to find her kindred spirit.

What better hiding place for an anthropomorphic shapeshifter than an X-rated Furry Convention? The irony made her laugh. The other woman could blend in and get laid with anonymity. Clearly the puma was self-controlled, or she couldn't mix with this famously passive group. The virus she contracted from the devil cat must have been greatly diluted at the time of her attack. Lucky break.

As Anika passed a portable bar, she dropped off her drinks tray and order pad. "I'm going to lunch," she said by way of explanation to the bartender, who clearly couldn't have cared less. She moved to her left. The scent grew stronger, and she picked up her pace. Her heart pounded blood to her ears, and her breathing quickened as anticipation shot through her system.

From a dimly lit alcove, the sound of a woman's melodious laughter rose above the din, luring her like a siren's call. The aroma she'd been tracking hit her senses like luscious perfume. Her sex grew damp.

Anika stepped into the shadows.

Her eyesight adjusted instantly to the dark. She honed on the small, slender woman standing with a trio of Furries at the back of the room. Others sat on a sofa accented by a coffee table and topped by wineglasses. The alcove was barely big enough to accommodate all the people and furniture, so they'd tucked in close.

Anika hovered near the threshold and watched as the YIFF

met her gaze and offered a shy smile. She slid her hand along her tail and waved the tip. Anika understood the signal and began to close the distance between them. When she reached the woman's side, she edged out the others, who hissed and snarled at her for interloping. Anika held her ground and resisted the urge to demonstrate what a real snarl sounded like.

"It's you," the woman said. "I've been waiting for you to find me." Her large eyes shimmered golden like a puma, and chestnut hair cascaded in thick tendrils past her shoulders. She wore a russet-colored bodysuit on her petite frame. Black high heels adorned her feet. She was clearly naked beneath the garment, since her prominent nipples and the outline of her round breasts pressed tightly against the fabric.

Anika could barely stop staring at the other cat's incredible body. "Why didn't you seek me out?" She searched the woman's mesmerizing eyes and caught her breath as they captured her and pulled her in.

"My sense of smell isn't fully developed. I merely got an inkling of you. I've been all over town, hoping you'd track me." A flash of long pink tongue swiped across her lips and disappeared again into her mouth. "My...uh...gifts arrived in other ways."

Electricity shot through Anika at the sight and she fought back a whimper. *Holy shit.* She thought she'd been the one in control. "I don't go out much anymore." Except for work and the grocery store, she'd learned to keep to herself. She took the smaller woman by the elbow and led her to the far corner along the back wall. "What's your name?" Anika moved so close she could feel the heat rising between them.

"Maya." The female stared up as Anika looked down. Warm breath brushed her chin. It smelled sweet, like strawberry daiquiri.

When their gazes locked, a thrill snaked up Anika's back. "Are there more like us?"

"You mean, puma? Or gay?"

At that, Anika had to laugh. "Both."

Maya smiled. "I'm puma, and *verrry* curious. I haven't met anyone else like us. In my dreams, I only see my mate in animal form. We play and hunt together in the mountains." Maya nuzzled Anika's cheek, and then dragged her raspy tongue over her jawline in a classic Furry *Nuzzlelick*. "She...you...taught me how to bond with another female."

"I've been alone in my dreams." Anika nuzzled her in return and swiped her tongue over Maya's plump bottom lip.

"You've never been alone," Maya murmured.

Desire and relief at finding her soul mate created a heady cocktail that almost undid her. She fought back the urge to suck her mouth and kiss her hard until the formalities were done. "But my dreams have taken me out of bed to track the demon."

"I know. I was there."

A new fear struck Anika's heart. She didn't want to believe they actually shapeshifted. No memories of Maya in puma form lingered. Yet the truth could no longer be denied. She nodded toward Maya's tail. "Mind if I ask if that's real?"

Maya twisted her hip and whipped the tail forward between Anika's thighs. She felt her eyes widen as the length began to move, stroking her slit slowly, before picking up speed. "It's costume. It expresses who I've become on the inside. That's why I love Fur Cons. I can act the part, whenever I want."

"Were you attacked? Bitten?"

Maya shook her head. "The mountain lion had me cornered after I got separated from the other hikers, but the sounds of approaching cyclists saved me. Before the puma ran off he, or she...swiped its tongue over my mouth."

"That was no ordinary puma. If the animal had the ability to change you, it was a shifter. I'm glad you weren't hurt. Still, its contact was enough to transfer the virus it carried."

Maya nodded as if she'd suspected that all along.

"I was barely scratched, but the wound changed me in odd ways." Anika gripped the moving tail and stopped the erotic play before things got out of hand. "Keep this up and we'll need to find a room."

Maya touched her wrist. "I have a room in the hotel. I've always wondered what it would be like to have sex with a beautiful woman." She swiped her long pink tongue across her top lip while she maintained eye contact. "I'm glad it will be you."

Anika shivered at thoughts of what Maya's cat-like tongue could do. "I should warn you, I become aggressive during sex."

Maya purred long and deep in her throat. "I like aggressive. It's yiffy." She retrieved her tail, and then leaned forward to kiss Anika full on the mouth.

The sensations of her soft, generous lips and flicking tongue nearly brought Anika to her knees. She nipped Maya's lips in return and cupped her breast, squeezing and massaging the softness before gliding a thumb over a tight nipple.

Maya trembled beneath her touch. "I've waited so long for you to find me."

Anika pulled back, panting with arousal. She had waited too, but she needed to stop this foreplay before she lost control. "I'm still on duty. Can you meet me in a couple of hours?"

Maya ran the palms of both hands along the inside of Anika's thighs and cupped her pussy. "I'll give you my room number."

Maya opened the door of her hotel room, wrapped in a towel, and pulled Anika inside. Her dark hair and lithe body were damp from a shower. Anika took Maya in her arms and buried her face in her hair. "You smell like clean mountain rain when it washes over the fields." She rubbed her cheek against the darker woman's temple. "I've smelled that scent in my puma dreams." Anticipation erased her former loneliness.

Maya ran her tongue along Anika's throat and laved the base of her neck at the hollow above her collarbone. "You taste like sweet and salt, excitement and danger." She let her towel drop to the floor and pool at her feet.

The aroma of arousal filled the air as Anika's hands glided over Maya's breasts and along her waist. The beast inside her awakened.

Maya's tongue continued to play over Anika's skin. The fluttery movements raised goose bumps that produced hot and cold shivers across her flesh. In a gesture of trust, Anika let her head loll back to grant Maya greater access.

Sure, steady hands unbuttoned her blouse and kissed the swell of her breasts as they unhooked the waistband of her shorts. A quick rustle of fabric and abandoned shoes freed Anika to follow, naked, to the king-sized bed.

Their pairing began tentatively and playfully, since it was their first time. Anika let Maya move at her own pace while she explored her body—tasting and touching each crevice, curve, and plane. She was a gentle lover, but as her desire grew, Anika sensed her animal lust taking control. Maya's scent changed too, and the pungent fragrance of sweat and pheromones heated Anika's blood.

Anika had been kissed many times in her life, but nothing had prepared her for the explosion of sexual energy Maya's feminine kiss aroused. Her full lips and warm breath were unlike any she'd ever tasted. When she deepened the kiss to explore Maya's amazing tongue, their connection turned kinetic. Need fired into Anika's nervous system like hot electrical charges.

Her desire surpassed anything she'd known before.

They broke their kisses, panting when they ran out of breath, and then met each other's gazes.

Anika stared down at the stunning woman on the bed and gave herself over to the need to stroke and caress her satiny skin. She massaged her firm, apple-shaped breasts and pinched her long nipples until she moaned and begged for more. Anika cupped the weight of her lover's breasts and kneaded their softness.

Anika closed her eyes with the tactile movements and savored the feel inside her hands. While she stroked, the invisible cord that connected her nipples to her clitoris tightened and pulled. If Maya stimulated her pussy right now, she'd come in a blink.

Anika shifted to her knees and guided Maya up to face her. She caressed her own breasts and rubbed her engorged nipples against the other woman's.

The friction between the hard points caused an erotic buzz that brought a cry to Maya's lips. Her eyes glistened. "This feels incredible."

Anika gasped too. She licked her mouth.

"I know a way to make you feel even better." Maya leaned down to simultaneously lick, suck, and stroke Anika's breasts and nipples. Maya let one hand drift down to Anika's stomach to toy with her navel.

The dark cat sank down against the mattress and pressed her cheek to Anika's sex while she stroked her thighs.

Anika trembled and released an anxious breath. She opened her thighs to offer Maya the first intimate look at her pussy.

Maya ran her hands over Anika's trimmed mound and then traced her slit with her thumbs to open her vaginal lips. Anika sucked air through her teeth when the delicate, pearly flesh inside was exposed.

* * *

"Your pussy is beautiful." Maya had never had intimate contact with another woman, although she'd fantasized about the experience for years. Anika's scent aroused her as much as the sight of her erect clit jutting from beneath its protective hood. Her mouth watered with the desire to lick and suck the swollen bud. She hoped to give her new lover the best orgasms of her life.

Anika gripped her by the shoulders and pressed her clitoris to Maya's mouth. Her pussy tasted slick, supple and wonderful. Maya pulled the sensitive folds between her lips and sucked in greedy little tugs while her finger played at the opening of Anika's channel. Her tongue teased the hard nub, which swelled again with the intimate contact. Maya began to lick Anika's clit in wide, deliberate circles with the rough surface of her cat's tongue.

Anika leaned back on her knees and arched her spine in response to the sensations. Her body trembled, and she began to gasp in tiny rhythms while Maya worked her pussy. When she sensed that Anika's climax drew near, Maya stretched out her tongue as far as it would go and thrust it inside her. Anika groaned while Maya's tongue flicked and then slid in and out. To take her over the edge, she returned to her peak and licked in short, quick strokes.

Anika screamed into the room and gushed against Maya's mouth. Her fingernails scored her arms while the spasms continued, but Maya refused to flinch against the pain. Finally, keening and little whimpering sounds followed. The fingers that clutched her relaxed.

The scent of feminine juices filled Maya's senses. She inhaled them while she continued to lick and suck Anika's tender folds until her tremors faded.

She stroked Anika's inner thighs while her climax wound down, gratified she could offer such pleasure.

Maya pressed her cheek against the downy blonde sex she'd tasted and waited while her lover recovered. When she had, Anika reached down, took Maya's hand, and kissed it.

Replete but ready for more, Anika rose up on her knees and watched while Maya sat and stroked her own breasts. She leaned down to nibble the tips of Maya's nipples and bite their fullness. Her mouth and teeth worked the firm orbs until the smaller woman began to masturbate slowly. "Do it too," Maya whispered.

They watched each other intently and exchanged languid smiles while they played. Anika's clit was so sensitive from her climax that it almost hurt to touch, but she continued to nudge the tiny bundle of nerves until she returned to a state of full arousal.

When she grew close to orgasm, she stopped pleasuring herself and ran her teeth over Maya's neck and shoulders and glided her hands across those lovely breasts, enjoying the feel of her soft skin.

Maya opened her legs to grant complete access to her sex. Anika dipped down to lick and suck her clit and vulva while her lover urged her on. As she nibbled, Anika slid one finger, then two, into her channel and began to fuck her fast and hard while her tongue flicked over her engorged nub.

Maya's pussy was everything Anika had hoped for, and more. Sex with her thrilled her beyond her wildest fantasies and Anika knew, without a doubt, that she wanted Maya as her partner. When Maya bucked and shouted with a climax so intense Anika had to fight to maintain oral contact, she knew she would never give her up.

They lay side by side to rest, but continued to kiss and stroke each other's bodies. "More," Maya said.

"Yes." Anika pressed her pussy against Maya's and began to rotate in small circles until the friction created erotic vibrations strong enough to bring climax. Her desire mounted until the primal urge for satisfaction took over.

"Lie on your back and open your legs." When Maya complied, Anika lay on top of her, missionary style, and then pressed their erect clits together. She relaxed her hips, but kept her torso elevated by resting her elbows on the bed.

Anika sighed at the sensual feel of indescribable softness against equally soft flesh and the meeting of their hard, swollen buds. She held her groin tight to Maya's and moved in circles until she found a rhythm.

The woman beneath her gasped with pleasure. She elevated her hips and matched Anika's movements until the sexual pressure building between them exploded.

Lowering her head, Anika sank her teeth into the base of Maya's neck while her climax bloomed. She nipped and bit until blood pooled just beneath the surface of her skin, but controlled the urge to bite down and drink.

Maya crooned and whispered words of endearment to both encourage and soothe her.

Anika's orgasm spiked so fast the room went dark. Powerful spasms shook her and blazing heat spiraled through her. Her nails scratched the arms that held her, but stopped short of breaking the skin. As the climax continued, Anika held on to her tempo, pleasuring Maya while she came.

Seconds later, Maya screamed with her climax.

As they lay together afterward, Maya cradled her in her arms. Anika kissed and licked the marks her teeth and nails had made. The aggression had been deeply satisfying, but for the first time since her change, a normal future seemed possible. Her need to bond had been stronger than her thirst for blood.

"I'm not going back to Fur Con," Maya told her. "I don't need to hide anymore. I want to stay with you."

Anika sensed she'd grow stronger with Maya by her side. "We'll hunt and kill the demon together."

"Then we'll be free."

Sleep came soon after. As she drifted into her dreams, Anika roused enough to cry out, but Maya soothed her. The fiery demon inside her quelled. "No hunting tonight, my love." Maya's embrace calmed her and chased the demon spirit away.

Anika nestled closer, safe in the knowledge they'd one day find peace in the Pocono Mountaintops.

TOTEM

Karis Walsh

S hay dipped her left wing and glided around the bow of the cruise ship. She flew by the next row of windows, glancing in each as she searched for Tala's cabin. In her human form, she would have laughed at these people who were here to experience rugged Alaska. Out of one eye Shay could see the fjords carved by glaciers, and the dense forests that reached to the shores of the deep channel and provided a home for wildlife, independent settlers, and native people who still knew the old ways.

Her other eye scanned the passengers who lounged in their rooms in silk pajamas and merely observed a tiny edge of the wilderness Shay called home. They would snap photos of an orca with their cell phones, eat crab legs and salmon at endless buffets, and take home a few Native American trinkets to remind them of their brief brush with nature. They would never understand what it was like to live the beauty of Alaska inside and out like Shay did. She only hoped Tala wouldn't be one of them—that she would choose to stay.

One more circuit of the enormous ship and Shay finally found the woman she was looking for. She perched on the far edge of the balcony and crab-walked along the railing until she could see past the heavy green curtains and into the small stateroom. Tala wore a towel, and her hair was damp from a shower. Shay hadn't seen her since she left college eight years ago, but the familiar rush of longing hit her as if they hadn't been apart for more than a day.

When Tala dropped her towel and reached for a pair of simple white panties, Shay nearly flew smack into the window in her longing to touch her mate.

Shay guiltily knew she was spying, but she couldn't resist sidling further along the rail so she could see inside better. She realized with a start that in their two years as lovers, she had never seen Tala naked in daylight. Theirs was a relationship that had belonged only to the dark screen of night, but Shay wanted nothing more than to have Tala know her in the day as well. Greedily, she watched Tala's slight form, her pale skin that too rarely left the confines of the museum, her nipples that puckered in the cool air.

They were the color of soapberries, but Shay knew from experience they would be sweet, and not bitter, on her tongue. She knew the other flavors of Tala as well, from her mouth to the skin of her neck to the moist heat she was hiding under those plain undies. A gust of wind coming down the channel caught Shay in her moment of distraction and nearly knocked her off the smooth wooden railing. She fanned her black wings and teetered for a moment as she struggled to regain her balance, talons scratching the teak rail.

Shay's hopes of remaining undetected were dashed as Tala's attention was drawn to the balcony. A four-foot wing span was difficult to hide when you were flailing all over the place, she thought with a sigh as she finally settled her wings back against her body. She knew she should simply fly away and confront Tala later, on shore and in human form, but their eyes locked and she was unable to move.

She saw the exact moment when Tala's green eyes widened in surprise and recognition. Tala hastily pulled on a shirt and jeans before sliding open the door and stepping onto the balcony.

"Shay," she whispered, as if it were a struggle to speak. As if voicing Shay's name in the presence of this non-human raven would turn her suspicions and fears into truth.

Shay sighed into her shift and felt her wings stretch, her thin legs lengthen and grow, her beak and feathers retract back into her soul. She perched precariously on the narrow railing, her knees drawn up in an attempt to protect herself from the rejection she knew she might face.

"Tala," she said, equally quietly. "You came."

They stared at each other. After stating the obvious, Shay found she had forgotten all of the speeches, the propositions and declarations she had practiced in her mind. They had sounded so convincing and irrefutable in her daydreams, but faced with the real Tala—the woman with shock and confusion etched over her delicate features and in her expressive eyes—all of Shay's words vanished as if she really were an animal incapable of human speech.

"They're true?" Tala asked. "All the stories you told me?"

Shay nodded. "You always knew they were." She and Tala had been unlikely roommates at Seattle's University of Washington, probably placed together because they both had Tlingit roots. She had been rebellious and wild, changing majors and girlfriends with equal rapidity. Tala had been—and clearly still was—serious and quiet. She had followed her lifelong goal into the field of museology, with never a step off the path she had chosen for herself. By day, the two barely spoke—and barely tolerated each other's presence. But at night, when Shay first began to shift and was terrified and confused without any tribal elders to explain her new abilities, she had turned to Tala instead.

She remembered that first time when she returned to their room after a frantic wolfen run through the shadows of the campus and stood mutely by Tala's bed. She smelled of wet grass and moonlight and fear, and Tala had wordlessly pulled the covers back and allowed Shay into her bed. From that night on they were lovers, unknowingly imprinting on each other every time the studious and introverted Tala opened her heart, her soul—and her legs—to a disheveled, half-wild-with-need Shay.

"What have you been doing since college?" Tala finally asked, standing pressed against the sliding glass door.

Shay laughed at the banality of the question in this situation that was anything but common or everyday. *Besides flying around cruise ships and peeping in at the passengers?* she wanted to ask. Instead, she followed Tala's lead and answered in as normal a way as possible.

"I'm an Alaska state trooper. I was in the bush for a few years, but I'm stationed in Sitka now. I'm planning to return to my people soon."

When I've chosen my mate, Shay added silently. Her grandmother, the clan's shaman, was getting old and Shay knew it was time to claim her birthright and reveal her ability to shift through her totem like her mother and grandmother could. But she didn't want to go alone. "You're still at the same museum," she stated. She knew the answer already since she had addressed her first tentative letters to Tala at the Pacific Northwest native art museum where she served as curator. Tala had answered with equally brief and impersonal notes, wavering indecisively over Shay's suggestion that she come to Alaska and see some of the art she catalogued and displayed in its real life setting.

Tala reached out and plucked at Shay's flannel sleeve. "Can you get down from that railing?" she asked nervously. "You might fall."

"If I do, I can just shift and fly away," Shay said with a laugh, but she climbed down anyway and stood close to Tala.

"You couldn't, not in front of all these passengers," Tala said, worry clearly showing in her eyes.

Shay stepped closer and curled her hand around the nape of Tala's neck. "Here I thought you were concerned for my safety," she said with a mock frown. "But all you really care about is what other people might think."

Tala shook her head and Shay's fingers tangled in the damp ash blond curls. "I don't want you hurt," she whispered as Shay's mouth hovered over hers. Tala was the one to bridge the distance, the years, between them as she pressed her lips to Shay's. The kiss was everything Shay remembered. Open and soft, inviting her inside, reconnecting a confused and untethered Shay back to her human body and spirit as only Tala had ever been able to do.

Shay reluctantly pulled away. She had read in novels about people drowning in kisses, but the opposite was true for her. Without Tala she was unmoored, sinking and helpless. With Tala at her side, in her home, Shay knew she would have the quiet harbor she needed to give her strength to be a tribal leader. But if Tala wasn't ready?

"I'll see you on shore," Shay said as she stepped back and pulled herself onto the railing. She wanted to stay, but she needed more than hidden kisses and secret trysts. Her one consolation as she slipped backward off the balcony and stretched her fingers until they feathered was that Tala watched and didn't turn away from her transformation. It was one step toward acceptance.

* * *

Shay stayed within the tree line, easily keeping pace with the small group of tourists who obediently followed their guide through Ketchikan's forest of totem poles. Tala was among them, listening intently to the lecture and looking as serious as she had in college. Shay was surprised she wasn't taking notes in case there was a test following the tour.

She snarled her impatience and waited until Tala looked her way, as if sensing her presence, before she slipped out of the cover of the woods and stood panting in plain sight. Tala's mouth opened to call attention to the large gray wolf before recognition again showed in her eyes. Shay dropped into play posture before she turned and sprinted a couple of yards into the woods. She returned and repeated the process a couple of times until she coaxed an actual smile from Tala.

It took several feints before Tala, with a last guilty look at her guide, broke away from the rest of the tourists and casually walked toward the stand of trees that hid Shay from view. Shay loped along happily, her tongue lolling out, as she made enough noise so that Tala could easily follow her trail. Lovingly, she guided her prey toward a small clearing. She pushed through the low branches, gradually drawing more erect, until she walked into the clearing in her human form. Then she stepped behind Tala, who stared at a lone totem pole.

Shay slipped her arms around Tala's waist. "This is my totem," she said quietly, nuzzling along Tala's neck while her wolf senses were still acute.

Tala leaned into her embrace. "You can shift into all of these animals?"

Shay stared at the red cedar pole that depicted the special totems of her grandmother, her mother, and all of the females in their lineage. Raven. Wolf. Seal. "Yes," she said. "And once

I take my place as shaman, I'll be able to shift into any of my clan's spirit guides."

She turned Tala in her arms so she could meet her eyes. "I want you to be with me when I do," she said, opening her soul to the woman she loved.

"That's crazy," Tala said as she averted her gaze and tried to pull out of Shay's arms.

"No," Shay said, her voice still sounding like a snarl after her recent shift. "I belong with my people, and you belong with me."

"I'm Tlingit, too," Tala reminded her as she stepped away, "but I don't change into animals. And I'm not going to give up everything I have in the city just to go back to some tribe."

Shay growled her frustration. Tala just didn't understand. She was Tlingit, but for two generations her family had been away from their clan. Now her only contact with them was behind glass, on velvet pedestals at her museum.

Shay had spent the first eight years of her life among her people before her mother was killed in a fishing accident. Her Russian-American father left the tribe with young Shay, raising her as Natasha Golikov in Seattle, but she had never forgotten her early years with her grandmother or the stories about shape-shifting she heard around the evening fires. Tala's idea of myth was her reality. How could she convince her that the Tlingit way wasn't just a fictional story, but a liberating, achievable truth?

Words failed Shay after a long few days of shifting. All she could do was grab Tala's upper arms and pull her close for a kiss. She kissed like a wolf, her teeth rasping against Tala's unprotected lips, snapping against the tendons on her neck. She fanned her arms around Tala like wings, wanting to protect her and rip her apart at the same time. Her skin slid along Tala's like the ocean, fierce and glorious in its power. She managed to unbutton

Tala's blouse without tearing it, wishing she could as easily break the shell of civilization that surrounded Tala like a coffin.

She shoved Tala against the totem pole and dropped to her knees, leaving long, thin scratches along Tala's abdomen as she zeroed in on the denim barrier denying her access.

Daylight. Public. Those thoughts raced through Shay's mind as she slipped Tala's jeans off her hips and down to her ankles. It was the first time Tala had trusted her like this, the first time she had let desire and need overrule her sense of propriety and acceptable behavior.

Shay's tongue delved into Tala's warm wetness and a sense of gratitude overwhelmed her. Gratitude for the fingers tangled in her hair, urging her on. For the thighs that parted, opening to her and surrounding her at the same time.

When Tala came with a rough cry, Shay's tears mingled with her wetness, forming a bond that was deeper than any that could be formed by blood or legal ties.

Shay stood up and pulled Tala against her. She could feel Tala's rapid heartbeat, her labored breathing. But worst of all, she sensed Tala's almost immediate withdrawal. She was going back, Shay realized with a stab of pain. Back to her protected world, back behind her museum glass.

They stepped apart. "I'm sorry," Tala whispered. She continued, her voice growing stronger as she spoke. "I love what you are," she said, gesturing at the totem pole behind her. "I love you. But I can't live like this. I can't leave my job, my home, my world just to follow you."

"They're your people too," Shay said, turning her head away since she was unable to face the conviction she knew was in Tala's eyes. Tala wasn't from her clan, but her roots were tied as deeply to the Tlingit people as Shay's were. They had to be.

"It's not the same," Tala said with a shake of her head. "You're closer to them. You've lived with your tribe, with their legends as your reality. *My* reality is in Seattle. In the museum."

Shay kept her eyes averted, her face as emotionless as the painted animals carved on the cedar totem pole. She had no more arguments, no more pleas. If Tala couldn't accept what tied them together, she couldn't force it on her. Tala waited in silence for a few moments before she struggled into her jeans and walked back to join the tour.

Shay couldn't resist following the cruise ship as it left Ketchikan's dock. She easily kept up with its slow pace, resurfacing occasionally to glance at Tala's empty balcony before arching into a graceful dive and ducking below the surface. She usually felt her most playful when she shifted to her seal totem, but today she only knew sorrow as her sleek body undulated through the icy ocean water. She both hoped for and dreaded one last glimpse of Tala as she watched the ship aim toward Juneau—and away from her. She believed Tala would easily recognize her in this form, but there was no sign of life in her stateroom.

Shay slowly swam back to her Cessna Skywagon. She reached a flipper toward the seaplane, her fingers lengthening and grasping the struts. She half slithered, half crawled onto the pontoon as her body slowly morphed back to human.

She had planned to resign from the state troopers and study with her grandmother until she could take on the role of shaman, but with Tala gone her confidence wavered. Perhaps another year with the force, either on the remote Aleutians or back to the isolated, expansive deep north. Shay grabbed a uniform shirt and pants off the pilot's seat of her plane and slipped them on. Then she sat on the pontoon, resigned and defeated, her feet dangling in the frigid water, when a flicker of movement made her look toward the shore.

With a body suddenly come to life, Shay hopped from the pontoon to the dock. She walked to the shore, to Tala, and came to a trembling stop a few feet away.

"I...I couldn't leave you," Tala said quietly. Shay didn't have to be told what a sacrifice that was for Tala. She couldn't leave Shay, so she chose instead to leave behind the world she knew. Shay silently vowed to make sure Tala never regretted her decision.

She reached up and cupped Tala's chin gently in her hands. "Welcome home," she said, kissing her with all of the fierceness and gratitude her totem animals inspired.

Tala shook her head, still not fully convinced. "*Your* home," she said. "You are so much more than—"

"No," Shay said firmly. "This world, these people are inside you too. Don't tell me you've never felt it, that urge to run, crawl, and swim right out of your own skin."

Shay slipped her hand to the nape of Tala's neck, tangling fingers in her hair, tugging gently as she stepped backward into the lapping waves. She could feel Tala's skin grow slick under her hand, see the dawning awareness in Tala's beautiful eyes, as together they dipped below the ocean's surface.

SNEAK

Giselle Renarde

It wasn't much to look at, inside or out, but this house had been a brothel of sorts for as long as Bess could remember. Only one woman lived here now, alone—or so she thought. She didn't know about Bess. At least, not yet.

Ah, Loralee, so unassumingly pretty underneath that thick foundation, the false lashes, the dark shadow. Her men only got to see her one way—made-up, falsified, cloaked in everything she wasn't. Her skirts were small, but her hair was big—teased and sprayed to retain dimension. It wasn't the real Loralee on that bed, just a body that looked like her. Cosmetics prevented the men, the adulterers and perverts, from seeing her true self. Loralee, pretty Loralee, was so vulnerable, so insecure...so like Bess.

Bess looked on, unnoticed, as some reeking cowboy took Loralee from behind. His shirt was half-off, dirty denim around his ankles, boots grinding mud into the worn-down carpet. They were all so lazy, these dirty, grunting men. Loralee deserved better, but the poor thing was resigned to her fate.

And how, exactly, did Bess know all this? Well, people tend to talk when they think they're alone. Loralee always talked to herself when the men had gone, while she stripped the bed. Poor girl always washed the sheets after a john had left.

Bess didn't blame her—she'd have done the same if fate hadn't blessed her so long ago. She hardly remembered being human. She hadn't much cared for it, as far as she could recall.

The cowboy pulled his cock from Loralee's pussy and shoved it up her ass. Bess cringed as Loralee screamed bloody murder. Loralee's hands, with their chipped-polish nails, balled the fitted sheet, tearing it from the mattress. The cowboy just kept ramming her, and Bess wondered how humanity continued to function with so many of these heartless bastards on the loose. He slapped her ass rosy, and when he pulled out, a trail of white stuff followed. Blood, too.

Without a word, he shrugged on his shirt, zipped up his jeans, and tossed a couple of bills on the tall dresser. They landed so close to Bess she could smell his putrid scent on them, and her stomach flip-flopped.

The ceramic tea light holder on the dresser was open at the back and had stars cut out in the front. It was a perfect hiding spot. Perched inside, Bess watched Loralee take heaving breaths, like she was trying to expel that man from her lungs. Pulling the sheets along with her, she slipped to the floor and sobbed.

"Oh God," she kept saying, over and over, like a pleading sort of prayer. "What kind of life is this for a person?"

Bess wished she could help, but how? Perhaps if she got close, that would provide comfort to the woman huddled in a pool of dirty sheets. Dipping through the hole she'd gnawed in the wall, Bess scurried down a familiar series of beams and brackets to her hole in the baseboards. She poked her head through, pulling her fat little body after her, and skittered close to Loralee. Black rivers of mascara coursed down the poor thing's cheeks. If only Bess could say something, talk to the girl...

"Ahhh! Mouse!" Loralee scooted back on the carpet, reaching for the largest volume on the bookshelf. It had to be the Bible—what else? With it, Loralee tried to thump what she obviously perceived as vermin. "Git, you!"

So much for that idea. Bess darted underneath the tall dresser, where even the vacuum couldn't reach, and encouraged her racing heart to settle down.

"Damn you!" Loralee's voice was hoarse.

Bess's heart fell until she peeked out and saw that Loralee's focus had shifted to the mirror. As usual, Loralee was talking to herself.

"Slut," she said.

Bess watched her reflection, observing Loralee's bruised and beaten body. When she was younger, she didn't have the varicose veins or the cellulite, but Bess appreciated her figure as it was now: a real woman's body, with life to show for it.

When Loralee dredged the blade from her underwear drawer, Bess hissed, "No, no, no..." but her words came out as squeaks. On the one hand, she didn't want to see this, but she felt the need to supervise in case things got out of control.

Loralee fell to the floor, swaddling herself in bloody, cum-soaked sheets. Leaning against the bed, she opened her legs and stared down at her cunt. She still had on that hideous animal print miniskirt, but no panties. The cowboy had torn open her purple blouse, so sheer her polka-dot brassiere showed through it even when it was buttoned up. Her big breasts bounced as she sobbed silently.

"Why?" she asked as she ran that blade across her thigh. She hissed when it sliced her flesh, a surface wound deep enough to bring forth blood.

"Don't hurt yourself," Bess pleaded, still more squeaks. "Oh, Loralee, you're such a pretty girl."

"Ugly," Loralee replied, as though she'd heard Bess. "Ugly, ugly, dirty whore." She sliced up her poor thigh in quick strokes, one cut after another. "Dirty whore."

Loralee drank a whole bottle of whiskey that night and passed out on the floor. Bess stood guard the whole night long, and well into the morning hours. It was afternoon before Loralee dragged herself to the toilet and her sheets to the old machine. She looked perfectly horrid with makeup spread across her cheeks, her mascara-laden false lashes askew. The poor thing didn't even wash, except the crusted blood from her thighs, pussy, and ass.

"Eat something," Bess pleaded. *Squeak, squeak, squeak.* "Oh, my poor darling..."

"Gotta pay the rent, pay the bills, pay the piper." Loralee traipsed about the place, one shoe on, one shoe off. Stopping at the fridge, she pulled out the orange juice. It was better than nothing.

Bess had seen so much self-destruction in her time, but Loralee got to her like nobody else. She couldn't watch any more of this. It was time to come out of retirement in the career she'd never begun.

How long since she'd taken human form? Long, long ago, in what she now thought of as her youth. She'd watched generations come and go since, trapped—though not unhappily—in this tiny, fuzzy form. Bess preferred life as a mouse. Humanity seemed too full of repercussions. And, of course, there was Old Gertie's spell...

With a hair-of-the-dog flask in hand, Loralee stumbled out

the door and tramped around back. She didn't drive anymore—license suspended, car impounded—and it was an hour-long walk to the bar. It worried Bess that Loralee cut through the brush and down the ravine, but that was her chosen path. That girl's life was full of shortcuts.

Bess pushed the small pot of Gertie's powder beyond the hole in the baseboard and stopped cold. What would she look like when she took human form? Would she be as old as her years? Bess shook her head. No time for worries—she was doing all this for Loralee. Without another moment's hesitation, she dipped her nose in the pearly white powder.

The transformation was swift, thank God, because it hurt like hell and left her naked and moaning on the floor. The room looked much smaller from this perspective. When she rose on shaky legs she was surprised to find a young face looking back in the mirror. She was never a great beauty—small, frizzy brownish hair, lackluster skin—but to see her own face was to come home. She held her cheeks in both hands, pressing, feeling the long-forgotten skin and bones. In that moment, gazing at her naked reflection, she knew she'd made the right decision.

Before seeking out her old clothing, Bess went in search of a telephone. She felt like a baby giraffe, so awkwardly gangling, but she knew she'd grow accustomed to this form soon enough. Bess had never used one of these telephones with the fancy rotary dials. It was all very modern age.

"Operator?"

The telephone made a noise, a low, steady buzz.

"Hello, Operator? Are you there?" And then she recalled watching Loralee dial numbers to place calls. Bess didn't know which number would get her through to Dorothy's Tavern, so she started with zero.

A woman answered. "Operator."

"Oh, wonderful!" That was a stroke of luck. "Could you connect me with Dorothy's Tavern, please?"

When the operator put the call through, Bess's stomach tumbled. Loralee couldn't possibly have arrived so quickly. Even if she headed home the minute she walked through those doors, Bess still had a good hour and a half. This plan was sure to succeed. But...what if it didn't?

Another woman answered, "You got Dorothy's Tavern, here."

"Wonderful," Bess repeated. "I'm looking for a patron of yours—a Miss Loralee."

There was silence on the line, and Bess was sure she knew why: the tavern owner was kind to Loralee and didn't care to see her in any trouble. "She ain't here just now...but she might be later on. You got a message, or what?"

"Yes." Bess twirled the telephone cord around her index finger. "Would you tell Loralee her next trick is waiting, and to please come home immediately?"

Bess didn't wait for a response. She dropped the handset and hopped up the stairs to the disused second floor. Everything was dusty. Loralee never came up here and neither did she. Too many memories. Bess didn't like to think about the old days.

She found her old frocks crammed at the very back of the cupboard. Amazing nobody had thrown them out in all these years. Grabbing the tawny one with the little flowers, she held it up in the muted sunlight. The collar had yellowed considerably, but Beth was happy to find something she'd stitched by hand, back in the days when she had hands and not paws. She looked at them now—the nails were quite long, and she raced downstairs to trim them.

Despite her lack of undergarments, Bess slipped into her dress before putting fresh sheets on Loralee's bed. It was too soon to put on tea—no, coffee, to sober the girl when she arrived. Bess paced the floor, smoothing her dress again and again.

Goodness, this frock did have a musty odor. *Now what? What's next?* Her stomach rumbled and she decided it was time to eat...as humans do.

After pacing and fidgeting indoors for a time, Bess paced and fidgeted outside. It felt so strange to be big, and clothed to boot. She hoped Loralee wouldn't notice she had no shoes on.

Crackling in the brush set off Bess's instinct to run, but she convinced herself to stay put. It was only Loralee, after all. "Yoo-hoo!" Bess called out, waving her hands. "Over here!"

Loralee emerged, leaning her weight against a tree. "Who the heck are you? Dorothy said I got a trick waiting at home."

"You do." Bess felt nervous under Loralee's scrutiny. "I'm it."

Tossing her head back, Loralee cackled. Her hair was sprayed so firmly in place even the tree trunk couldn't dent it. "But you're a girl."

"Yes..." *Better a girl than a mouse!* "I'm a girl with money." *Money I took from your nightstand.*

Loralee considered Bess gravely. "You're not some freaky chick, here to kill me or whatnot?"

Bess shook her head. "I'm just a girl who wants a little pleasure out of life...like you?"

"Oh, sister, you got me all wrong." Cackling again, Loralee pushed herself away from the tree with her foot and stumbled toward the kitchen door.

Bess's heart palpitated as she followed. "I took the liberty of brewing some coffee. Want a cup?"

A grin bled across Loralee's lips. "I surely would. Thanks a bunch." She sat at her own kitchen table and allowed Bess to serve her.

As Loralee sipped her coffee, her hazy eyes found the glimmer of youth. She'd been so vibrant before the drinking, before the whoring. Bess had watched from the walls as girls grew up too fast in this house. She would have been one of them if not for Old Gertie's magic, and there was more guilt in that thought than Bess could bear.

"Could I help you take a bath?" Bess asked, watching Loralee's strong hands grip her mug.

Loralee looked up from the table, questioning, and then grinned. "Why, sure. What's your name, anyhow?"

"Bess," she replied before contemplating whether she ought to give a false one.

Rising from the table, Loralee said, "Well, that's a pretty little name. How's about you wait here while I use the commode, and then we can get on with that bath?"

With a polite smile, Bess sank into Loralee's vacated chair. What a luxury, all this indoor plumbing—hot water that flowed right through the taps.

When Loralee opened the bathroom door, she was naked as a jaybird and the tub was full of bubbles. The whole room smelled like lavender and heat, and the steam made it tricky to breathe.

"I gotta admit, little Bess, I ain't too sure what you wanna do with me."

Did Bess know, herself? Her desire for Loralee was a thick pulse at the center of her being. The few times she'd shifted into human form, the transformation was spurred by this same pounding within. Loralee's nude form, her breasts soft and full, wide hips, and gentle thighs made Bess feel faint. She stood before the tub, shielding the fiery hair below her navel, as though she were shy for Bess to see it.

"You certainly are a pretty woman." Bess looked over that pale flesh. "Let's wash you up."

It wasn't until Loralee hissed upon sinking into the warm bath that Bess realized her mistake: Loralee hadn't been shy of Bess seeing her pubic hair, but rather the cuts on her thighs. Bess's heart sank as she wondered if this might all be a terrible idea, but how else could she act as savior to this poor woman?

Perching on the edge of the tub, Bess scooped water into her hands and let it trickle down Loralee's full, weighty breasts. It felt funny to do all this, to touch things.

Loralee sighed and leaned back in the water, sinking her big hair below the crackling bubbles. When she emerged, her hair was dark, saturated, sheets of water flowing from it. Her makeup ran off in black lines.

Bess reached for the flannel and ran a plain white bar of soap across it. "Mind if I help you wash up your face?" When Loralee jerked away, she said, "I promise I'll be gentle."

"Well…" Loralee sat a little straighter. "What can I say? You're the john, Jane."

"Bess," she corrected before recognizing the joke.

They both chuckled. Bess was so nervous she scarcely touched Loralee on the first pass. She gasped when the girl took her by the hand. There was such longing in Loralee's gaze, and Bess felt a glittering sensation all around her heart. It coursed downward, too, like the wet bubbles running down Loralee's breasts, a hot tremor between her legs.

Loralee rinsed her face when Bess finished scrubbing those ground-in layers of makeup. Years of cosmetics, caked on, forming a mask against her skin. Now it was gone, and all that remained was Loralee, her face rosy red from the heat and the pressure.

"Why, you're even prettier now than you were before," Bess sighed. Loralee must have believed it because she didn't contradict her, not even a laugh. "Can I wash your hair now?"

With a wink, Loralee said, "Nah, I'll deal with that mess. You work my front, doll."

Bess's heart beat wildly, and she wasted no time running her washcloth down Loralee's long neck. Despite her fierce desire, Bess was shy about touching. She stared at Loralee's dark puckered nipples. Her heavy breasts had a funny sort of tan from low-cut blouses, diagonal lines running down to meet where her pushed-up cleavage would sit in a brassiere, lines separating dark from light.

Loralee had her hands over her head now, pressing shampoo against her scalp and lathering suds. She looked like a princess, and that made Bess even more anxious about touching her.

"Ain't ya gonna wash my chest?" Loralee's voice was downy and welcoming even as she stuck out her breasts and waved them side to side. Bess was mesmerized by the motion. "Aww, don't be shy."

Bess swallowed past the lump in her throat. Her washcloth hovered above Loralee's breasts, droplets falling gently on those pert nipples. While Loralee washed her hair, Bess courageously pressed soapy cloth to skin, rubbing round and round. She even worked up the nerve to touch one breast with her bare hand, and the sensation made her dizzy. Oh, Loralee's flesh was softer than Bess ever imagined. This girl wasn't as hard, as calloused and secure, as those wretched men thought. Loralee was precious, and Bess wanted her to remember that.

"Want to wash my pussy?" Loralee rose and sheets of sudsy water coursed from her body. She leaned against the tile wall.

Staring straight into that dark bush, Bess gulped in fear and in awe. There were so many things she'd like to do with that pussy, but cleaning it seemed like a good start. She pressed her palm flush to Loralee's bush. The girl moaned when Bess moved her hand up and down, hoping she'd strike the girl's clit if she kept at it. She gazed at the puffy pink wounds Loralee had inflicted the night before, and whimpered.

When Bess pressed two fingers inside Loralee's pussy, she couldn't believe how hot it was, how slippery wet. The yearning sigh that passed through Loralee's lips made Bess's pelvis throb. She pressed the meat of her palm against the engorged clit poking out between plump pussy lips. The glistening redness drove Bess out of her senses, and she lunged for Loralee's breast, sucking with brutish intensity.

"Oh, little Bessie!" Loralee cradled Bess's head in her hands. "Baby, that feels so nice!"

Bess moved to the other tit, licking and sucking that pebbled nipple. Loralee's flesh tasted like white soap and lavender, so clean and fresh. As her arousal built, Bess's body took over. Her fingers, three now, fucked Loralee's pussy hard, pausing only momentarily so her palm could mash that distended clit. Loralee gasped and groaned, bunching Bess's hair with wet hands.

"Is this what you came here for?" Loralee squealed and moaned. "You're paying to make me come?"

"Yes!" Bess cried, pressing her cheek against one breast while she lapped the other. "I want you to feel good."

Climbing into the tub, soaking the hem of her dress, Bess kissed Loralee's mouth. It tasted like coffee, and the flavor was exhilarating. Loralee's tough tongue danced with hers, and the heat rendered Bess breathless. She let herself collapse against Loralee's wet chest, but that only made her wish she were naked, too. When she fiddled madly with her buttons, Loralee laughed. "Come on now, little one. Let's get in the bedroom and do this right."

Loralee didn't seem to realize her hair was still a beehive of white bubbles until Bess pointed it out. Stepping out of the tub, she crouched over the ledge to wash it out. Bess's torment only increased as she observed the sway of Loralee's plump backside. She reached out to touch it, and surprised herself by squeezing that rounded flesh, digging her fingernails in and grabbing on.

Swinging around with surprise, Loralee splashed the tile with wet hair. After a moment, her expression faded from alarm to arousal. She quickly stole a towel from the hanger and swaddled her sopping locks.

"That's it, you!" Loralee leapt from the bathroom, streaming toward the boudoir. "To bed, I said! And get yourself out of them clothes, you hear?"

Bess abandoned her frock while Loralee retrieved a bottle of scented oil from her dresser. "Am I going to rub you with that?" Bess asked.

"Not if I get you first!" Loralee chased her naked onto clean sheets, straddling her waist and pouring the sweet-smelling oil between her breasts

When Bess stole the bottle away in a fit of giggles, Loralee laid hands on Bess's sizzling flesh, tracing oil in circles around her tits, taking their peaked nipples between her fingers and squeezing. Of course, Loralee's hands were so slip-slidey with oil they couldn't get a grip, but it sure seemed like fun trying. That's why Bess sprinkled thick droplets of oil across Loralee's big breasts and traced her hands around those globes. Gosh, Bess could never get tired of this.

And then Loralee slowed the pace and her laughter subsided. In slow back-and-forth motions, she brushed her big bush over the wispy hair of Bess's little pussy. Bess was mesmerized by the sensation. It wasn't enough, just barely a feather touch, but she was sure, oh so sure, it would evolve into something more.

In silence, Bess watched the pendulous sway of Loralee's breasts, the towel toppling from her hair, allowing wet strands to fall across her shoulder. Water dripped down her tits as she moved too softly against Bess's tortured pussy. Droplets fell from her nipples and landed cool against Bess's warm belly.

"Oh, more!" Bess begged. All she could feel was the faint kiss of clit on clit through a curtain of pubic hair. It just wasn't enough. "Please, more!"

Loralee winked, and her smile seemed genuine. "You're the boss, little lady." Sneaking one leg underneath Bess's thigh, Loralee leaned back so far Bess could no longer see her head beyond those mountainous breasts.

When the wet heat of Loralee's pussy met hers, Bess gasped. The sensation was so vast and yet so direct she started to pull back, but forced herself to stay. Loralee rolled her hips in slow circles, rubbing Bess's slick lips and clit with every pass. Everything, every slight motion, made her tingle all over, and her pelvis filled with a buzzing sort of pleasure she hadn't experienced in a very long time. Her skin was hot, her nipples so hard they hurt. Her pussy pulsed as she writhed against Loralee.

The motion continued, hypnotic, the same tight circles, pussy on pussy, clit kissing clit. Even minor variations—a wider loop, a diagonal splash—made her squeal and buck against Loralee's curves. They were trapped together like this, caged by one another's bodies, and the tremulous pleasure went on and on until Bess was trembling and moaning, until she couldn't control herself anymore. She pinched her nipples and squeezed those buds, pressed her eyes closed, and pounded her pussy hard against Loralee's wetness.

"Easy, little one." Loralee laughed. "You'll be sore in the morning."

"I don't care!" Bess cried, smashing her clit anywhere that would receive it—Loralee's pussy lips, thigh, and then fingers… oh, those wonderful fingers! Loralee squirmed from the bed and planted them inside Bess's cunt, ducking between her legs.

Bess had never in her life been so wild with pleasure. She screamed and cursed, groping for Loralee's head and grabbing hold of her long wet hair. Loralee shrieked now, too, but Bess couldn't stop. Her desire drove her into realms unknown, and even when the pleasure of Loralee's tongue was so good it hurt, she trapped the woman's face between her thighs and held her there.

The explosion was monumental. Bess's belly flip-flopped while her bum bounced against the mattress. She released Loralee's hair and pinched her nipples until the sensation zapped through her body and ignited her clit. It was too much now, too much to bear, and she closed her legs, curling in on herself and moaning while Loralee joined her on the bed.

"I don't know where you came from, little Bess, but you're the best thing that's happened to me in donkey's years." Loralee folded an arm around Bess and pulled up the quilt.

Was it too soon to tell all? She'd wondered how she would reveal her plan to Loralee, but now that her exhilaration was wearing into exhaustion, it seemed easy. Bess turned around in the bed. When they were nose to nose, she could smell her pussy on Loralee's breath, and the image of that pretty woman between her legs came roaring back.

"Loralee, I know this'll sound crazy, but I'm the mouse that's been living in your house."

She expected Loralee to laugh, but Loralee didn't do anything, just lay there waiting for more.

"I was raised here a long time ago, and told it was my fate to become what you are now. Well, I just couldn't do it, and I went to Old Gertie who knew spells and such, and I asked her to release me from my fate. She gave me some powder that would turn me to a mouse, and I been living like that ever since. I could turn human if I wanted, for a while, but if I were to stay like this Old Gertie said I had to switch places with another girl. Somebody had to live the fate."

Loralee nodded solemnly, pulling Bess in so close their soft breasts touched. "Yeah, I heard about you from the girls I grew up with. Never knew if any of that were true."

Bess nodded, hooking her chin around Loralee's smooth shoulder. "It's true. And now I want to trade places. I'll take on your life and you can be the mouse in my house."

Pulling away quickly, Loralee left Bess with a cold front even under warm covers. "You don't want my life, little girl. Hell, I don't want it neither, but being a got-dang whore's just about killed me. I wouldn't wish that on nobody."

With a giggle, Bess leaned in and kissed Loralee's lips. "Don't you worry, 'cause I got a plan: you'll be my one and only trick. Never was any rule saying I couldn't go out and get some other job, too. I could work in town, be a modern secretary. Nobody knows me there. I'll give you the money, and you pay me for pleasure—that way I'm technically still a whore. I'm just your whore, exclusive-like."

"You'd make love to a mouse?" Loralee screwed up her brow.

"Silly girl." Bess pulled her in close. "You can take human form for hours at a time. Aren't I pretty human-looking now?"

Loralee looked at her funny, and then petted something at the side of Bess's head. "Well, you did until this little mousy ear sprouted up." Looking her straight in the eye, Loralee conveyed about as much gratitude as any one person could rightly feel. "Imagine—me, a mouse! Bet I'll do a lot of sneaking around inside your walls, huh?"

With a smirk, Bess replied, "I bet you will and all."

PURRFECT
IN VENEZIA

Myla Jackson

Natalie checked her body-hugging, nearly see-through leotard, adjusted the cat ears nestled in her mane of tawny gold hair, and dared to smile for what felt like the first time in a year.

From her room's window in Hotel Eden, she glimpsed the beauty of nighttime in Venice. Lights reflected off the still canals, the occasional motorboat cruised by, barely stirring a wake. A gondola skimmed the inky, black waters, its oarsman guiding a young couple through the watery streets of the ancient city, a deep, otherworldly song echoing off the decaying buildings.

A year ago she'd sat in this room, dressing to go out on the town for a little fun at the annual *Carnevale di Venezia*. Eager to dance among the elaborately costumed patrons, she'd hurried out her door and down the hallway to what she thought was the exit. Just one wrong turn was all it took to change everything.

With a last glance in the mirror, Natalie picked up her clutch containing a photo of her mother and father and the blood-red ruby ring and letter her grandmother had left to her. She slipped the ring on her finger, recalling the message contained in the letter.

My darling Natalie, as I reflect on my life, I have but one regret—not following my heart. If I could bequeath only one thing to you, it would be the strength to make the right choice in love, even if it means leaving behind all things familiar and safe. The ruby ring is a family heirloom. Some say it is only a ring. I choose to believe it has magical qualities. Wear it with love and let it guide you to your heart's desire.

Within days of giving her the letter and ring as an engagement gift, Natalie's grandmother had passed away. Natalie had worn the ring to Italy on a working vacation prior to her wedding. It was in Venice she'd discovered magic, both in her grandmother's bequest and in the city of love. What she had intended to be a one-week working holiday had changed her life forever.

Engaged to a man patiently awaiting her return to the States, Natalie had been hesitant to accept the gift the ring and Venice had offered. Now, a year later, she prayed she wasn't too late.

Heart pounding, hands clammy and shaking, she stepped into the hallway and opened the secret, mirrored door. It led down a dark corridor to another door marked Room 307.

Natalie twisted the ruby on her finger, trying to recall exactly what she'd done over a year ago, the precise way she'd touched the ring and then the doorknob to the secret room. With her breath lodged in her throat, she twisted the knob and pushed the door open. Instead of a hotel room, steps led down into an alley.

Natalie descended, leaving the door ajar. If her plan didn't work as hoped, she'd go home, back to her world, and live the rest of her life wondering what would have happened if she'd been less cautious back then.

Darkness engulfed her, more pronounced than anywhere else in the city. A gas street lamp flickered to life as if beckoning her. Heart thumping, she abandoned the doorway.

A shadow moved in the darkness, skittering away, just far enough to entice Natalie further.

She pursued the silhouette, at first moving slowly. Soon she ran to keep pace with the aberration flitting amongst the murky streets.

Several twists and turns later, Natalie lost the mysterious form and slowed to a halt. She stood at the base of a bridge arching over a narrow canal. For the first time, she realized she was completely alone. A cold finger of apprehension slithered down her spine. Had she made a mistake? Was this all a trick?

Trick or not, she had to find her. Had to get back to that magical place that had captured her heart, imagination, and desire. She glanced behind her one last time, squared her shoulders, and crossed the bridge.

Lights and music streamed from an ancient palace, rising up before Natalie. Its Roman columns and gilded frescos spoke of wealth, beauty, and enchantment. The decaying buildings of Venice vanished with the darkness, revealing an island city so bright and beautiful, Natalie's heart suspended, beating as she drank it all in. Nothing had changed from her previous visit.

She blinked to clear her vision and climbed the steps, lured by music and laughter, her chest swelling with hope and purpose. As she neared the stately doors, they swung open. A gasp slid past her lips as the view below her exploded in an array of twinkling illumination and sound. Beings of different shapes, colors, and sizes glided around a grand ballroom, dressed in every manner of clothing, costumes or nothing at all. Before her lay a sea of creatures both human and not so human, their bodies swaying together to the music filling the cavernous space.

Natalie entered the ballroom from above, her gaze panning the faces of those dancing and talking as they spun around the floor. She searched for one unique face, one that had haunted her memories, reminding her of all she'd walked away from.

After several minutes, Natalie's excitement waned, and she sighed in frustration. She hurried to the sweeping staircase leading to the ballroom floor. Adjusting the headband holding her cat ears in place, she descended the stairs one deliberate step at a time, her hand sliding down the smooth balustrade, all the while looking for *the one.*

Had her lover changed? Would Natalie still recognize her? Would she have moved on and found someone else to love when Natalie had gone back to the States?

Natalie's breathing grew labored, tears wadding like a sock in her throat as she stepped out on the dance floor. She stopped a cat-man gliding by with a smile and a tail that twitched with each step.

"Do you know Bella Gato?" she asked.

"Bella?" The creature looked over his shoulder and pointed. "Near the orchestra. You can't miss her."

"Thanks." Butterflies swarmed Natalie's belly as she crossed the crowded floor, weaving her way through *Carnevale* merrymakers. Just when she thought she'd never find her, the crowd parted, and she spotted Bella mingling with a group of revelers, her head thrown back, laughing merrily.

Natalie halted, mouth dry, pulse racing, her mind unable to form a coherent thought but for the incredible beauty standing before her.

Bella.

Long, pale blond hair hung down around her waist in cascading natural curls. Ice-blue eyes with the strange elongated irises twinkled in the party lights. The fine sheen of hair coating every inch of her supple body glistened like silk. Scraps of a dress she wore barely covered her nipples, hugging her waist and falling to just below the juncture of her thighs, her perky tail flicking gently from beneath.

A tall, lean male with the distinct coloring of a Bengal curled his fingers around her hip. Pulling her against his body, he whispered in her pert, pointed ear.

Bella tipped her face toward him, a smile curving her lush, full lips.

Natalie's heart plummeted, her hand rising to touch the fake cat ears mounted on a headband tucked into her hair. How could she compete with the real thing—creatures she'd never known existed and didn't in the world beyond the mystical bridge?

Bella's lips straightened, her body tightening, ears rising in alert.

The male Bengal nodded toward Natalie.

Natalie tensed, her heart hammering against her ribs. Her breath froze in her throat, waiting for the moment...

Slowly, as if in a dream, Bella turned. Her clear blue gaze captured Natalie's.

Music faded into the background, the people dancing around her blurred, and all Natalie saw was the cat-woman who'd haunted her dreams.

Bella's hand rose to her chest, her eyes blinked closed, then opened quickly, as if she was afraid what she saw wasn't real. "Natalie?"

Natalie's head raised and lowered. Her body quivered. Could it be Bella hadn't forgotten her? Could she still share the same feelings they'd explored for that incredibly magical week of *Carnevale*? Hope burgeoning, Natalie moved forward at the same time as Bella.

Natalie couldn't believe she'd found her. The ring...the bridge...*Venezia*! All were truly miraculous.

Bella stopped after only a couple of steps, a frown pulling her pretty brows together. "What are *you* doing here?"

Her heart plummeted to her belly. Natalie closed the distance, her footsteps faltering, hope and joy evaporating at the flash of anger in Bella's eyes.

Natalie refused to give up. She'd come too far. Her chin tipped upward. "I came back to find you."

The Bengal who'd been holding Bella a moment ago stepped behind her, his lip curled in a snarl. "What do you want with *mia Bella*?"

Her belly flipped over the male Bengal's claim to the beautiful Bella, but Natalie remained firm. "We had feelings for each other...once." Natalie's gaze flipped from Bella to the Bengal and back. "Perhaps those feelings were on my part alone." Head held high, Natalie turned to leave, her heart breaking into a million pieces.

Before she'd gone two steps, Bella caught her arm. "Natalie, wait."

Natalie stood with her back to Bella. "Why? It's obvious you belong to him. I should have expected someone as beautiful as you would move on after so long. There's nothing here for me."

Bella's hand tightened on her arm. "I belong to no one." She tugged on Natalie's elbow. "I choose who I want to be with."

That desperate spark of hope flared in Natalie's gut. The hand on her arm reminded her of all they'd shared. She turned to face Bella.

The Bengal slid an arm around Bella's waist and nuzzled her ear, his gaze capturing Natalie's.

A stab of jealousy pierced Natalie's heart. "Are you sure you belong to no one?" She leaned backward, tugging her arm loose, praying she wouldn't break down in front of Bella and the Bengal.

Natalie's jaw tightened. She was with Bella—the one she loved—a relationship worth fighting for. She couldn't give up now.

Bella grasped her hand. "Please. Stay. Perhaps my welcome was less than polite. Come, we will find a quiet place to talk."

The Bengal growled.

Her brow wrinkling, Bella touched his arm. "Shh, *Leandro*, you will scare her away."

"Exactly." He growled again.

Bella hooked Natalie's elbow and guided her to the end of the ballroom. A corridor branched off, leading deeper into the palace. "Come to my room. We can talk there."

Natalie cast a glance behind her where Leandro followed. "Can't we be alone?"

"I need Leandro. He stays with me."

When Natalie hesitated, Bella moved to stand in front of her, a hand rising to cup Natalie's cheek. She stared at Natalie with unblinking blue eyes. "When you left, you broke my heart. You can understand my hesitance to give it away again, no?"

Natalie nodded, her gaze straying to the well-muscled Bengal. "You've obviously found someone else. Why bother with me?"

Bella raised another hand to trail across Leandro's chest. "I have much love to give." She laughed and dragged Natalie down the corridor. "Come, I will show you."

Leandro trailed behind, the fierce frown marring the silken fur of his brow.

After climbing several flights of stairs and racing down a long hallway, Bella pushed a door open to a spacious room with lofty ceilings. An enormous bed commanded the center, draped in plush throws and satin sheets.

The door closed behind Natalie, and she spun to find Leandro leaning against it.

Throwing her arms out to her sides, Bella danced into the middle of the floor. "See? There is more than enough room in my home and heart for both of you."

Natalie shook her head. "I don't do threesomes."

Bella stopped, a teasing smile quirking her lips. "Have you ever tried?"

"No." Natalie's mouth pressed into a thin line.

"Then how do you know?" Bella laughed. "A year ago, did you think you'd make love with a cat-woman like me?" Her hands rose to loosen the bow around her neck. The front of her dress fell to her waist, exposing voluptuous breasts, pert nipples pointing tightly. The fine sheen of fur coating her body blended so well with her skin tones, Natalie could barely tell Bella wasn't human. Memory reminded her of how soft and silky she was.

Her core heated, juices stirring to life. Natalie clenched her tingling fingers and glanced at the cat-man leaning against the door.

Bella nodded at the Bengal. "Leandro, show Natalie how wonderful a threesome can be."

Natalie backed away. "I didn't come to be with him. I came for you."

"If you want me, you must do as I say." Bella crossed her arms over her lovely breasts. "Do you want me?"

Natalie sighed. This wasn't how she'd envisioned their reunion. "Yes, I want you."

"Take off your costume and show Leandro how beautiful you are." Bella's lips curled, and her eyelids drooped in a secretive smile.

Natalie hesitated, her gaze moving from Bella to Leandro. To prove she was earnest about coming for Bella, Natalie's hands rose to the neckline of the leotard hugging her body. She tugged the stretchy material over her shoulders and pushed it down to her waist, exposing her nakedness. The cool air of the room wafted across her skin, teasing her nipples to attention.

"Leandro, help my friend out of her suit."

Leandro hesitated.

"Go on." Bella waved her hand at him, urging him forward.

Leandro stepped up behind Natalie and peeled the leotard down her body. His hands skimmed over her body, down her legs and calves to her feet, where he helped her slide out of her sandals and the outfit.

Natalie refused to look at him, her gaze on Bella. She had no interest in the Bengal, yet his furry hands on her skin made her want Bella even more.

Bella tapped her finger to her chin. "Leandro does not make your blood burn? I am told his touch has inspired birds to sing and cats to purr."

"I'm not here for him." Natalie stood naked, her shoulders thrown back, her heart pounding. "I came for you."

Bella closed the distance between them. "You left me once for a man. How can I be so certain you will not leave me again?" She leaned in and nuzzled Natalie's neck, sliding upward until their bodies pressed together, breast to breast.

Natalie's breath caught in her throat, and she fought to keep from reaching out to touch Bella. "I called off my wedding because of you."

The cat-woman danced away. "How do I know? I cannot see into your world."

"I'm here, aren't I?" Natalie went after Bella, grabbed her

arm and hauled her back against her, her heart rejoicing at the feel of her silken body. "I came back because of you."

"We are of different species," Bella argued, keeping her back to Natalie.

"That didn't make a difference the last time we were together." Natalie's hands settled on Bella's hips, all thoughts of Leandro pushed to the back of her mind. She pulled Bella close, the softness of her fur caressing Natalie's skin. Her fingers convulsed, her pussy creaming.

Bella leaned into her, her long blond hair sweeping across Natalie's chest. "Our species didn't matter then."

"Does it now?" Natalie's fingers rose up Bella's sides, luxuriating in the sleek, silky fur. She palmed Bella's breasts, weighing each before tweaking the taut nipples into tight little buds. "I love your hair, the fine fur coat covering your body, the way your eyes glow in the dark." Natalie buried her face in Bella's throat, rubbing her cheek against her neck.

A soft rumbling resonated from Bella's chest, rising up to escape her lips. "I remember." She pushed one of Natalie's hands lower, to the juncture of her thighs.

Joy leaped in Natalie's heart as she parted Bella's folds, pressing two fingers into her, swirling in her juices. "You make my blood run hot."

Bella spun in Natalie's embrace, her eyes wide, filled with tears. "You hurt me."

"I'm sorry." Natalie cupped Bella's face in her hands. "I promise never to do it again, if only you let me love you."

"I don't know if can." Tears slipped from the corners of Bella's eyes.

"I've loved you from the day I left."

"What took you so long to return?"

"I had to tie up loose ends."

"For a year?" Bella's words came on a sob.

Natalie sighed. "I was afraid to see what was in my heart."

"And now?"

Natalie smiled. "I'm here."

"Hold me."

"What about Leandro?" Natalie glanced over her shoulder at the cat-man with the fierce frown creasing his brow.

"You must love him as well."

"If that's what it takes to be with you, I will." Natalie waved a hand in Leandro's direction. "Would you like him to join us?"

"Not now. I want you to make love to me alone." Bella clutched Natalie's hand and led her toward the giant bed. "Show me how much you missed me. Perhaps then, I can open my heart to trust you again."

Bella stopped beside the mattress and faced Natalie. Her furry hands slid across Natalie's shoulders and over her breasts. She pressed a kiss to Natalie's collarbone, trailing her lips lightly downward to one distended nipple.

Natalie inhaled deeply, her breasts rising to meet Bella's coarse cat-like tongue. The roughness made her skin tingle, her nipples beading into tight little nubs. "I love it when you do that." She cupped the back of Bella's head and pressed her closer until the cat-woman sucked more of her breast into her mouth.

Every cell in Natalie's body burst to life. Her hands closed on Bella's shoulders, and she forced her away. "Get on the bed."

"But I thought you liked that." Bella shook her head, her blue eyes glazed, and her pretty pink lips wet and full.

"Too much. I want to make you feel as good." Natalie walked her backward until Bella's legs bumped against the mattress and she sat down. Knees draped over the sides, Bella smiled up at Natalie and opened her thighs, dropping to her back on the bed.

Her hand skimmed over her belly and down to part her folds, fingering her clit.

A wash of desire burned across Natalie's chest and spread downward to her core. She wanted to be with Bella in every way imaginable. Her own knees buckled and she dropped to the floor, hooking Bella's thighs over her shoulders. Then she touched her tongue to the inside of Bella's legs, the layer of fur thinner there, allowing her to taste the tender skin beneath.

She trailed a path to Bella's center, lapping at the glistening juices rimming her entrance.

Bella clutched her hair, her hand closing around the fake cat ears. She laughed and tossed the headband to the corner. "You don't need to be anyone but you, my lovely."

"Good, because I want only *me* inside *you*." Natalie slid her tongue inside Bella's cunt, swirling around the walls of her channel, thrusting in and out. She traced the ring of Bella's ass with her finger and poked inside, mimicking the rhythm of her tongue strokes.

"Oh, my!" Bella's back arched off the bed, her purring transitioning into squeals as Natalie intensified her assault. By the time Bella climaxed, she would know Natalie wasn't going to settle for less than forever.

Natalie licked her way upward, pushing Bella's hands aside and replacing her finger strokes with long, wet caresses, interspersed with nibbles and nips. With one digit in Bella's ass and her thumb pressing into her vagina, she had Bella crying her name out loud.

"Natalie!" Bella's body rocked the bed, faster and faster. She drew her knees up, digging her heels into the mattress, her fingers threaded into Natalie's hair. "There! There! Oh, yesss!" All movement stopped but for the thrusts of Natalie's tongue. Bella stiffened, every muscle trembling, cum coating Natalie's thumb.

When Bella fell against the blankets, her golden hair spread out in a silken fan around her, Natalie climbed up beside her and pulled her into her arms. "I came back for you. Do you believe me now?"

A slow, sexy smile slid across Bella's face and she nuzzled Natalie. "I believe you."

"Will you let me love you?"

Bella shook her head.

Natalie's chest tightened. "No?"

"No." Bella sat up and pushed her hair out of her face. "Not until I show you how much I can love you in return. I will never be able to go with you to the other side."

"I know that. I'm here to stay."

"What if you stop loving me? What if you decide to return?"

"I won't."

"You'd give up your life in your world for me?"

Natalie nodded. "I'd even share you with Leandro, if I had to, just to keep you by my side."

Bella laughed. "And you *will* have to share my love with him."

Disappointment threatened Natalie's bubble of happiness. She breathed deeply and nodded. "As you wish."

"I wish." Bella touched Natalie's breast. "I've been a bad girl. You two haven't been properly introduced."

Natalie tugged the covers over her breasts as Leandro approached the bed. She sat up, clutching the blanket. "Hi."

Leandro grinned, his gaze sweeping over her. "The pleasure is mine." He clasped her hand and bent to kiss it.

"Natalie," Bella said, "This is Leandro, my brother."

Natalie gasped and jerked her hand from his. "Your brother?"

Bella laughed. "He feels some misguided sense of responsibility where I'm concerned and gets all protective." She leaned up and touched him, her nakedness not bothering her in the least. "I love him dearly and would gladly share him with you to satisfy your...other needs."

Natalie frowned, her gaze drifting down Leandro's torso. "Thanks, but I like what you and I have together."

With a shrug, Bella drifted back against the pillow and sighed, her hand reaching out to cup Natalie's breast. "Then let me please you this time."

"If you're all right, Bella. I'll leave you two alone." Leandro gave Bella a pointed look.

"I'm more than all right." Bella smiled. "I couldn't be more purrfect."

Leandro backed out of the room and closed the door.

Alone at last, the cat-woman sighed. Her fingers drifted across Natalie's cheek and down the length of her throat. "I'm afraid if I close my eyes, you will disappear again."

"Don't be afraid." Natalie clasped Bella's hand in hers and guided it to her pussy.

Bella didn't need more encouragement. Her fingers parted Natalie's folds, and she stroked her clit. She leaned close and captured Natalie's lips in a tender kiss. "I've missed you more than you can know." She brought her long, sleek tail up to Natalie's mouth and drew a line across her lips, dragging the fur downward, following the contours of Natalie's throat. "I was inconsolable for months." The tail slid lower, skimming over the swell of Natalie's breasts, flicking several times over each.

Natalie stopped breathing, the touch of Bella's tail so erotic she couldn't suck air into her starving lungs.

"My brother couldn't cheer me." Bella captured one of Natalie's nipples between her teeth and scraped her sharp incisors over the delicate tip.

Natalie's back arched off the bed, pressing her breast into Bella's mouth. "I was engaged," she gasped.

"You made love to *me*." Her teeth nipped harder, sending a delicious stab of pain rocketing across Natalie's nerves.

"Oh, Bella. You don't know how often I cursed myself for leaving. But I had to break it off with him."

Bella's tail brushed beneath Natalie's breast and across each rib as if memorizing the rise and fall of skin over bone. As the trail edged lower, dipping into her belly button, the short silky hairs tickled.

Natalie smiled. "I wanted to come sooner but didn't have the funds to fly back. It took time to save."

The tail slipped between her thighs, snaking along the ultra-sensitive skin. "You should never have left."

"I had to." Natalie's knees fell to the side.

Bella's tongue followed the tail's lead, coarse where the tail had been soft, a titillating contrast that set Natalie's nerves on fire. She writhed against the sheets, wanting to touch the cat-woman and make her just as crazy.

As Bella worked her way down Natalie's body, Natalie positioned Bella's knees on either side of her head, sliding beneath her, urging Bella to widen her legs, dropping her low so that Natalie could tongue the center of her desire.

A single stroke on her clit made Bella jerk and cry out. She captured the cat-woman's hips, fingernails digging in, pulling the fur-clad body close enough to suck the swollen nub into her mouth. She gnawed on the delicate flesh, savoring Bella's sweet musky scent.

Teeth grazed Natalie's folds; sharp claws sank into her thighs, parting them wider. Her tongue snaked out and entered

Natalie's pussy. The coarse texture, as it scraped the slick lining, added to the barrage of overwhelming sensations blowing Natalie away. Longer than a human's, Bella's tongue slipped deep inside Natalie.

Natalie's nails dug into Bella's hips, holding her steady, as she tongued her clit. The pretty cat-woman bucked and thrashed above her as waves of lust washed over Natalie, pushing her higher to that tingling explosion of the most magnificent orgasm she'd ever experienced.

Bella threw back her head and cried out, her voice a mix between a cat's yowl and a woman's wail.

Her body pulsing with the aftershocks, Natalie drifted slowly back to earth, in a bed with Bella, not flying high among the stars. "I didn't know you could do that," she whispered.

Bella collapsed beside Natalie, her hand resting on Natalie's mons. "I didn't know anyone could make me feel so complete."

Natalie lay for several long minutes, spent, too tired to move. She wanted to say so much, to tell Bella of all that had happened since they'd last seen each other, but she couldn't find the energy. Time was on their side. Natalie would never cross over the bridge again. Her heart and home was with Bella. She knew it now; she'd known it a year ago, even as she'd re-entered her own world.

Bella's hand tightened over Natalie's mound. "Any regrets?"

Natalie slid her thigh over Bella's hip. "Not one."

A soft purring sound rumbled against the sheets and Natalie smiled, fingering the ruby ring. No regrets.

THE DRAGON DESCENDING

Sacchi Green

"My first woman? As well ask if I recall my first dragon!" Seok-Teng, still afloat in the ebbtide of the fierce coupling that followed battles won and prizes taken, scarcely realized she spoke aloud.

Han Duan lay intensely still beside her. When she spoke again, her tone was a study in idle curiosity. "Your first dragon, then. Surely not old Mountain of Wealth?"

"Blasphemy!" Seok-Teng managed a chuckle. "With a tentacle in every profitable pot, Madame Lai Choi San should be called Old Octopus, never the Dragon Lady of Bias Bay." Best to pursue this much safer line of conversation. "And you know well that I was no more a virgin than you when we met as her bodyguards."

"Yet even I," Han Duan admitted, "learned much from her beyond the management of pirate ships."

"Is that how you formed your knack for domination of our young crewmembers?" Seok-Teng relaxed, confident that the dangerous topic had been circumvented. Han Duan held firmly to disbelief in her captain's visions of dragons, yet as second in command she followed with complete trust wherever Seok-Teng led. Seok-Teng, and her *kris,* the short undulating blade passed down through generations of her family until a woman was the only heir. A demon blade, Han Duan would say, in a tone that meant she did not believe in such things; but demon or no, the *kris* had bonded with its inheritor according to the old traditions. Always, after Seok-Teng's dragon dreams, the *kris* would point the way the ship must sail, where they would find women skilled in the ways of the sea, or captives on their way to slavery, who would gladly join such a pirate crew.

Seok-Teng did not wish to speak now of dragons. "Those sleek young pearl divers we rescued were certainly eager for your domination." *Dalisay and Amihan should be good distractions.*

But Han Duan would not be distracted. Not this time. "What color were their dragons in your dream?"

For once, Seok-Teng would be open. Han Duan deserved that of her, and more. "They were the blue-green of shallow southern seas, and twined about each other in a wheel like the yin and yang, spinning through the sky."

Han Duan nodded, but pulled Seok-Teng closer against her lean body and murmured into her ear, "And what of your first dragon?"

A shuddering sigh swept Seok-Teng. Whatever the cost, she would be open at last with the comrade and lover who had been her lifeline for so many years.

"My first dragon, and first woman as well. Not a dream, nor yet a vision, unless visions leave scars."

"Ah! These?" They knew each other's bodies as well as they knew each inch of their ship. Han Duan moved so that her fingers could trace the line of short pale ridges along Seok-Teng's sides from armpit to hip. "Truly a dragon of a woman!"

"A woman who was truly a dragon," Seok-Teng said flatly. "But take it as merely a tale, if you wish. A tale worth hearing..."

Ha Long, Bay of the Descending Dragons. Seok-Teng had heard of its beauty and legends, but had never seen its labyrinths of vertical, time-carved islands until the day she sailed her junk-rigged boat through them in pursuit of her father's killer. No time then to stare at its wonders, only to maneuver among them, searching always for the small motorized vessel whose lines were etched indelibly into her memory.

Rival smugglers who resented her father's incursion this far north came in the night, while he slept. Only chance kept them from finding Seok-Teng, whose teenaged energies had sought outlet in a night swim, naked, of course. If they had seen, they could not have mistaken her for the adolescent boy she pretended to be. She had seen their boat, and the first flames of the fire they set as they left; but all she could do when she reached her floating home was put out the fire, weep and curse over her father's body, and take up the ancient blade he had not had a chance to grasp.

The *kris* was cold to her hand. Such blades descended from father to son, bonding to their owners, tradition said, and a danger to any other who would try to wield them. This time there was no son. Seok-Teng swore, though, that she would sink the blade into the bodies of his murderers, and as she raised it in the direction they had gone she felt a subtle vibration, an almost imperceptible warming, that gave her hope. For this revenge, at least, she must trust the weapon to accept her right to hold it.

Twice she had found the killers moored in tiny villages, and twice she had swum from her boat, now repaired and disguised, and slit a smuggler's throat. One remained. One terrified killer now fleeing from what he thought to be a demon. Perhaps he was right.

Once in Ha Long Bay, it should have been impossible to find one small boat hiding among the thousands of limestone islands with their caves and grottoes and thick pelts of greenery clinging to sheer walls. Impossible for a man—or even a girl with a warrior spirit—but not for the *kris*. It showed the way, through three days of a winding course.

On the third evening, the blade took on a glow that told Seok-Teng her prey was so close that she must approach with caution. She anchored and waited through the night. This time she would make sure her prey saw his doom coming.

At last the dawn mist began to dissipate, the islands took shape, and the sun's first rays struck the leafy crest of the nearest island in a blaze of green like emerald flame.

Seok-Teng slid into the water wearing nothing beyond the *kris* belted to her naked hip. The boat she sought was there, just beyond the island, perhaps fifty feet away. When she reached its side, she listened for several minutes until she heard the man stirring, moving slowly about, then standing on the lee side and, by the sound, relieving himself into the sea. The perfect moment!

She was up over the side, *kris* unsheathed and raised, before he could turn; yet even at such a time he had kept a dagger in his hand, and parried the longer blade. Seok-Teng spun and struck again, knocking his weapon this time from his grip. He grasped her knife-wrist so tightly with his other hand that it took all her effort to keep from dropping the *kris*. Or almost all. Her knee tensed, began its upward strike toward his groin—but he fell back before it connected. She had only a fleeting glimpse of his eyes, widened in horror as he looked at something beyond her, his face as contorted as though her blade had pierced his belly.

Seok-Teng stumbled, unbalanced, and still managed to slice the *kris* across his throat before he toppled backward into the sea.

She swung around and saw what he had seen. A golden eye gazed down at her from the island's greenery, and then two eyes, in a long, elegant, emerald-scaled head that lifted to regard her full-on.

"I had him! He was mine!" Seok-Teng's blood-madness still ran so hot that she felt no fear, no amazement that a dragon such as she had seen only on painted screens or the prows of festive longboats was here before her in the flesh. If indeed dragons were made of such. "I needed no help!"

The dragon seemed to laugh, although what difference there might be between a dragon's laugh and its snarl Seok-Teng did not know. Indeed, as her blood slowed, she scarcely knew whether she herself dreamed, or imagined, or even lived. She held the *kris* upright, flat between her breasts, as talisman rather than weapon; it quivered, but gave off no heat.

Heat of another sort did warm Seok-Teng's flesh as the dragon's gaze moved slowly along her body. Did dragons lust after human women? She had never heard such tales, but after all, she herself lusted after women, though so far only in her dreams.

"Why not?" The voice was not her own, yet unmistakably female—and it spoke from inside her head. "Who can know so well how to please a woman as another woman?"

A dream, then. That sort of dream. Already Seok-Teng's loins stirred with longing. Her bedroll would be damp and tangled when she woke. If only this dream would take her far enough for relief.

The boat she stood upon had floated nearer to the island. Seok-Teng looked full into the golden eyes, not flinching when the dragon's green coils, their scales textured to resemble leaves, loosened from the rough limestone enough that its neck could arch outward above her and descend. Even when a flickering forked tongue, impossibly long, darted across her belly, Seok-Teng held her ground, though she could not suppress gasps and jerks at the tantalizing sensations it aroused.

"Set aside your noble blade," the voice said, "if you would taste of more tender delights."

She sheathed the *kris* but kept it belted at her hip. This time the dragon's laughter echoed inside her head, drowned out soon by Seok-Teng's own cries as the deep-coral tongue lapped at the paler coral tips of her high breasts, teasing and tweaking at them until they hardened and darkened and sent bolts of pleasure close to pain down through her belly into her cunt.

"How brave are you, girl? Enough to follow me?" The voice seemed uneven now, almost breathless. The long tongue reached down between her thighs and slick lips to find the jewel of pleasure there, and a low, rough moan was wrenched from deep in Seok-Teng's throat, followed by a keen wail as the stimulation ceased.

"Come, if you dare!" The dragon launched suddenly from the rock, leaving it nearly bare, and dove into the water. Seok-Teng followed so swiftly that the wake of the great long tail swept her briefly off course. Attuned from birth to all the motions and secrets of the sea, she was back on course in a moment, and when the waters stilled beside an island much larger than the first, she dove unerringly through an underwater passage to come up in a pool within a grotto infused with green light.

On its far side stalactites hung nearly to the floor, chiming like bells as the dragon's emerald scales brushed them. Nearer, an arc of sandy beach edged the water.

The voice came again. "One more challenge, if you are truly

brave." But this time it felt more like a plea than a dare. "Your blade...will you trust me with your blade?"

The *kris* was extended in Seok-Teng's hand before she could even recall drawing it from the sheath. "The blade chooses for itself, always," she said. "It appears to have done so already."

"Place it between my teeth."

Seok-Teng advanced along the beach. Fear, which she had not felt until now, weighed on her like anchor chains. The dragon's rows of sharp teeth could easily take off her arm; she would have parted with that rather than lose the weapon that embodied the soul of her lineage; but indeed, the blade had chosen. She watched in amazement and horror as the bright undulating curves of metal slid, seemingly of their own accord, down the dragon's throat. Her hand jerked upward as though reaching out to reclaim the *kris*, whatever the cost, but it was too late.

"Turn away!" This was a desperate plea and a command, all in one. "Go below the water!" Seok-Teng turned, not quite in time to miss the sight of her sacred blade's tip slicing through the emerald scales from within; then she dove into the pool.

She could always hold her breath for several minutes. This time she waited even longer. When hands—human hands!—reached down to pull her forth, she was too dazed for a moment to brush the water from her eyes, and when she did, the vision before her seemed no more believable than an erotic hallucination caused by lack of air.

The woman was taller even than Seok-Teng herself, and as strongly built, with hair as wild and dark but glinting with green highlights. Her curves were both voluptuous and graceful, while her face, like Seok-Teng's own, would have been as beautiful on a man as on a woman. In the grotto's subdued light her golden eyes were muted to amber.

The womanly parts swept away all thought of other matters. They came together on the beach, heat sparking wherever skin met skin and spreading like a raging fire. A very human tongue found Seok-Teng's nipples, and a human mouth tugged and sucked them to peaks of glorious soreness. Her own mouth yearned to taste the other's flesh, but for the moment hands sufficed, filling with sweet, bountiful breasts and tweaking coral nubs that grew ever harder in their demand for more, and yet more.

Someone whimpered. Someone moaned, long and low. Voices had better uses than mere words. Seok-Teng's hunger grew, and her hands left the other's breasts to explore the further delights of a female body not her own. What her fingers had often done for herself, she tried on this dragon-woman, with the same effect and more. So soft and yet firm—wet, slick to enter, then clenching, hips thrusting forward for more, until the need to taste her sent Seok-Teng to her knees and her mouth to those demanding folds and depths. Her own tongue felt as long as the remembered dragon's tongue, thrusting deeper, deeper, while hot sea-flavored flesh pressed and ground against her face, and her thumb worked the jewel of pleasure to its peak. The woman's cries rang out so loud and high that the stalactites chimed again in unison.

Seok-Teng held on until she could stand it no longer, then rammed a hand against her own aching cunt. In moments it was knocked away, replaced by a mouth and fingers infinitely more skilled than hers. They teased, tormented, swept her to the brink and left her hovering there time after time—until, when at last she tangled her fingers in the dark hair and held the mouth fiercely against her need, she was allowed to plunge over the edge. Her whole body reverberated like a temple gong, subsided for a moment, and then reached for new heights and plummeted into new depths, over and over, until at last she had not enough breath for further screams, or even whimpers.

"Rest for a bit," came the voice. "Regain your strength. You will need it all, for there is yet more that I must have."

So, of course, Seok-Teng's strength surged again, with scarcely more than time for her breathing to recover. "I am ready," she said, "for anything. But first," and she dared to place her hands on the beautiful face leaning above her as they sprawled on the sand, "tell me now who you are, and how this comes about, for I may die of pleasure before I can ask again."

"You may choose your tale. They are plentiful enough." The voice paused for a long minute. "Have you not heard how, long ago when China first threatened this land, dragons were sent by the gods to protect it? They spat out gems that became the tangle of islands, and found the bay so beautiful that they stayed for a time. The mother dragon's children stayed in their turn, some becoming islands themselves." The dragon-woman shrugged. "As good a story as any. There are few of us now, and we sometimes sleep for eons as men count time, but I will tell you this one true thing." Her laughter rang in Seok-Teng's head. "A woman like you is so rare a gem that her approach will always wake me."

At this, Seok-Teng wrapped arms and legs about the other, and they grappled again in a delirium of lust and laughter, bodies finding joy in any contact, any stroke or pressure.

Gradually laughter ceased, and hunger surged again. The dragon-woman rolled on top, face and body tense. "You must be strong now. I must...there are no words..."

She moved as they had moved before, but harder, pummeling Seok-Teng's body with her own, grinding into her until it seemed that bone must break bone. Her face twisted, became wilder, neither human nor dragon, only savage passion personified.

Seok-Teng thrust back in response, adding her own strength and savagery, heedless of pain even when the hands gripping her hips and sides spread farther and claws sprang forth that pierced her skin. When the voice roared in her head with the fury of a great volcano, her own voice followed as closely as any merely human voice could.

Sound, pain, pleasure—it was all too much. Blackness closed in around Seok-Teng.

When she woke the daylight filtering through crevices in the limestone had faded almost away. The grotto was deserted except for herself, and the faintly glowing *kris* beside her.

She sat up and grasped the blade's hilt. There was a wetness on the blade; when she touched her tongue to it the taste was of sea salt and blood.

Outside the grotto, catching the last reflected light of sunset, her own boat lay anchored, though she had left it some distance away. "Thank you," she thought, for her body was now stiff and aching and bleeding from her punctured sides, and she was glad to be spared the swim.

A faint, far voice answered from within. "You owe me more thanks than you know. Since you have tasted my blood, some day, when you have need, dreams of dragons may lead to warriors with spirits like yours, just as you came into my dreams."

Seok-Teng's story ceased. She wondered, for a time, whether her tale had put Han Duan to sleep; that might be just as well.

But Han Duan stirred. "So you dreamed of Gu Yasha, too, and many others." Gu Yasha, the strong, tall gunner as silent as her cannons were loud, had appeared in a dream as a dragon of golden amber.

Seok-Teng heard the hurt in her companion's voice and knew where this was going. "Yes. But I have never lain with any as

I do with you, and never will, not merely as a matter of maintaining authority." She turned toward Han Duan and stroked the weathered face that moved her more than any beauty. "I had no dragon dream of you, because there was no need. You, I found for myself, as you found me. That makes all the difference."

And that was enough.

ALL THE COLORS OF THE SUN

Victoria Oldham

She walked on water. Well, not really on it, but over it, like the sun shot her from a ray across the top of the ocean to drop at my feet on the hot white sand.

She hit her knees, backlit by the sun, and her silhouette was beautiful.

I jumped up to help her, trying not to shake sand on her.

She looked up at me, and the sun had settled in her eyes, reds battling oranges to consume her pupils. I blinked hard, since the sun had obviously blinded me. When I looked into her eyes again, they were a beautiful light blue, contrasting perfectly with her long black hair.

She brushed her hair from her eyes and ruefully took my hand. "Thanks. I got caught up in the riptide, and it's taken me forever to get out. I think I'm a bit shaken up."

"No problem. Want a drink?" I turned away to grab water from the cooler, more than a little worked up. Her navy blue bikini was shot through with vines of green and looked painted on; her long wet hair hugged her sides and wrapped around her flat stomach. She was the hottest woman I'd seen in ages, and I didn't want to blow it. "Do you want me to grab a lifeguard?"

"Water would be great. I don't suppose you have an extra towel? The current pulled me pretty far from my stuff, I think." She leaned over and wrung out her hair on the sand, letting loose a waterfall before wrapping it in a bun-thing on her head. I tugged at my swim shorts, suddenly glad they were loose enough not to show how wet I was getting looking at her.

I handed her the towel I had been using as a pillow and yanked a T-shirt over my sports bra. I was vaguely disappointed when she wrapped the towel around herself, hiding that gorgeous figure.

"I'm Cree, by the way," I said, holding out my hand.

"Ashley. But please, call me Ash."

I shook her hand and nearly pulled away in surprise. Her skin felt as hot as a branding iron.

"Wow," I said, "I can't believe how warm you are with the water as cold as it is."

"Warm blooded, I guess." She looked at me and smiled, and I felt like a kid being given the best gift ever on a perfect spring morning.

"I'm going to walk down the beach to find my stuff. Thanks for the water." She took off the towel and handed it back to me, and once again I focused on how perfect and soft her body looked.

"Yeah, sure. No problem." She walked away, and her firm ass under her tiny bikini bottoms made me sweat. "Hey! Maybe I could walk with you? I mean, what if you don't feel well or something?" Okay, so it was lame. But her body had me tongue-tied.

"I'd like that. Thanks."

She grinned, and I handed her the towel again. I needed to sound like a reasonably intelligent human being, which meant she'd have to cover up a bit.

"I thought I was the only one to brave this area of the beach in March," I said, keeping my eyes on her silver toe rings. One was a bird of some kind, and the other a tiny little sun.

"I like the peace. I don't like crowds, so the beach this time of year is perfect. I avoid it the rest of the time. How about you?"

"I'm a water rat, really. I'll come all year long, but the off season is the best, when it's just you and the waves."

She nodded like she understood. "So you live around here?"

"Yeah. Two blocks away. It's tiny, but being so close to the ocean makes it worth living in something the size of a closet. You?"

She frowned and shrugged. "For the moment. I move around a lot."

"A free spirit, huh?" I said jokingly.

"Yeah, something like that." She looked at me so seriously for a moment I wondered if I'd said something wrong.

"Cool." I curled my toes in the sand, not sure what to say. How do you speak to a woman who almost literally washes up at your feet? At least in a club you have the music to keep you from having to make conversation. With only the crashing waves as a soundtrack, though, I was at a loss.

She stopped suddenly and looked around. "I'm sure I left my stuff by this lifeguard tower. I mean, it was only a towel and my keys, but I'm sure I left them here."

I looked around at the nearly deserted beach, an idea forming. "Damn, that sucks. A lot of the homeless will grab whatever they can to keep warm this time of year. They must have taken your stuff when you weren't around to keep an eye on it."

She was looking at me with her head tilted to the side, and it made me think of the way a bird will watch you from the trees, which in turn made me giggle a bit.

"Is it funny?" she asked with a small grin.

"No, not at all. Sorry. In fact, if you want to walk to my place with me, I probably have some clothes that might fit you. Then I can take you to your place, or wherever you need to go."

"Are you always this solicitous to total strangers?"

The heat from her touch scorched me when she placed her hand on my forearm. I felt like the yin-yang tattoo under her hand could spin right off my skin.

"No. I mean, if someone's in trouble I try to help, but you know, I mean, you did fall at my feet." I stopped talking, feeling the heat rise to my face. I ran a hand through my hair, thinking it must be sticking up in all directions after my day in the sun.

"I'm teasing. Obviously I could use the help. Thanks."

I motioned the direction we should walk and tried to ignore the way her breasts swelled slightly over the top of the towel.

"So, is there someone waiting at your place for you?" I asked, unable to think of a smoother way to find out if she was single.

"Nope. All alone. You?"

"No one. My girlfriend and I broke up about a year ago, and I haven't felt like going back on the dating scene." I waited, hoping she'd take the bait and tell me she was a lesbian.

"I'm sorry. Breakups are terrible. Even if they're a long time coming, they're never easy." She looked so sad for a second I felt bad for bringing it up.

"Well, like you said, it was a long time coming. We were from different worlds, you know? She wanted to stay in one place forever, raise a family. I'm not that type. I like to travel, I want to see the whole world before I die."

She looked at me again, with that same quizzical look. "I

enjoy traveling as well. That's why I'm rarely in one place for long. It's a hard thing for some people to deal with."

"Maybe we could travel together," I said, grinning to show her I was kidding and not some crazy stalker person who latches onto total strangers.

She grinned back at me, and my stomach dropped to my toes. Her almond-shaped eyes crinkled slightly at the corners, and a dimple appeared in her right cheek. "You never know. Stranger things have happened."

We arrived at my place, and as I unlocked the door I prayed I hadn't left underwear lying around.

I went to my bedroom and pulled sweats and a baggy sweat-shirt from the closet. She was a few inches shorter than me, but at least my clothes wouldn't be too small. I threw on warmer clothes myself, since the evening fog was rolling in, and it was getting cold.

I took the clothes back to the living room and stopped dead.

She was on all fours, the towel draped across the arm of the couch, eye to eye with my cat, Mrs. Pufferfish. The cat stared into her eyes like it was hypnotized, and seeing Ash on all fours, that perfect ass framed only by her bikini bottoms in the air, made me nearly double over with desire.

I must have made some little sound, because she looked up at me and laughed. "I like your cat. She's beautiful." She rose gracefully, and Mrs. Pufferfish wound around her ankles, purring so loudly she sounded like a motorboat.

"She normally doesn't like anyone," I said, handing over the clothes and trying to hide my trembling hands. "And I've never seen someone...interact...with her that way."

She pulled the clothes on, and I melted at the sight of her in my baggy sweats. She looked adorable, and with her covered up it was a bit easier for me to breathe through the haze of lust I had felt since she appeared at the beach.

"Animals like me. So, is the offer still on to take me to my place? If not, I can catch the bus."

"No! I mean, yeah, of course. Let me grab my keys. I think my shoes are all too big for you, but I can grab you some socks if you like...?"

She wiggled her toes. "No thanks. I'm almost always barefoot. I hate my feet being bound up." She looked a bit queasy at the thought, so I let it drop. I mean, who was I to tell her she shouldn't have cold feet?

We pulled up in front of her place, and I realized just how out of my league she was. Her house was beach front, about two miles from mine, in one of the most expensive areas in the state. Floor-to-ceiling windows took up the first and second floors, all looking out at the ocean. Stairs led down the rocks to the sand, with the roof of a gazebo visible through the tall garden bushes. She grabbed a key hidden under a rock behind a bush and led me inside.

"Holy crap," I whispered, looking around her living room. Artwork decorated the walls, mostly of women from various mythological stories in sensual poses. A huge deck with a Jacuzzi spread outside the windows, which looked onto the endless expanse of ocean.

"Drink?" she asked from the kitchen, reappearing with two bottles of Spanish beer.

"Thanks. I have to admit, I feel pretty stupid, having taken you to my place. I mean, wow. Your place is amazing."

She looked around as though seeing it for the first time. "I like it. It's home for now, anyway." She slid open the doors to the deck, and we sat there, watching the sun go down through the light fog. "This is my favorite time of day. There's something so sad and beautiful about the sun disappearing behind the water the way it does."

"I've never thought of it that way."

She shrugged, her eyes reflecting the sun. "It always comes up again. But I always wonder if it hurts at all, to die that way and have to come up the next day, over and over again."

"But it doesn't die, does it? It comes up somewhere else, in another part of the world. You just don't get to see it for a while. And we wouldn't appreciate it without the night to balance it, would we?"

She sipped her beer and stared at me for a long time, so long I became uncomfortable and remembered the way she'd looked at my cat.

"Thanks for the beer. I should probably get going."

She stood with me and stepped close. She placed her hand on my face, and I was amazed once again at the heat coming off her skin. "Thank you, really, for all you did for me today. Can I take you to dinner sometime to thank you?"

Yes. This gorgeous, amazing, sexy woman wanted to have dinner with me. "Sure. But you don't need to thank me. I'm glad we met."

"Me too. Tomorrow night? Pick me up at eight?"

"Eight is good. See you then."

I left, feeling like I'd won the biggest jackpot in history. I glanced over my shoulder, and stumbled. Once again she was backlit by the setting sun, and her silhouette seemed to have... wings. I turned around fully and squinted, and realized it was just the bushes on either side of her doorway.

"What the hell is wrong with you?" I mumbled to myself, already thinking about what to wear for our date.

* * *

The next day I arrived at exactly eight, feeling good in my tight black jeans, black button-down shirt, and big-ass boots. I knocked, and then rang the bell when she didn't come after a few minutes.

I heard her heels on the marble floor before she got to the door, and when she opened it, I nearly fell to my knees.

Her navy blue dress hugged her body like a second skin, a forest green band under her breasts pushing them forward while the rest of the dress dropped in folds beneath them. A pendant hung between her breasts, a bird with the same blue and green of her dress, the wings tipped with the colors of fire. Then I realized there was no chain—it wasn't a pendant, it was a tattoo. One her bikini must have covered the day before, although that didn't seem possible, given the scarcity of material in her bikini top.

She cleared her throat, and I realized I'd been staring at her breasts.

"Sorry. You look amazing. I was looking at your tat. It's gorgeous." I shoved my hands in my pockets, wanting the marble floor to swallow me whole.

"Thank you," she said softly. "I need to finish my makeup if that's okay. I'm running a bit late. Help yourself to a beer or whatever." She ran back up the stairs, and I admired the way the dress swung around her.

I walked out to the deck and stared at the multitude of colored feathers scattered around the deck. The breeze picked one up, and I watched it slide into the air, the orange and blues in it catching the lights from the house before it was taken away by the wind. The other feathers, mixes of blues and greens and reds and golds, all took to the wind as well, and by the time Ash came back downstairs, they had all gone.

"It was the weirdest thing," I said when she came out on the deck, "When I came out there were all these really beautiful feathers, but in colors I've never seen."

She froze, and I grabbed for her when the color drained from her face, afraid she was going to faint. "Are you okay? What's wrong?"

"Nothing. Nothing at all, sorry. I must have stood up too fast. Shall we go? I've forgotten to eat much today."

"Of course. I've made reservations at Gladstones. I hope that's okay." I let go of her, but not before I noticed that her hand was shaking slightly. "Are you sure you're okay?"

She nodded, quickly gathering her purse and other girlie stuff. "I'm fine, I promise. I just need food." She smiled at me, and like every time she smiled, I felt like the sun was coming up just for me.

Dinner was perfect. We sat by the window, and unlike the day before, conversation was easy and comfortable. Occasionally, she reached across the table and touched my hand, and by the end of dinner I ached to touch her, to kiss her beautiful red lips, to feel her pressed against me.

For weeks we followed the same pattern. Every week I was desperate to take her to bed, but every time the evening ended she gave me a soul-scorching kiss at the front door and sent me on my way.

On the way back to her place after dinner at a particularly beautiful seaside restaurant, I took a gamble and held her hand, placing it on my upper thigh, and was glad she didn't pull away. I raised it to my mouth and kissed it, amazed at how soft her skin was. I felt her tremble slightly and skimmed my lips over her knuckles, meeting her eyes briefly when I heard her intake of breath.

I pulled up in front of her house, and we sat looking at one another for a moment. I could see her wrestling with whether to ask me in, and I waited patiently. I desperately wanted more time with her, but I didn't want to push and scare her away. Something about her told me that she wasn't the type to be pushed into anything.

Her shoulders straightened, and she raised our linked hands to her mouth and kissed my hand the way I'd kissed hers. My eyes closed at the heat of her lips and the soft tip of her tongue as she nipped at my knuckle. "Will you come inside?"

"Do you need to ask?" I said, knowing my voice was shaky but not caring. She climbed from the truck and we walked hand in hand to the door. While she unlocked it, I put my arms around her from behind and nuzzled her neck. "You smell so good."

She pressed back into me, and I groaned softly when her ass pressed against my jeans, my clit already hard.

Once inside, she went straight to the stairs, leading me up to her bedroom. There we no blinds, no curtains on the floor-to-ceiling windows, just an amazing view of onyx ocean under a blanket of stars.

I pulled her to me, sliding the thin straps off her shoulders and following my hands with my mouth, kissing her neck, her shoulders, along her collarbone. Her skin was the silkiest thing I'd ever felt, so soft, so sweet, so smooth. Her head fell back, and I took the offering, kissing and nipping down her neck to the beautiful tattoo. I traced it with my tongue, and she shivered hard in my arms. If possible, it was hotter than the rest of her skin, which was already making me sweat as heat poured off her.

I walked her back to the bed, never taking my lips from hers, the feeling of her full lips under mine driving me to distraction. I needed her like I'd never needed anyone in my life, and although it didn't make any sense, I went with it, desperate to make love to her, to hear her cry my name.

I unzipped the dress and let it fall to the floor. "Jesus, baby. You're so beautiful." Her bra was the colors of fire—reds, blues and oranges. I remembered the feathers and wondered briefly if she had some feather lingerie or something. All thoughts fled, though, when I undid the bra and slid it from her creamy shoulders, exposing full, high breasts with nipples the color of cherries.

The sight shattered the last of my control, and I let our combined weight carry us onto her bed, where we sank into a feather duvet. I took her nipple in my mouth, sucked it, bit it, made love to it as I wanted to the rest of her body. Suddenly dizzy, I realized I was overheating. I quickly pulled my top and jeans off, leaving my boxers and sports bra on, and pulled her panties off as well.

"Please, Cree. Please make love to me," she whispered, her eyes closed and her hands pulling me on top of her.

"Yes, God, yes. You're so beautiful. So gorgeous, baby."

I licked and sucked my way down her body, across the flat plane of her stomach, over her protruding hip bones, between her thighs. I looked at her before taking her clit in my mouth, but her eyes were closed tightly, her hands bunched in the covers. She cried out when I slid my tongue over her, her back arching.

"Please. God. Please, Cree. I'm begging, baby."

I pressed my tongue against her clit, sucking it into my mouth as I entered her with two fingers, pushing deep. She pressed against me, inarticulate cries filling the room.

She was sweet, like honey. Like ice cream on an August day, like nectar to a hummingbird. She gave herself to me, and I took all she could give. I felt her start to orgasm, felt it rising inside her.

And then I felt something else.

The muscles in her stomach clenched, her thighs tightened. And in my peripheral vision colors exploded through the room. Fire red, the blue of the ocean, the green of a forest, the gold of the sun. I raised my head and as her orgasm crashed through her, I pushed deeper, harder, taking her over the edge.

She opened her eyes, and her pupils had expanded so that there was only a thin, brilliant circle of citrus orange. She stretched her arms over her head.

Her body exploded into a cacophony of color and feathers. Enormous wings spread from beneath her, like all the colors of the sun, and she gazed at me. Fire spread through her eyes, burning me as she came in my hand.

For the briefest second I was scared. But the very next moment I took in her beauty, the dazzling, insanely sublime beauty of her, and I lowered my mouth to her again, taking orgasm after orgasm from her, even when her wings folded around me and pulled me hard against her.

I moved up her body and straddled her thigh, sliding my fingers inside her to the same rhythm I rocked my clit on her. Her wings caressed my back, tickling my shoulder blades and stroking my thighs. I came hard, pushing inside her and taking her over the edge with me.

I collapsed on her, but quickly became aware of how fragile she seemed beneath me. I looked into her eyes, and she was looking at me quizzically. Although unnerving, it was also unspeakably beautiful.

"Your tattoo is gone," I said softly, brushing my hand over the area it had been.

"Because I've changed. It only shows up when I begin to change more often," she said, and her voice had a strange clip to it, not unpleasant, but not really human either.

"What are you?"

"A phoenix." Her wings flexed and lifted from me, spreading out at least six feet from the bed.

I thought about it, and tentatively touched her feathers, feeling their softness and the subtly different textures that went with the different colors. "That's why you're so hot. And why you look like the sun when you smile." I grinned, and felt my stomach jump when she smiled back. "Wait. Isn't there something about burning up and being reborn, or something?" I said, suddenly nervous she'd do some kind of internal combustion thing, and I'd be accused of killing her.

She shifted, motioning to the door. She handed me a robe, which I quickly threw on, feeling more than a little drab compared to her Crayola splendor. I watched as she wrapped her wings around her body, covering herself from ankle to shoulder.

I followed her onto the deck, realizing where the feathers had come from.

"Yes. The phoenix lives for two hundred years, then burns to ash. She rises three days later, newborn."

"Newborn, like a baby bird? Or newborn, as in you but not you?" I flushed. "I'm sorry. I sound pretty stupid."

She wrapped me in the incredible softness of her wings, pulling my back against her chest so we could continue to gaze at the ocean. "You've just made love to a bird woman. I don't think you sound stupid at all." She nuzzled my neck lightly, and I shivered, even with the heat radiating from her skin. "I am reborn into my adult self, just a bit older than before I burned. So I age, but very slowly."

"And you're kind of immortal, right? I mean, you die, but you come back to life?"

I felt her deep sigh against me. "Yes."

I turned in the embrace of her wings and pulled open my

robe, pushing our breasts together. "How cool is it that I'm with a phoenix? Are there many of you out there? Like, a flock or something?"

She made a noise I assumed was a scoff. "A few. Fifteen, maybe, in the world. You're really not bothered?"

I pulled away so I could look into her exquisite eyes. "You've got the body of a goddess. Your smile makes me think of the best day of surfing ever. You make me want to go to bed with you and stay there forever. I want to know everything about you, as long as you want to keep me around."

She rested her head against mine, and I watched as tiny tears slid down her cheeks.

"It is difficult being one of a small species who has to hide. I would love to have you with me. I want to feel your touch and taste your lips. I'll tell you what you want to know, but you can't ever tell anyone about me. Obviously."

"Well, yeah. I mean, no offense, but people would think I'm kind of nuts." I squeezed her butt and grinned at her sharp intake of breath.

Her feathers started to tickle my calves, and then slid up my thighs and tickled between my legs. I moaned.

"Then let's get started, shall we?" she asked, and led me back to the bedroom.

THE HANDLER

Tahira Iqbal

'm in. My wolf body is always a neat fit once I transform. Commanding my cells, breaking them down one by one in milliseconds doesn't hurt—well, not anymore. At my first change, I'd screamed then howled in agony as minutes ticked into hours. Hours of horror. Gradually, I'd learned to transform with effortless ease, my initial pained gasps and pants gone. It's all been replaced by a sharp inhalation of breath that ends with a euphoric shiver along my spine, a forthright twinkle in my eye as I wake the wolf.

The need to transform had begun at dusk. I'd paced the slate of my kitchen floor naked, watching, waiting for the sun to set. Wanting, needing dark, the crawl in my veins both pain and pleasure.

My spirited run is on the hundreds of acres of land adjacent to my home, through tangles of woods, across broad streams that are nearly frozen.

Winter has made the land hard; the earth underfoot barely

gives as I thunder along it, slumbering birds launching into the air as I pass by. They know I'm...different. The deer, the stags, even the foxes and rabbits—they know that I run here. I haven't seen them for years now.

My lungs inhale, long, deep; my tongue tastes the night air, accepting the ferocious chill that's rolling over the lush planting of my land. Snow has been forecast for this region, having already settled in other parts of the country in thick droves.

I hit the cold brick of my driveway about an hour later, panting hard, my breath visibly rising before me. Courtesy lights pick me out; I'm a broad black charge against the chill azure of the beams.

"You're back." The cool voice of Remis, my Handler, drifts like the smoke coming from the Cohiba in his mouth.

I sit back on my haunches and let out a soft growl.

"Okay, okay, no smoking in the house," he says.

Rising, I head for the handsome, middle-aged man who's my closest friend in the world.

"Technically, I'm not in the house, I'm at the front door..." he says.

Again, I growl, edging past him, coming up to the middle of his thigh. I flick my tail against the muscle.

"Hey! Watch it!" Remis closes the door after stubbing out the cigar in the crystal ashtray he's been holding.

I bound upstairs.

"Dinner's in ten, Allegra."

With a bark of agreement, I head toward my bedroom. The door is already open, lamplight casting a soft, welcoming glow.

Taking a soft breath, I wrap my senses around the moment that I'm in. I go from four legs to two, three foot nothing to five-ten in a heartbeat.

I step into the bathroom. My trembling body is streaked with sweat and dirt from my run; my nipples have peaked from the cold.

I shower quickly and shove on sweats, leaving my jet-black hair in a damp fall down to the middle of my back.

Dinner is with Remis, as it always is, in the kitchen diner. I eat two sixteen-ounce steaks, four jacketed potatoes, and a mini-pyramid of green vegetables before I push away my platter.

Running, transforming, it takes all that I have, and I've gotten used to this over the years. Always eating, always nurturing my cells to make sure they have enough power when the time comes to be the wolf. You'd think that I'd be overweight, but I'm a powerhouse. Long, lean, and athletic.

"Seconds?" Remis asks.

With a shake of my head, I reach for water. "I'm going to go for a walk."

He stops loading the dishwasher. "You've already taken a run this evening."

"I know…"

"I'm not questioning it. But you have been…" Remis looks at me, but I avoid his gaze to search the water in the glass. "Overly twitchy recently."

I rise.

"Allegra…"

"I'm fine," I say, painfully aware there's a catch in my throat.

After collecting my down jacket from the hall closet, I trek down the winding driveway, which is lit sporadically by spears of lights embedded in the ground.

Damn it. Overly twitchy.

Remis was right. He always was.

He'd been appointed to the position of Handler by my father when I'd first transformed eight years ago. I'd been at my twenty-first birthday extravaganza at this very estate, puking in the toilet, thinking I'd caught food poisoning at my own party...only the face staring back in the mirror had extraordinary starlit eyes.

The rapid rapping at the door had been my father demanding that I let him in. I did...and his eyes were the same as mine, worry spiking them that unholy color. He'd then relayed a crazy story that had made me jump in places, gasp in others. Words like *twenty-one...ascension...wolf*...had fallen from his lips.

At his request, because I'd transformed the second I'd officially turned twenty-one (normally there was some sort of grace period), I'd left the world behind, joined the ranks of my kin, opting for the seclusion required to deal with this new way of life.

Some wolves are members of royal families, some own Fortune 500 companies, and some of them even run 7-Elevens. Those wolves are older, able to control the need to transform. I'm still a relative newcomer. Eight years and counting. And my father has been gone for seven of them. I inherited this estate and his billion-dollar empire upon his death.

Twitchy... Twitchy? No... No, that's not it.

My heart shimmers at the realization. *Lonely.*

I'm lonely.

Eight years, I've been living like this. I don't know when I'll be bold and brave enough to venture outside of the walls of the estate for longer than a few hours. Leaving my home is a sporadic occurrence, perhaps once or twice a month, early in the day when I've eaten enough and the need to transform isn't a siren's song in my head. Sometimes, it's for special occasions, like Remis's birthday, mine, or a meeting at work that requires my physical presence. But it is only for hours—three at the most.

I shake out of my thoughts as the tall wrought iron gate at

the end of the drive appears just as the hard patter of ice-cold rain descends, hitting the leaves of the dense planting. I give the dark road beyond the railings a long look.

Lonely.

I lower my head, turn around, and walk back.

Remis stubs the cigar out as I saunter up the driveway, shivering from the rain lashing my face.

"How was the walk?"

Good, I want to say, but I can't. Tears rise into my eyes.

"Oh, Allegra..." He reaches for me, holding me close. I get his stained breath against my neck. As much as I love Remis, I wish with all my heart it was my father holding me.

I wake early the next morning, dreams of my father lingering in my waking moments. I'd been the one to find him...knifed in the gut. I'd held his paws, wrapped my hands around his belly, his muzzle against my chest, howling through the pain. Hunters. The Hunters had gotten him.

Down in the kitchen, Remis has prepared enough breakfast to feed a family of five. I pick a china platter and load it with cut fruit.

"Carbs, Allegra."

I pick up a roll and bite. It's still warm from the oven.

"I've got to head to the city today, last-minute thing. Do you need anything?"

"No, I'm fine. I have the merger stuff to work through today. The Tokyo office should have sent some documents—did they arrive?"

Remis nods. "I put them in your office. You'll stay on the grounds?" He lowers his gaze to mine. "I hate last-minute things, but apparently it's important. Handler stuff. But I'll be back before dark; more snow is forecast for later, and I don't want to get stuck in the city."

"I'll stay. The run yesterday, the walk, did me good. I'll be fine for a few hours," I say with a smile.

He pours coffee straight into his commuter cup, then grabs a couple of the rolls. For the road, I think, until they land on my platter.

I head to my desk at eight, log onto the network, and immediately start dealing with the eight-billion-dollar merger that has had my staff and I working fourteen-hour days for the last six weeks.

I power through a steady swath of business, rapidly arriving red-flagged e-mails, and conference calls until noon, some of which require me to converse in Japanese. My stomach rumbles so hard it feels like a cramp. I'd left the two rolls... Remis will have a fit.

Shaking like a diabetic, I bumble my way to the kitchen, down orange juice straight from the carton, and then chew leftover steak from the fridge without heating it.

It really is better to work from home. That way I can raid any one of the six Sub-Zeros without water cooler gossip about the boss and her freaky eating disorder.

The intercom beeps.

I check the color screen. There's a man at the gate who's not Remis. Remis doesn't forget his keys or the ten-digit entry code. And no one visits us.

The beep goes again.

I don't do anything except stare at the screen. He's probably got the wrong house. He'll realize that soon.

Beep. Beep. Beep.

I press the talk button. "Hello?"

"Thank God..." The man straightens up on the screen. "There's been an accident... My wife...she's trapped in the car!"

I watch him carefully, his face now tilting up towards the

camera. There's a dark patch of blood on his shirt, leaking from a wound on his forehead.

"My phone's dead... Can you..." He puts his hand out, reaching for the gate to support himself, but misses.

"Shit..." I watch aghast as he crumples in a heap beside the gate. "Shit!"

For long seconds, I stare at the image. He's not moving. He's really not moving.

I exit the house, hitting the drive at an athletic run. Sunlight cascades through the trees, causing my eyes to contract painfully. Cold air freezes my lungs as I charge my run.

Minutes later, I push the code into the intercom. The gates swing inward. Kneeling beside him, I press two fingers against his pulse. Good, he's not dead. I take stabilizing breaths, catching the strong scent of the wound, which bashes into my heightened senses.

Wait...

That's not real blood.

The man's eyes snap open; his hand snags my wrist. I stare directly at cold dark eyes as he hauls us both upright.

"You're a Hunter," I whisper.

"Got it in one, sweetheart."

I fight him off. It's easy to do; I'm stronger, imbued with crazy strains of strength. I punch out, catching him in the jaw. It barely registers. He's muscle with well-trained reflexes. He pulls a gun from the folds of his jacket. I can't tell whether it delivers a tranquilizer dart or a silver bullet. Either way, it's still shit creek.

I'm about to transform with the shock, my cells jumping like Mexican beans. I'd run faster, dart with more stealth as a wolf. I know the estate like the back of my hand...but the gates have already closed behind me.

Hands. I need hands to input the code!

Suddenly, a black car hurtles over the rise in the road, the engine growling hard.

Ignoring it, I size up the Hunter who's taking aim. Out of the corner of my eye, I see the car switching its trajectory. It's coming... Holy shit! It's coming straight for us!

I throw myself out of the way. The vehicle, doing at least sixty, hits him. The Hunter cannons into the air, tossed over the car, landing in an oddly angled, bloodied-for-real heap, yards away.

The Mercedes skids to a halt. The door pops open. A young, striking woman with dark honey blond hair to her shoulders, dressed entirely in black, steps out. "Get in."

I pant where I lay, my heart racing.

"Remis sent me. Get in, Allegra!"

I scramble up, shaking hands meeting the handle as I slide into the car. "What's going on?"

The car reverses, then barrels down the country road, cranking up speed.

"My name is Olivia. Remis was attacked. He managed to get away, but whatever he had to go into the city for was a diversion." She looks at me; eyes the color of jet sparkle. "They wanted you." She twists the wheel to take on a sharp bend.

"Remis is hurt? Is he okay?"

"I'll know more soon."

"Where are we going?"

"Somewhere safe."

And for the next hour, neither of us speaks.

The car halts on a bricked drive in front of a small house with a wraparound weathered deck. The woodlands surrounding it are dense, planted close to the house. I don't think there's much acreage to run...and I'm burning up with the need to eat, to run, to make sense of today.

"You'll be safe here," Olivia says.

I tremble as I follow her to the door, my steps tangling.

"You need to eat." She takes my elbow, walking me through the house to the kitchen. "Sit."

I take a seat at the breakfast bar, wiping the sweat from my forehead with fingers that are vibrating.

A cooler hits the counter a minute later.

"Here." She picks out a fat parcel, handing it to me. I immediately tear it open. It's a triple-layered steak sandwich. I thank my lucky stars. Handlers always know how to cook.

I eat two sandwiches, down a quart of water, then another.

"Better?"

I nod, but I'm exhausted.

"You need to rest before you transform."

"What about Remis?"

"I'll get an update," she says, her tone briskly efficient. "Come on, I'll show you the bedroom."

It's upstairs, and it's gorgeous. White luxury linens on a king bed, stacked with a fluffy quilt, plump feather pillows, and broad throws.

"You've had a shock, so just rest." Olivia heads to the door.

"Hey... I...uh..." I breathe, "Thank you." I try to stop the tears, but fail.

"Rest," she says softly. The door clicks shut.

As soon as I'm alone, I push back the covers and kick off my Nikes. Climbing into bed, I fall fast asleep without bothering to get out of my jeans and T-shirt.

I wake, sitting immediately upright, watching as flakes of snow brush the window, making dusk even darker than usual. My hands flatten against the linens as a pulsing anxiety rips through my veins. I've never slept anywhere other than my own bed since becoming a wolf. I rush out of the covers.

I find Olivia downstairs, pacing on a call. Sensing my arrival, she looks up. "She's awake. Sure... Hold on." She extends the cell phone, "It's Remis."

I exhale sharply, take the call. "Are you okay?"

"I've got a broken arm." His deep voice is roughened. He sounds tired.

I fight tears as I hear the pain in his voice. "I shouldn't have left the estate..."

"You thought someone was hurt... I downloaded the security footage. That guy should get an Oscar."

"Is he dead?"

"Yeah, Olivia versus bad guy usually ends in death," Remis says, wry humor in his voice. "And don't worry about his body; it's been taken care of."

"Remis... Hunters..." A shiver rolls through me as I process the boldness of the attack.

"I know, Allegra, but you're with one of the best. Trust Olivia, okay?"

I quietly assure him that I will, then Remis urges me to rest and then transform.

Later, Olivia and I eat from the cooler. I'm alight with pressure; the deepest corners of my body throb with the need to run, to vault along land at terrific speed. I need to feel grass under my paws until they're bloody. I need to feel this run. To claim it. But the terrain will be unfamiliar—strange dips and highs. I won't be able to fully expel all this adrenaline.

Olivia must have sensed my distress because she wipes her hands on a napkin, rises off the stool, and says, "Follow me."

Moments later, we stand at the door of a spare downstairs room, bare except for one thing.

"A treadmill?" I snort.

One finely arched brow lifts. "Custom made. You want to run

forty miles an hour? That deck will take it. And you can set a time limit—if you're worried about the no-hands thing."

I let out a shocked laugh. It looks like a regular treadmill, except the controls are at the side and the belt is wide, perhaps twice the size of a regular treadmill.

And it works. I run as a wolf for nearly two hours, and according to the console, I've gone over twenty-seven miles.

I transform, emerging sweat-soaked and nude. I'm reaching for the towel when Olivia comes back into the room.

She stops at the door. Her gaze travels downward in a lazy line, lowering until they hit the darkness between my legs. Then it rises, settling on my breasts. Remis, as my Handler, has seen me nude before, but his glance never made me blush like this.

I hastily wrap the towel around my frame.

"Better?" Her voice is soft, low.

I nod shakily.

"Meet me in the kitchen once you're ready. There's a shower room across the hall."

The way illuminated by low lights, I find Olivia. The stillness in my system means I'm not preoccupied with the buzzing of my cells, the need to transform. My attention is all on her—her incredibly lithe figure that is clearly honed for the work she does. She turns, and instantly there's a new, vivid heaviness in my pelvis.

"Are you hungry?" She reaches for the cooler.

I shake my head.

"What's wrong?"

The distinct rhythm in my core fires. My breath is shallow. Off.

"Allegra?"

Lonely.

Lonely.

My gaze rises to hers, which darkens like the night under my appraisal. Her lashes are impossibly long. Her cheeks flush with color.

Something clicks deep inside.

"You should get some sleep, Allegra."

Like a spell being broken, I blink out of my reverie. Snaking desolation fills my veins, confusing me more.

It's nearing midnight. I'm not sleeping, not even close. Every time I close my eyes... Olivia is there. Under me. Over me. In me.

I kick out of the covers in frustration. Water. I could do with some water.

I head downstairs, nude except for my panties and fitted tee.

Olivia is there. The boards creak softly under my feet, making her look up from her cell phone. "That was Remis. He's moving to a safe location."

I halt. My shoulders start to shake. Soft cries leave my throat as I'm hit fully by the crazy significance of the day. I don't even realize she moved until her arms wrap around my frame.

"He could have died..." I whisper.

Olivia draws back and looks at me. "I know Remis. It would have taken a lot more than a beating to take him down."

"But still... He's hurt because of me." I wipe away the tears.

"We're Handlers. If we get hurt and you don't, then we're doing our job."

"Will there be more Hunters coming for me?"

She nods.

"I don't understand why they want to hurt us..." I sob my words.

"Shh... It's okay, Allegra."

I watch those sparkling eyes, those lips. Energetic scenarios suddenly vault into my head where I'm kissing her, where I'm pushing my tongue into her mouth. My pulse spirals. I'm panting, tingling in new, very new places.

"You're shaking..." Olivia says.

I squeeze my eyes shut, wondering if I'm going to transform due to the stress.

"Allegra..."

I don't open my eyes, afraid of the moment. I take rapid breaths, hoping that these sensations pass.

Then I get pressure.

Lips.

Her lips.

On mine.

"It's not transformation...what you're feeling... It's attraction. Arousal." Olivia's pupils go wide; her lips part in a soft sensual smile.

"Is that why I'm..." I blush hard as her hand disappears into my panties.

"Wet," she whispers as her mouth moves against mine, making me groan.

We're in my room now. Olivia kicks off her trainers, unzips her denims, sliding them down toned thighs. I see the black of her panties against the healthy color of her skin. The sight of her brings on another crushing heaviness in my pelvis that sends a trail of wetness into my panties.

Olivia presses her lips against mine again, opening my mouth with her tongue. I put my hands on her shoulders as her fingers slip into my panties again. Amongst the heat in my system, there's another surge...newer, more potent. Almost electric.

"Oh!" My back arches, knees are about to give way, as she rubs, softly, thoroughly, until I'm breathing in short bursts.

"Let go..."

And I do. Muscles seize, blood boils, stars cross my vision. The orgasm is hot, furious, thundering along my every nerve. I bite my lip to stop from screaming out; my eyes are tightly shut, water leaking from the corners.

"Open your eyes."

I do, seeing Olivia taking her shirt off, standing there in a matching black bra.

Lonely.

That's what I'd said.

Be careful what you wish for.

We're on the bed now, Olivia sitting over me, fully naked. She has a tattoo, three straight jet-black lines like a bar code on her hip. I trail my fingers there.

"A line for each wolf I've handled," she breathes.

I smile. "That's nice."

She's wet, really wet. I can feel her warmth on my body. Olivia leans in, taking my erect nipple into her mouth. She teases it, driving me mad. I want to touch her. I want to taste her, but she's my guide. And as if she can read my mind, she takes my hand, bringing it between her legs.

"Touch me..." She undulates softly over me, tipping her head back as my fingers slide into her warmth. She lets me have free rein.

I know what I should be feeling for, but I've never done this to another person... Oh... I find it with my index finger; then softly, ever so softly, I caress her clit.

Olivia's eyes are closed. Her hands cup her breasts. Short, rough breaths leave her throat. "Allegra... I'm close..."

My finger slides faster.

She undulates, muscles catching, holding, then releasing sharply. She's bolder than I could ever be. Her scream of satisfaction is a wonderful crash against my ears.

I wake hours later. Olivia is curved in the sheets beside me, sleeping. I slide out of bed, shaking softly. I raid the cooler, eating three bars of chocolate.

I let out a broken exhale. It's not enough... I'm going to pop any minute. The French doors... Fresh air might help...

I unlock them, push, and step onto the deck, the snowy night taking my breath away, but still I jog down the steps. Toes sink into the frozen grass. Flakes stick to my bare body. I hope the multiple pinpricks of cold will distill the volcanic tension.

Hands reach for my shoulder. Press softly. Olivia. Naked.

"I'm going to transform..."

"It's okay..." She palms my hair. "It's okay."

I take a breath, arching into the heat claiming my muscles. I gasp unevenly, and then I'm staring at her kneecaps. I back off, my chest filling with air, confusion making me whine softly.

"Easy..." Olivia kneels, holding out her open hand.

I go into it. Her hand works softly through my damp pelt. She smoothes it back in a caring gesture. I nuzzle her neck, whining softly. If I'd been human, I would have been crying.

She leads me back into the house, closes the doors, then sets a fire in the hearth.

We lay together on the rug. Her hand runs through the fur on my back. I lay my muzzle on my paws. She kisses the top of my head. I let out a soft moan. A moan!

"Welcome back..." she says, smiling.

I'm staring at my own hands, my own skin. I twist, propping myself on my hip. Her hand reaches for it, bringing me closer. Her lips go to mine, and then travel down my body as she pushes me to my back and parts my thighs.

"You're safe..." She plants kisses on the inside of my thigh, then her tongue finds my clit.

My body fires positively and toes curl. I weave my hands into her hair. I have to ensure that she stays...*right there.*

My orgasm is swift, dragged from the pit of my soul as she flicks my clit, teasing it until I cry out with delight.

"I'll gladly add another line on my hip if Remis wants early retirement," she breathes, rising to claim my mouth.

I smile into the kiss, the heady suggestion setting off bold fireworks within my blood that make me feel like I've run for hours. And tomorrow...? Tomorrow, I'll deal with the threat of the Hunters.

BOUND WITH BRONZE

Chris Kouju

R ain, warm and silky, was misting through the canopies of my jungle the first time I saw her. She was desecrating the sacred tree.

My claws dug into the soft earth as I watched her in my clearing. Power radiated down her sleek, human body in tremors subtle as sin. Her hair obscured part of the darkening sarong wrapped around her, but I caught glimpses of the garment's colors, patterned like wet leaves molding on the ground of the rain forest.

Thick flecks of wood flew as she sent her right hand, shaped into a claw much like mine, scouring across the bark. A bronze bangle, as aged as an ancient promise, enclosed her other hand.

She and I were the same, after a fashion. Mortal men named her *hantu raya*, as if by proclaiming her greatness they reminded all other spirits and jin in Malaya how they must be subservient. What surprised me was her kind were usually male. *She* obviously was not.

I padded forth from the shadows. "Stand away," I challenged, baring my fangs. Men have scurried over themselves from me, for the tiger was the undisputed ruler of the jungle, and thus what better shape for a guardian?

She turned. Dying sunlight reflected eyes an unnatural green, eyes as evasive as the heart of a rain forest.

Her brows furrowed. She, too, recognized what I was. Her kind might be royalty, but I dared her to ignore the threat of a feline poised to lunge, hot glowing eyes and heavy paws capable of rending heads from necks. "I have cause to be here," she said.

"As do I. You are on sacred land."

"I was not told a *hantu keramat* guarded this place. Will you not let me fulfill my task?"

"Do you not care what you desecrate?" I growled, scattering birds from their branches.

She glanced towards the scratched bark. "I know that beneath the roots of this angsana, a great scholar of Islam lies buried. I know this man was a descendant of Iskandar Zulkarnain, he who has conquered the world. I know despite his lineage, the scholar remained humble, gaining favor in the sight of Allah, the All Compassionate. Small of stature, weak of body, he is said to have spent tireless days spreading the faith, using the rivers to brave the jungle, to reach the most forsaken of villages." She smiled at the startled look on my face, and then the smile became cutting. "I care nothing for these things. I do as my master bids."

I narrowed my eyes. I recalled the irony of her kind: that although they stood superior over all spirits, the *hantu raya* served mortal masters. No, she and I were different after all. My kind lived free. "And what bidding is that?"

She let her arm fall, her paw blurring into the smooth fingers and thumb of a human. Her feminine beauty was distracting, and I wondered at the reason for her shape.

Careful.

"A more recent descendant of this scholar offended my master," she said. "And thus I am bid to destroy this tree, to dig up the bones and scatter them."

I sneered. "Then I cannot allow you to do that."

"As a lesser spirit, you are obligated to yield to me."

"I yield nothing. I wield power of my own. The boundaries I protect are not yours to violate."

She frowned, an imperfection that deepened the fullness of her lips. Then she smiled and tilted her head. Hair damp from the rain slid to one bare shoulder. "Brave words. But like you, honored one, I have obligations." She peered straight into my eyes.

In that instant, I sensed her mind penetrating mine. Her touch was halting at first, like the caress of a new lover. Then I felt her stroke fingers down my spine, heard the whisper of her voice warm against my ear. I *jerked* when her lips brushed the side of my neck. She'd not taken a single step towards me.

"Leave!" I snarled.

She wrenched her mind from mine, looking startled that I had broken her hold. She laughed, shakily. "Will you not listen to reason?"

"Be gone," I said with a fearsome growl, the sound thrumming with disgust and threat and contempt. "Or neither of us will leave unscathed."

Something shifted in her face. For a moment I imagined her eyes betraying a human sadness.

She nodded. "As you wish."

The "great spirit" faded from sight, into the shadows.

The jungle felt strangely empty. I sank to my haunches to steady the pounding of my heart.

* * *

I knew she had to return. Her master sounded like a petty creature, arrogant in his desires.

I stretched my body at the base of my tree and waited. We of the *hantu keramat* could be infinite in our patience. It helped that we spirits were beyond mortal needs to eat or mate or love.

Once I was such a wretched soul.

I did not miss that time.

I did not move from my place.

On the sixth day, she appeared just as the evening, cool and heavy, had stolen the last rays of the sun. A half-moon, outshining the fireflies, hovered above her against that patch of sky visible from my clearing.

She said nothing, at first, just watched me as if she expected me to follow at her heels. I lay there, lazily defiant. I almost pitied her.

"Will you step aside?" she murmured.

"Only if you destroy me."

I sensed her frustration, although not a ripple flickered across her face.

And then she said, "Let me sit with you, then."

I tilted my feline head. "If this is some trick..."

"No trick. You will obviously not abandon your duty, and I shall not dissuade you." Her eyes sank closed. "I am weary and would rest a few moments before my master sends me on another thankless errand."

I should have known better, but found myself saying, "Very well." I watched her approach me, both of us cautious and spare in our movements.

She sat on her legs, adjusted the folds of her sarong. We said nothing more, our eyes on the jungle, on everything but each other.

I was keenly aware of her nearness, her scent sandalwood, a touch of cassia and pelaga spice. And then I felt her stir. My senses snapped awake. This could be it, her moment to strike.

"Show me your true form," she said.

I blinked my eyes open.

She was leaning far too close to me.

It took me a moment to remember her words. "Why would I do that?"

"I am curious."

"I am no weaker in my other shape," I warned.

"Then there is nothing wrong with revealing it." She smiled, and my throat tightened. "Or are you afraid?" she teased.

I leaped to my paws with a snarl. Her eyes flickered wide, alert, as I swung to face her. I gloried in what I imagined was her fear as my tail lashed back and forth, as I let her see the sharpness of my fangs.

And then I began to change. My forelimbs first; I had to take care everything matched. Fingers and thumbs on the grass, then toes. One forgets, after a while. My fur retreated, I ended up on my knees, back arched, my hair long enough to drift to my breasts. I regarded her with head held high, reckless.

Her eyes began tracing a line ever so slowly from my face to my collarbone, from my chest to my belly, to the juncture where my thighs met. Her gaze crawled back up. Her lips curved.

My face turned hot. I readied myself for an attack.

I was right. She pressed her face to me. Her lips brushed against mine, her mouth soft as the feathers of a nestling bird. It was...pleasant.

I tugged my head away from her, narrowed my eyes. "If you are trying to—"

"Be silent," she said, clasping the sides of my face, to resume this touch, this kiss, the word for it flitting across my mind.

She smelled like warm rain. Mossy stones from a stream, patterns of afternoon sunlight wandering within the shade. I shivered as her hands carefully combed into my hair, gathered the strands together, stroked up and down the back of my neck as if she were soothing a skittish animal.

I caught her shoulders and pushed her back. She met my gaze, calm and sure and brazen. She did not look sorry, the impudent spirit.

I kissed her harder, teeth sinking against her mouth. She didn't question, giving off a moan as I pressed her against the bark of the tree. At first, it had been play. I'd been determined to prove she would not rule me, no matter her heritage. And now all I could think about was feeling her touch and shoving into the source of my ache. My fingers dragged on the folds of the sarong barely clinging to her skin. She caught my wrists, bit hot into my lips.

We stopped. Pulled away. For a moment we just breathed, staring at each other.

And then I released her. "You should go," I whispered.

She was still hunched against the tree. Her hands gathered the sarong to her body, and she nodded. She rose and disappeared, leaving me. My uncovered body shook.

It was only later I realized I did not know her name.

My name is Zaleha. I knew this once.

I had stopped questioning how I came to my duty. I simply did. I had murky memories of running alongside paddy fields, of my home amidst shapeless huts beneath the shade of a hundred coconut trees. What was clearer was the scent of the sea, sharp in the air. My feet had been bare, caked with mud, as hard as my hands were now.

Standing in my sacred clearing, I looked down at those

hands. They belonged more to an old woman. With a snarl, I sank back to my paws in the shape of a tiger, mighty and callous once more.

For the first time in a decade I ranged far from my trees. They were bound to me, as I was bound to them. I would know if something threatened. For now, I felt the need to hunt.

I sought out Sang Gajah. For some time now his herd of elephants had been ravaging a village's plantations. I could still feel the echoes of despair rippling throughout the jungle, of the farmers crying out at harvests lost. There was no reasoning with Sang Gajah. There was a bitterness in him. That bitterness was infecting the jungle. Soon it might threaten my clearing.

It didn't take long to track the herd to a river. I waited for the bull to dip his trunk into the water before I lunged. The other elephants stampeded away. Sang Gajah trumpeted and tossed me off his head. I rolled across the ground, roared as he charged me. I leaped towards him.

Afterwards, my entire body bruised and shivering with a human exhaustion, I sank my jaws into his neck. I dragged the carcass, slowly but surely, towards the river. There the grateful pack of crocodiles waited, jaws already agape.

"You've been restless lately," called a voice above me.

I didn't have to look to know who it was. Pak Tua preferred wings to carry out his duty—his sacred place was over the river.

"Have I?" I sank to my haunches, watching the crocodiles tear at their meal. Blood was still on my tongue. I told myself I was witnessing balance being restored.

Pak Tua glided down to melt into the shape known to mortals, that of a kindly old man. Instead of weighing down his back with a tottering basket of durians, he let me see the large brown wings of the coucal.

"A mortal insists on sending his *hantu raya* slave to destroy my sacred tree," I said.

Pak Tua cocked his head. "Ahhh. The chieftain of the coast."

"You know him?"

"He has inherited great magic. His family has several *hantu raya* at their command. You should be careful."

I scoffed. "He cannot harm us."

"Can he not?" the old man mildly said. "He has many warriors. Some say his followers swarm like ants. Perhaps someday he might sweep across your jungle."

"That changes nothing."

He smiled, and I remembered his sacred place—a crumbling temple—was much closer to this chieftain than my jungle home. The threat to him was greater.

"Pak Tua—"

He unfurled his wings. "There is something different about you. I like it. It has been ages since I saw you hunt." His eyes twinkled. "You should see her again."

The elder laughed when I snarled at him. I watched him leap into the air with an explosion of feathers, flying around me once before sweeping back toward his territory.

She told me her name was Aryani.

She began visiting more. She called them "visits" even though we both knew she had been summoned here. It had become our tradition for her to formally ask that I give way, and for me to just as formally decline. We would smile. Then we would find somewhere to sit—a moss-covered log, or the branch of a giant tualang tree—and spend the remaining hour holding hands. We'd say little, just bask in the murmurs of the jungle, the way the trees and the hidden animals shared a single heartbeat.

Sometimes, we'd speak about nonsense things, human things, as I learned the rhythm of her voice.

One time, she gathered both my hands in hers to look at them, and I tried to curl the fingers closed.

"My hands are broken," I said, wary.

She gazed at the cracked nails, the lines that reminded me of the years I'd spent as a girl, smashing the endless sheaves of paddy to loosen the husks. *Bapa* had a voice that spoke softly only during the holy month of Ramadan, and his children could not stop working.

"Aryani," I protested.

"I think they're beautiful," she said at last. She lifted my hands to press her lips against the roughness of my palms, one after another.

I closed my eyes, accepting this gift. And when I thought her guard was lowered, I touched the bronze bangle snaring her wrist. "What does he do to you, when you return with nothing?"

She did not answer.

"His warriors have begun moving into the jungle," Pak Tua said. "I see them carry parangs, and soon they will begin cutting into my trees."

I marveled at his calm. We had taken to meeting by the river lately, both of us too tense to leave our animal shapes. "What do they want?"

"Who can say? They talk of land for their families. The chieftain has promised them such."

"What will you do?"

"If they enter my sacred place, I will challenge them, of course."

"But you said he has many warriors. Many *hantu raya* at his command."

"Did you not say no harm could befall us?" He smiled. "It is the will of Allah, young one. You accept what you are given."

I rose to my paws. "Don't go."

"All things end," he said, unfurling his wings. "And some things begin."

As the coucal soared towards the north, I wondered if the heavens looked with kindness upon the spirits.

It had been a month since I saw Pak Tua. A year since I first met Aryani that rainy afternoon, watching her scar one side of my tree.

I fretted in my clearing but did not dare leave. Once, twice, I might have heard distant shouts across the river, but I was now no longer sure. I had a duty. It was important that I be here, important that I preserve the bones of the past.

But when Aryani appeared before me again, the first words that sprang from my throat were, "Do you love him?"

She halted in surprise. She gazed down upon me with those eyes, as much a mystery as during our first meeting, while I crouched as if prepared for a blow. A year ago I had not been so humbled.

In the end, she whispered, "I thought so once."

"And now?" I could not help the hope surging in me. If I could sway her from her master—

She sank down to her knees and wrapped her arms around me. "Fly with me," she murmured, burying her face against the fur of my neck. "There is a lake where the sun shines on one end and the light of the moon on the other. Have you been there?"

"I have heard of it." It is a pool no mortal has swam in, for the roots of the trees surround the borders of the lake, drinking deeply of its waters. Spirits resided in every branch.

"I wish to swim with you there," she said into my ear, her

fingers smoothing down my fur. "They say that any soul who bathes in the waters realizes their life's purpose."

"A double-edge blade," I said. But I agreed.

I took to the air as a hornbill with wings as black as pearl, my beak the bright amber of the tiger. She shivered free of her human form and became a kingfisher, her wings flitting like leaves whipping in the wind. We soared between trees that touched the sky, the earth surging away beneath us.

She brushed against me first, feathers teasing my chest mid-flight before her smaller body dipped away. When she did it a third time, I shifted into a serpent eagle and playfully snapped my beak at her. Aryani gave off a sound like a laugh, blurred into the form of a swiftlet, and ducked beneath me. From there we circled each other, shifting, grazing each other even as we descended.

The game didn't stop once we touched ground just short of the lake. She dropped to the grass as a clouded leopard, spotted tail lashing, head bent as if ready to pounce. I became a sun bear, my mark a blazing orange beneath the neck. With my curved claws, I wrapped my arms around her and pulled her close. She shrank into a mouse deer and slipped free on tiny hooves. Over and over we changed shapes, reacting to each other, until we confronted each other as snake and mongoose.

We fell silent. I sank my serpentine head low, aware our choice of shapes could not be coincidence. And then the mongoose leaned forward to blatantly rub its face against mine. In shock, I shifted back to human, and so did Aryani.

She ended up straddling me, her legs around my waist, her hair brushing my lips. She smiled as she stroked my face, seeming to enjoy pinning me on the grass.

"Move," I said.

"Uncomfortable?" She grinned when I sent her a mock

growl. "Come," she said, taking my hand, helping me up.

I found myself laughing as we ran towards the lake. The trees parted for us, and then we were plunging into the waters. There, I grabbed her sarong and dragged it down. While she gasped, it was my turn to wrap my arms and legs around her from behind and kiss her over her shoulder. My hands explored while she nuzzled breathlessly against my mouth. My fingers played across the curve of her breasts so modestly hidden, stroked down to her quivering belly, until I found the softness between her thighs. I slid a finger in, stroking inner flesh where I would sometimes touch myself—when I'd weakened and changed to human, gasping and thrusting fingers in while curled up on the forest floor, waiting those endless hours for her.

Aryani whimpered in my arms, our two bodies as one in the water, heat sliding against skin. I kept her like this, held her prisoner while my fingers caressed and teased deep and made love to her, while I kissed her neck and listened to the sharp, breathless sounds. Her own hand tangled and tightened in my hair as I finally slid my finger out to seek a particular sensitive bead of her flesh. I knew I'd found it when she jerked in the water, protesting and calling my name in the same breath. I yearned to kiss her there but instead rubbed, gentle at first and then faster and faster until she quivered violently, thrashed once, and slumped in my arms. I smiled, satisfied I had won this game of ours, and nipped my teeth against her shoulder.

That was when I noticed something else her sarong hid. I froze when I spotted the marks across her back, so similar to the lines scarred across wood.

"Zaleha?" she whispered.

She stiffened, understanding what I had seen.

"I will kill him," I hissed.

She turned around in the water, throwing her arms around my neck. "They fade with time."

"I will tear his heart out, the miserable dog. How could you let him—"

"It doesn't matter. Stay with me." Her voice was edged with despair.

"Stay with you? Why—" Realization dawned. I should have known. No, a part of me must have known, but did not want to believe.

I looked back. Even with the towering trees, I could see the tendrils of smoke. I caught the scent of burning wood.

I pushed her away.

Her eyes were wide and tearful. "Zaleha," she began.

"You betrayed me."

"I gave you warning," she said.

"You lured me away!"

Her voice became dull. "Of course I did. I was ordered to. I am not like you, free to do as you please. Do you think it so easy, to live the way you do?"

"What happened to Pak Tua? The spirit guarding the temple across the river?"

"I had to spare you his fate. Don't you see? I had to make you safe."

I clenched my hands. "Come with me. You don't have to exist like this."

"You know very well that if I break my oath, I am condemned to the fires of Hell."

"There has to be a way."

"There is no other way!" Aryani snapped. "I am bound to *his* blood for eternity. I thought you less a fool than this."

"Whom do you love more? Him or me?"

She stared at me as if struck. "I thought you would understand."

"What is there to understand? He will never care for you as much as I."

She pressed hands to her face with a sob. "This is torment. Stay in your jungle, Zaleha. Stay there and live forever."

She began to fade. I shouted, but she was gone.

For a while I floated in those waters, feeling as if she'd sunk talons into my chest and clawed my heart out. And then I tore out of the water in the shape of a serpent eagle.

Heat and smoke blasted my eyes as I swept over the heads of the men setting fire to the trees. For a moment, gliding on heated air, I remembered the flames that surged and danced as they devoured the paddy fields of my childhood, unleashed to make the soil richer for the planting.

The men were moving fast, as if rushing to inflict as much damage as possible. When they approached my sacred tree, I plunged among them as a tiger. Fear seized their faces, but there were so many of them. Were these the ones who had murdered Pak Tua? The ones who desecrated his temple? Would they end me as they had my friend?

I took little joy as I ended lives with a slash of my paws, a snap of jaws onto throats and heads. Again and again they came, but not once did I feel the usual satisfaction as bones cracked under the weight of my teeth. It didn't matter anymore.

Nothing mattered anymore.

I sank to the ground, bathed in blood and gasping for breath. Around me the trees blazed, the wood groaning before branches snapped off to plunge to the ground.

I curled up there. The flames crept closer. I watched them with a kind of wistfulness.

Live, she'd said. *Live forever.*

She would want me to fly, to soar free, unfettered.

Bleeding from a dozen wounds, feeling my most mortal in centuries, I felt the revelation stir within me. Not from a magical lake, but within an inferno.

I want to tell her—

The smoke thickened, became choking. Noxious.

I shoved my body up. I bent forward, forced paws to sprout feathers. Made flesh condense inwards, caused bone to crack and shrink and become hollow. The last thing I saw before taking to the sky were the flames engulfing my sacred, scarred tree.

The chieftain did not look that surprised when I landed in his court and shed the shape of a coucal—my tribute to a lost friend. Followers and warriors gasped as I stood there, human, naked. Hands reached for their weapons, but Aryani's master raised a hand.

He'd noticed I made no move to attack. "Why are you here?" he asked.

I studied the layers of a hundred charms and magics protecting him, and found them cast with undertones of fear and desperation. When I peered into his face, I saw ambition. Greed. I relaxed. His charms were powerful, true. But given some effort, a decade or two perhaps, and I could crack through them. I had time. I had all the time in the world.

My gaze flitted to Aryani, who stood beside her master's chair. Her face was pale with shock. She shook her head sharply, urging me to flee while I could. Behind me, I felt the brimming hostility of the mortal's other guardian spirits, all of them fierce and strong. They wanted to shred me to pieces for daring to breach their master's house.

But I smiled, for her alone.

"I have come to serve you," I answered. And I raised a hand, for the chieftain to fasten the bronze bangle he uses to enslave his spirits.

He hesitated. I had the feeling no *hantu* or jin had ever chosen to enter his servitude. He licked his lips. "Are you certain?"

I nearly laughed, and thrust my hand forward again while his warriors muttered around us.

Soon the chieftain was whispering the ancient words of binding as he secured the thing around my wrist.

My eyes were only on Aryani.

"Do you miss the jungle?" she whispered, many nights later.

"Not really," I said, sedately.

She laid her head on my shoulder as we sat on the window of our master's house. The moon was a pale maiden drifting across gardens rich with spices and promise. On nights like these, I did not mind the weight on my hand.

"You are a terrible liar," she decided.

I laughed, nestling her close. She sighed and leaned into my arms.

CATNIP

Delilah Devlin

Mallory set the rusted box back on the rickety shelf. Had it been in better shape, the Bionic Woman lunch box would have made a nice addition to her collection.

Disappointed, she sighed and turned away. This was the last sale she'd circled in red from the classifieds. She was ready to call it a day. This Saturday morning's haul was pretty pathetic—a painted brass ink stand of indeterminate age and manufacture, a tomato-head plaque with a broken thermometer, and a vermeil stick pin, perhaps from the Victorian era, but with the gold wearing away in spots. Not that she truly minded. Finding unique and valuable treasures among the junk wasn't the point. She enjoyed the search—the feeling she got reaching into a dilapidated cardboard box and pulling out something unexpected. Something intriguing.

Some of her treasures sat on shelves in her home for her to enjoy—until their luster faded and she sold them through her eBay store. She was fickle that way. As many times as she'd moved in her lifetime, she never grew truly attached to things. She enjoyed them for a while, and then let them go. Rather like the many girlfriends who'd passed through her life.

Mallory waved to the old woman who sat at a metal table with a cash box beside her. As she passed, heading to her car, the woman reached out and caught the bell sleeve of her peasant blouse.

The old lady's grip was surprisingly strong. "Didn't you find anything of interest?"

A cool shiver trickled down her spine. Something about the sharp-eyed gaze in the hawkish face made her heartbeat stutter. It would have been impolite to shake off the withered hand, so Mallory forced a smile. "Not particularly."

"Did you look inside the shed?"

Tamping down an irritated sigh, Mallory scanned the make-shift tables and shelves scattered on the lawn in front of the old clapboard home. Behind the house, down a rutted gravel path, stood a small weathered shed, leaning on its foundations. The door was closed. "I didn't know to look in there. There aren't any signs."

The old woman's gaze narrowed. "Go look. You might be surprised."

Again, a chill prickled her skin. Maybe it was the wind, which had picked up in the last few moments, or maybe it was the gap-toothed yellow smile the woman flashed. At this point, Mallory was eager to take the woman's suggestion just so she'd let her go. "Thanks. I'll take a look."

The woman's grasp eased away. Her features relaxed into a docile and somewhat dazed expression.

Mallory wondered if she suffered from dementia, but shrugged, relieved to end the awkward encounter.

As she passed the tables that earlier had seemed stacked with haphazard junk, she discerned there was a theme, an ominous one, and certain items stood out, as though haloed by the fading sunlight. A crow-shaped weather vane, a silver chalice with the figures of three crones engraved on it, a worn but shiny wooden mortar and pestle—the bowl beginning to rot and resembling a blackened skull.

The shed door creaked open on rusty hinges, swinging through thick cobwebs. Mallory grimaced, but reached up and swept them away, then stepped through the door and into a grimy darkness lit only by rays creeping through the slats of the wood siding.

Rustling sounded, and she jumped. Mice, most likely. Usually, she wouldn't have reacted, but the old woman had creeped her out. She took a deep breath, wondering how long she had to pretend to hunt through cardboard boxes stacked along shelving that looked like a slight breeze might send it crashing to the floor.

Light shone on a box, the folded top opened on one side. A shimmer of fur caught her eye. Curious, she reached inside. She pulled out a toy, not the stuffed animal she'd been expecting, but a doll with molded features—a pretty cross of tiger-striped kitten and human woman. A Barbie with tufted cat's ears, fur coating its pronounced curves, but with a smooth cherub's face.

She brushed her fingers over the fur and dust billowed. Grime streaked its cheeks, and there was a tear at the base of the doll's long tufted tail. The eyes were deep emerald green and so glossy, they appeared to be filled with tears.

The doll was of no intrinsic value, not something that would earn more than five bucks in her online store, but it appealed to Mallory's sense of whimsy. "I have just the spot for you on my shelf."

Relieved she'd found something to satisfy the old woman,

she retreated from the gloomy lean-to and headed back to pay.

Only now, three old women stood behind the table, all gray, all their gazes fixated on the doll she held.

Mallory hoped they wouldn't think she'd be gulled into paying more for it than it was worth. To forestall any haggling, she reached into her pocket. "I'll give you two dollars."

The women never glanced among themselves, but their sharply honed features eased. The one who'd grabbed her arm held out her bony hand. "Done."

Mallory set "Miss Kitty" on the bookshelf beside her computer. She'd brushed away as much dust as she could before sponging away the grime. She'd reattached the tail with tiny stitches. While she'd worked, she'd admired the craftsmanship of the strange little doll. The fur suit was seamless and molded to the figure. The small face wasn't hard plastic, but something softer, with the texture of real skin. The lips, with their cat's cleft at the center, were parted with a row of individually attached teeth beneath them. She'd stroked her thumbnail over the soft lashes surrounding those shining eyes—each lash appeared to be embedded in the lids.

Perhaps there was more to the doll than what she'd originally believed. Promising herself to do a little Internet search in the morning, she turned off the bedroom light and climbed into bed.

Her head no sooner hit the pillow than she heard something drop to the floor. The sound was soft, but solid.

She sighed and reached to turn on the bedside lamp. Glancing in the direction of the sound, she scanned the floor, but found nothing out of place. Only mildly perturbed, Mallory reached for the light, then paused. Her gaze flicked to the bookcase. Her new doll wasn't on the shelf where she'd placed it.

Dammit. She'd never sleep until it was back where it belonged. She crawled from the bed and searched the floor beneath the shelf. Nothing. She pulled out her desk chair to see if it had somehow tumbled beneath her desk. "Weird," she said under her breath as she pushed the chair back into place.

A skittering sounded in the closet beside the shelf, and her heart rate accelerated. "What the hell?" The sound was too small to be a hidden intruder. Wary, she approached the closet. The door was open only a crack. Did she have a mouse? The mystery over the doll was forgotten as she worried how she'd trap it. Inching the door open, she reached inside for the string attached to the lamp on the ceiling.

A loud thump came from the back of the closet, and Mallory jumped back. *Too freaking big to be a mouse. Fuck!* She backed up two steps, then ran for the bedroom door.

Before she'd gone three steps, something pounced on her back, taking her to the carpet. Hands wrapped around her wrists, pinning them to the floor. Mallory bucked, panic making her breaths come in short, shallow sobs.

"Don't be afraid," purred a feminine voice from right beside her ear.

The raspy quality of the voice caressed nerves Mallory chose to ignore. "Get off me," she ground out.

"I think I'll stay here for a moment. I don't want you bolting again, because I wouldn't like to hurt you. You smell good."

"What the fuck were you doing in my closet? What do you want?"

The body covering her back resettled, curves molding to Mallory's. "I'm not sure why I'm here. Are you a witch?" The woman's hips undulated, grinding against Mallory's ass.

Which made it very hard to think. "Am I a wha—"

A snarl sounded. "Just shut up a second. I can't think."

A rumbling purr vibrated against her, growing louder as the woman on her back nuzzled her neck.

"What are you doing?" Mallory asked in a very small voice, wondering if she was going to be raped by the woman and why that thought didn't terrify her more.

"*Mmm...* I'm doing what I couldn't when you groomed me."

"*Groomed* you?" A sandpaper tongue licked behind her ear. "Jesus! Get off me."

Pffft. Nails dug into her shoulders, but the woman released her hands and climbed off her.

Mallory rolled to her side, caught a glimpse of her attacker, and screamed. She scrambled backward on her hands and butt, halting when she hit the bed. "You—you..." She pointed, hyper-ventilating.

The woman who knelt on all fours in front of her was the spitting image of Miss Kitty. Well, mostly. Her body was still Barbie Doll perfect, but the tiger-striped fur was a shorter, shining down, which did nothing to hide the lovely tuft of fur at her mound or the pert, brown nipples of her breasts. Her face was still smooth, still beautiful and round, the eyes a wide, unblinking green. Long brown hair fell down her back, parted by small cat's ears atop her head. A long striped tail curved around one thigh—the white, tufted end flicking lazily side to side.

Mallory drew deep breaths and shook her head. This wasn't happening. Beautiful women didn't visit her bedroom, never mind the fur suit. "All right. I'm asleep. Or high. Maybe that old witch at the garage sale had some LSD in the goo she rubbed on my hand when we shook."

The cat-woman's small, triangular nose twitched. "Old witch?"

"Not important right this minute," Mallory bit out. "I'm being punked, right? Although why me, I don't know. I'm not a celebrity. I don't have any friends here."

Miss Kitty's head canted, curiosity in her large mirrored eyes. "What are you talking about? And could you please speak more slowly? I'm still having trouble—" Her eyelids slid halfway down, and she sniffed the air delicately. "Your smell— it's delicious." Her cat's lips, with the pretty cleft on the upper bow, lifted. White teeth, the eyeteeth honed to scary sharpness, flashed.

"Are you going to eat me?"

The cat's eyes blinked. Her lips twitched. "Only if you're good," she purred.

Again, an unwanted stir of arousal tightened Mallory's nipples; her pussy clenched.

The cat-woman knew it. Her nose twitched again. Her sniffs grew deeper. Her lovely green eyes narrowed. She stepped closer on her hands, her head sinking between her shoulders, looking like a stalking tiger.

However, the only flesh she pursued was Mallory's pussy. Her mouth was level with it as she approached Mallory's bent, splayed legs.

Mallory stiffened, but couldn't help watching with fascination as Miss Kitty nuzzled the crotch of her pajama shorts.

"Will you remove them or do you want me to tear them?"

"I don't want you to do anything," Mallory said, but her whisper lacked conviction.

The arching brow of the creature poised between her legs mocked her. The cat-woman lifted one small hand, and her nails protracted, curving like a cat's claws as they lengthened.

Mallory's breath caught, and she froze as with one swipe, the cat-woman shredded the fabric without grazing her skin.

The creature's mouth curved. "Did you like that?"

She started to shake her head, but her sex was exposed,

oozing excitement. This strange turn of events might be only a dream. A drug-induced fantasy. Why should she deny it?

"This is no dream."

"You can read my mind?"

"You give your thoughts away. You're torn. You're frightened, and yet you're aroused." The cat stuck out her small pink tongue and lapped Mallory's clit. "You think too much. And I'm suddenly ravenous."

The claws retracted, and human fingers, small but with surprising strength, slipped beneath her ass and raised her. The cat's head dipped, and her rasping tongue licked with abandon.

Mallory's thighs tensed; her toes curled. Her breaths were chopped apart by fear and elation. The roughened tongue pulled and petted her folds.

"I want more," the cat growled, sliding fingers up Mallory's cunt to coax more fluid with swirls and thrusts.

Panting, Mallory braced her hands on the floor and raised her bottom, pulsing her sex up and down, eager for the climax surging through her body. She gave a muffled shout, her hips grinding against the cat's smooth muzzle until it faded away.

When she opened her eyes, it was to find the cat, draped over her legs, *grooming* the fine hairs cloaking her cunt. Mallory gasped. This was way too real.

Ears pricking, the cat lowered her ass to the floor, then gripped Mallory's ankles and dragged her forward until she lay flat on her back. "I want more."

Before Mallory could think to roll away, the cat jumped over her, knees landing on the carpet beside her hips. The cat lowered her torso, breasts mashing against breasts and her cat's mouth poised above Mallory's. "We should play. Night will pass, and tomorrow we will visit the crones."

"Crones?" Mallory whispered, curious about what that cleft

lip would feel like against her own.

The cat pressed her sex against Mallory's mound. "The three witches who gave me to you. They have the power to release me from this curse."

"You're cursed?" Mallory parroted, unable to follow the conversation because silky down rubbed her breasts and belly as the cat undulated.

"Stop talking."

"I'm taking orders from a fur-ball?" Mallory muttered.

"My name's Katya."

"Of course it is."

Katya grinned, then sat up, straddling Mallory's middle. "A name, or I'll call you 'Catnip,' because I'm getting drunk on the taste of you."

Something in the way the cat commanded her made it impossible for her to refuse. Who knew she was this submissive? Then again, it wasn't every day a naked cat-woman pinned her to the floor. "Mallory," she said, breathlessly.

"Mallory," Katya purred. "Can you handle a tail in front of your face?"

"I suppose."

The cat turned gracefully before setting again, then glanced over her shoulder, her expression amused, and backed up her beautifully rounded bottom. Her tail was erect, the tip jerking with excitement.

Mallory watched, her hands flattened to the ground as the brown-furred twat edged over her face. "Does one call a cat's pussy a...pussy?"

Katya purred. "You may call it anything you like so long as you lick it."

"And what will you be doing?"

"*Grooming.* Now, raise your knees."

Mallory complied without hesitation. When she was arranged to Katya's satisfaction, the cat wrapped an arm around one thigh and curved her lithe body to lap Mallory from clit to crack.

Mallory jerked as the raspy tongue plied her asshole with licks, but the sudden lowering of Katya's very wet sex muffled her gasp. It glazed her nose, but Mallory didn't mind because the scent that wrapped around her head was entirely human and completely luscious. Damp humid heat surrounding her, she palmed the down-soft thighs and rubbed her thumbs over Katya's outer lips.

The cat's purr deepened, vibrating against her belly and between her legs. Taking a deep breath because she was committing to pleasuring the creature, she dove in, at first licking with broad strokes between the spread labia, then thrusting her pointed tongue into her opening to swirl around and around.

Moisture seeped to coat her tongue, and she gave her own little growl. She burrowed into the bottom of the folds, seeking the hard little knot straining from under the hood. Latching her lips around it, she sucked, mashing her tongue against it as she drew. She thrust two fingers into Katya's vagina, and was rewarded with a stiffening at the base of the cat's tail and rapid back and forth toss of its tufted end.

Lord, she'd missed this—not the tail swishing, but the taste and sounds of sex that didn't have a thing to do with a vibrator. Although the purring added a texture to their lovemaking that Mallory could appreciate.

Katya licked at Mallory's clit and coaxed more fluid to trickle down between her buttocks. Then she used the fluid to moisten a fingertip and pressed against the tight rosette.

Mallory grunted and tried to close her legs, but Katya leaned on her splayed thighs to press them wider. The finger penetrated, pushing deep then withdrawing, then sinking once again until the burning discomfort faded with the unaccustomed pleasure.

Her body writhed, spurred by the wet rasp on her clit and the fingers fucking her ass, but also by the quivers in Katya's thighs. Katya's clit swelled, becoming erect and allowing Mallory to get her mouth around the base of it while she sucked. When Katya began to hump Mallory's face in shallow dips and swells, Mallory curled her own hips upward, begging for more.

Another finger stretched her asshole. Mallory groaned and turned her head side to side, pulling on Katya's clit. Then she let it slip from her mouth, ignoring Katya's muffled complaint. She pinched the she-cat's clit between her thumb and forefinger and pulled and pushed on it, fucking it quickly while she continued to plunge fingers into her strange lover's pussy.

Katya's body arched, her fingers still buried in Mallory's ass, and a loud yowling, scream echoed in the small bedroom.

Mallory let go of the clit she'd tortured and lapped it gently. She withdrew her soaked fingers and licked the feminine cum smeared on Katya's sex. She *groomed* her until the body above her relaxed, and the tail fell limply to the floor.

Kisses landed on her own inner thighs. The fingers in her ass fucked with renewed strength, in and out. Centering her face, Katya lashed her tongue against Mallory's clit, then slid between the folds.

Mallory humped her hips, faster and faster despite the weight crushing her against the carpet. She was close, so close. "Please, Katya, please." Frustrated, Mallory turned her head and sank her teeth into Katya's thigh.

Katya yowled and withdrew her fingers. Before Mallory could wonder what was next, she was rolled, forced onto her knees with her mouth against the carpet. "I thought you'd like a little nibble," she grumbled.

"I liked it a lot. It inspired me." Katya gave a sultry purr.

"To do what?" Mallory asked, suddenly nervous.

Katya eased away and something bristly stroked the backs of her thighs.

Mallory lifted her head to look behind her, but a hand slapped her bottom. The blow stung. "Ow!"

"No peeking."

The bristles tickled her already abused clit, and she hissed between her teeth.

"Too much? Poor baby." The bristles brushed between her folds.

With her forehead resting on the carpet, Mallory concentrated on the sensations. The bristles softened with her moisture, and then Katya used them to paint her outer lips.

"It's your tail, isn't it?"

"Of course. It's not as limp as my doll's tail. There's bone in it."

Mallory's breath caught as the bristled tip of the tail played with her opening, swirling and swirling around it. When Katya pressed it inside, and then kept feeding it inch by inch into her pussy, Mallory's whole body grew rigid. Her pussy clamped around the tail, the fine hairs abrading her tender inner tissues. The girth of it was just enough, just right. Fluid gushed to ease its way as Katya pushed and pulled her tail, fucking Mallory with it. When a finger tapped her asshole, Mallory moaned.

"Will you miss my tail?" Katya asked slyly. The finger poked inside her ass, then stroked in time with the tail fucking in and out.

Mallory couldn't even imagine what this looked like. This was pure perversion. A Kubrick dream. She moaned and rocked her head side to side, fingernails digging into carpet.

When little sharp nips to her fleshy parts were added to the delirious pleasure, she muttered and widened her stance, dropping her back to raise her bottom higher.

"Just like a little girl cat." Katya pulled her fingers free and shoved her tail deeper inside until it crowded against Mallory's cervix, and then slipped an arm beneath her to bring her up. They knelt, spooned closely together. The soft, velvety pads of Katya's fingers played with Mallory's tightly budded tips while she remained impaled upon Katya's meaty tail. At first the she-cat teased, cupping the soft undersides of Mallory's breasts and sliding her thumbs to tiddle the swollen buds.

"I could eat you right up."

"You already have," Mallory groaned, squeezing around the thick tail. She rested against Katya's down-cloaked body and reached behind her to spear her fingers through her lover's hair. "Make me come," she groaned.

Katya's claws lengthened and curved. She scraped the points down Mallory's belly, not hard enough to break skin, but just enough to leave white threads. She reached down and scratched the tops of her thighs, then the tender insides, coming closer and closer to her pussy, until she used two claws to comb through her bush.

Mallory squirmed and sighed, then pinched her own nipples as she rubbed her back against Katya's silky skin.

Claws retreated. A finger skimmed over her clit, then returned to push on it and rub until Mallory whimpered and plucked her nipples and came apart in a shattering climax.

Katya reached between Mallory's legs and slowly removed the end of her tail. She flicked it under her nose and sniffed, then lapped at the moist bristles. "*I shall miss my tail.*"

Mallory giggled and turned around, gripped Katya's shoulders, and shoved her to the floor. Climbing over her body, she straddled her, damp curls to wet fur, and snuggled against the cat-woman's chest. She yawned. "Tell me."

Katya glided her hands over Mallory's back, soothing her. "I was a witch, or at least an apprentice, until I tried to steal something from the crones."

"What did you want?"

"Their grimoire. I only intended to borrow it and copy their spells, but Rosemary caught me."

"What did she do?"

"She brought me to the others and told them what I'd done. Margery said that I should be punished. They threw so many horrid punishments around that I curled into a ball and wept.

"Agnes took pity on me. Said they'd never had a familiar. They made me into a cat, but I couldn't seem to keep out of things. I was constantly searching for the book they hid although I couldn't have used it—not without a voice to cast the spell."

"So they turned you into a doll?"

"Yes, until Agnes took pity again today."

"She was the one with the money box?"

Katya's head nodded, rubbing against Mallory's cheek.

"If she was the nice one, I'd hate to be alone with the other two."

"Today was the first time I shifted."

Mallory pulled back and glanced at Katya, whose features were still. "Why do you think you changed?"

"It might be because this is the first time I've been away from them. Maybe the spell weakened."

"Maybe it had something to do with the goo Agnes rubbed on my hands."

Katya picked up Mallory's hand and sniffed it.

"I washed my hands."

Katya's lips curved. "But you must have touched me with it,

then transferred it back to your hands. It's only catnip and an oily base to make it cling to your skin."

Disappointment speared Mallory. "So you were only attracted because of the catnip?"

Katya's eyelids dipped, and her mouth crimped into a flat catlike smile. "Baby, you groomed and petted me like a new friend. I hadn't known kindness in a long time."

"So you're grateful. This was all about gratitude."

Katya's expression softened. "Are you afraid I won't want you once you've bathed?"

"You won't need me once you've been returned to human form."

The she-cat's glance hardened. "Or I can stay like this. Your pet."

Mallory sighed. "Even though I'd never tire of this, I'd be horribly selfish if I didn't let you go."

Katya blinked and glanced away. "I'll still need somewhere to stay. Someone I trust."

"I have room. A bed."

One feline brow arched. "Yes, you do, although we have yet to use it."

Feeling more hopeful that this strange exotic creature wouldn't slip away, Mallory nodded. "So how about a bath first, then dinner."

Katya wrinkled her nose. "Cats don't bathe. We groom."

The next day, Mallory pulled the car close to the doorway for Katya, dressed in a long trench coat to hide her tail and a straw hat to hide her cat's ears, to run quickly to the door and jump in.

The trip to the old crones' house didn't take long. The whole time Mallory thought about things she wanted to say to Katya, but didn't have the courage.

For her part, Katya remained mute, watching the changing scenery through the passenger window.

She'd never thought to ask how long she'd been under the crones' spell.

"Fifteen years I've been away." When she saw Mallory's startled expression, she blinked. "You asked."

"Actually, I didn't."

They turned into the long driveway. The tables were gone.

At Katya's sharp inhalation, Mallory patted her knee. "See? You haven't changed back. It doesn't have a thing to do with this place."

"How'd you...?" She shook her head. "Maybe we do read each other's minds."

They exited the car, Katya tossing the hat onto the seat and shaking out her hair.

The wind caught it and Mallory thought she looked like a Brazilian cover model dressed for Carnival.

They knocked but no one answered. They tried the latch, and it depressed. The door swung open.

A quiver of unease shook Mallory. "Maybe we should wait. The last time you went snooping, they turned you into Garfield."

"No, I think we're okay." Katya walked through the foyer and down a darkened hallway that opened into a large kitchen with an equally large cauldron bubbling on the gas stove.

"Someone has to be here," Mallory whispered. "We should leave while we can."

Katya scanned the kitchen, and then froze.

Mallory followed her gaze. A large leather-bound book sat on a counter. "Baby, that's a real bad idea."

"The little one is cautious while you are bold."

The creaky voice behind her startled Mallory so badly she jumped and shrieked.

Agnes's sharp features peered at Mallory. "I thought you'd be the one; the others weren't sure. But look what we have…" Her gaze sliced toward Katya. "You still wear your pride."

Katya's eyes narrowed. "I don't know what you mean, but you know why I'm here."

"You're sure you don't want to keep a remnant or two of your punishment to keep you humble?"

Katya's chin jutted. Mallory nearly asked for the tail. Katya's gaze cut her way, and a slight smile curved one corner of her mouth.

The old woman clapped her hands delightedly. "You hear one another! Marvelous! What fun you shall have."

Mallory reached for Katya's hand and took a step toward the door, intending to make a run for it.

"Where are the other two?" Katya asked softly.

"There are always only three. Rosemary and Margery are at rest. When my niece, Melisande, arrives, so too shall I be."

Katya's hand tightened around hers, and she pulled her against her side, anchoring her there.

And even though she knew she ought to tear out of the embrace and try to escape some horrible fate, she didn't much care what happened, not with Katya's arm around her. "So are you going to make us into a matching pair of Beanie Babies?"

Agnes chuckled. "No, but I should leave you two alone. You have a lot to talk about."

Mallory turned to Katya, and then blanched. Katya was her human self again. Still as shapely, but with a longer nose and human ears and skin as smooth as alabaster.

"That's a rather trite description."

"What's going on?"

"Didn't you hear her? There are always three."

"And that means something to you, but three sounds crowded, and she's not coming to my bed." Mallory shuddered.

Katya laughed and the sound was like bells ringing. Gone was the purr, the raspy growl. "If you miss your Miss Kitty so much, you can always learn the spell to change me. I'll even stand still while you blow the powder at me."

"Me, cast a spell?"

"You really are slow." Katya shrugged off the trench coat and opened her arms. "Darling apprentice, we're home."

A week later, a car door slammed. Katya drew off her apron. Mallory brushed off flecks of crushed lavender from her fingers. Agnes had been teaching them to cast a love spell. The ingredients had been crushed in the old mortar and then burned like incense in a silver bowl. "Do you think it's her?" Mallory asked.

She glanced around, saw Agnes walking down the dark hallway toward the front door. The old woman pushed open the screen door, waved to whoever had just arrived, then disappeared in a shimmer of golden light.

Mallory gasped.

Katya gave her a smile. "It's going to be all right." She grasped Mallory's hand and together they stepped out onto the porch to welcome Melisande.

BELLING
THE CAT

J.L. Merrow

Y ou're doing it again, Kat," Belle said, in that oh-bloody-hell-here-we-go-again tone of voice that these days just screams Belle to me.

Don't get me wrong, she's a really good mate, Belle is. Always ready to drop work and have a natter, and she makes sure she keeps a tin of tuna in the cupboard, which is a much more important quality in a friend than most people think, I've always found. We work together, always have—well, not together, together, but for the same firm of accountants. She's in audit; I'm in tax, which is handily on her way down to the ladies'. That's where we were just then. Well, if smokers can have a ten-minute fag break in the morning and again in the afternoon, I don't see why the rest of us can't have a ten-minute pee-and-a-chat break every now and then, do you?

I twisted around from where I'd been sitting on the counter, swinging my legs, to have a look in the mirror. Yep, couldn't deny it. I mouthed a couple of curses at my reflection and set to with the breathing exercises.

"You're going to have to do something about that, Kat. What if it happens at your desk? Or worse, in a meeting?"

"Aaannnnnnddd *out*, two, three," I said aloud. You can't actually do breathing exercises while speaking, but I was trying to make a point. "You know, given that this seems to be stress-related, I don't think coming up with worst-case scenarios is really helping, do you?"

"You think that's a worst-case scenario? What if it happens in the middle of the wedding?" Belle asked, hands on her hips giving her even more of an hourglass figure. "There we are, walking up the aisle behind Amie, her all radiant in that bloody meringue dress we couldn't talk her out of buying, and suddenly—"

"*Not* helping, okay?" I said brightly. "Look, I'll be fine. I just need to relax, that's all. Center myself. Find my 'Calm Place.'"

Fat chance of that, I admitted to myself after she'd gone back to her desk, leaving me alone in the ladies' trying to visualize a pile of warm, fluffy towels in my mum's walk-in airing cupboard. The problem with Belle was, she was the problem.

Ever since I'd seen her in the slinky satin dress Amie had, against all the odds, chosen for us as her bridesmaids, well, I hadn't been able to get the picture out of my head. And it was totally inappropriate, because Belle and I had been mates for ages. Ever since we both started working at Cuthbert & Co. on the same day, September before last. Fresh out of college we were, both of us—totally unprepared for the world of work.

Well, I was, anyhow. Belle's one of those people who always seems prepared for anything, and she's so nice with it you can't help liking her, even so.

I'd noticed her straight off—hard not to, as she's almost six foot tall with the sort of looks that have strangers coming up to her in the street and asking if she's a model and if not, why not.

Poor sods. They don't know what's hit them when she goes off on one of her tirades about objectification of women and propping up an archaic, misogynistic fashion industry. We hadn't really spoken much, but then on my second day I was sent off to do some photocopying (three hundred pages, double sided, and twenty-seven copies) and it all went pear-shaped really quickly, because I didn't realize the machine couldn't handle all that at once.

Belle rescued me. She slipped into the little photocopying room and dug me out of the avalanche of paper that had buried me alive, as if Swiss mountain rescue had started employing sleek black panthers instead of Saint Bernards. She even changed the toner when it ran out halfway. "I did work experience in my mum's office over the summer," she explained.

We ended up going out for a drink after work, and I told her I was a dyke, but not to worry, she wasn't my type—because she wasn't, at least not as far as I knew back then—and she just laughed and said she reckoned she could fight off any unwanted advances.

And when I developed my little problem, she was right there to support me, and spent hours on the internet Googling for a cure. Which she didn't find, obviously, but then she just started helping me to deal with it.

Which not a lot of mates would do. I mean, it's not something straightforward like a case of thrush.

So I did my best to be glad for her when she had boyfriends, which never seemed to be that often, actually. I think a lot of blokes have a problem with a girl who's taller than them. And even though I had a few dreams about curling up in her lap while she stroked me and stroked me, I never said a word.

But then we had the fittings for the dresses, and, well—like I said—I just couldn't get the picture out of my head.

* * *

Amie's wedding day dawned bright and warm, and I had to rouse myself from the sunny spot on the armchair in the front room to get over there on time. We were all changing together at her house, and I really should have known. I mean, it started out all right. Amie was all excited, even before she cracked open a bottle of bubbly to get us in the mood. Trouble was, once we started getting our kit off to change, what with the alcohol and all, I was more than in the mood. And then there was Belle in her lacy stockings and push-up basque—I didn't need her startled look to know I needed to go and compose myself.

So I ran into the box bedroom in my boring cotton underwear and I tried to think calming, and unsexy, and above all, human thoughts.

But then the door opened, and Belle walked in. "Don't look at me!" I wailed, because who wants the girl of their dreams to see them all hairy? Not to mention the...other thing. Even sensible cotton underwear can only hide so much. But she just kept coming, and then I felt her stroke my hair, again and again, and it was so soothing I just forgot myself and leaned into her.

"Oh, Kat," Belle said softly, cuddling me. "I wish..." She scratched my chin, and I nuzzled into her touch.

"Wish what?" I wanted to say, but it came out as, "Miaow?"

Belle seemed to understand anyhow. "I wish I was your type," she said, and I was so shocked I changed back into human in her arms without even trying.

"Really?" I squeaked. "It doesn't bother you—all the going furry and, um," and here I blushed, "growing a tail?"

Belle blushed too, but then she kissed me. "You know I've always loved you as a cat. And it really is a beautiful tail." Her hand slid around to my bottom, and I realized—because she was stroking it—that the big, long, furry unmentionable thing was still there, poking out the leg of my knickers.

I'd always wondered why cats go all squirmy when you stroke their tails. I didn't have to wonder anymore.

My hand crept up to her breast all on its own, and I checked quickly to make sure there weren't any claws. Belle was all lace and satin and little bows, like a really posh birthday present, and I couldn't wait to unwrap her properly, but Amie would be banging on the door any minute demanding to know where her bridesmaids were. So I slid Belle's panties down over her suspenders, smoothed her dark little curls, and lapped her up like a saucer of cream, and it didn't take a moment before she shuddered and gasped.

Then she pulled me up, and her lips were on my lips, her soft tongue tasting mine. "I'm not sure you've washed properly today," she said, and as I shivered she licked her way all down my throat. "I think you missed a bit just here." Her hot breath tickled my skin as she licked a slow track around my nipple. "I think this bit's filthy." Belle's tongue was like silk sweeping over my nipple again and again, and I mewled as her hand crept into my knickers.

"Oh!" I said, and "Oh!" again, watching that little pink tongue make promises Belle's fingers more than fulfilled. "Don't stop!"

"Don't worry," she whispered. "I'm going to get you all sparkling clean." Her fingers stayed where they were while her tongue moved over to my other breast, laving it first softly, and then harder. The heady scent of her, all shampoo and body lotion and the sweet musk that was my Belle, rose up to tickle my nostrils.

Warmth spread through me, and when her other hand grabbed my tail and stroked it from root to tip, I exploded with heat and joy. "Oh!" I breathed, as stars shone around me, winking cheekily.

And then we kissed again, quick and wet and sweet, and we tidied ourselves up and checked that my tail had finally gone before we ran out, giggling.

All right. Maybe one of us was purring.

ABOUT THE AUTHORS

ANGELA CAPERTON writes eclectic erotica that challenges genre conventions. Look for her stories published with Black Lace and eBury Publishing, Cleis, Circlet, Coming Together, Drollerie, eXtasy Books, Renaissance, and in the indie magazine *Out of the Gutter.*

CHRISTINE D'ABO loves writing in the worlds of sci-fi, BDSM, and romance. By combining the elements of those genres, Christine creates the types of stories she loves to read. Christine is currently published with Ellora's Cave, Samhain Publishing, Carina Press, Berkley Heat, and Cleis Press.

KATE DOUGLAS, lead author of Kensington Publishing's Aphrodisia erotic romance imprint, which is home to her bestselling *Wolf Tales* series and upcoming *Dream Catchers* and *Spirit Wild* series, lives in the beautiful mountains of Lake County, California with her husband of forty years.

ADELE DUBOIS is an award-winning, multipublished erotic romance author and former newspaper and magazine columnist, features writer, and foreign correspondent. When not on the beach, she and her family enjoy their rural eastern Pennsylvania home, where she is currently working on her next novel.

SACCHI GREEN writes in western Massachusetts. Her stories have appeared in a hip-high stack of publications with erotically inspirational covers, and she's also edited or co-edited seven volumes of erotica, including *Girl Crazy, Lesbian Cowboys* (winner of the 2010 Lambda Literary Award for lesbian erotica), *Lesbian Lust,* and *Lesbian Cops.*

TAHIRA IQBAL is a UK-based writer who currently works in the film and TV industry, but writing is and will always be her first love. You can find her work, an erotic vampire short story "The Queen," in the *Red Velvet and Absinthe* anthology published by Cleis Press.

MYLA JACKSON pens wildly sexy adventures of all genres including historical westerns, medieval tales, romantic suspense, contemporary romance, and paranormals with beasties of all shapes and sizes. When not wrangling words from her computer with the help of her canine muses, she's snow skiing, boating, or riding her ATV.

MICHAEL M. JONES is a writer, editor, and book reviewer, which often leads to interesting conversations at family get-togethers. His stories have appeared in *Rumpled Silk Sheets, Like A Queen, Like A God's Kiss, Masked Pleasures,* and more. He is the editor of the forthcoming *Like A Cunning Plan: Erotic Trickster Tales.*

CHRIS KOUJU, a Malaysian writer, usually pens fantasy, science fiction, and an obscene amount of slashfic. Although lesbian erotica is not something she typically writes, she will lay hands on anything. Armed with a master's in creative writing, she is determined to finish her first novel in gorgeous, chilly Scotland.

ANNA MEADOWS is a part-time executive assistant, part-time Sapphic housewife. Her work appears in six Cleis Press anthologies, including *Girls Who Bite*. She lives and writes in northern California.

J.L. MERROW is that rare beast, an English person who refuses to drink tea. She writes across genres, with a preference for contemporary gay romance and the paranormal, and is frequently accused of humor.

VICTORIA OLDHAM is an editor of lesbian fiction and has published erotica in *Girls Who Bite*, *Where the Girls Are*, *Women in Uniform*, *Skulls and Crossbones*, and *Blue Collar Lesbians*. She lives in England with her partner and enjoys tromping through ruins.

GISELLE RENARDE is a queer Canadian, avid volunteer, contributor to more than fifty short story anthologies, and author of dozens of electronic and print books, including *Anonymous, Ondine*, and *My Mistress' Thighs*. Ms. Renarde lives across from a park with two bilingual cats who sleep on her head.

PAISLEY SMITH is a full-time freelance writer and can usually be found in front of her computer either writing, chatting, promoting, or plotting. It's a glamorous life...working in one's pajamas. She attended college in the Deep South, where she obtained a slew of totally useless degrees and developed an unrelenting sense of humor.

KARIS WALSH is a horseback riding instructor in the Pacific Northwest. She is the author of *Harmony* and *Worth the Risk* (January 2012), both from Bold Strokes Books.

ABOUT
THE EDITOR

DELILAH DEVLIN is a prolific and award-winning author of erotica and erotic romance with a rapidly expanding reputation for writing deliciously edgy stories with complex characters. Whether creating dark, erotically charged paranormal worlds or richly descriptive historical and contemporary stories that ring with authenticity, Delilah Devlin "pens in uncharted territory that will leave the readers breathless and hungering for more..." *(Paranormal Reviews)*. Ms. Devlin has published more than ninety erotic stories in multiple genres and lengths. She is published by Avon, Berkley, Kensington, Atria/Strebor, Black Lace, Harlequin Spice, Ellora's Cave, Samhain Publishing, and Cleis Press. Her published print titles include *Into the Darkness, Seduced by Darkness, Darkness Burning, Darkness Captured, Down in Texas, Texas Men, Ravished by a Viking,* and *Enslaved by a Viking.* She has appeared in Cleis Press's *Lesbian Cowboys, Girl Crush, Fairy Tale Lust, Lesbian Lust, Passion, Lesbian Cops, Dream Lover, Carnal Machines,* and *Best Erotic Romance (2012).* In 2011, *Girls Who Bite,* Delilah's first effort as an editor for a Cleis collection, was released.

Out of This World Romance

Buy 4 books, Get 1 *FREE**

Steamlust
Steampunk Erotic Romance
Edited by Kristina Wright

Shiny brass and crushed velvet; mechanical inventions and romantic conventions; sexual fantasy and kinky fetish: this is a lush and fantastical world of women-centered stories and romantic scenarios, a first for steampunk fiction.
ISBN 978-1-57344-721-8 $14.95

The Sweetest Kiss
Ravishing Vampire Erotica
Edited by D.L. King

These sanguine tales give new meaning to the term "dead sexy" and feature beautiful bloodsuckers whose desires go far beyond blood.
ISBN 978-1-57344-371-5 $15.95

Dream Lover
Paranormal Tales of Erotic Romance
Edited by Kristina Wright

A potent potion of fun and sexy tales filled with male fairies and clairvoyant scientists, as well as darkly erotic tales of ghosts, shapeshifters and possession.
ISBN 978-1-57344-655-6 $14.95

Fairy Tale Lust
Erotic Fantasies for Women
Edited by Kristina Wright

Award-winning novelist and erotica writer Kristina Wright goes over the river and through the woods to find the sexiest fairy tales ever written.
ISBN 978-1-57344-397-5 $14.95

In Sleeping Beauty's Bed
Erotic Fairy Tales
By Mitzi Szereto

"Who can resist the erotic origins of fairy tales from Little Red to Rapunzel's long braid? Szereto knows her way around the mythic scholarship and the most outrageous sexual deviations in Pandora's Box." —Susie Bright
ISBN 978-1-57344-367-8 $16.95

---

* Free book of equal or lesser value. Shipping and applicable sales tax extra.
Cleis Press • (800) 780-2279 • orders@cleispress.com
www.cleispress.com

Ordering is easy! Call us toll free or fax us to place your MC/VISA order. You can also mail the order form below with payment to: Cleis Press, 2246 Sixth St., Berkeley, CA 94710.

ORDER FORM

QTY	TITLE	PRICE
_____	_____	_____
_____	_____	_____
_____	_____	_____
_____	_____	_____
_____	_____	_____
_____	_____	_____
_____	_____	_____
_____	_____	_____

SUBTOTAL _____

SHIPPING _____

SALES TAX _____

TOTAL _____

Add $3.95 postage/handling for the first book ordered and $1.00 for each additional book. Outside North America, please contact us for shipping rates. California residents add 8.75% sales tax. Payment in U.S. dollars only.

* Free book of equal or lesser value. Shipping and applicable sales tax extra.

Cleis Press • Phone: (800) 780-2279 • Fax: (510) 845-8001
orders@cleispress.com • www.cleispress.com
You'll find more great books on our website

Follow us on Twitter @cleispress • Friend/fan us on Facebook

13

Should You Vote for the Candidate—or the Party?

In 1960 the Republicans and Democrats agreed to have their presidential candidates confront each other in a series of TV debates. After one round between Kennedy and Nixon, a Chicago woman was asked by a reporter which candidate had persuaded her to vote for his party.

"I'm voting for Kennedy," she replied. Asked why, she explained, "Because of Nixon's eyes. Especially the left eye. Something about his eyes bothers me!"

Marshal McLuhan, authority on TV's impact on audiences, observed, "Without TV, Nixon had it made."

Some Americans vote for candidates principally because of their stand on crucial issues. Others vote largely because of party affiliation. Still others vote because of personality.

A great many voters identify with one political party or the other, often because "everybody in my family has always voted that way." Some vote for a party because it represents the value they believe in. Most Republicans tend to be conservative, high status or middle-class. Most Democrats tend to be liberal, low-income or lower middle-class. Many acquire their party loyalty even before reaching voter age.

Americans unclear about the issues in a political campaign usually play safe and vote the ticket they most trust. Since registered Democrats outnumber registered Republicans three to two, a straight party vote could almost always elect Democratic nominees, however unworthy. Fortunately Democrats refuse to give their party that power, often voting with Independents according to their own judgment of each candidate.

This is the value of a multi-party system. In any country that legalizes only one party, voters are denied a choice. The result is dictatorship instead of democracy.

Many great leaders in our history, however, did not value political parties very highly. George Washington opposed forming them, declaring in 1796, "The spirit of party . . . agitates the community with ill-founded jealousies and false alarms; kindles the animosity of one party against another; foments occasional riot and insurrection."

John Adams agreed in 1808: "Neither party will ever be able to pursue the true interest, honor, and dignity of the nation. I lament the narrow, selfish spirit of the leaders of both parties. . . . They are incorrigible."

But a twentieth century president, Republican Warren Harding, declared in 1923, "I believe in political parties. These were the essential agencies of the popular government that made us what we are. We were never perfect, but under our party system we wrought a development under representative democracy unmatched in all proclaimed liberty."

Lyndon B. Johnson, a staunch Democrat, nevertheless reminded votes of a higher loyalty. "All of us are Americans," he said, "before we are members of any political organization."

More and more Americans today are moving away from rigid party loyalty. A Michigan study made during the 1970s found that only 24 percent of that state's voters considered themselves Republicans and only 42 percent called themselves Democrats. Among voters under 30 it was found that Independents outnumbered both parties together. These findings dramatized the change since a 1958 survey found that 74 percent of voters had voted for the same party their parents had.

The new independent trend has resulted in much split-ticket voting for a presidential team on one ticket and congressmen on both tickets. This is how in 1980 voters elected Republican Reagan president, yet voted for a Democratic House.

Because TV now projects candidates into the nation's living rooms, voters can rely less and less on party affiliations and more on their own perceptions of how the candidates look and what they say. Candidate image clearly matters today far more than party image.

The print media are equally influenced. Doris A. Graber's 1972 study of 20 papers covering the 1968 Humphrey-Nixon race found that almost all reportage of the candidates' presidential qualities dealt with their personality traits, rather than with their abilities or beliefs.

The sparkling personalities of candidates like Adlai Stevenson and John F. Kennedy attracted lots of new young people into the Democratic Party. Likewise, the TV images presented by such attractive political candidates as John Lindsay, Charles Percy, Mark Hatfield, and Howard Baker brought many new enthusiasts into the Republican Party.

By the 1980s many voters seemed to have grown more politically sophisticated, more knowledgeable about the issues. Split-ticket voting was especially common among voters dedicated to special causes—for or against equal rights for women, nuclear weapons, abortion, cleaning up the environment, etc. Millions cast their ballots for candidates who had promised to advance their own passionate interests.

The most important elections in our history, in fact, have been those in which voters' choices of the issues clearly turned the country in a new direction.

When voters elected Jefferson over Adams, they opted for weaker government control of the economy and for limiting federal powers. When they voted for Polk over Clay in 1844, they approved of U.S. territorial expansion. When they made Lincoln president, they did so in opposition to slavery. When they chose Roosevelt over Hoover in 1932, they wanted the

Depression ended by government intervention. And when they elected Reagan over Carter in 1980, they agreed with his program to slash federal taxes and spending to "get the government off our backs."

Sometimes a candidate who seizes on an issue becomes a "one-issue candidate" as a way of standing out from rivals and winning media attention. California Senator Alan Cranston did this in his drive for the 1984 Democratic presidential nomination by embracing the nuclear-freeze issue as his own. He won headlines but risked alienating those millions of voters who were opposed to the nuclear freeze.

Many candidates have wooed the anti-communist vote, calling for a tough stand against the Russians. "They will outbid each other in escalating the arms budget and applying a discredited policy around the world," observed Pulitzer Prize winner Robert Lasch, retired editor of the respected *St. Louis Post Dispatch.* "We should demand something more of our leaders. . . . It is long past time that we began . . . leaving it to the people of every country to pursue their own destiny, socialist or otherwise."

Sometimes when a candidate has the courage to take an unpopular stand on a controversial issue, voters respect his integrity enough to vote for him anyhow. That was the case in the 1970s when Ed Koch was running an uphill race to become mayor of New York. Talking to an audience of homeowners who favored a multi-billion-dollar highway project that he opposed, Koch told them, "I am not going to change my mind about it. If it means the difference between getting your vote and losing your vote, then I am not going to get your vote." One man rose to declare he would vote for Koch anyway, primarily because Koch didn't just tell them what they wanted to hear. Koch was elected.

Civil rights have been, and still are, a key issue in American elections. Black voters are determined to enforce those rights by electing black candidates. In 223 cities that have large black populations, there are now black mayors, 17 of them governing

Whether a voter chooses to cast his or her ballot for the party or the candidate, this machine won't be used. It's a ballot box from the late nineteenth century.

When Lincoln was elected in 1860, the nation had made the decision to oppose slavery. Voters' choices of issues often decide elections. HALFTONE REPRODUCTION OF DRAWING.

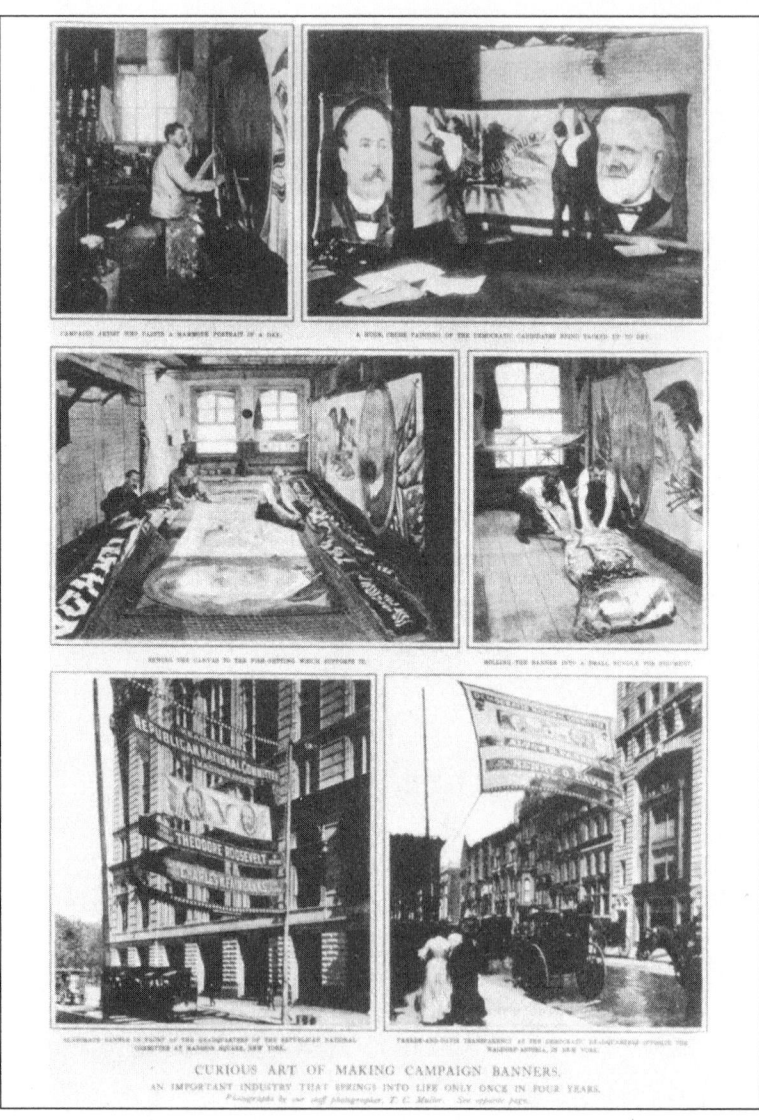

CURIOUS ART OF MAKING CAMPAIGN BANNERS.
AN IMPORTANT INDUSTRY THAT SPRINGS INTO LIFE ONLY ONCE IN FOUR YEARS.
Photographs by our staff photographer, T. C. Muller. See opposite page.

Today, television brings candidates into the voter's home, but prior to that, campaigning was conducted via less direct means. This series of 1904 photos shows the process of making campaign banners. REPRODUCTION OF PAGE FROM LESLIE'S WEEKLY, 1904.

cities with populations of over 100,000. The number of black voters has increased by 4 million in the South alone since federal enforcement of voter registration.

"I can remember back in 1968 when Andy Young and I were arrested in Atlanta for lying down in front of some garbage trucks during a strike," recalled Rev. Joseph Lowery, president of the Southern Christian Leadership Conference (SCLC) in the early 1980s. "Today Andy is the mayor and in charge of the garbage trucks."

There are now also 21 black congressmen, over 340 black state legislators, and some 5,000 black local officials. Usually they have won those offices on the Democratic ticket.

Many whites vote for black candidates, either because they agree with the justice of increasing black political power to give them proportionate representation or because they simply agree with the candidates' views. Thus in Missouri, black state legislator Alan Wheat won a congressional seat in a district that was over 75 percent white.

Similarly, blacks will vote for a white candidate, even one running against a black candidate, if they favor his or her stand on the issues. Thus black votes were crucial in electing liberal white Congressman Wyche Fowler Jr. of Georgia over his conservative black opponent.

While issues are emerging increasingly as more important to American voters than party labels, voters are still strongly influenced by a candidate's image. If they are irked by their party's nomination of a candidate they dislike, they are apt to stay home on Election Day or vote for the opposition.

14

How Lobbyists Influence Elections

Railroad barons in the late nineteenth century, who were major sources of campaign funds, exerted tremendous influence over American elections. Candidates they opposed were seldom elected to either state or national office.

James Bryce, an English barrister visiting the United States in 1881, was awed by the railroad lobby. "They have power," he wrote, "more power than perhaps anyone in political life except the president and the speaker, who after all hold theirs only for four years and two years, while the railroad monarch may keep his for life. When the master of one of the greatest Western lines travels toward the Pacific on his palace car, his journey is like a royal progress. Governors of states bow before him; legislatures receive him in solemn session."

Powerful lobbies are still with us today, seeking favors or legislation to benefit their special interests. They pressure legislators who are indebted to them for large campaign contributions and hope to retain their support for reelection.

There is nothing intrinsically evil in lobbying. The right of any group to "petition the government for a redress of grievances" is guaranteed by the First Amendment. But the Bill of Rights never intended the redress of grievances to be influenced by whether or not legislators received campaign contributions from petitioners.

"About 95 percent of campaign funds at the congressional level are derived from business," observed Senator Russell Long, chairman of the Senate Finance Committee. He pointed out that legislators helped their supporters get juicy government contracts, voted to cripple government agencies that regulated industries, blocked agencies seeking to enforce environmental protection laws, and voted to give government subsidies to special interests.

After being in charge of House military budgets for twenty years, Congressman Clarence Long of Maryland accused powerful corporate lobbies of controlling American foreign policy under any administration through campaign contributions. Arms and aid programs adopted by Congress, he charged, were designed to protect corporate investments overseas.

Similar concern was expressed in President Eisenhower's farewell address in 1961, when he voiced his fear that the pressure of lobbies greedy for munitions contracts and fat profits, plus the power of the Pentagon, could stampede Congress into militarizing the nation dangerously. "The potential for the disastrous rise of misplaced power exists," he warned, "and will persist."

Over twenty years later, syndicated columnist Jack Anderson pointed out, "It is doubtful that even Ike foresaw the extent to which the sweetheart relationship between Big Business and the brass has taken control of the single biggest slice of the federal government's budget pie."

In 1979 the *New York Times* reported that in the previous fall's congressional elections, special interests had contributed almost $1 million to the campaigns of just eight congressional leaders. Few realists expected those congressmen to vote against any bills the lobbies wanted passed.

Corporate lobbies exercise even greater power in state legislatures, where they can push their bills through much more easily and cheaply. State legislatures tend to meet infrequently and briefly, because salaries paid are generally so low that the legislators must maintain businesses or careers during their terms in office. Often, in their haste to adjourn, they rush through bills by voice vote—bills they have scarcely read, let alone studied. Many of these bills are written for legislators by the lobbyists.

Philadelphia reporter Bernard McCormick once noted that in the Pennsylvania legislature, the lobbyist for Sun Oil was "often referred to as the fifty-first senator," and the lobbyist for Penn Central Railroad was "considered the fifty-second."

"I have no hesitation in stating my deep conviction," declared Senator Joseph S. Clark of Pennsylvania, "that the legislatures of America . . . are presently the greatest menace to . . . the successful operation of the democatic process."

In 1983 California Secretary of State March Fong Eu warned that if the legislature didn't act to control "the unbelievable spending that is turning elections into auctions," she would introduce a citizens' initiative to control campaign spending. She pointed out that an incredible $150 million had been spent on the state's 1982 elections.

Mark Twain once observed sardonically, "I think I can say, and say with pride, that we have legislatures that bring higher prices than any in the world."

A Ford Foundation study also found that some governors accepted payoffs disguised as campaign contributions from business lobbies, in return for state contracts awarded without competitive bidding. Baltimore contractors testified that they had made such payoffs to Spiro Agnew, when he was governor of Maryland and when he was vice-president. Convicted of tax evasion, he was fined, then forced by Nixon to resign.

As early as 1852, congressional lobbies were a cause for concern. James Buchanan wrote to President Franklin Pierce, who had beaten him for the Democratic nomination, "The host of contractors, speculators, stock-jobbers, and lobby members which haunt the halls of Congress, all desirous . . . on any and every pretext to get their arms into the public treasury are sufficient to alarm every friend of his country."

Three years later a congressional investigation found that lobbyist Samuel Colt, inventor of the Colt .45 pistol, had paid a congressman $10,000 to get him a patent extension and had sought the favors of other congressmen by providing them with food, liquor, and women.

In 1873 Wisconsin Chief Justice Edward Ryan warned, "Money as a political influence is essentially corrupt . . . dangerous to the free and just administration of the law. . . . Who shall fill public stations—educated and patriotic free men, or the feudal serfs of corporate capital?"

The National Association of Manufacturers (NAM) lobby pulled its strings in 1902 to defeat labor bills for an eight-hour workday and a ban on strike injunctions. Congressmen who refused to oblige the lobby were defeated in the 1904 elections by heavy NAM contributions to their rivals' campaigns.

When Theodore Roosevelt sought reelection that year, he received large campaign contributions from the Navy League, made up of munitions makers and industrialists with Navy contracts, as well as from multimillionaires like J. P. Morgan, John D. Rockefeller, and Jay Gould. All were well repaid when Roosevelt revised the Monroe Doctrine to proclaim the right of U.S. armed forces to invade any Latin American country failing to meet its financial obligations to foreign (U.S.) banks and wealthy investors.

A group of investigative reporters whom Roosevelt derisively labeled "muckrakers" exposed the connection between corporate lobbies and the politicians they controlled. Lincoln Steffens declared, "Our political leaders . . . conduct the government of the city, state, and nation, not for the common good, but for the special interests of private business."

Often legislators who were voted out of office were rewarded by the lobbies they had served by being hired, in turn, as lobbyists. They were expected to capitalize on their former associations to influence ex-colleagues.

Thus in 1934 the electric light and power lobby was headed by two former senators. An investigation led by Montana Senator Thomas J. Walsh characterized it as "the most formidable lobby ever brought together . . . representing capital to the amount of nearly ten billion dollars." He predicted wryly that no action would follow his committee's investigation of the lobby's corrupt practices "because it will dry up the sources of campaign funds for the next election."

In 1951 the Kefauver Senate Crime Committee hearings revealed that three men had met in a Florida hotel room to put up $150,000 each as a campaign fund for Fuller Warren's race to be governor. Apart from this half million, Warren received only $15,000 in public contributions. Soon after his election, the partner of one of Warren's three backers wrote a bill that Warren steered through the Florida legislature, freeing the billion-dollar citrus industry from all state taxes.

Look magazine reported in 1960 that lobbyists had scattered a quarter of a million dollars around the Louisiana legislature to assure passage of a right-to-work (anti-union) bill.

The Watergate scandal during the Nixon administration was, in part, about illegal campaign finances. Contributions to Nixon's Committee to Reelect the President (CRP) had been "washed" through a series of banks to conceal their sources.

Big-business lobbies, however, are not the only ones that influence elections. In 1924 organized labor provided large campaign funds that helped elect many congressmen. The new Congress passed the Railway Labor Act, giving labor more latitude in strikes. Similarly, labor's support of Franklin D. Roosevelt's campaigns was rewarded by passage of the Wagner Labor Relations Act, compelling collective bargaining.

In 1943 the Congress of Industrial Organizations (CIO) formed a political action committee (PAC) to mobilize the CIO's 5 million members in electing pro-labor candidates. When the CIO merged with the American Federation of Labor (AFL) in 1955, they organized the Committee on Public Education (COPE), which today is labor's lobby for political action.

Many other lobbies pursue what is called "single-issue politics." The Right to Life (anti-abortion) forces, for example, were responsible for defeating Iowa Democratic Senator Dick Clark's 1978 bid for reelection. Lobbies like Jerry Falwell's Moral Majority, Inc., were active in seeking to defeat congressmen who opposed prayer in the schools or who favored the Equal Rights Amendment.

Crediting lobbying by the Moral Majority for the election of Ronald Reagan in 1980, Falwell proudly asserted that "Christian people came out of the pews into the polls and caused this avalanche."

Single-issue lobbies who came to Washington empty-handed have not always received a cordial welcome. In 1894 when a severe depression led Jacob Coxey to organize a national coalition of the unemployed, Coxey's Army, to march on Washington to demand jobs, Congress turned a deaf ear. Coxey and his lobbyists were jailed for walking on the grass.

And in 1970, when half a million Americans went to Washington to lobby against the Vietnam War, Nixon's Attorney General, John Mitchell, ordered mass arrests that totalled 13,400 people.

Lobbying efforts by Common Cause in the 1970s and 1980s claimed to have as their objective "returning the government to the people." This organization exposed big corporations with defense contracts that paid off helpful politicians with big campaign contributions. It also exposed how much money candidates were collecting, and from whom. Some senators and congressmen were shown to have received donations from contributors who had business before committees on which they sat in judgment.

Angry business lobbyists pointed out that the Common Cause lobby itself had spent over $442,000 in the 1982 off-year

The powerful lobbies that exist today are a far cry from this 1930s parade in New York City in which children marched for better housing conditions. AN INTERNATIONAL NEWS PHOTO.

Theodore Roosevelt, here with Admiral Evans aboard the *Mayflower*, repaid the Navy League for its large campaign contributions in 1904 by revising the Monroe Doctrine to increase the rights of U.S. armed forces. PHOTO BY WILLIAM H. RAN, COPYRIGHT 1908.

elections, almost 25 percent more than any other registered lobby. Its president, Fred Wertheimer, replied, "Many of the organizations that spend substantially more money than we do don't report at all." Other lobbies, he said, used loopholes in the disclosure law to conceal expenditures.

Some lobbies that reported spending over $100,000 each on the 1982 campaign included Handgun Control Inc., the American Petroleum Institute, the Sierra Club, the American Postal Workers Union, the American Medical Association, the Citizens Committee for the Right to Keep and Bear Arms, the U.S. League of Savings Associations, the AFL-CIO, the American Farm Bureau Federation, and the National Rifle Association (which also gave $85,000 to members of the Senate Judiciary Committee the year before it approved a bill making it easier to buy and sell firearms).

Some lobbies contribute campaign funds to both major candidates in an election, so that no matter which one wins, the lobbies are guaranteed the ear of the winner.

The political action committees, or PACs, were set up by lobbies to get around laws setting limits on a candidate's contributions from single sources. The PACs spend funds on behalf of favored candidates, ostensibly without the knowledge or control of those candidates' official campaigns. The use of PACs allows lobbies to put ten or more times the money behind a candidate than the law would allow them to contribute to his own campaign fund. During the 1981–82 election period, some 2,000 PACs contributed up to $90 million to congressional campaigns. Corporate and trade association PACs ("big business") contributed over twice as much as labor PACs (unions). PAC spending on federal campaigns was expected to reach half a billion dollars by 1992.

One of the most powerful union PACs is the National Education Association, whose teachers won from President Carter the creation of a Federal Department of Education. In 1982 its

PAC spent nearly $1.5 million to back 334 candidates in the mid-term elections and helped elect 250 of them.

In 1983 Republican Party leaders appealed for a removal of federal limits on political party expenditures for candidates. "Surveys repeatedly show that the public is overwhelmingly opposed to taxpayers' financing of elections," declared Nevada Senator Paul Laxalt, Republican Party chairman.

The change would lessen the influence of PACs, said Indiana Senator Richard Lugar, chairman of the Senate Republican Campaign Committee, and strengthen the role of the parties. Democrats objected because the Republicans, with access to much wealthier private financing, would benefit most.

The Democrats, meanwhile, went to a federal court to try to block conservative PACs from spending tens of millions of dollars to reelect President Reagan in 1984.

In 1983 three of the six declared candidates for the Democratic Party's presidential nomination—former Vice-President Walter Mondale, Colorado Senator Gary Hart, and Florida Governor Reubin Askew—declared they wanted no PAC support. "A president who owes his election to narrow interests," Hart explained, "risks an administration that is owned by them."

It is unquestionably true that lobbies can, through campaign contributions, affect the outcome of elections. And to the extent that they can claim credit for a candidate's victory, they can influence his decisions while in office.

The problem may never be solved until the amount of money that can be spent on election campaigns is strictly curbed by law. This change would probably require a rigid shortening of the campaign period to reduce expenses; a ban on private contributions or PACs; public funding of candidates; and apportioned free TV time for political speeches and debates.

Such reforms might mean the saving of vast millions in unnecessary expenses, fairer opportunities for all candidates, and more honest representative government for all of us.

15

Stealing Votes

In a special Georgia election held shortly after World War II to replace deceased Governor Eugene Talmadge, his son Herman was elected. *Presumably* elected, that is. It turned out that 32 votes for him were cast by the same man under 32 different names. Only 10 of 48 write-in votes for him were legitimate; at least two voters were dead men; five had moved away; five said they hadn't voted; and another dozen voters couldn't be found. The *Atlanta Journal* won a Pulitzer Prize for exposing Herman Talmadge's stolen election.

There are many ways to steal votes. Some candidates' supporters have done it by outright fraud; some by frightening opposition voters away from the polls; some by using technicalities to disenfranchise the opposition; some by rigging election results.

Stealing votes has a long and dishonorable tradition. Colonial parties in America used mobs to terrorize opposition voters away from the polls. One of the first election riots occurred in 1742 in the Pennsylvania colony, when Scotch-Irish frontiersmen making up the Proprietary Party sought to disenfranchise Quakers. They organized a mob of 70 sailors, arming them with clubs that they "flourished over their heads with loud huzzas, and in a furious and tumultuous manner approached the place of election."

The polls were on a courthouse balcony, to which voters mounted from a street staircase. Rushing the staircase, the mob clubbed and drove off all Quakers seeking to vote. But the ordinarily non-violent Quakers quickly organized their own mob.

Throwing the sailors off the staircase, they locked up 50. The election then proceeded peacefully, with a Quaker victory.

Federalist President John Adams feared the votes of French and Irish immigrants who favored Jefferson over him. So he passed the Alien and Sedition Acts to prevent aliens from becoming citizens for 14 years. Anyone daring to criticize this theft of votes was thrown in jail. Becoming president, Jefferson instantly made the Acts dead letters, so that it was easier for aliens to become citizens and vote.

In the first half of the nineteenth century, as Democrats succeeded in organizing the immigrant vote in the big cities, members of the Know-Nothing Party intensified their efforts to keep foreign-born voters from the polls. The immigrants fought back. Killings on Election Day were commonplace during the 1840s and 1850s.

In 1855, Know-Nothing mobs in Louisville, Kentucky, took control of the polls, beating, shooting, and stabbing Irish and German immigrants seeking to vote. When some Irish killed several rioters, enraged mobs invaded their neighborhoods, burning buildings and shooting down fleeing tenants. Twenty people died. Know-Nothing candidates swept the elections, with almost no Irish or German votes recorded.

In New York City from 1860 to 1871, police looked the other way when Boss Tweed's gangs of Tammany toughs invaded election precincts to frighten off or beat up opposition voters. Tweed also bought and bribed votes and rigged elections, until the Tammany machine was finally overthrown.

During that same period down South, it was the Ku Klux Klan that stole elections. In 1868 a congressional investigation found that in the three weeks prior to Election Day, 2,000 blacks had been murdered, wounded, or flogged in Louisiana. The message to blacks was loud and clear.

In the late nineteenth century, organizations proliferated whose aim was to stop "undesirables" from voting. These included the Immigration Restriction League in the East; the

American Protective Association in the Midwest and Far West; the Klan and similar organizations in the South. They sought to drive away from the polls not only immigrants and blacks, but also Catholics, Jews, Mexican Americans, and Chinese.

In some cities, political bosses stole elections by outright fraud. Shortly after the turn of the century, muckraker Lincoln Steffens reported that St. Louis boss Edward R. Butler would walk out of a polling place and call across a cordon of police to men lounging at the curb, "Are there any more repeaters out here that want to vote again?"

Fraud was even more blatant among Philadelphians. Steffens reported that they had "no more rights at the polls than the Negroes down South. . . . The machine controls the whole process of voting, and practices fraud at every stage. The assessor's list is the voting list, and the assessor is the machine's man." A Municipal League report revealed 250 votes cast in a ward with less than 100 registered voters, the list padded with the names of dead and imaginary persons.

In one Philadelphia election, some 80,000 out of 204,000 votes were found to be fraudulent. Police had enabled repeaters to vote "without intimidation," arresting only voters who dared to protest. With the machine's own officials counting the ballots, there was no way its candidates could lose.

During the Prohibition era in Chicago, Al Capone and other gangsters contributed $300,000 to the reelection of Republican Mayor William Hale Thompson in 1927. On Election Day two Democratic precinct clubs were bombed, two election judges kidnapped and beaten, and voters driven from the polls by gangsters opening fire. Other voters prudently stayed home as police squads cruised the city with machine guns and tear gas. There were very few votes against Mayor Thompson.

In 1948 stealing votes was routine in Louisiana's Plaquemine Parish, bossed by Leander Perez. When Russell Long won election to the Senate that year, he freely admitted receiving several thousand votes stolen for him by Perez. When Perez introduced a law letting him plunder the local treasury, the parish's 3,000-odd registered voters were credited with 5,361 votes in favor and 3 votes against.

During U.S. Senate Judiciary Committee hearings on why so few blacks were registered to vote in his parish, Perez explained that some white Louisiana voters charged $10 for their votes, and others charged $5, while blacks and poor whites could be bribed for only $2. "People of low character," he said, "are a little cheaper. . . . The $5 and $10 voters would not ride in the same automobile with the $2 voters when they are being brought to the polls. It was beneath their dignity."

The astonished investigator asked, "You segregated the voters according to how much you paid them?"

"Yes, sir," replied Perez blandly. He denounced any federal intervention to protect the rights of black voters as both "un-American" and "communistic."

"That," snapped Republican Senator Everett Dirksen, "is as stupid a statement as has ever been uttered in this hearing!"

Stealing elections in the old South was routine until the Civil Rights Act of 1957 established a Federal Civil Rights Commission to investigate complaints and report to the president and congress. Before then, even in communities where blacks far outnumbered whites, white officials won almost all public offices by the simple expedient of barring black voters through poll taxes that they could not afford and through hard literacy tests that only blacks were compelled to take.

Literacy tests were also used in California to exclude Hispanic citizens who didn't speak English. Ironically, the original U.S.-Mexican treaty required all California laws and proceedings to be in both Spanish and English, with the rights of Spanish-speaking citizens respected. The law that kept them from voting was passed "to protect the purity of the ballot box from the corrupting influences of the disturbing elements that come from abroad." The California Supreme Court finally set this law aside as unconstitutional in 1970.

One of the oldest and most skillful methods of stealing votes is called "gerrymandering." It was named after a signer of the Declaration of Independence, Massachusetts Governor Elbridge Gerry, who re-districted his state in 1812 in such a way that his party could win more seats in the legislature with far fewer voters than the opposition needed.

Gerrymandering works this way: Voting-district boundary lines are redrawn so that, say, a district of 40,000 largely Republican voters can elect only one representative, while another district carved out of only 3,000 largely Democratic voters is given one representative also. In effect, the voting power of 37,000 voters has been stolen.

When Gerry re-carved voting districts for this purpose, the boundaries of one had so curious a shape that a legislator suggested it resembled a salamander. "No," replied one wit dryly, "a Gerrymander." The name stuck to the political trick.

In the late 1950s a group of blacks charged Alabama with gerrymandering the election district of Tuskegee from a square shape "into a strangely irregular 28-sided figure," which had the effect of "fencing Negro citizens out of Tuskegee."

The Supreme Court rejected Alabama's claim that it had the right to shape its political subdivisions as it saw fit. No state legislature, said Justice Felix Frankfurter in 1960, could isolate "a racial minority for special discriminatory treatment." Three years later, Justice William O. Douglas upheld the right of the federal government to rule on the fairness of districting. "The conception of political equality . . . can mean only one thing—one person, one vote," he declared. Otherwise, he pointed out, a resident of Georgia's smallest county would have 99 times the political power and influence of a citizen of Atlanta.

All state legislatures were finally forced to undertake reapportionment on a one-person, one-vote basis. District boundaries were redrawn to equalize the number of people in each election district, regardless of geographical size.

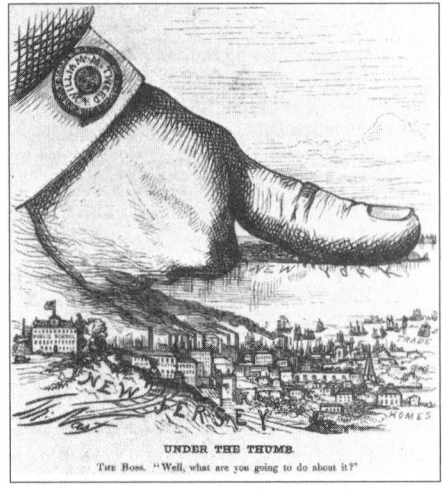

From 1860 to 1871, Boss Tweed bought and bribed voters in New York and New Jersey, putting voters "under his thumb." WOOD ENGRAVING AFTER THOMAS NAST IN *HARPER'S WEEKLY*, JUNE 10, 1871.

Fraud was blatant in Philadelphia, Pennsylvania elections in the late 1800s and early 1900s. In one election, some 80,000 of 204,000 votes were fraudulent. Voting lists were sometimes supplemented by the names of dead or nonexistent men. WOOD ENGRAVING FROM SKETCHES BY BERGHAUS IN FRANK LESLIE'S ILLUSTRATED NEWSPAPER, 1872.

The voter in this 1837 cartoon could well have been a 1948 voter, for that was when Louisiana Plaquemine Parish boss Leander Perez went so far as to segregate bribed voters by how much he had paid them. The range was from two dollars to ten dollars. LITHOGRAPH BY N. SARONY.

This cartoon shows the 1871 arrest of Boss Tweed, with the ghostly figure of an avenging Justice standing over him. WOOD ENGRAVING AFTER THOMAS NAST IN *HARPER'S WEEKLY*, 1871.

Politicians still sought to carve election districts in such a way as to tip the balance of power in them as far as possible in favor of one or the other party. In 1983 Republican George Deukmejian of California threw Democrats into an uproar by announcing a special election to try to redistrict the state so that the Republicans could win the legislature.

No other group of Americans was rendered as powerless through having their votes stolen as Southern blacks, even as late as the 1960s. After the passage of civil rights acts, when Northern sympathizers went South to aid in black voter-registration drives, many were terrorized and beaten. Some were murdered.

Fannie Lou Hamer, a black militant, reported in 1964, "I tried to register in 1962. I was fired the same day, after working on the plantation for eighteen years. . . . When my employer found out I'd been down to the courthouse, she said I'd have to withdraw or be fired. 'We are not ready for this in Mississippi' she said. 'Well, I wasn't registering for you,' I told her, 'I was trying to register for myself.'"

One voter-registration drive was mounted in 80 percent black Lowndes County, Alabama, in the spring of 1965, because out of 15,000 resident blacks, not a single one had been allowed to register.

The Voting Rights Act of 1965 suspended literacy tests and other means used to bar blacks from the polls. Federal examiners were appointed for all voting districts where less than half the population was registered to vote. Anyone trying to stop a citizen from registering or voting was made subject to arrest on criminal charges. Shortly afterward the Supreme Court ruled all poll taxes unconstitutional.

The effect of the Voting Rights Act in Mississippi was impressive. Before its passage, only 35,000 blacks had been registered in the whole state; after passage, the number jumped to

Elbridge Gerry, looking rather satisfied in this portrait, redistricted his state of Massachusetts in 1812 so that his party would win more seats in the legislature. Gerrymandering is one of the most effective ways of stealing elections, but no state can get away with it today. ENGRAVING BY J. B. LONGAGRE FROM A DRAWING BY VANDERLYN.

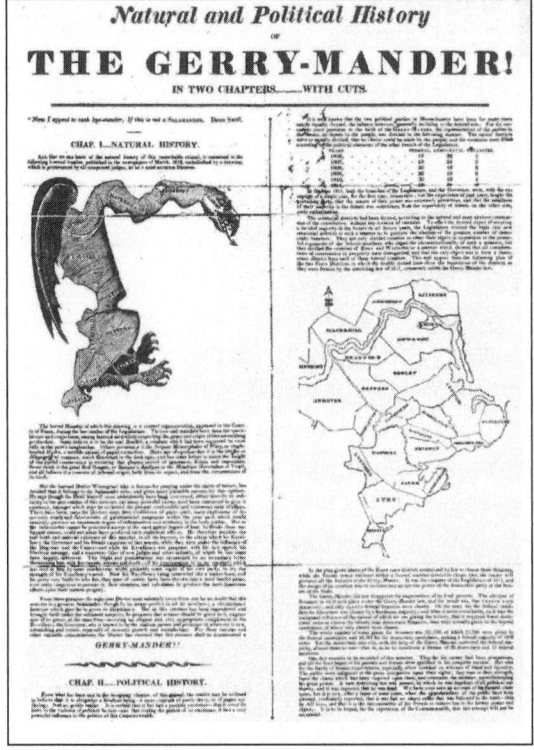

When a legislator suggested in 1812 that the boundaries of one newly founded district resembled a salamander, someone else dubbed it a "Gerrymander." Gerrymandering became the subject of political cartoons such as this. BROADSIDE, 1815.

President Lyndon Johnson signed the Voting Rights Act in 1965, which suspended literacy tests used to bar blacks from the polls.

200,000. By November, 1967, they were able to elect 22 blacks to public office in the state.

Even so, black votes were still being stolen by 1983, when black leader Rev. Jesse Jackson challenged William Reynolds, chief of the Justice Department's Civil Rights Division, to join him in rural Mississippi for a firsthand look at voting rights abuses. Reynolds discovered registration offices that closed at county officials' whims; employers who refused to let blacks leave work to register; polling places moved from black to white neighborhoods without notice; black voters turned away by white imposters posing as federal officials.

"I never heard of anything like that before," Reynolds admitted. He dispatched federal examiners to five Mississippi counties to stop such abuses and register black voters.

Today, because of changes in the law and stricter enforcement, elections are generally more honest, for the most part, than they were in darker periods of our history. There will always be some vote stealing here and there, just as there is some dishonesty in law, medicine, business, or any other facet of American life. But the vast majority of us can count on voting, and on our vote counting—unless we rob ourselves of our vote by failing to go to the polls.

16

"What Difference Does My Vote Make?"

Ever hear of President Charles Evans Hughes?

You would have, if just one more voter in each California district had voted for him, sending him to the White House instead of letting Woodrow Wilson remain in it in 1916.

Many Americans don't bother exercising their franchise, feeling that the vote of one more person isn't going to make any difference in the results of an election. Some explain that they're too busy or have more important things to do. Others shrug and say that they're simply not interested in politics.

In 1964 a public-opinion poll found that three out of four Americans trusted the government to do what was right most of the time. But another poll in 1978 found only 28 percent expressing such trust, with 65 percent by then convinced that the government was run on behalf of a few big interests.

One might have expected such disillusionment to result in a widespread determination to "vote the rascals out." Instead, 65 percent expressed the belief that ordinary people had little to say about what the government does. Their apathy was reflected by a sharp decline in registration and voting.

Yet even presidential races have often been so close that they were decided by the few extra votes of citizens who cared enough to cast their ballots. In 1884 Grover Cleveland was elected over James G. Blaine when, out of over a million New Yorkers who voted, just 1,149 more chose Cleveland.

And in 1960 John F. Kennedy was sent to the White House instead of Richard Nixon by an average of less than a single vote per election precinct.

Even world history could have been changed by a single vote. That was the margin by which Adolf Hitler was elected leader of the Nazis in a 1932 party election. Had he lost by a single vote instead, there might have been no World War II.

Sometimes minorities feel discouraged from voting because they are always outnumbered. Then something happens that lets them discover their strength when anger drives them to vote.

After the Civil War, President Andrew Johnson sought to pacify white Southerners by weakening the Civil Rights Act. In 1868 angry blacks went to the polls in record numbers to vote against him. The black vote proved decisive in sending Ulysses S. Grant to the White House.

Since 1872, there have been eight presidents who went to the White House with less than a majority of the popular vote— Hayes, Garfield, Cleveland, Harrison, Wilson, Truman, Kennedy, and Nixon. The significance of this is that had the small number of third-party votes gone to their opponents instead, those eight presidents would not have been elected. The importance of even a handful of votes cannot be overestimated.

While your vote may or may not be crucial in an election, casting it gives you the healthy satisfaction of acting out your convictions. "Always vote for a principle, though you vote alone," advised John Quincy Adams, "and you may cherish the sweet reflection that your vote is never lost."

Some citizens who ignore the polls on Election Day feel that it doesn't matter because plenty of others will be voting. If everyone felt the same way, of course, there would be no elections and, in a little while, no more democracy.

"The whole system of American government rests on the ballot box," President Calvin Coolidge declared in 1926. "Unless citizens do their duties there, such a system of government is doomed to failure."

One might expect young Americans who pass their eighteenth birthdays to rush enthusiastically to the ballot box in an election year to exercise their right to choose the leaders they want. Ironically, records show that young people 18 through 25 have the poorest voting turnout of any age group. A 1974 Census study found only about 40 percent registered to vote.

This lack of participation disturbed presidential candidate Hubert Humphrey, who resented criticism of American politics by youths who failed to vote. "If you think politics is a little dirty," he challenged them, "why don't you get a bar of Ivory soap and get in and clean it up instead of sitting out there in the bleachers?"

At a 1980 rally of Reagan supporters, Paul Weyrich, director of the Committee for the Survival of a Free Congress, admitted frankly, "I don't want everyone to vote. Our leverage in the election quite candidly goes up as the voting populace goes down. We have no responsibility, moral or otherwise, to turn out our opposition. It's important to turn out those who are with us."

If you have the vote and fail to use it, you may allow a candidate you oppose to slip into office by a slim margin. Then, despite barely escaping defeat, he may claim that his election represents a "mandate from the people" to put into effect the very laws you fear and oppose, ignoring the fact he was elected by only a minority of registered voters.

One of the most valuable services any young American can perform, whether of voting age or below, is to help get out the vote, making certain that as many eligible voters as possible register and express their choices at the polls. The larger the turnout, the more the results will represent the true will of the majority. The smaller the turnout, the easier it is for pressure groups to steamroller an election.

"A registration and get-out-the-vote drive is hard work," admitted John Bailey, a past chairman of the Democratic National Committee. "There is little glamour in it. But it is the most essential of all political activity. It is what puts the votes in the ballot box on Election Day."

There is a wide choice of volunteer jobs awaiting those willing to join in getting out the vote. Needed are checkers to work at the polls and note registered voters who haven't shown up; messengers to convey this information; telephoners to contact the absentees; drivers to take voters to the polls; and baby-sitters to take care of youngsters while their parents vote.

When racist opposition was intense in the South during the early 1960s, many idealistic Northern youths volunteered to go South in buses to help get out the black vote. They persisted in the drive even when some were shot, beaten, gassed, whipped, and jailed. One youth, his arm in a sling after being beaten by a police baton, told a reporter, "If blacks can't register to vote, then what's all this democracy we hear so much about?" Since that drive, the number of black voters in the South has jumped to over 4 million.

More and more American blacks up North, too, were realizing that the answer to many of their problems lay in getting a better deal from their local, state, and federal governments. And the only way to do that was to get out the black vote to support candidates who would work toward that goal.

When black Harold Washington ran for mayor of Chicago in 1983, his campaign attracted a huge black voter turnout. Among black youths 18 to 25, only 10 percent of whom normally voted, fully 90 percent flocked to the polls. Washington's election thrilled and inspired blacks everywhere.

As a direct result, over 100 black young volunteers showed up in Boston to organize voter-registration drives for the 1984 presidential election, even though this was 19 months off.

What difference can one vote make? In 1932, Adolf Hitler was elected leader of the Nazi Party by only one vote. In a less spectacular but nevertheless close election, Grover Cleveland was elected president in 1884. PHOTO COPYRIGHT APRIL 1, 1908.

Like Cleveland, President John F. Kennedy was elected to the office by less than a majority of the popular vote. Other presidents with this distinction: Hayes, Garfield, Harrison, Wilson, Truman, and Nixon.

"It's unheard of," marveled black City Councilor Bruce Boiling. "Generally people don't think about registration until two months before the election."

Other ethnic groups like Mexican Americans and Cuban Americans were impressed. They began cooperating with blacks to support candidates pledged to help minorities. All political parties began paying more attention to the minority vote.

"In the final analysis, it is up to you," Patrick J. McGarvey, a former CIA agent, reminded American voters. "It is the boom of your voice that will bring about the necessary changes. As an individual you no doubt have a feeling of impotence when it comes to influencing your government. Collectively, however, you have tremendous impact. It requires only that you get a slight ground swell started."

Turning out the vote is one way to do that. Any citizen of any age with a burning desire to stop injustice and a willingness to get others to sign on is a one-person dynamo.

"What old people say you cannot do, you try and find that you can," Thoreau advised youth in Walden. "Old deeds for old people, and new deeds for new."

Thomas Carlyle reminded us, "Every new opinion, at its starting, is precisely in a minority of one." And as Henrik Ibsen pointed out, the majority of· today was the minority of twenty years ago, because it takes that long for progressive ideas to prevail and transform popular opinion.

If you want to participate in getting out the vote, you can join 120,000 Teen Age Republicans in any of 50 states, or the Young Democrats of America in over 40 states. The American Student Association has branches in many colleges. COPE, the AFL-CIO's political-action arm, recruits young volunteers. The League of Women Voters is a nonpartisan organization devoted to working for open and responsive government. The National Organization for Women (NOW) works for policies that will bring women into the mainstream of American society. And there are many third parties that would eagerly welcome the aid of as many young volunteers as they can get.

Check your local phone book for the names and phone numbers of the organization you'd like to work with. If it isn't listed, phone the local office of your state or federal representative for this information.

It's your country. If you care about it, use your vote when you have it, and help your fellow citizens use theirs.

Or would you rather turn the country over to political bosses to run it as they please?

17

Is Your Job Done When Your Candidates Win?

In 1964, while the Vietnam civil war raged, Americans voted for Lyndon Johnson as president because of his promise of a "Great Society" program, which would end poverty in America, and his assurances about Vietnam: "We don't want our American boys to do the fighting for Asian boys. We don't want to get . . . tied down in a land war in Asia."

Yet Johnson let his Great Society program go by default, throwing America's resources instead into sending half a million American boys to fight the most unpopular war in our history. His broken promises outraged millions of Democrats who had voted for him. They flooded the White House with tons of protesting mail and staged huge anti-war demonstrations.

Johnson did not dare to run for another term

As when your favorite baseball, football, or basketball team wins the season's honors, it's highly satisfying when your favorite candidate or political party wins an election. But the consequences are vastly more important. One week after a sports team is victorious, the event is ancient history and has no further impact on your life. But for the length of an election term, the victorious candidates or party will affect your life by the laws they pass.

If you have voted for or helped get out the vote for the winning side, you may feel that your job is done. Your choices are in place, and now it's up to them to do all the things they promised during the campaign. It's okay now to sit back and "let George do it." Right?

Wrong. Often much of what has been promised during a campaign turns out to be empty oratory. Elected officials or the party may give halfhearted lip service to the goals they promised to the electorate, but then they take no real action to achieve them through legislation. Or they may enact a watered-down, weak, ineffective law that is really a betrayal of their pledge.

Moreover, as new problems arise, a candidate you elected may take a position in dealing with them that you strongly oppose. Just because you've elected leaders to represent you, does that mean you're obligated to support everything they do? Those in office are responsible to the people who elected them. They need to hear from their constituents when their decisions are disappointing, especially in issues of such life-and-death importance as peace and war.

A case in point was the decision of President James Polk to declare war on Mexico in 1846 in order to seize huge areas of Mexican land. Far from docilely accepting this decision, the voters of every New England state reprimanded him sharply. The Massachusetts legislature even flirted with charges of treason by resolving that it was the patriotic duty of "all good citizens to join in efforts to arrest this war."

Similarly, in 1916 Woodrow Wilson campaigned on the slogan, "He kept us out of the war." And just one year earlier he had promised, "We will not ask our young men to spend the best years of their lives making soldiers of themselves!"

Then in 1917 Wilson reversed himself and took the country into World War I. There was deep bitterness among those who had voted for him to keep America at peace, and many dared to speak out openly against the war. Hundreds, including Eugene Debs, were imprisoned under a new Sedition Act rushed through Congress to make "disloyal language" a felony.

No group of Americans is better qualified to testify as to the broken promises of government officials than Native Americans. Despite dozens of treaties signed with Native American tribes, the government has broken almost every one, seizing their best lands and driving them onto arid reservations.

Government officials turned a deaf ear to their complaints until finally Senator Robert Kennedy headed a new subcommittee to investigate conditions on the reservations. "I am doing my best," he told a group of Native American students in one state, "to get you your civil rights."

"Never mind our civil rights, Senator," one young man replied wryly. "Just get us back our country!"

Voters weary of being deceived about Vietnam under the Johnson administration listened to Republican candidate Richard Nixon promise, "It's time we once again had an open administration—open to the ideas from the people and open in its communication with the people—an administration of open doors, open eyes, and open minds." He also promised voters an administration dedicated to "law and order."

Voters elected him in 1968, only to get an administration that proved one of the most dishonest and lawless administrations in the history of the country—the administration that expanded the Vietnam War for four more years and that ended in the Watergate scandal.

But as Nixon himself noted in his book *Six Crises,* "Voters quickly forget what a man says." He proved it by winning a second term despite his broken promises, largely because the full extent of his criminal behavior had not yet been exposed by Election Day of 1972. When it was, however, public outrage was so great that an avalanche of angry mail forced even Republican congressmen to announce they would vote for his impeachment.

The media serve America well when they remind voters of the discrepancy between what politicians say and what they do. This makes it more difficult for them to shift positions when it is politically expedient. When California Senator Alan Cranston announced his candidacy for the 1984 Democratic presidential nomination, he sought to unite all the nuclear-freeze forces behind him. He declared himself "convinced that, in the long run, we cannot revive our economy—or save our society—until we end the incredibly dangerous, shamefully expensive arms race." That won much liberal support.

But the media pointed out that Cranston had supported President Reagan's decision to revive the costly B-1 bomber, which would be built in Cranston's home state. Was expediency, the media asked, more important than principle?

Australian correspondent Elisabeth Wynhausen, stationed in Washington, found discrepancies between President Reagan's claims and his performance. Checking on his claim that as governor of California he had reduced the public payroll, she found that during his governorship, the number of state public servants had increased by 21 percent instead.

Campaigning for president, he had promised a balanced budget by 1984. Elected, he declared that it was unrealistic not to expect a national deficit of $100 billion at least. He had campaigned with promises to weed out "waste, fraud, and mismanagement." Elected, he had demanded record billions for the Pentagon, which all government agencies agreed was the worst culprit in waste, fraud, and mismanagement. Campaigning, he had attacked arms control negotiations with the Soviet Union as "appeasement." Elected, he promised to speed up arms control talks with the Russians.

Widespread public protest forced Reagan to backtrack on some of his initiatives. When he violated the 1980 Republican platform plank opposing the withholding of a percentage of interest and dividends for the Internal Revenue Service, a deluge of protest mail caused Congress to delay his proposal indefinitely.

Even *Reader's Digest*, an enthusiastic Reagan supporter, criticized him for his appointees to head the Environmental Protection Agency (EPA), whom he praised as well qualified to provide the nation with clear air and water. The *Digest* revealed that, by secret agreement with White House officials, the agency's assignment to clean up dangerous dumps and spills was sabotaged, protecting the industries responsible.

A different Republican president, Dwight D. Eisenhower, had declared, "There may be some cynics who think that a platform is just a list of platitudes to lure the naive voter—a sort of facade behind which candidates sneak into power and then do just as they please. I am not one of these."

Most historians agreed that he was not.

It needs to be pointed out that some candidates do honestly try to keep their campaign promises when they win election. Often, however, they depend heavily on campaign funds contributed by special interests that expect legislation favoring them. Such candidates have to weigh conscience against practicality. They may listen to their conscience if enough voters pressure them to vote in the public interest.

There are several ways you can try to hold elected candidates to their campaign promises, forcing them to pay attention to your disagreement with their policies. The easiest and best is to write them letters. Representatives and senators, state as well as national, are sensitive to voter reactions in their mail. So are presidents, governors, and state, county, and local officials. They also pay attention to letters to the editors of newspapers and magazines, because such letters are read and considered by thousands of voters.

Public officials pay particular attention to letters of protest from those who have helped to elect them, whether by contributions, votes, or helping in their campaigns. They hope that they can count on the same support for their reelection campaigns. Thus it becomes important for them either to change their stand or to persuade dissatisfied supporters that their stand is a correct one.

Another way to express disapproval of elected officials' behavior in office is through state primary elections. When you vote against a president, governor, senator, representative,

A vote for James Polk in 1844 was a vote for U.S. territorial expansion, but when he declared war on Mexico in 1846 so the U.S. could seize Mexican land, every New England state opposed his decision. LITHOGRAPH BY P. HAAS, 1844.

When the Narragansett Indians offered shelter to Roger Williams, little did the Native Americans realize what was to follow. Despite dozens of treaties that U.S. government officials signed, the government broke almost every one and stole the Indians' land, confining them to reservations. ENGRAVING BY J. C. ARMYTAGE AFTER A. H. WRAY.

mayor, or other elected official in a state primary, you are sending that candidate a message. The size of the official's reduced vote lets him know clearly how much he has failed to live up to his constituents' expectations.

If enough voters are disillusioned, and the official is defeated, his successor will also get the message. The chances are then brighter that this time you will get the kind of administration you voted for.

18

How Other Countries Choose Their Leaders

An intriguing view of early American elections through European eyes was provided in 1835 by a young Frenchman, Count Alexis de Tocque-ville, when he wrote a book about his visit to America four years earlier. Tocqueville was dubious about French interest in borrowing the American practice of universal suffrage. He felt that the animosity of the masses toward the better-educated classes would result in the election of uneducated incompetents to public office.

That had already happened in America, he noted. The election of roughnecks like Andrew Jackson, Sam Houston, and Davy Crockett to public office showed "how far wrong the people can go . . . to be represented by people of their own kind." It was deplorable that a "David Crockett, who has no education, can read with difficulty, has no property, no fixed residence, but passes his life hunting," should be considered qualified to help make the nation's laws in Congress.

Tocqueville sympathized with leading Americans who refused to seek public office: "To win votes one has to descend to maneuvers that disgust distinguished men. You have to haunt the taverns and dispute with the populace: That's what they call *electioneering* in America."

He expected all New World democracies to become tyrannies through the abuse of power by their elected incompetents.

"It's through this . . . evil," Tocqueville predicted darkly, "that the American republics will perish."

The election of President Andrew Jackson horrified French Count Alexis de Tocqueville, who wrote that it exemplified "how far wrong the people can go . . . to be represented by people of their own kind." This picture is of Jackson's inaugural reception in 1828. COLONIAL AQUA-TINT BY ROBERT CRUIKSHANK IN THE PLAYFAIR PAPERS, 1841.

The secret ballot is as old as the ancient Roman Republic, where it was first adopted in 139 B.C. But the kings who ruled Europe for centuries afterward did not take kindly to any kind of ballot, secret or otherwise. Prince Clemens von Metternich, who forged the Holy Alliance of European monarchs in 1815, warned them that a growing demand for popular elections threatened their thrones.

"Rule must come from above, not below," he cautioned.

But the spread of the Industrial Revolution doomed the old order. Constitutional government gradually spread throughout Europe in the nineteenth century, even though many monarchs were allowed to remain on their thrones as figureheads.

For the first half of the century, votes had to be cast openly under the grim observation of powerful monarchist factions, who could mark opposing voters for reprisal. Finally public pressure forced France to adopt the secret ballot in 1852. Italy followed the trend in 1859. England resisted secret voting at parliamentary and municipal elections until 1872.

The twentieth century saw the rise of a new threat to the institution of free elections in Europe—dictatorship.

When the old Czarist regime in Russia was overturned by revolution in 1917, the Russian people won the right to vote for the first time in their history. But not for long. The Bolshevik Party soon seized power, substituting a "dictatorship of the proletariat" for elected public officials. Only a small band of dedicated Marxists, the communists insisted, was qualified to govern a nation for the benefit of the masses. Elections were scorned as a bourgeois system by which the ruling classes deceived and controlled the people for profit.

The next important challenge to free elections came in the Italy of King Victor Emmanuel, when Fascist leader Benito Mussolini ran for a seat in the Chamber of Deputies in 1921. His Blackshirt followers organized torchlight parades, tossed bombs into socialist meetings, and beat up opponents and forced castor oil down their throats. A year later, Mussolini led a march on Rome, seizing power as prime minister. "We Fascists throw poisonous ideas about liberty on the rubbish heap!" he roared in a balcony speech to a huge crowd. "Italians are tired of liberty. They want and need order, authority, discipline!" Although he scoffed at voting as a "childish game," Mussolini held fraudulent elections in 1924 to "prove" to the world that the Italian people supported his dictatorship. His Blackshirt squads broke up rival meetings, terrorized voters at the polls, stuffed the ballot boxes, then tallied the votes and announced their leader's "victory."

From then until Mussolini's downfall during World War II, the only elections held were those in which Fascists alone were permitted to run. "I prefer fifty thousand rifles to five thousand votes," Mussolini once cried. "A party in power has the duty to defend itself against all!"

Mussolini's example inspired Germany's Adolf Hitler, leader of the Nazi Party, whose Brownshirts waged street warfare against working-class and Jewish districts. By 1932 Hitler had captured over a third of the popular electoral vote and was able to compel his appointment as chancellor of Germany. He lost no time in seizing total power as dictator.

"The man who feels called upon to govern a people has no right to say, 'If you want me or summon me, I will cooperate,'" he explained. "No! It is his duty to step forward!"

That was the end of free elections in Nazi Germany.

Another dictatorship arose in Spain, when Generalissimo Francisco Franco, with military aid from Hitler and Mussolini, led a revolt against the legally elected republican (Loyalist) government in 1936. After the Fascists had shot their way to power three years later, Franco proclaimed himself Caudillo, Chief of State for Life. His firing squads executed 30,000 republican prisoners. He ruled Spain with an iron fist until his death in 1975, when liberal King Juan Carlos took power and subsequently restored free elections to Spain.

Portugal became a republic after the overthrow of its monarchy in 1910. But in the next sixteen years, there were 24 revolutions and 44 changes of government. Finally, in 1926 the military seized power, establishing a dictatorship under Antonio de Oliveira Salazar. When several thousand Portuguese signed a petition urging free elections, Salazar had his secret police locate these "Red intellectuals"[5] for "correction."

Pressured by Portugal's Western allies, Salazar announced elections for 1949. When a political opponent took him seriously and tried to run, Salazar denounced him as a public enemy, compelling him to withdraw his candidacy. The tactic was repeated in 1951. Unopposed, Salazar "won" each time.

Not until 1958 did an air force general, Humberto Delgado, dare defy Salazar by stumping the country to campaign against him. Rigging the election as usual, the dictator declared Delgado the loser. The Bishop of Oporto indignantly cried fraud. Salazar promptly went on TV to announce that he was abolishing popular elections and punishing all "agitators." Delgado, who prudently fled to Brazil, was subsequently murdered.

Illness forced Salazar's retirement in 1968. After several succeeding military dictatorships, popular discontent finally restored elections to Portugal in 1975.

For centuries most Asian people were governed by either autocratic monarchs or Western colonial powers. The first break in this pattern came in 1912, when forces led by republican Sun Yat-sen finally overthrew the Manchu dynasty in China. But his republic was quickly subverted by warlords and their ally, Chiang Kai-shek, who kept China a dictatorship.

In 1948 communist forces led by Mao Tse-tung overthrew Chiang and the warlords, only to establish a Marxist dictatorship under which free elections were still forbidden. That situation still prevails in the China of today.

In 1954, inspired by Mao, Vietnam communist leader Ho Chi Minh led Vietminh revolutionists against ruling French colonial forces and defeated them. A peace settlement at Geneva was guaranteed by the British, the Russians, the Chinese, and the Americans, who withdrew, however, while promising not to interfere with the Geneva Accords.

This agreement decreed that the French were to withdraw to the south, and Ho Chi Minh's forces to the north, to prepare for nationwide elections two years later that would determine a unified government for all Vietnamese.

"I have never talked or corresponded with a person knowledgeable in Indochinese affairs," President Eisenhower subsequently admitted, "who did not agree that had the elections

Italian dictator Benito Mussolini held fraudulent elections in 1924 to prove that people supported him. His Blackshirt squads terrorized voters and counted the votes themselves to guarantee his victory. Mussolini's tactics were a source of inspiration to Adolf Hitler and his Brownshirts. PHOTO BY UNDERWOOD & UNDERWOOD.

Hitler and Mussolini aided Generalissimo Francisco Franco in establishing his dictatorship in Spain. Franco proclaimed himself Chief of State for Life, and he had 30,000 republican prisoners executed to seal that proclamation. He died in 1975, after ruling Spain for almost 40 years. PHOTO BY ALFONSO.

been held as of the time of the fighting, possibly 80 percent of the population would have voted for Ho Chi Minh."

They never got the chance because Eisenhower's secretary of state, John Foster Dulles, was determined to sabotage the Geneva Accords. He set up a puppet government in South Vietnam, which rejected the scheduled elections. The result was the disastrous Vietnam War, involving an American intervention with troops that was denounced by most nations in the world.

When outraged American public opinion finally forced the Nixon administration to sign a peace that extracted U.S. forces from the Vietnamese quagmire, North Vietnam quickly overran and defeated South Vietnam. They could then have held the long-postponed national elections and probably have won. The elections were never held. As in other countries where the communists won power militarily, there were no further free elections. Elections represented a dangerous precedent for the future.

After World War II, African nations began to fight off the yoke of colonialism. The first to succeed was the Belgian Congo, now called Zaire, which won its freedom and the right to hold its first election in 1960. Almost 200 tribes speaking 400 different languages and dialects participated. Murders of each other's candidates were not uncommon. Polling booths were wrecked, election officials beaten. Rival tribes speared each other in the streets. The elections left some 60 dead, hundreds wounded.

The omens were not too bright for the peaceful transition of other former African colonies to new democracies.

Closer to home, the Cuban people had suffered under the tyrannical and corrupt rule of U.S.-supported dictator Fulgencio Batista until 1959, when he was overthrown by a popular revolution led by Fidel Castro. Castro instituted sweeping reforms benefiting the poor Cuban masses at the expense of the middle classes, many of whom fled to the United States.

Most journalists who covered the Cuban revolution agreed that if elections had been held, Castro would have been the overwhelming choice of the people. But he resisted all demands for elections, saying, "They would be unfair because I would be swept into office."

At a May Day rally in 1961, he told a huge crowd that elections were unnecessary: "A revolution expressing the will of the people is an election every day, not every four years; it is a constant meeting with the people, like this meeting. The old politicians could never have gathered as many votes as there are people here tonight to support the revolution."

When he asked the crowd to express their will, they roared back the answer he wanted: "No elections!"

One bitter opponent, Urrutia Lleo, declared, "Castro's maneuver was successful. He knew that the people would reject the kind of elections that had been held so often before in Cuba, and he did not offer them better ones, democratic, honest elections."

The U.S. State Department cited Castro's refusal to hold elections as proof that Cuba was a communist state. But Castro did not turn to the Soviet Union for aid until Washington had rejected his appeal for a U.S.-Cuban accord and had instead sought to overthrow him by the Bay of Pigs invasion.

In India, Prime Minister Indira Gandhi was found guilty in 1975 of violating the election laws to win her seat in Parliament. Faced with demands for her resignation, she declared a state of emergency instead and assumed dictatorial powers. Tens of thousands of her political opponents were jailed. Censoring the press, she suspended further elections. Angry dissenters fought running gun battles with police.

Turmoil in India grew so great that Gandhi was finally forced to dissolve Parliament in 1977 and announced new elections for March. She tried to rig them against the opposition, but she failed. Voted decisively out of office, she sought to mollify the citizens by restoring civil liberties, abolishing censorship, freeing political prisoners, and then resigning. But she was imprisoned awhile for her misdeeds.

Nevertheless three years later the Indians forgave her, electing her to a second chance as prime minister. This time, she promised, India would continue to operate as a democracy.

Fresh political storms brewed in 1983 over a scheduled election in the state of Assam, where Hindus were enraged over the heavy immigration of Muslim Bengalis from Bangladesh. Boycotting the election, which the Bengalis were expected to win, the Hindus demanded that Gandhi cancel it. Perhaps because her party would gain from the Bengali vote, she refused. The result was a horrifying massacre.

Ten thousand Hindus in Assam marched with guns, spears, and arrows against 50 Muslim villages. They burned huts, chased the villagers into cornfields, and hunted them down like rabbits. Women and children were killed. As village after village burned to the ground, the death toll exceeded 3,000.

Such are the lethal passions that can swirl around foreign elections deciding supremacy between mortal enemies.

The British electoral system differs from ours in a number of significant ways. We vote for a president. The English vote for a party; the party that wins the most seats in Parliament forms a government, and its leader becomes prime minister. Our president's term is four years. Each Parliament sits for five years, but it can be dissolved by a vote of no confidence in the government or by new elections called sooner by the prime minister.

Traditionally, Britain has given its voters a choice between the Conservative Party and the Labor Party. A split in Labor's ranks, however, has produced a third-party alliance of Social Democrats and Liberals. This split allowed Conservative Prime Minister Margaret Thatcher to remain in power in a 1983 election with only 43.1 percent of the total vote.

Britain also has its share of tiny splinter parties, many of them expressing the British sense of humor at the cost of a $240 filing fee. There are the Nobody Party, the Independent Mushroom Party, the Ban the Old Fogeys Party, the Best Party I've Ever Been To Party, Freddie's Alternative Medicine Party, and Jim the Fish Conservative Independent Party.

The Official Monster Raving Looney Party ran against Thatcher in her own home constituency. Its leader, Screaming Lord Sutch, campaigned with the slogan: "Give a vote for insanity. You know it makes sense!"

Australia offers its voters a choice between the Labor Party and the conservative Liberal/Country Party. Voting is compulsory, with fines for any citizen who fails to vote in a national election. In 1983 an Australia newspaper accused the American CIA of secretly interfering in a previous election in order to defeat the Labor Party.

The French elect their president for a seven-year term. He appoints the premier. The French Parliament consists of a National Assembly and Senate. The president has the right to dissolve the Assembly and call for new elections.

There are many different French parties, no one of which holds a majority in Parliament. Most laws are passed by a coalition between parties. France turned socialist in the spring of 1981 with the election of Frangois Mitterand as president. In municipal elections 22 months later, the dissatisfied French voted heavily anti-socialist. But like him or lump him, Mitterand would remain their president for another five years.

After World War II, a defeated Germany was divided into the Federal Republic of Germany (West Germany), a democracy allied to Europe and the U.S.; and the German Democratic Republic (East Germany), a communist state linked to the Soviet Union. More than the ugly Berlin Wall erected by East Germany divides the two German governments.

West Germany is governed by a Parliament, whose *Bundestag* members are elected for four-year terms. Together with an appointed upper chamber, the *Bundesrat*, they elect a president for a five-year term. The *Bundestag* alone chooses the chancellor, or prime minister. The major parties are the Social Democratic Party and the Christian Democratic Union/Christian Social Union Party.

Something of a stir was created in 1983 when a new party called the Greens, supported by German youth, won five seats in the *Bundestag*. They marched to Parliament wearing jeans and sweaters, in a festive parade featuring banners, bongo drums, and flowers. The Greens vowed to work against nuclear power plants, acid rain, the East-West arms race, and NATO.

West German elections have a remarkably high voluntary voter turnout. A European Community study found the levels of political discussion in West Germany to be the highest on the continent, a remarkable turnaround for a people who, under the Nazis, did not dare express a controversial opinion.

East German citizens have little to say about how they are governed. That is determined by the Socialist Unity (communist) Party, which handpicks the 500 deputies who are "elected" to the People's Chamber for five-year terms. The Chamber chooses the Council of State and Council of Ministers who carry on executive functions. But the real power in East Germany is suggested by 400,000 Soviet troops garrisoned there.

On the other hand, in communist Yugoslavia, non-communists can run for office. There is also relative freedom to criticize the government, unusual in a communist society, although advocating its overthrow could result in arrest.

Yugoslavs vote for delegates, who then vote for the councils that run the nation's six republics and the federal government. A policy of rotating the national leadership annually gives each republic's council representative a chance to be president. This system prevents any one official from becoming a dictator or any one republic from becoming dominant.

Hungary, too, is liberalizing its regime. Non-communist candidates have been permitted to run for office in 39 of the nation's 352 parliamentary districts. Under new proposals for 1985 sponsored by communist officials, up to 85 percent of seats in the National Assembly will be open to non-communists.

From 1967 to 1974 Greece was a dictatorship ruled by a military regime known as "the Colonels," who seized power. A public uproar finally compelled them to agree to elections, which brought about a socialist government. Most Greeks I spoke to during my visit there in 1983 told me that it had made little difference in their lives, except that they now felt free to say anything they pleased in the daily political discussions that go on in the *tavernas*.

Television plays a major role in many West European countries. Britain, Sweden, Denmark, Norway, the Netherlands, and West Germany give generous TV coverage to important political debates. No political advertising is permitted at election time, but free time is made available for party broadcasts.

Twelve political parties in the Dutch Parliament are given ten minutes of TV time four times a year, with extra time at elections. In Britain political broadcasts are shown on all channels, so that viewers cannot escape exposure.

No elections have been more controversial than those in Central America. In El Salvador revolutionists sought to overthrow a brutal government that used army troops and rightist "death squads" to murder dissenters and innocent villagers. Despite its persistent human rights violations, which included the murders of four American nuns, the government was supported by the Reagan administration.

In 1982 the junta in power, prodded by President Reagan, staged elections in El Salvador, which, however, were supervised by its brutal troops. The rebels led a boycott of the election, warning that leftists who tried to vote were likely to be seized and shot. The junta assured a large turnout by letting it be known that Salvadorans who couldn't show proof of having voted might be suspected of being rebel supporters.

The junta won the election, which the rebels disdained as unfree and unrepresentative. President Reagan sought to increase military and economic aid to El Salvador, calling it a vital ally in fighting the spread of communism in Central America. But Congress was appalled when the junta arrested 23 Salvadoran teachers for "terrorism," while the army also kidnapped scores of trade-union and political leaders. Amnesty International protested the junta's capture and torture of political prisoners.

Refusing to increase any aid to the brutal regime until there was proof it was reforming, Congress also demanded that President Reagan compel the junta to enter into negotiations with the rebels for a peaceful solution to the civil war.

What about elections in the nation that is the leading challenger of the United States for world influence?

In the Soviet Union, nomination is tantamount to election. One candidate for each local post is chosen in small, closed meetings controlled by the Communist Party, the union committee in a factory or commune, or often by both together.

Asked why two or more candidates were not nominated for a post, a Soviet official replied, "It would mean you think one of them is not good enough for the office. We don't want to insult our candidates."

Nominations for deputies to the Supreme Soviet take place at a club or Palace of Culture. Officials in the Communist Party apparatus indicate who is to be nominated. Speeches are made on behalf of the candidates. Their nomination, voted on by a show of hands, is always approved unanimously.

Candidates chosen are usually Party members who excel in their jobs and in demonstrated civic concern. Nominated because of the respect they command in their communities, they often have little knowledge of the workings of government.

This is not considered important as long as they follow the Party line. Important legislation does not originate with the Supreme Soviet, which is largely a rubber stamp for decisions made by the Party's *Politburo,* the ruling body of the Soviet Union. Deputies facilitate execution of policy, not its formulation.

"The old deputies will tell me what to do," one newly elected deputy explained, "and I'll carry out my assignments."

During the last ten days of election campaigns, voters are visited by candidates and Party workers speaking in their behalf. These occasions also allow voters to voice grievances they would like the candidates to take care of.

Elections are viewed basically as a public vote of confidence in the Soviet regime. As Election Day draws closer, scarce food items suddenly become abundant in the stores. Soviet papers overflow with praise for communist accomplishments since the Revolution. Bookstores display brochures attacking Western bourgeois elections. These charge that monopolists manipulate and control those elections through fraud and bribery; that blacks and minorities are prevented from voting; and that candidates can be elected by a minority vote, unlike Soviet candidates, who usually get 100 percent of the vote.

On Election Day, polls are set up in schools, Palaces of Culture, and other public places. They are usually decorated with flowers, pictures of Lenin, and red banners with communist slogans. Sometimes there are refreshments and a brass band to reward voters. There are no voting machines. Since there is usually only one candidate for each post, voters can either mark their ballots or just drop them in an urn.

All voters have their names checked off a voting list that tells poll·watchers who has failed to vote. By mid-afternoon nonvoters are contacted and reminded of their civic duty. This follow-up has different implications in the Soviet Union than in Western democracies like ours. Soviet elections have something like a 99 percent turnout because few Russians care to attract suspicion, by refusing to vote, that they are dissenters.

On the rare occasions when an angry Russian may enter a voting booth, scratch off the name of the official candidate, and write in his own choice, his vote is invalidated because his candidate has not been nominated and approved.

Soviet elections cost only a tiny fraction of what is spent on American elections. Most campaign workers are unpaid volunteers. Candidates pay nothing in campaign expenses.

The significant difference between Soviet and American elections is, of course, that Russian voters never have the option of turning out one government and installing a new one. They cannot reject and reverse a government policy they don't like. And they have no real choice of candidates to represent them. No free elections, in the Western sense, can be said to exist in the Soviet Union.

It would boggle the mind if 70 percent of American candidates elected to Congress were suddenly to be arrested and executed by the president of the United States. Yet former Premier Nikita Khrushchev revealed that in 1934 Josef Stalin had done just that to Soviet deputies: "It was determined that of the 139 members and candidates of the Party's Central Committee who were elected at the Seventeenth Congress, 98 persons, i.e., 70 percent, were arrested and shot."

Western democracies, with all their shortcomings, still offer their citizens a free choice of candidates and programs.

Dictatorships have an advantage in that their unlimited powers enable them to act more swiftly than democracies. It only takes a change of mind by one person or a few people to change the whole course of government.

A constitutional democracy, on the other hand, is deliberately slowed down by checks and balances. Power and authority are divided among a president, Congress, and Supreme Court; or a prime minister, Parliament, and High Court.

These precautions also make it difficult for any one person or group in a democracy to gain enough power to impose a dictatorship upon its people. That is the great strength of all democratic electoral systems, including our own.

19

What's Good and What's Bad About Our System

No one would claim that our electoral system is perfect.

We have had notable presidents like Thomas Jefferson, Abraham Lincoln, and Franklin D. Roosevelt. But our system has also put into the White House presidents who were "eminently forgettable" mediocrities like Millard Fillmore, Franklin Pierce, and James Buchanan; and presidents like Ulysses S. Grant, Warren Harding, and Richard M. Nixon whose administrations were corrupt.

Certainly no electoral system can guarantee that only the finest, most intelligent and honest chief executive will emerge victorious. But one has to question why Americans have so often made poor choices.

During the Nixon administration, the American public was shocked by disclosure of the Watergate scandal. They were stunned further when tapes of conversations within the White House were made public, revealing the president and his aides as cynical, vulgar, dishonest, and corrupt. After Nixon was forced to resign and many of his aides went to jail, millions wondered how they could have been so misled as to have voted for such an administration not just once, but twice.

Perhaps we need to pay less attention to political propaganda and self-serving pitches by candidates and parties, and more to factual campaign information provided by such organizations as the League of Women Voters and Common Cause.

Some voters are dissatisfied with the convention system of the two major parties because often the candidates chosen, instead of being the best each party can offer, represent a compromise between opposing factions within each party. The electorate is then faced with a choice of two unexciting major candidates. Consequently, many disgusted voters either stay home on Election Day or protest by voting for a third party.

During the 1960s and early 1970s, voters became disillusioned about professional politicians after Vietnam and Watergate. Democrat Jimmy Carter won election promising that his administration would stay close to the people because he was not part of the Washington Establishment. Similarly, Republican Ronald Reagan won election by promising voters to "get the federal government off our backs."

The election of presidents who lack national experience is a mistake, argues Nelson W. Polsby of the University of California at Berkeley in his book *Consequences of Party Reform*. "That our two most recent presidents [Carter and Reagan] should be arguably the two most nationally inexperienced in American history," he declares, "cuts directly across the grain of common sense that tells us that duties of the presidency are not smaller today than when more seasoned candidates . . . were routinely the only ones considered qualified for the job."

Our turnout at the polls, poor at best in the past, seems gradually to be growing even worse. In 1960 slightly over 3 in 5 citizens voted in a presidential election. This percentage steadily declined until the 1980 election, when only 53.9 percent of the population—slightly over half—bothered going to the polls. Thus Ronald Reagan was elected president by less than 28 percent of Americans eligible to vote.

Perhaps one reason is that we're too engrossed in our private affairs to pay attention to shaping the government we live under. As long ago as 1896, M. I. Ostrogorski, a Russian visitor observing American politics, reflected, "The desperate race for wealth has absorbed the citizen and has not left him time

THE CRADLE OF THE G.O.P.

FIRST REPUBLICAN CONVENTION HELD AT LAFAYETTE HALL, PITTSBURG, PA, FEB, 22ᴰ 1856.

LITHOGRAPH BY ARMOR LITHOGRAPH COMPANY. 1897

TRYING TO KICK IT OVER.

POLITICAL CARTOON BY LEON BARRITT, OCTOBER 1, 1904

Perhaps voters should turn their attention from political propaganda and self-serving campaign speeches to factual information provided by organizations such as the League of Women Voters and Common Cause.

BEN SHAHN PHOTO

LITHOGRAPH PRINTED BY B. THURSTON, 1856

to attend to the public welfare; it even encouraged his want of public spirit and converted it almost into a virtue."

George E. Reedy, former press secretary to President Lyndon B. Johnson, thinks the problem lies in public dissatisfaction with mediocre, muddling White House leadership. Perhaps we need to shake off resignation and apathy by getting mad instead—mad enough to "turn the rascals out."

On Election Day, that is our time-honored form of peaceful revolution, one of the great strengths of our electoral system. As long as we enjoy the right to vote against candidates, parties, and programs we oppose, we can feel confident of living in freedom. Even if our choices are mistaken, as they often are, we will always have another opportunity to reverse them at the next regular election . . . if only we take it.

One serious defect in our electoral system is the advantage large campaign funds give to some candidates. As the law presently operates, huge sums can be spent on behalf of a candidate's campaign as long as he presumably does not have control of those expenditures himself.

Trade association, labor union, corporation, and other PACs were revealed to have spent $83 million on behalf of 1982 congressional candidates. "When PACs give money they expect something in return other than good government," observed Republican Senator Robert Dole, chairman of the Senate Finance Committee.

Democrat Representative Thomas Downey declared, "You can't buy a congressman for five thousand dollars, but you can buy his vote on a particular issue." There are 3,371 PACs of all kinds, only a quarter of them pro-labor.

"The financing of elections must be altered if there is to be authenticity in our society," insists Professor Art Pearl. "A campaign *by* Big Money must also be a campaign run *for* Big Money. That leaves us no alternative but to think small—to spend no more money than needed, to build a mass base of large numbers of persons contributing modest amounts. . . . If contribution is monopolized by the few, the quality of life must suffer for the majority."

England's campaign period is only one month. If we could shorten ours, the cost of running for election could be reduced tremendously. There would be many benefits. Candidates would have less need of PACs. Money would be less of an obstacle to running for office. Fewer voters would be bored by yearlong campaigning, and more would be willing to pay attention during the month before Election Day.

On the other hand, our present lengthy campaigns do serve to help educate voters. During the 1960s, for example, the clashing campaigns of Barry Goldwater and Lyndon Johnson made voters think deeply about the issues of nuclear war. The campaigns of George Wallace, Strom Thurmond, and Robert Kennedy made voters sensitive to racial issues. The campaigns of Hubert Humphrey, George McGovern, and Richard Nixon made them think deeply about the Vietnam War. Such campaigns serve to crystalize views of controversial problems.

Public-opinion polls are both a minus and a plus in our electoral process. Critics charge that they don't merely sample public opinion, but also create or change it. A poll may ask a loaded question that elicits answers favoring one candidate or position. Polls also create a "bandwagon effect." People like to vote with a winner, to bet on a favorite.

If polls show a candidate in the lead for either nomination or election, a certain number of voters are likely to be influenced to jump on that bandwagon. That candidate also finds it easier to win financial support from PACs, which desire to back a winner who will be obligated to them.

Polls can't, of course, be outlawed. They're part of a free press, of the people's right to know. And they do satisfy public curiosity about how well candidates are doing, who seems to be forging ahead, and which issues are prevailing. In that sense they serve the electoral process well, because they contribute to the interest in a campaign race.

Perhaps what's needed is greater public awareness that polls are only straws in the wind. Voters' minds change from week to week with new developments. Schools could also help by educating tomorrow's voters to think for themselves, rather than follow the herd just to "be with a winner."

There is controversy over the role of the media in our elections. Conservatives accuse them of being biased in favor of liberal candidates because many reporters and editors are liberals. On the other hand, liberal and radical candidates accuse the media of being under the thumb of their wealthy owners and big advertisers, slanting campaign coverage to favor conservative candidates.

Presidential candidates have often complained about the media's scrutiny, which Democratic Senator George McGovern labeled often "beyond reason." When he had delivered a major campaign address, the media had largely ignored it, playing up instead a personal feud between two of his staff members.

When a newspaper had attacked the wife of Democratic Senator Edmund Muskie in 1972, he was moved to tears of outrage in public.

The media blew up the incident as an alleged indication of instability, and Muskie's presidential candidacy was destroyed.

When Republican Governor George Romney reversed his support of the Vietnam War, explaining that he had been previously "brainwashed" by the administration's "snow job," the media ended his chances by calling him "the brainwashed candidate."

When Republican President Jerry Ford sought to be elected to a term of his own, he said, in answer to a question, that he didn't think the Polish people considered themselves dominated by the Soviet Union. His error was magnified by the media into an indictment that he was totally ignorant about foreign affairs. It helped defeat his candidacy.

Presidents complain, too, about media reportage once they are elected. But with all their faults, the American media are still free—which means free to make mistakes and free to be unfair from time to time. Would anyone trade them for controlled media that report only what the government allows?

A major flaw in our electoral system is its discrimination against women. They have a hard time unseating male officials in office, who have decided advantages as incumbents—name recognition, party support, favors done for constituents, easy access to campaign funds. They are also handicapped by the myth that women aren't qualified to be politicians.

PACs contribute to far more men than women. One reason is contacts made by men on golf links, at business lunches, at fraternal organizations, at the Chamber of Commerce, etc.—opportunities that are mostly closed to women. When women do get contributions, those are usually only a fraction of the money given to male candidates.

One of the more urgent needs for reforming our electoral system, most political experts agree, is the abolition of the Electoral College, so that citizens can vote directly for their presidential choice instead of for electors with that power.

Unless we make that change, it is quite possible that a candidate may become president even though most of us vote for his opponent. If he wins a state's popular vote by just a single ballot, he gets that state's entire electoral vote. Many similar slim wins give him a lot of electors. Thus he may win the election with a majority of Electoral College votes, even though his opponent gets a majority of the popular vote.

Countless efforts have been made in Congress to abolish the Electoral College, but none have succeeded to date because of reluctance to tamper with our traditional electoral machinery. We can expect a fresh public uproar, however, the next time a candidate wins the White House while losing the popular vote.

The increasing practice of American voters in splitting their tickets, instead of voting for all candidates of a single party, has resulted in what some see as a weakness of our electoral system, while others regard it as a strength.

A president may be of one party, while the majority of one or both houses of Congress may be of the other. The same is true of a governor and his legislature. This can create serious problems if what a president or governor wants, the Congress or state legislature doesn't. Or vice versa. Thus there may be constant squabbles, a series of executive vetoes, and legislation piling up un-passed.

On the other hand, this division of power also provides a series of checks and balances. Neither the chief executive nor the legislators get their way entirely. Often they are compelled to compromise, so that the final legislation that emerges does not ride roughshod over the wishes of the voters who support either party.

The quality of our elections might improve if some way could be found to make voters blind to the color of a candidate's skin. Too often the campaigns of black or Hispanic candidates provoke a backlash of racism, with many voters casting ballots out of prejudice, regardless of the candidates' qualifications or the excellence of their programs.

It is understandable that such prejudice would anger blacks and Hispanics into voting as a bloc for minority candidates. But one can only hope for the day when *all* of us vote for candidates purely on the basis of their character, qualifications, and record, and what they pledge to accomplish in office.

A minor flaw in our electoral system is the time difference in reporting election results, because of the three-hour lag between closing of the polls in the East and on the West Coast. In 1980, when it became clear that Republican Ronald Reagan had won decisively over Democrat Jimmy Carter, Carter graciously and publicly acknowledged defeat soon after early results began coming in, and while the West Coast was still voting.

California's Democratic candidates were furious. They lost votes when many of the state's Democratic voters, hearing Carter's concession on TV, didn't bother going to the polls. They demanded that, in the future, either no election results be broadcast until California voting had ended or all polls shut down at the identical moment, regardless of the different time zones. This would require a compromise as to the hours all polls would be open.

The United States has probably the most elaborate, complicated, and expensive electoral system in the world. It operates according to a kaleidoscope of national, state, and local party rules, state statutes, and special rulings by federal, state, and local courts.

Political maneuvering also goes on for much longer than in any other country. Some critics complain that no sooner is an administration elected than it prepares for the next election.

Yet, with all its shortcomings, our system is recognized as one of the best and most flexible in the world. Consider how we have been able to transfer power peacefully in the most turbulent of times, as during the Vietnam War, civil rights riots, and the Watergate crisis, instead of by violence or armed insurrection. Even when America has been at war abroad, or within itself as during the Civil War, we have continued to hold our elections on schedule. And each time, citizens have been free to vote whether to continue an administration in office or to end it.

When a dictator or junta seizes power, the people of that country have no voice in their own destiny. Even when a coup or uprising with sincerely patriotic motives overturns a tyrannical government, the longer the new dictatorship remains in power without free elections, the more it begins to resemble the tyranny it overthrew. "Power tends to corrupt," said the British historian Lord Acton; "absolute power corrupts absolutely."

That is why, in the United States, we give no presidential administration longer than four years in office without compelling it to submit to new elections. As President Wilson once said, "America is safe only because we do not know who the presidents of the United States are going to be."

In his book *Landslide*, Professor Art Pearl urges students—the voters of tomorrow—to get involved in the electoral process as early as possible. This requires, he says, that "everyone gets with some *political* organization, pays dues, and gets involved in policy determination and candidate selection. . . . *Now* is the time to be involved . . . in your community."

To participate properly in the machinery of our democracy, we need to attend political meetings and work for causes and candidates we believe in. If we don't, a handful of activists are likely to operate and control our governments—local, state, and national. We need to understand the direct link between politics and our personal benefit. If we fail to look after our own interests, why should we expect strangers with different goals to do it for us?

When there is misgovernment in Washington, state capitols, or local offices, it is easy to blame political leaders. But those leaders did not get in power without our votes. As Lincoln Steffens once observed, "The misgovernment of the American people is misgovernment *by* the American people."

We need to work inside the political parties to help select candidates of the highest integrity, instead of permitting political bosses to foist their choices on us. To keep the power out of their hands, more of us have to seek election as convention delegates.

We need to be aware, moreover, that there are among us some who would like to see elections outlawed. They are not many, but they are often tightly organized in paramilitary groups seeking to establish an American dictatorship.

For example, in California, John Capricorn heads a paramilitary group called Orion Nebula 18. "The military order will take possession of the government," he predicts. "What this country needs is a good military dictatorship . . . to straighten out people's perspective."

The only way to keep groups like this at bay is to make certain, by our participation, that the electoral system remains the only way to change our government. "The ballot," Lincoln said, "is stronger than the bullet."

Another way you can participate in the political process is through writing your local officials, state legislators, Senators, and Representatives, letting them know what you think about the issues that concern you. This is an excellent way of making your voice and your views heard, and you don't have to be of voting age. Even if a thirteen-year-old youth writes, an elected official needs to pay attention, because that youth probably has at least two adult voters in the family.

"I read every letter written me by a constituent," declared Arizona Representative Morris K. Udall. "A staff member may process it initially, but it will be answered and I will insist on reading it and personally signing the reply."

Sometimes the candidates we vote for turn out to be terrible choices. As one wit put it wryly, "I'm superstitious—I believe that voting brings four years of bad luck." But lots of other decisions we make also turn out wrong. That doesn't stop us from trying to make better decisions in the future.

And we *have* had some outstanding Americans serving us in the White House, Congress, governor's mansions, and city halls. If we learn all we can about the candidates and the issues and get involved in the electoral process, we're bound to elect a lot more fine leaders.

One of them, in fact, might eventually be you.

ACKNOWLEDGMENTS

For their generous assistance in helping me to shed light on our intricate electoral system, to make it understandable and entertaining without being simplistic, I wish to thank:

My friend Professor Arthur Pearl of the University of California, himself once a candidate for Governor of Oregon; Jean G. Birch, Secretary, and William I. Greener III, Director of Communications, of the Republican National Committee; the National Teen Age Republicans (TARS); Rick Boylan of the Democratic National Committee; the Young Democrats of America; Raymond O. Heaps, G. W. Brown, and William K. Shearer of the American Independent Party; Donald Davis of the Socialist Workers Party; the Young Socialist Alliance; Robert Bills, National Secretary of the Socialist Labor Party; the AFL-CIO Committee on Political Education; and various individuals in Greece, Yugoslavia, France, Northern Ireland, England, and West Germany who discussed their countries' electoral systems with me.

My appreciation, too, to the Knight Publishing Corporation for allowing me to adapt my article "The Man Who Clowned His Way to the State Capitol" (ADAM Magazine), in somewhat different form, for Chapter 12 of this book.

Jules Archer
Santa Cruz, California

APPENDIX

Presidential Winners and Losers

DATE	WINNER	LOSER
1789	George Washington (F)	John Adams (F)
1792	George Washington (F)	John Adams (F)
1796	John Adams (F)	Thomas Jefferson (D-R)
1800	Thomas Jefferson (D-R)	Aaron Burr (D-R)
1804	Thomas Jefferson (D-R)	Charles C. Pinckney (F)
1808	James Madison (D-R)	Charles C. Pinckney (F)
1812	James Madison (D-R)	De Witt Clinton (F)
1816	James Monroe (D-R)	Rufus King (F)
1820	James Monroe (D-R)	John Quincy Adams (N-R)
1824	John Quincy Adams (N-R)	Andrew Jackson (D)
1828	Andrew Jackson (D)	John Quincy Adams (N-R)
1832	Andrew Jackson (D)	Henry Clay (N-R)
1836	Martin Van Buren (D)	William Henry Harrison (W)
1840	William Henry Harrison (W), replaced by Vice-President John Tyler (W) in 1841	Martin Van Buren (D)
1844	James K. Polk (D)	Henry Clay (W)
1848	Zachary Taylor (W), replaced by Vice-President Millard Fillmore (W) in 1850	Lewis Cass (D)
1852	Franklin Pierce (D)	Winfield Scott (W)
1856	James Buchanan (D)	John Charles Fremont (R)
1860	Abraham Lincoln (R)	Stephen A. Douglas (D)

1864	Abraham Lincoln (R), replaced by Vice-President Andrew Johnson (R) in 1865	George B. McClellan (D)
1868	Ulysses S. Grant (R)	Horatio Seymour (D)
1872	Ulysses S. Grant (R)	Horace Greeley (D/Lib. R)
1876	Rutherford B. Hayes (R)	Samuel Jones Tilden (D)
1880	James A. Garfield (R), replaced by Vice-President Chester A. Arthur (R) in 1881	Winfield Scott Hancock (D)
1884	Grover Cleveland (D)	James Gillespie Blaine (R)
1888	Benjamin Harrison (R)	Grover Cleveland (D)
1892	Grover Cleveland (D)	Benjamin Harrison (R)
1896	William McKinley (R)	William Jennings Bryan (D, Pop.)
1900	William McKinley (R), replaced by Vice-President Theodore Roosevelt (R) in 1901	William Jennings Bryan (D)
1904	Theodore Roosevelt (R)	Alton Brooks Parker (D)
1908	William H. Taft (R)	William Jennings Bryan(D)
1912	Woodrow Wilson (D)	Theodore Roosevelt (Prog.)
1916	Woodrow Wilson (D)	Charles Evans Hughes (R)
1920	Warren G. Harding (R), replaced by Vice-President Calvin Coolidge (R) in 1923	James Middleton Cox (D)
1924	Calvin Coolidge (R)	John William Davis (D)
1928	Herbert Hoover (R)	Alfred Emanuel Smith (R)
1932	Franklin D. Roosevelt (D)	Herbert Hoover (R)
1936	Franklin D. Roosevelt (D)	Alfred M. Landon (R)
1940	Franklin D. Roosevelt (D)	Wendell Willkie (R)
1944	Franklin D. Roosevelt (D), replaced by Vice-President Harry S. Truman (D) in 1945	Thomas Edmund Dewey (R)
1948	Harry S. Truman (D)	Thomas Edmund Dewey (R)
1952	Dwight D. Eisenhower (R)	Adlai Ewing Stevenson II (D)
1956	Dwight D. Eisenhower (R)	Adlai Ewing Stevenson II (D)
1960	John F. Kennedy (D), replaced by Vice-President Lyndon B. Johnson (D) in 1963	Richard Milhous Nixon (R)

1964	Lyndon B. Johnson (D)	Barry Morris Goldwater (R)
1968	Richard M. Nixon (R)	Hubert Horatio Humphrey, Jr. (D)
1972	Richard M. Nixon (R), replaced by Vice-President Gerald R. Ford (R) in 1974	George Stanley McGovern (D)
1976	James E. Carter (D)	Gerald R. Ford (R)
1980	Ronald Reagan (R)	James E. Carter (D)

POLITICAL PARTY LEGEND

F = Federalist

D-R = Democratic-Republican

N-R = National-Republican

W= Whig

R = Republican

D = Democrat

Prog. = Progressive

Pop. = Populist

Lib. R = Liberal Republican

BIBLIOGRAPHY AND
RECOMMENDED READING

Archer, Jules. *Angry Abolitionist: William Lloyd Garrison.* New York: Julian Messner, 1969.

———. *Battlefield President: Dwight D. Eisenhower.* New York: Julian Messner, 1967.

———. *Colossus of Europe: Metternich.* New York: Julian Messner, 1970.

*———. *The Dictators.* New York: Hawthorn Books, Inc., Publishers, 1967.

*———. *The Extremists: Gadflies of American Society.* New York: Hawthorn Books, Inc., Publishers, 1969.

———. *Famous Young Rebels.* New York: Julian Messner, 1973.

———. *Fighting Journalist: Horace Greeley.* New York: Julian Messner, 1966.

———. *Hawks, Doves, and the Eagle.* New York: Hawthorn Books, Inc., Publishers, 1970.

———. *Ho Chi Minh: The Legend of Hanoi.* New York: Crowell-Collier Press, 1971.

———. *Indian Foe, Indian Friend.* New York: Crowell-Collier Press, 1970.

———. *Laws That Changed America.* New York: Criterion Books, 1967.

*———. *1968: Year of Crisis.* New York: Julian Messner, 1971.

*———. *The Plot to Seize the White House.* New York: Hawthorn Books, Inc., Publishers, 1973.

---

* Indicates recommended reading.

*————. *Police State.* New York: Harper & Row, Publishers, 1977.

*————. *Resistance.* Philadelphia: Macrae Smith Company, 1973.

*————. *Revolution in Our Time.* New York: Julian Messner, 1971.

*————. *Riot! A History of Mob Action in the United States.* New York: Hawthorn Books, Inc., Publishers, 1974.

————. *The Russians and the Americans.* New York: Hawthorn Books, Inc., Publishers, 1975.

————. *Strikes, Bombs, and Bullets: Big Bill Haywood and the I.W.W.* New York: Julian Messner, 1972.

————. *Superspies: The Secret Side of Government.* New York: Delacorte Press, 1977.

————. *Thorn In Our Flesh: Castro's Cuba.* New York: Cowles Book Company, Inc., 1970.

————. *They Made a Revolution: 1776.* New York: Scholastic Book Services, 1973; St. Martin's Press, 1975.

————. *Treason in America: Disloyalty Versus Dissent.* New York: Hawthorn Books, Inc., Publishers, 1971.

————. *Twentieth-Century Caesar: Benito Mussolini.* New York: Julian Messner, 1964.

————. *Uneasy Friendship: France and the United States.* New York: Four Winds Press, 1972.

————. *The Unpopular Ones.* New York: Crowell-Collier Press, 1968.

*————. *Washington vs. Main Street.* New York: Thomas Y. Crowell Company, 1975.

*————. *Watergate: America in Crisis.* New York: Thomas Y. Crowell Company, 1975.

*————. *Who's Running Your Life?* New York and London: Harcourt Brace Jovanovich, 1979.

*————. *World Citizen: Woodrow Wilson.* New York: Julian Messner, 1967.

*————. *You and the Law.* New York and London: Harcourt Brace Jovanovich, 1978.

*————. *You Can't Do That to Me!* New York and London: Macmillan Publishing Co., Inc., 1980.

*Atkins, Chester G. *Getting Elected: A Guide to Winning State and Local Office.* Boston: Houghton Mifflin Company, 1973.

Bailey, Thomas A. *Presidential Greatness.* New York: Applet on-Century, 1969.

Baker, Kendall L., Russell J. Dalton, and Kai Hildebrandt. *Germany Transformed.* Cambridge and London: Harvard University Press, 1981.

*Barber, James David, ed. *Choosing the President.* Englewood Cliffs, N.J.: Prentice Hall, Inc., 1974.

*Broder, David and staff of the *Washington Post. The Pursuit of the Presidency: 1980.* New York: Berkley Books, 1980.

*Bruno, Jerry and Jeff Greenfield. *The Advance Man.* New York: William Morrow and Company, Inc., 1971.

Clavir, Judy and John Spitzer, eds. *The Conspiracy Trial.* Indianapolis/New York: The Bobbs-Merrill Company, 1970.

*Deuel, Wallace R. *People Under Hitler.* New York: Harcourt Brace and Company, 1942.

*Domhoff, G. William. *Fat Cats and Democrats: The Role of the Rich in the Party of the Common Man.* Englewood Cliffs, N.J.: Prentice Hall, 1972.

*Dorman, Michael. *Under 21.* New York: Dell Publishing Co., Inc., 1970.

*Douglas, William O. *The Right of the People.* New York: Arena Books, 1972.

Durant, John and Alice. *Pictorial History of American Presidents.* New York: A. S. Barnes and Company, 1955.

*Ferguson, Thomas and Joel Rogers, eds. *The Hidden Election.* New York: Pantheon Books, 1981.

Gosnell, Harold F. and Richard Smoka. *American Parties and Elections.* Columbus, Ohio: C. E. Merrill, 1976.

Green, Timothy. *The Universal Eye.* New York: Stein and Day, Publishers, 1972.

*Greenfield, Jeff. *Playing to Win: An Insider's Guide to Politics.* New York: Simon &, 1980.

*Gregory, Dick. *Dick Gregory's Political Primer.* New York: Harper & Row, Publishers, 1972.

Haldeman, H. R. *The Ends of Power.* New York: Times Books, 1978.

Harnsberger, Caroline Thomas. *Treasury of Presidential Quotations.* Chicago: Follett Publishing Company, 1964.

*Hoopes, Roy. *Getting With Politics.* New York: Dell Publishing Company, 1968.

Johnston, Mary. *Roman Life.* Chicago: Scott Foreman and Company, 1975.

*Lebedoff, David. *Ward Number Six.* New York: Charles Scribner's Sons, 1972.

Leinwand, Gerald, ed. *Civil Rights and Civil Liberties.* New York: Washington Square Press, Inc., 1968.

Leish, Kenneth W. *The American Heritage Pictorial History of the Presidents of the United States* (3 vols.). New York: American Heritage Publishing Co., Inc., 1968.

Levy, Mark R. *The Ethnic Factor: How America's Minorities Decide Elections.* New York: Simon and Schuster, 1972.

*Mandel, Ruth B. *In the Running: The New Woman's Candidate.* New Haven and New York: Ticknor & Fields, 1981.

Martin, Michael and Leonard Gelber, eds. *The New Dictionary of American History.* New York: Philosophical Library, 1965.

Masters, Nicholas A. and Mary E. Baluss. *The Growing Power of the Presidency.* New York: Parents' Magazine Press, 1968.

*McGinnis, Joe. *The Selling of the President: 1968.* New York: Trident Press, 1969.

Morris, Richard B., ed. *Encyclopedia of American History.* New York: Harper & Row, Publishers, 1965.

*Mote, Max E. *Soviet Local and Republic Elections.* Stanford: Stanford University Press, 1965.

*Murphy, William T. Jr. and Edward Schneier. *Vote Power: How to Work for the Person You Want Elected.* Anchor Press, 1974.

Nash, Gerald D. *The Great Transition.* Boston: Allyn and Bacon, Inc., 1971.

*Neuborne, Burt and Arthur Eisenberg. *The Rights of Candidates and Voters.* New York: Avon Books, 1976.

*Nie, Norman H., Sidney Verba and John R. Petrocik. *The Changing American Voter.* Cambridge & Boston: Harvard University Press, 1979.

*Paizis, Suzanne. *Getting Her Elected: A Political Woman's Handbook.* Sacramento, Calif.: Creative Editions Publishing Co., 1977.

*Papele, Henry. *Banners, Buttons, and Songs: A Pictorial Review of America's Presidential Campaigns.* Cincinnati: World Library Publications, Inc., 1968.

*Pearl, Arthur. *Landslide.* Secaucus, N.J.: The Citadel Press, 1973.

*Polsby, Nelson W. and Aaron Wildausky. *Presidential Elections: Strategies of American Electoral Politics.* New York: Charles Scribner's Sons, 1980.

Quigley, Charles N., exec. dir. *On Participation.* Los Angeles: Law In A Free Society, 1973.

Reedy, George E. *The Twilight of the Presidency.* New York and Cleveland: The World Publishing Company, 1970.

Rosenbloom, David Lee. *The Election Men: Professional Campaign Managers and American Democracy.* New York: Quadrangle, 1973.

*Roseboom, Eugene Holloway and Alfred E. Eckes. *A History of Presidential Elections.* New York: Macmillan Publishing Co., Inc., 1979.

*Russell, Francis. *The President Makers.* Boston/Toronto: Little Brown and Company, 1976.

Saul, Mort. *Heartland.* New York and London: Harcourt Brace Jovanovich, 1976.

*Sandoz, Ellis and Cecil V. Crabb, eds. *A Tide of Discontent: The 1980 Elections and Their Meaning.* Washington, D.C.: Congressional Quarterly Press, 1981.

Seldes, George. *Freedom of the Press.* Indianapolis/New York: The Bobbs-Merrill Company, Publishers, 1935.

*Sherrill, Robert. *Gothic Politics in the Deep South.* New York: Grossman Publishers, 1968.

Sinkler, George. *The Racial Attitudes of American Presidents.* Garden City, New York: Doubleday & Company, Inc., 1971.

*Spero, Robert. *The Duping of the American Voter.* New York: Lippincott & Crowell, Publishers, 1980.

Steam, Gerald Emanuel, ed. *Broken Image: Foreign Critiques of America.* New York: Random House, 1972.

*Steffens, Lincoln. *The Shame of the Cities.* New York: Hill and Wang, 1957.

*Thompson, Hunter S. *Fear and Loathing on the Campaign Trail '72.* New York: Popular Library, 1974.

*Weingast, David E. *We Elect a President.* New York: Julian Messner, 1966.

*White, Theodore. *America in Search of Itself: The Making of the President 1956–1980.* New York: Harper & Row, Publishers, 1982.

*Wolfinger, Raymond E. and Stephen J. Rosenstone. *Who Votes?* New Haven: Yale University Press, 1980.

Also consulted were issues of *Newsweek, The Nation, Reader's Digest, Life, Commonsense, Variety,* the *Australian National Times,* American Civil Liberties Union reports, and political materials provided by various political parties.

INDEX

Abel, Jules, 126, 134

Abolitionists, 23, 89–90, 106–107

Abortion, 20, 100, 116, 118, 169, 179

Acid rain, 218

Acton, Lord, 233

Adams, John, 5, 7, 40–42, 75, 168–169, 184

Adams, John Quincy, 37, 39, 43, 46, 195

Adamson Act, 74

AFL-CIO Committee on Public Education (COPE), 13, 181, 199

Africa, 214

Afro-American Unity Party, 113

Agnew, Spiro T., 54, 56, 176

Alabama, 9, 16, 30, 54, 78, 115, 187, 190

Alaska, 3

Aldrich, Winthrop W., 65

Alexander, Herbert, 65

Alien and Sedition Acts, 5, 184

Allen, George, 51

American Beat Consensus, 113

American Civil Liberties Union (ACLU), 13

American Farm Bureau Association, 181

American Federation of Labor, 112, 178

American and Foreign Christian Union, 105

American Government: Democracy at Work, 129

American Independent Party, 54, 103, 115–116

American League Against War and Fascism, 22

American Medical Association (AMAJ), 181

American Party, 89–90

American Party of the United States, 103

American Protective Association, 185

American Protestant Society, 105

American Railway Union (ARU), 111

American Revolution, 75

American Student Association, 199

American Vegetarian Party, 113

Amnesty International, 220

Anderson, Jack, 175

Anti-draft demonstrations (*see* Anti-war rallies)

Anti-Federalist Party, 41, 73, 104

Anti-Mason Party, 126

Anti-Saloon League of America, 110, 161

Anti-semitism, 113

Anti-war rallies, 55, 83, 115, 132, 201

Appraisal of U.S. electoral system, 224–235

Arizona, 32, 67, 88, 235

Arms race, 204, 218

Asians, 10, 34, 53, 201, 212

Askew, Reubin, 182

Assassinations, 53, 71, 83, 92

A Tide of Discontent, 26

Australia, 22, 217
    Labor Party, 217
    Liberal/Country Party, 217

Bailey, John, 197

Baker, Howard, 13, 169

Bangladesh, 216

Barnburners Party, 106

Batista, Fulgencio, 214

Bayh, Birch, 12, 86

Bay of Pigs invasion, 83, 215

B-1 bomber, 204

Bedford, Roger, 16

Belgian Congo (*see* Zaire)

Berkeley High School, 14

Berlin Wall, 217

Big business, 26, 64, 66, 73, 88, 92, 107–108, 175, 178, 181

Bilbo, Theodore, 142, 154

Bill of Rights, 2, 174

Birney, James G., 106

Blacks, 6, 9, 34–35, 45, 53, 58, 85, 145, 156, 170, 173, 184–187, 190, 192, 197, 232
    mayors, 58, 156, 170
    vote, 9, 34–35, 85, 156, 170, 173, 186, 190, 192, 195, 197

Blackshirts, 210, 213

Blaine, James G., 194

"Bloody Sixth" ward, 76

Boling, Bruce, 199

"Boll Weevil" Democrats, 54, 56, 81, 100

Bolsheviks, 210

Bonus Army march, 95

Borah, William E., 120

Boray, Alvin, 89

Boston Irish, 77

Bouchet, Edward, 13

Breckinridge, John C., 44, 78, 82

Bridges, Harry, 154

Brown, G.W., 116

Brown, Edmund G., 53

Brown, Pat, 154

Brownshirts, 211, 213

Bryan, William Jennings, 47–48, 50, 78–79, 82, 92, 108, 128, 130

Bryant, William Cullen, 90

Bryce, James, 174

Buchanan, James, 90, 176, 224

Bular, William J., 140

Bull Moose Party, 78, 94

Burr, Aaron, 42–43, 46, 47

Bush, George, 29

Busing, 100, 116

Butler, Edward R., 185

Byrne, Jane, 70

Cajuns, 35

California, 3, 4, 9, 14, 17, 23, 35, 53, 63, 70, 77, 90, 101, 116, 124, 141, 145, 146, 154, 170, 176, 186, 190, 194, 203, 204, 225, 233, 234
    Supreme Court, 10, 186

Campaigning, 15, 20, 29, 48, 52, 60, 67, 70, 84, 85, 94, 134–137, 145, 148, 149, 155, 156, 163, 204
   funds, 55, 58, 59, 64, 65, 66, 85, 174, 178, 181, 205, 228, 231
Candidate requirements, 57–72, 167–173
Capitalism, 80, 110–111, 118, 134, 139
Capone, Al, 185
Capricorn, John, 234
Carlyle, Thomas, 199
Carter, Jimmy, 3, 26, 29, 56, 58–60, 63, 66, 69, 84, 133, 151–152, 170, 181, 225, 232–233
Cass, Lewis, 78, 107
Castro, Fidel, 214–215
Castro, Genoveva, 9
Catholics, 5, 31, 48, 58, 74, 105–106, 141, 143, 144, 156, 185
Celler, Emanuel, 117
Censorship, 100
Central America, 219, 220
Chappaquiddick incident, 67
"Checkers" speech, 146
Chiang Kai-shek, 212
Chicago, 13, 54–55, 58, 70, 85, 111, 113, 124, 126, 128–129, 132, 141, 144, 150, 156, 167, 185, 197
Chicanos (*see* Mexican Americans)
Child Labor, 112
China
   Manchu dynasty, 212
   People's Republic, 99

Chinese, the, 185, 212
Chisholm, Shirley, 68, 70
Chotiner, Murray, 145, 146
Christian Front, 142
CIA, 199, 217
Civil rights, 6, 34, 54, 80, 85, 115, 170, 186, 203, 233
   Acts, 6, 74, 145, 186, 190, 195
   Commission, 186
Civil War, 5, 44, 54, 61–62, 78, 83, 91, 107, 201, 220, 233
Clark, Dick, 179
Clark, Champ, 130
Clark, James, 78, 79, 130
Clark, Joseph S., 176
Clay, Henry, 43, 106, 135, 169
Cleveland, Grover, 38, 47, 78, 107, 137, 194, 195, 198
Cold war, 83, 145
Collective bargaining, 48, 112, 178
Collins, Lisa, 119
Colombia, 92
"Colonels, the," Greece, 219
Colonialism, 212, 214
Colt, Samuel, 177
Committee to Reelect the President (CRP), 55, 178
Common Cause, 179, 224, 226
Communism, 51, 80, 97, 99, 101, 104, 111, 113, 116–118, 134, 142, 146–148, 210, 212, 214–215, 217–221
Communist International, 112
Communist Party, U.S.A., 103, 111, 117

Congress, 2, 3, 5, 6, 9, 17, 23, 29, 30, 35, 37, 42–44, 47, 56, 59, 65, 66, 68, 80, 81, 92, 96–98, 100, 104, 106–108, 110, 114, 117, 135, 145, 149, 154, 175–179, 202, 204, 208, 220, 222, 231–232, 235
Congress of Industrial Organizations (CIO), 178
Connecticut, 4, 70, 132
Consequences of Party Reform, 225
Conservation, 88
Conservative Party, 104, 113, 116, 216
Conservatives (*see* Right Wing)
Constitution, 1, 2, 7, 9, 13, 41–42, 110
Constitutional Convention, 40
Constitutional Party, 116
Conventions, political, 40, 68, 122–133
    Cook County, 129
    delegates, 32, 48, 122–133, 234
Coolidge, Calvin, 63, 94–95, 112, 140, 195
Costigan, Howard, 165
Cotton, Douglas MacArthur, 34
Coughlin, Charles E., 113
Cox, James, 139
Coxey's Army march, 179
Cranston, Alan, 63, 170, 203–204
Crockett, Davy, 136, 208
Croker, Richard, 139
"Cross of Gold" speech, 48, 50, 128
Cuba, 78, 83, 92, 105, 118, 215

Cuban missile crisis, 83
Cuban Americans, 3, 199
Czarist Russia, 210

Daley, Richard J., 54, 132
"Dark-horse" candidates, 48, 67, 85
Davis, Bob, 138
Davis, John W., 140
Dayton, Mark, 65
"Debategate" controversy, 151
Debs, Eugene, 109, 111, 139–140, 143, 202
Decatur, Stephen, 45
Defenders of the Christian Faith, 142
Defense, 80, 88, 179
Delaware, 40, 78
Delegates (*see* political conventions)
Delgado, Humberto, 212
De Leon, Daniel, 110
Democratic Party, 12, 31, 40, 42, 43, 58, 70, 73, 74, 79–81, 83–84, 86, 88, 90, 97, 99, 101, 117, 145, 154, 155, 169, 182
    National Committee, 86, 153, 197
    1968 Chicago convention, 132
    reforms, 74
Democratic-Republican Party, 5, 41–43, 46, 73, 75, 104
Denmark, 219
Denver, 3
Depression, 51, 79, 95, 112, 141, 169, 179
Deukmejian, George, 190

Dewey, Thomas, 81, 96, 122, 144–145, 147

Dictatorships, 23, 88, 168, 210–213, 219, 222–223, 233–235

Dirksen, Everett, 186

Disarmament conference, 94

Discrimination, 5, 74, 100, 119, 231

Dix, I. F., 163

Dixiecrat Party, 80

Dole, Robert, 228

Dore, John F., 158–158, 162

Douglas, Helen Gahagan, 145–146

Douglas, Stephen, 44, 78, 82, 90

Douglas, William O., 187

Downey, Thomas, 228

Draft resistance (*see* Anti-war rallies)

Dulles, John Foster, 96, 214

Durenberger, David, 65

Dyke, William, 16

East Germany, 217
    People's Chamber, 218
    Socialist Unity (communist) Party, 218

Education, 14, 15, 35, 89, 101, 104–105, 118, 120

Eighteenth Amendment (*see* Prohibition)

Eisenhower, Dwight D., 35, 51–52, 59, 61, 64–65, 81, 96–98, 118, 146, 148–149, 166, 175, 205, 212, 214

Elections, 21–28
    close, 194–200
    costs, 222, 229
    election day, 1, 36, 91, 139, 146, 154, 173, 184–185, 195, 197, 203, 221, 225, 228
    fraud, 185, 188, 204, 221
    procedures, 22, 40, 43, 75, 113, 123, 229, 234
    riots, 183

Electoral College, 35, 37–44, 47, 52, 78, 111, 231

El Salvador, 100, 105, 118, 219–220
    "death squads," 219

Enforcement Act of 1870, 45

England, 210, 216, 229
    Conservative Party, 216
    Labor Party, 216
    Parliament, 216
    Social Democrat-Liberal Party, 216

Environment, 28, 116, 169, 175

Environmental Protection Agency (EPA), 204

Epton, Bernard, 156

Equal Rights Amendment (ERA), 20, 71, 100, 118, 179

Equal Rights Party, 44

Eskimos, 3, 34

Eu, March Fong, 70, 176

Europe, 4, 94, 96, 209–210, 217

Extremists, 77, 88–89, 97, 100, 105, 120, 150

Fala, 144

Falwell, Jerry, 179
Farenthold, Frances, 68
Farley, Jim, 165
Farm aid, 79
Farmer Labor Party, 112–113
Farm relief, 107
Fascism, 22, 113, 142
"Favorite son" candidates, 124–125
FBI harassment, 117
Federal budget deficit, 100
Federal Communications Act, 119
Federal Election Campaign Act of
     1971, 55
Federal Election Campaign Reform
     Act of 1974, 119
Federal Election Commission, 65
Federalists, 41–42, 46, 75, 104, 184
Feinstein, Dianne, 70
Fifteenth Amendment, 4–5, 45
Fillmore, Millard, 90, 106, 109, 224
Financing the 1980 Election, 65
Fitzgerald, "Honey Fitz," 77
Flexner, Abraham, 120
Florida, 4, 35, 45, 78, 137, 178,
     182
Ford, Gerald, 56, 69, 84, 99
Foreign policy, 88, 92, 175
Founding Fathers, 2, 30
Fowler, Wyche, Jr., 173
France, 210, 217
Franco, Francisco, 211, 213
Frankfurter, Felix, 187
Freedom Rides, 6
Free enterprise (*see* Capitalism)
Free silver, 47, 107, 128
Free Soil Party, 89, 106–107

Fremont, John C., 90–91, 93
French Canadians, 35
French Parliament, 217
French Revolution, 75
Fusion Party, 103

Gandhi, Indira, 215
Gang wars, 48, 110, 114
Garfield, Arthur, 195, 198
Garner, John, 71
Garrison, William Lloyd, 23, 107
Geneva Accords, 212, 214
Geocaris, John, 156
George, Henry, 110
Georgia, 40, 56, 58, 70, 78, 173,
     183, 187
German-American Bund, 142
Germany, 140, 217
     Nazis, 21, 80, 96, 113, 142,
          195, 211, 218
Gerry, Elbridge, 187, 191
Gerrymandering, 187, 191
Getting Her Elected, 68
Ghetto riots, 53
Glenn, John, 66
Gold standard, 47, 116
Goldwater, Barry, 88, 115, 150, 229
Gould, Jay, 177
Gould, Simon, 113
Government
     ownership, 108, 112
     regulation, 94, 118, 175
     spending, 99, 116, 170
Graber, Doris A., 169
Grant, Ulysses S., 44–45, 61, 137,
     195, 224

Grasso, Ella, 70
Great Society, the, 53, 83, 201
Greece, 219
   Ancient Greece, 22
   Greeks, the, 35
Greeley, Horace, 62, 76–77, 89–91,
   93, 105, 136–137
Greenback Party, 107, 113
Gregory, Dick, 27
Grenada invasion, 101, 118
Guam, 92
Gun control, 116, 181

Hague, Frank, 21–22, 24
Haiti, 6, 105
Hall Leonard, 73, 154
Hamer, Fannie Lou, 190
Hamilton, Alexander, 2, 41–43, 46
Hanna, Mark, 91, 128
Harding, Warren G., 63, 94, 98,
   130, 139, 140, 143, 168, 224
Harper's Weekly, 189
Harrison, Benjamin, 38, 47, 198
Harrison, William, 61, 62, 136
Hart, Gary, 66, 182
Hart, Philip, 15
Harvard, 52
Hatfield, Mark, 16, 169
Hay, John, 91
Hayes, Rutherford B., 37, 45, 49,
   195, 198
Haymarket Square incident, 111
Hepburn Act, 92
Hicks, B.N., 161
Hindo-Muslim riots in Assam,
   216

Hispanics, 10, 34, 35, 74, 123, 186,
   232
Hitler, Adolf, 142, 195, 198, 211, 213
Ho Chi Minh, 212, 214
Holy Alliance, 209
Homosexuals, 100
Hone, Philip, 137
Hoover, Herbert, 11, 16, 48, 51, 79,
   95, 112, 141, 143, 169
Housing Acts, 74
Houston, Sam, 208
Hughes, Charles Evans, 112, 194
Humphrey, Hubert, 32, 53, 54, 55,
   116, 132, 150, 196, 229
Hungarians, 64

Ibsen, Henrik, 199
Idaho, 4
Illinois, 12
Immigrants, 3, 5, 64, 74, 77, 105,
   106, 184, 185
Independent vote, 120, 168, 173
India, 215–216
Indiana, 47
Indians, 9, 61, 163, 206, 216
Industrial Revolution, 209
Inflation, 83, 87, 100
Iran hostages, 56, 84
Irish, the, 35, 76, 77, 184
Isolationism, 96
Israel, 35
Italian Americans, 35
Italy, 96, 210

Jackson, Andrew, 37, 39, 40, 43, 46,
   61, 73, 126, 135, 208, 209

Jackson, Jesse, 58, 192

Jackson State demonstrations, 55

Japan, 96

Jefferson, Thomas, 5, 40–42, 46, 52, 63, 73, 75, 76, 104, 169, 184, 224

Jersey City, 21

Jews, 35, 74, 185, 211

Johnson, Andrew, 44–45, 195

Johnson, Lyndon B., 6, 16, 18, 35, 53, 54, 83, 88, 101, 115, 150, 168, 192, 201, 203, 28

Juan Carlos, King, 211

Kansas, 90, 108, 142

Kefauver Senate Crime Committee, 32, 178

Keyserling, Harriet, 17

Kennedy, Edward, 26, 67

Kennedy, John F., 31, 35, 52, 57, 63, 81, 130, 149, 169, 195, 198

Kennedy, Robert, 53, 58, 203, 229

Kent State demonstrations, 55

Khrushchev, Nikita, 222

King, Martin Luther, 28

Kings, 209–210

Know-Nothings (*see* American Party)

Koch, Ed, 170

Korean War, 79, 97

Krajewski, Henry, 113

Ku Klux Klan, 6, 184

Labor Party, 107

Labor unions, 26, 66, 74, 88, 110, 116, 228

La Follette, Robert, 112, 114, 140

La Guardia, Fiorello H., 103

Landon, Alf, 142, 154

Landslide, 234

La Plante, Laura, 161

Lasch, Robert, 170

"Law and order," 55, 104, 115, 203

Laxalt, Paul, 182

League of Nations, 79, 140

League of Women Voters, 17, 20, 27, 32, 199, 224, 236

Lease, Mary Ellen, 108

Lebanon, 100

Lee, Robert E., 61

Lefkowitz, Louis J., 15

Left Wing, 88, 117, 154

Lemke, William, 112–113

Lenin, Vladimir Ilyich, 221

Lewelling, L.D., 108

Liberal Party, 104

Liberalism, 74, 75, 81, 84, 100, 125, 140, 167, 204, 230

Liberal Republican Party, 137

Libertarian National Committee, 104

Lincoln, Abraham, 1, 44, 54, 62–63, 67, 68, 89, 90, 91, 106, 120, 126, 169, 171, 224

Lindblom, Louise, 30

Lindsay, John, 169

Linton High School, 14

Lippmann, Walter, 146

Literary Digest poll, 154

Lleo, Urrutia, 215

Lobbyists, 174–182

Long, Clarence, 175

Long, Huey "Kingfish," 142
Long, Russell, 174, 185
Longworth, Alice Roosevelt, 145
Louisiana, 35, 45, 78, 142, 178, 184, 186
Lowery, Rev. Joseph, 173
Lugar, Richard, 182

Madison, James, 16, 39, 40, 41, 75, 151
Maine, 28, 35, 142, 157
Manatt, Charles, 153
Manchu dynasty, 212
Manifest Destiny, 77, 145
Mao Tse-tung, 212
Marcantonio, Vito, 146
Marines, the, 100–101
Massachusetts, 35, 67, 84, 106, 187, 191, 202
Massachusetts Bay Colony, 5
Masters, Edgar Lee, 128
McCarthy, Eugene, 32, 54
McCarthy, Joseph, 80, 97
McClesky, Clifton, 26
McCombs, William, 130
McCormick, Bernard, 176
McGarvey, Patrick, 199
McGary, Thomas, 144
McGovern, George, 13, 55, 66, 83, 84, 132, 133, 229, 230
McKinley, William, 47, 48, 62, 91, 92, 108, 128,
McLuhan, Marshal, 167
Mechanics Union, 104
Medical care, 74, 119
Metternich, Clemens von, 209

Mexico, 77, 78, 105, 202, 206
Mexican Americans, 9, 185, 199
Mexican War, 77, 106
Meyers, Vic, 158–166
Miami, 3
Michigan, 3, 15, 56, 78, 114, 168
Military-industrial complex, 97, 177
Minimum Wage Act, 74
Mississippi, 3, 6, 34, 53, 55, 78, 142, 154, 190, 192
Mississippi delegation fight of 1968, 124
Mitchell, John, 179
Mitterand, Frangois, 217
Mondale, Walter, 59, 182
Monopolies, 104, 107, 112
Monroe Doctrine, 177, 180
Monroe, James, 40, 75
Montana, 3
Montgomery, Robert, 52
Moral Majority, Inc., 179
Morgan, J. Pierpont, 79, 177
Moriarty, Charles, 163
Morrison, Cameron, 140
Morton, Thruston, 150
Moss, Frank, 16
Muckrakers, 92, 177
Muskie, Edmund, 150, 230
Mussolini, Benito, 210, 211, 213

NAACP, 144, 156
National Anti-Monopoly Party, 107
National Association of Manufacturers (NAM), 177

National Association of Student Governments, 25

National debt, 83, 95

National defense (*see* Defense)

National Education Association, 181

National Guard, 55

National Organization for Women (NOW), 20, 199

National Republicans, 42, 126

National Rifle Association, 181

National States Rights Party, 104, 113, 115

National Teen Age Republicans (TARS), 12, 101, 236

National Union Party, 44, 91

National Women's Political Caucus, 20, 70

National Youth Administration, 16

National Youth Caucus, 25

Nation, Carrie, 110

NATO, 218

Navy League, 177, 180

Nazi Party, 80, 96, 113, 142, 144, 195, 198, 211, 218

Netherlands, the, 219

New Deal, the, 51, 79, 84, 113, 141, 142

New England Association of Farmers and Mechanics, 105

New Hampshire, 35, 67, 85, 132

New Jersey, 3, 21, 22, 24, 26, 40, 79, 113, 138, 139, 188

News media, 116, 119, 144, 155, 169, 205, 217, 230–231

New York, 3, 11, 12, 14, 15, 21, 22, 30, 33, 35, 36, 40, 43, 47, 54, 65, 68, 76–79, 81, 88, 89, 90, 93, 103–105, 110, 113, 117, 139, 170, 184

   Board of Education, 14

   General Organization Council, 14

   Legislature, 15

   Supreme Court, 15

Nicaragua, 100, 118

Nineteenth Amendment, 4

Nixon, Richard M., 7, 25, 26, 52–56, 63, 65, 84, 97, 99, 115, 116, 145–155, 167, 178, 179, 195, 198, 203, 214, 224, 229

Northern states, 6, 77–78, 81, 85, 197

Norway, 219

Nuclear freeze, 170, 204

Nuclear power plants, 28, 119, 218

Nuclear war, 27, 62, 83, 150, 229

Ohio third party controversy, 117

O'Neill, Thomas P. ("Tip"), Jr., 71

Order of the Star-Spangled Banner, 105

Order of United Americans, 105

Oregon, 12, 16, 236

Orion, Nebula Eighteen, 234

Ostrogorski, M.I., 129, 225

O'Sullivan, John L., 77

Paderewski, Ignace Jan, 163

Paizis, Susanne, 68

Panama Canal, 92, 98

Peace movement, 88, 113, 132, 184, 202

Pearl, Art, 23, 101, 153, 228, 234, 236

Pearl Harbor, 96

Pennsylvania, 3, 176, 183, 188

Pentagon, the, 175, 204

People's march on Washington, 47, 53, 179

People's Party (*see* Populists)

Pepper, Claude, 138

Percy, Charles, 12, 88, 169

Perez, Leander, 185–186, 189

Philippines, the, 92

Pierce, Franklin, 176, 224

Pilgrims, the, 9, 44

Plunkett, 33

Political Action Committees (PACs), 66, 178, 181, 182, 228, 229, 231

Polk, James K., 77, 78, 106, 137, 169, 202, 206

Poles, the, 39

Police brutality, 119

Polsby, Nelson W., 225

Poor Man's Party, 113

Poor, the, 5, 10, 39, 41, 53, 61, 74, 83, 87, 104, 106, 107, 128, 186, 224, 225

Pope, the, 48, 106

Populists, 107, 108

Portugal, 211, 212

Portuguese, the, 35

Prayer in schools, 20, 100, 179

Precinct caucuses, 32

Primary elections, 6, 12, 123, 160, 205

Private enterprise (*see* Capitalism)

Progressive Party, 81, 112, 114, 130

Prohibition, 48, 89, 110, 161, 185

Prohibition Party, 108, 113, 114

Proprietary Party, 183

Protective tariffs, 116

Protestants, 31, 89, 106

Public opinion polls, 32, 58, 64, 115, 194, 229

Puerto Rico, 92, 105

Pullman railroad strike, 111

Pure Food and Drug Act, 92

Puritans, the, 5

Quakers, the, 183–184

Quay, Mat, 47

Racism, 156, 197, 229, 232

Radical Republican Party, 45, 91

Railroads, 92, 108, 111, 112, 174, 176

Railway Labor Act, 178

Ray, Dixie Lee, 70

Rayburn, Sam, 122

Reader's Digest, 204

Reagan, Ronald, 4, 12, 29, 54, 56–60, 63, 66, 81, 85, 86, 89, 99, 100, 101, 133, 151, 152, 156, 169, 179, 182, 186, 204, 219, 220, 225, 232

Recession, 100

Reed, Thomas Brackett, 157

Reedy, George E., 88, 238

Reeves, Donald St. George, 14

Republican Party, 5, 41, 42, 44, 45, 54, 73, 75, 78, 85–97, 101, 103, 104, 128, 141, 152, 169, 182
  National Committee, 47, 51, 73, 148, 153, 154, 236
Revolution, 23, 56, 75, 80, 111, 118, 139, 210, 214, 215, 221, 228
Reynolds, Robert, 140
Reynolds, William, 192
Rhode Island, 5, 13, 35
Ribicoff, Abraham, 132
Right Wing, 64, 88, 89, 100, 133, 150
Rockefeller, John D., 177
Rockefeller, Nelson, 12, 54, 65, 88
Rogers, Will, 87
Roman Republic, 57, 209
  Senate, the, 57
Romney, George, 230
Roosevelt, Franklin D., 16, 51, 57, 59, 71, 79, 83, 84, 86, 112, 124, 141, 142, 154, 178, 224
Roosevelt, Theodore, 6, 57, 64, 78, 91, 92, 98, 100, 111, 129, 139, 177, 180
Root, Elihu, 129
Rural Electrification Act, 74
Ryan, Edward, 177

Salazar, Antonio de Oliveira, 211–212
Salem, Eric, 1
San Francisco, 3, 70, 88
Schroeder, Pat, 71

Schurz, Carl, 45
Seattle campaigns, 158–166
Secret ballot, the, 40, 42, 209, 210
Sedition Act, World War I, 202
Senate Judiciary Committee hearings, 181, 186
Seward, William H., 126
Shakespeare's *Coriolanus*, 57
Share the Wealth program, 142
Sheridan, Phil, 61
Sherman, William Tecumseh, 61
Sherman Anti-Trust Act, 107
Sierra Club, 181
"Silent Majority, the," 55
Single Tax Party, 110
Six Crises, 203
Slavery issue, 41, 44, 78, 89, 90, 106, 169, 171
Slum Clearance Act, 74
Smathers, George, 137–138
Smith, Al, 11, 48, 103, 141, 143
Smith, Margaret Bayard, 40
Smith, "Sugar Jim," 138
Social Security, 74, 79, 111, 141
Socialism, 51, 104, 108, 111, 134
Socialist Labor Party, 104, 110, 111, 113, 115, 236
Socialist Party, 104, 109, 110, 111, 112
Socialist Workers Party, 104, 113, 117, 118, 236
Soglin, Paul, 16
South Carolina, 4, 17, 45, 78, 80, 145
Southern Christian Leadership Conference (SCLC), 173

"Southern strategy," 54

Southern Democrats (*see* Boll Weevils and Democratic Party)

Southern states, 5, 44, 45, 47, 54, 78, 80, 81, 85, 91, 108, 115, 137, 145, 173, 190, 195

Soviet Union, 83, 96, 150, 204, 215, 217, 220, 221, 222, 230
elections, 220–222
Politburo, 221
Supreme Soviet, 220

Spain, 91, 211, 213

Spanish-American War, 91, 92

Spencer, Susan, 14

Split tickets, 168, 169

Stalin, Josef, 222

Stanton, Elizabeth Cady, 43, 46

State conventions, 37, 126

State elections, 205

State legislatures, 30, 104, 105, 175, 187, 232

Steffens, Lincoln, 177, 185, 234

Stevenson, Adlai, 32, 51, 52, 58, 59, 64, 135, 148, 169

Stock market, 95

Strikes, 111–112, 173, 177, 178

Student Non-Violent Coordinating Committee (SNCC), 34

Student revolts, 53

Suffragettes, 43

Sun Oil Company, 176

Sunset High School, 12

Sun Yat-sen, 212

Supreme Court, 3, 13, 15, 47, 65, 112, 117, 186, 187, 190, 222

Sutch, Lord, 217

Sweden, 219

Taft, Robert A., 96, 122

Taft, William H., 78, 92, 129, 139

Talmadge, Eugene, 183

Talmadge, Herman, 183

Tammany Hall, 33, 47, 78, 111, 139

Taylor, Zachary, 78, 107

Tax Cut Party, 113

Taxes, 4, 6, 27, 28, 74, 89, 95, 100, 107, 110, 113, 116, 158, 170, 176, 178, 186, 190

Teapot Dome scandal, 94

Teel, Steven, 14

Teen Dem Clubs, 12, 86

Television, 26, 52, 54, 63, 65, 69, 119, 122, 123, 132, 146, 150, 151, 153, 155, 167, 172, 182, 212, 219, 233

Television debates, 52, 63, 69, 151, 167, 182

Tennessee, 13, 116

Tennessee Valley Authority (TVA), 74

Territorial expansion (*see* Manifest Destiny)

Terrorists, 100

Texas, 3, 16, 68, 78, 113, 124

Thatcher, Margaret, 216, 217

Third parties, 80, 84, 85, 89, 90, 94, 103–121, 141, 195, 216, 225

Thomas, Norman, 112

Thompson, Hunter S., 25

Thompson, William Hale, 185

Thoreau, Henry, 199
Thurmond, Strom, 80, 145, 229
Tilden, Samuel J., 37, 45, 47, 49
"Tippecanoe and Tyler, tool"
　campaign, 136
Tocqueville, Alexis de, 208, 209
Tories, 75
Townsend Plan, 141
"Trickle down" theory, 89
Truman, Harry S, 32, 51, 61, 62,
　67, 72, 73, 80–82, 96, 97, 145,
　195
Truth Squad, the, 148
Twain, Mark, 176
Tweed, Boss, 184, 188, 189
Twenty-fourth Amendment, 4, 6
Twenty-sixth Amendment, 1–2, 7, 8
"Twenty years of treason," 80
Tyler, John, 136

Udall, Morris K., 67, 235
Unemployment, 74, 79, 80, 100,
　112, 142
Unemployment insurance, 74, 120
Union Party, 112
Unions, 74, 79, 88, 220, 228
United Nations, 116
United States Bank, 105
USSR (*see* Soviet Union)
Utah, 16, 113
Utilities, 120

Van Buren, Martin, 107, 135, 136,
　152
Van Rennselaer, Steben, 43
Vatican, the, 141, 143

Vermont, 4, 142
Victor Emmanuel, King, 210
Vietnam War, 1, 25, 26, 53–55, 83,
　99, 132, 150, 179, 203, 214,
　229, 230, 233
Virginia colony, 5
Volstead Act, 110
"Voodoo economics," 29
Voting
　compulsory, 23, 217
　districts (precincts), 32–33
　fraud, 77, 80, 108, 155, 183,
　　185, 188, 204, 212, 221
　registration, 6, 13, 31, 173, 190,
　　192, 194, 197
　requirements, 4, 6, 30, 39, 77,
　　119
　student vote, 4, 14, 234
　turnout, 22, 85, 196, 197, 218,
　　219, 222, 225
　Voting Rights Act of 1965, 190,
　　192
　wards, 32, 76, 77, 156
　write-in votes, 183
　youth vote, 2, 11, 25, 26, 196,
　　199, 235

Wagner Labor Relations Act, 178
Walker, Felix, 135
Wallace, George, 54, 112, 115–117,
　229
Wallace, Henry, 80
Wall Street, 108
Walsh, Thomas J., 178
War, 94
War Democrats, 44, 91

Warren, Fuller, 178

Washington Commonwealth
Federation, 165

Washington, state of, 159, 166

Washington, George, 5, 61, 75, 168

Washington, Harold, 85, 156, 197

Washington Post, 50, 55, 99

Watergate scandal, 26, 84, 99, 151,
178, 203, 224

Webster, Daniel, 40

Welch, Doug, 159

Welfare, 25, 74, 88, 111, 228

Wertheimer, Fred, 181

Western states, 47, 108, 174, 211,
212, 221, 222

West Germany, 217–219
Christian Democratic-Social
Union Party, 218
Green Party, 218
Parliament, 217–218
Social Democratic Party, 218

West Virginia, 31

Weyrich, Paul, 196

Wheat, Alan, 173

Whigs, 42, 44, 75, 76, 77, 89, 90,
93, 104, 136, 137

White Citizens Councils, 115

White House, 7, 16, 23, 31, 37–40,
48, 51–53, 55–57, 59, 61–65,
67, 72, 75, 77, 80, 81, 85, 94,
95, 99, 111, 120, 136, 137, 139,
141, 143, 145, 151, 152, 194,
195, 201, 205, 224, 231, 235

White, Robert, 129

Wicker, Tom, 83

Williams, Roger, 5, 206

Wilson, Woodrow, 26, 52, 64, 78,
79, 94, 101, 111, 130, 138–140,
143, 194, 198, 202, 234

Winrod, Gerald B., 142, 144

Wisconsin, 16, 80, 148

Women candidates, 17, 20, 27, 68,
231

Women's Rights Convention, 44

Women's vote, 5, 68, 74, 111, 161

Woodhull, Victoria Claflin, 44

Workingman's Labor Party, 104,
105, 110, 118

World War I, 79, 94, 111, 139, 143,
202

World War II, 51, 79, 80, 96, 145,
183, 195, 210, 214, 217

Wynhausen, Elisabeth, 204

Young, Andy, 173

Young Democrats of America, 199,
236

Young Socialist Alliance, 117, 119,
236

Yugoslavia, 218, 236

Zaire, 214